Dear Reader:

Season's Greetings, and welcome to what has become a favorite tradition at Silhouette! The publication of *Silhouette Christmas Stories 1989* marks the fourth year we've brought together a collection of heartwarming stories with a Christmas theme, and we're looking forward to many more.

I think you'll be moved by Marilyn Pappano's story of the reconciliation between an estranged husband and wife in "The Greatest Gift." And you can't help but be captured by the warmth that is unlocked when a lonely woman discovers an abandoned baby and is welcomed into a widower's home in Bay Matthews's "A Christmas for Carole." Lass Small's distinctive style gives you a poignant and humorous look at a small town in "The Voice of the Turtles." And Brittany Young has chosen Salzburg, Austria—birthplace of the famous carol—for her own touching and tender "Silent Night."

Created by four of your favorite authors, these stories will make you laugh, make you cry and reaffirm all that is precious about living, loving and the joy of giving.

Happy Holidays to you and yours from all of us at Silhouette.

Isabel Swift
Senior Editor
Editorial Coordinator

Silhouette Christmas Stories 1989

MARILYN PAPPANO • LASS SMALL
BAY MATTHEWS • BRITTANY YOUNG

Silhouette Books

Published by Silhouette Books New York

America's Publisher of Contemporary Romance

SILHOUETTE BOOKS
300 East 42nd St., New York, N.Y. 10017

Silhouette Christmas Stories
Copyright © 1989 by Silhouette Books

ISBN: 0-373-48218-3

First Silhouette Books printing November 1989

The publisher acknowledges the copyright holders of
the individual works as follows:

The Greatest Gift
Copyright © 1989 by Marilyn Pappano

The Voice of the Turtles
Copyright © 1989 by Lass Small

A Christmas for Carole
Copyright © 1989 by Penny Richards

Silent Night
Copyright © 1989 by Brittany Young

CONTENTS

THE GREATEST GIFT

Marilyn Pappano

A recipe from Marilyn Pappano:

My favorite holiday food is my mother's dressing for the turkey, but she's one of those cooks who use a little of this, a little of that. She gave me the recipe for our first Thanksgiving away from home, but it consisted of adding ingredients until the dressing looked, smelled or tasted "right." Since I never mastered that dish, I'm including, instead, one of my son's favorite holiday dishes. These cookies—thin brownies, really—cook best in disposable foil pans. Cleanup is easy.

FUDGY BROWNIE COOKIES

3 squares unsweetened chocolate, chopped coarse
2 large eggs
1 cup granulated sugar
¾ cup all-purpose flour
½ cup butter or margarine, at room temperature
½ cup semisweet chocolate chips
1 tsp vanilla
¼ tsp baking powder
¼ tsp salt

Preheat oven to 350° F. Grease 13″ × 9″ disposable foil pan. Set aside.

Sift together flour, baking powder and salt. In a 3-quart saucepan, melt butter. Remove from heat. Add unsweetened chocolate. Stir until chocolate is melted. Stir in sugar, vanilla and eggs. Add flour mixture and chocolate chips. Stir until blended.

Spread mixture evenly in pan. Bake 20 to 25 minutes, or until top is firm when lightly touched. Let cool in pan.

Carefully remove from pan. Cut away crusty edges. Cut into Christmas shapes with cookie cutters. Decorate with colored frosting.

Chapter One

It was a frigid November dawn, and the Montana sky overhead was leaden, heavy with the threat of snow. Neil Sullivan lay on his back, looking up at the ominous dark clouds, feeling a hundred little aches in his body, each slowly increasing until they equaled the single big ache in his head. Nearby, the stallion that had thrown him to the ground tossed his head and twisted his body, trying to lose the saddle fastened securely to his back. He was a magnificent sight, Neil admitted admiringly—sleek and powerful and filled with fury.

Neil shifted, and the pain doubled in intensity. "If I've broken anything, you worthless son of Satan, I'll kill you," he grumbled while he took stock of his injuries. His forehead had struck an outcropping of rose-colored granite, and blood was flowing steadily down the side of his face. Other than that and an ache in his belly, everything seemed minor—but painful, he thought with a grimace. He was going to be covered with bruises tomorrow.

He gathered his strength to sit up, but at the first movement, the ache in his abdomen exploded into agony, and he fell back against the frozen ground. He swore loudly, viciously, trying to outlast the pain, but it came in waves, fierce, intense, clawing inside him, ripping him apart, destroying him, killing him. He tried to fight it—tried to breathe, to control it, to hold his own against it—but it was defeating him steadily, brutally. He had to hold on. He couldn't die. He was afraid of dying, afraid of giving in, of losing....

An image of Elizabeth, clear and bright and beautiful, appeared before him, and his will ebbed. Elizabeth was the only important thing in his life, and she was gone. He had nothing to lose but life itself, and it was being taken from him anyway, bit by torturing bit.

His belly was on fire, spreading its pain until every part of his body throbbed. Every beat of his heart was like a blow, and every small breath of air he dragged into his lungs was agonizing. The pain was so incredible that his vision went dark, and the picture of Elizabeth disappeared in a swirl of heavy, dark reds and browns and blacks. He tried to speak, but his mouth wouldn't work—tried to move, but his limbs were paralyzed. There was nothing but pain...fear.... And hope. He was afraid of dying...but he was tired of living alone. Death could be his release from a world of loneliness, of emptiness. Death could be his salvation from a life without Elizabeth.

Slowly the strength left his body, and he felt his life going with it. There was darkness around him, and warmth—an enveloping, comforting, close warmth. The pain in his abdomen lessened, and the black, paralyzing fear eased its grip as he gave up the struggle to live.

His eyes opened one last time. His hand clenched, and he whispered one last word.

"Elizabeth."

Stopping inside the doorway, Elizabeth removed her coat, folding it neatly over her left arm, and took a deep breath to control the trembling inside. She tried to remember the last time she'd been in a hospital, to visit some long-ago friend who'd had a baby. Then it had meant the beginning of a life. Now it might mean the ending of one.

The desk was only a few feet from the emergency entrance, but it took her long moments to reach it. "Excuse me," she said, her voice shaking with emotion. "I got a call that my husband was brought here. Can you tell me where he is?"

The clerk looked up, her expression guarded. "You're Mrs. Sullivan?"

At Elizabeth's nod, the clerk gestured to a nurse to join them. "Carol, this is Neil Sullivan's wife."

The woman extended her hand. "I'm Carol Anderson, Mrs. Sullivan. I'm a critical-care nurse and the health-care administrator for the surgical intensive care unit."

Elizabeth looked blankly at the woman's hand before shaking it, then raised her eyes to her face. The nurse's expression was just as somber as the clerk's, and the panic began rising again. She had been fighting it ever since the phone call had come from Clara, Neil's housekeeper. It had been punctuated with sobs and filled with terrifying words: *accident... bleeding... critical... dying...* Now the panic threatened to overwhelm her. "Where is my husband?" she demanded in a hoarse, frightened whisper.

Carol Anderson shifted the clipboard she held to her other hand, took Elizabeth's arm and guided her down the broad hallway. "He's in surgery, Mrs. Sullivan. I'll take you to the family waiting room outside the surgical intensive care unit. The doctor will meet you there as soon as the surgery is over. Is there someone I can call for you?''

Elizabeth mutely shook her head. She couldn't speak for fear that the delicate strands holding her together would come apart and let her shatter.

They took the elevator to the next floor, then walked past a large waiting room, where a television was tuned to an early-morning news show. Farther down the hall was a smaller private room, with a window that faced north, a couple of sofas and chairs, a telephone and another television, this one turned off. ''Please sit down,'' Mrs. Anderson said, closing the door behind her.

Elizabeth obeyed, perching on the edge of the worn leather sofa, holding her coat in clenched hands on her lap. She looked around, carefully avoiding the view out the window, focusing on all the questions she needed to ask and the answers she was afraid of hearing. *What had happened? How had he been hurt? What were they doing to him? Would he live? Dear God,* she silently prayed, *please let him live.*

Mrs. Anderson sat in an armchair at an angle to the sofa and leaned forward. ''Your husband was injured in a riding accident, Mrs. Sullivan. He has a concussion, and there's some swelling of the brain. The more serious injury, though, is the ruptured liver. That's what they're repairing in surgery now.''

Elizabeth tried to remember what the function of the liver was, but she couldn't. All she knew was that you couldn't live without one. Clenching her hands together, she turned away from that thought. ''Was he conscious when he came in?''

''No.''

"Then how could you do surgery on him? He couldn't give you permission, and you can't operate on someone without permission." It was an awkward and clumsy way of asking, but she couldn't come right out with the real question: how serious is it? Is he going to die?

The other woman drew a deep breath. "When your husband came in, Mrs. Sullivan, his condition was very critical. If the doctors had waited for you to get here to sign the consent form…he would have died."

Elizabeth felt a chill sweep over her from the inside out. How could she live without Neil? How could she live in a world that didn't have him in it?

"This is the consent form for the surgery. Even though your husband is already undergoing surgery, for our records, we need you, as his next of kin, to sign this. I also need you to fill out the admissions form underneath it." She showed Elizabeth the lines for her signature, then held out the clipboard and pen. "Dr. Carter is repairing the liver now. Then, as soon as they're done, they'll take your husband down to radiology for a CAT scan to determine the extent of the head injury. After that, he'll be admitted to the surgical intensive care unit, which is right down the hall."

Elizabeth slowly took the forms. She read a few lines, then raised her eyes. "Is he going to be all right?"

Mrs. Anderson hesitated. She wished she could say yes, of course he would, but it might be a lie. His condition upon arrival had been worse than critical. There had been only a slender thread of life in the man. Finally she shrugged. "After the surgery, he'll be very closely monitored in the unit. We'll know more tomorrow."

"Tomorrow?" Elizabeth sprang to her feet, dropping the clipboard and the pen, knocking her coat to the floor, and paced to the end of the small room. "I can't wait until tomorrow to find out if he's going to be all right!"

Mrs. Anderson picked up the coat and laid it over the arm of the sofa, then retrieved the clipboard and pen. "I'm sorry. I know this is very difficult for you. Are you sure there's no one I could call—a relative or friend?"

Elizabeth shook her head. She hadn't seen her parents, who lived in Texas, in years, and she had no other relatives. Peg White, her best friend and boss, would come the minute she called, but she would be too concerned, too sympathetic, and Elizabeth would fall apart. No, she would be strong for herself, would rely on herself.

Returning to the sofa, she completed the forms, then handed them to Mrs. Anderson. "I'd like to be alone now."

"Are you sure?"

She nodded. She was very sure.

The nurse accepted her decision with a nod. "My extension is next to the phone. If you need anything..."

Elizabeth nodded once more, then waited for her to leave. When the door closed and she was alone in the small room, she placed a phone call to Peg. As she had expected, her friend offered to come to the hospital and wait with her, but Elizabeth politely turned her down. It was enough that *she* would be out of the shop; there was no reason for Peg to close up completely.

After promising to keep in touch, she hung up and sank back against the cushions, shuddering with fear, shock, sorrow. When she raised her hands to cover her face, she saw the slim gold band on her left hand. The matching diamond was at home, tucked away in the back of a drawer. She had removed it the day she'd left Neil and had sworn to never wear it again. But she hadn't been able to take off the wedding ring. Although they were separated, although for all practical purposes their marriage had ended a year ago, removing the ring was a step she couldn't take. In her heart, she would always be married to Neil, would always belong to him, and the ring was a symbol of that.

She rubbed the ring with the tip of one finger, back and forth, until it was warm from her touch. It sometimes seemed that Neil had been a part of her life forever, that she had loved him forever. Since she had first met him, when she was just eighteen and out of high school, on her own for the first time ever, she had loved him. He had been two years older, strong, handsome, with a wicked smile and a sexy drawl and a sensuous, gentle touch. He had promised her love and marriage and happiness for always, but they had been empty promises. Promises that she had lived on for two years, promises that she had dreamed of and prayed for, promises that had finally broken her heart.

With a soft sigh, she stood and walked to the window. Out there in the distance was the Sleeping Giant, a formation of rocky mountains that resembled a man asleep on his back. She could make out his forehead, nose and mouth, the slender column of his neck, the broad chest. It was the most distinctive landmark in the valley. She saw it every morning from her bedroom window, each day when she left her apartment, almost every time she looked outside. It was where Neil lived, where she had once lived with him.

He was a proud man. He'd been poor when she had met him, barely scraping by, but he'd been determined to be a success, to make something of himself. He had succeeded, all right. His ranch was one of the biggest in the state, his stock the best, his business among the most prosperous. He had everything he'd always wanted: wealth, power and respect. And what had it cost him? Nothing but his relationship with Elizabeth—twice. The first time she had left him because she had believed he didn't love her. The second time she'd left him because she had *known* it.

But *she* loved *him*. God help her, she loved him more than life itself.

When the door opened behind her, she stiffened, then, pressing her hands together in a prayerful pose, slowly turned. She was hoping for the best, but expecting the worst. When she saw that the newcomer was a man dressed in jeans, boots and a heavy coat and not a member of the medical staff, she gave a sigh of relief. "Hello, Roy."

Roy Harper, Neil's foreman, closed the door and came hesitantly into the room. He held a cowboy hat in chapped hands, turning it in nervous circles. "Have you heard anything?"

She shook her head. "The doctor's supposed to come here when the surgery is finished."

"You want some coffee or something?"

Once again she shook her head. "What happened, Roy?"

He laid his hat on the chair, then shrugged out of the coat. "It was that damned horse, Elizabeth."

When Mrs. Anderson had mentioned the horse, she had suspected that it was Thunder. "That damned horse" was legendary in western Montana. He was the meanest, most vicious animal she had ever seen, and she had often urged her husband to get rid of him, but Neil had refused. He had loved that horse, had admired his spirit and respected his power.

"Thunder." Roy scoffed at the stallion's name. "Demon is more like it. That horse has a mean streak a mile wide."

Her smile was weary. "About as wide as Neil's stubborn streak." How many times had she pleaded with him not to buy the stallion, not to ride him, not to risk his life on the horse? But he had laughed at her fears, had insisted that nothing could hurt him. And he had been wrong. The horse had damn near killed him.

"We don't know for sure. He rode out alone early this morning. When Thunder wandered home by himself, we went looking for Neil and found him unconscious. I guess that damned horse threw him."

Elizabeth shook her head in denial. "Neil's too good a rider to just get thrown. He's the only man in the state who can control Thunder."

"He's been a little…preoccupied lately," Roy said, shifting his gaze away from hers.

She looked away, too. She knew what had distracted Neil this morning—the same thing that had been on her mind for weeks now. Today was November twentieth. The second anniversary of their marriage. And the first anniversary of their separation.

She twisted the gold ring on her finger. "I'm sorry."

Roy moved to the opposite end of the window. "It's not your fault."

She wasn't sure what she was apologizing for, or what he was excusing her for. Neil's accident? Or her leaving? Both, or neither?

Maybe none of it was her fault…but maybe it was. Maybe she had asked too much of Neil, more than he was capable of giving. He had been a good husband to her, had given her everything she'd ever wanted—except his love. When she had left him a year ago today, she had asked for his love, had pleaded for it, had done everything but get on her knees and beg for it, but he had withheld it. He was a proud, honest man—too proud to pretend an emotion he didn't feel, too honest to lie.

"How long do you think it will be?"

"I don't know." She stared hard at the Giant until her vision blurred. "The nurse said he almost died. She said that it will be tomorrow before they'll know if he's going to be all right."

Roy heard the emotion in her low voice and shifted uncomfortably. He didn't know the boss's wife well, but he knew that she loved her husband, knew that she had loved him better the day she'd left than she had the day she'd married him. The breakup of their marriage had come as a shock to everyone at the ranch, including the boss. No one had known what had gone wrong except Neil, and he hadn't been talking. In the past year he had never mentioned his wife's name, had never acknowledged to anyone that he even had a wife living twenty miles away. But he hadn't forgotten. Roy knew *that*, too, from the look in his eyes. "I imagine he'll be all right," he said awkwardly. "He's pretty tough."

She nodded once. He had always been tough. He'd had some bad breaks in his life, but he had made it past each of them, stronger, bolder and more deter-mined than ever. She prayed that he would make it through this.

With a sigh, she looked at her watch. The slim gold bracelet loosely encircled her wrist, and the diamonds that ringed the face winked even in the dreary light. It had been a Valentine Day's gift from Neil, typical—like the diamond ring at home—of his extravagance. Sometimes she thought he had tried to buy her. Since he couldn't love her, he had given her beautiful, ex-pensive gifts, bribes to quiet her demands, to placate her growing unhappiness with their marriage.

But she had never wanted money—not eleven years ago, when he didn't have any, when she had returned his engagement ring and left the state; and not a year ago, when she had turned her back on his beautiful home and beautiful gifts. All she had ever wanted was his love, and that was the one thing, for all his money, that he couldn't give.

"Clara sends her best."

Elizabeth managed a faint smile at the thought of the woman who was Neil's housekeeper and Roy's wife. She was a sweet, gray-haired, motherly type who treated Neil like the mother he'd never known. She had been good to Elizabeth, too. "How is she?"

"She's fine. Says she's missed you." He pushed his hands in his pockets and rocked back on his heels. "I reckon everyone has."

He meant Neil. Elizabeth wondered if it were true. Had he cared that she was gone? Or had she been like the occasional business deal that fell through—just one more venture that didn't work out? She remem-bered the way he had looked one year ago today, when she'd given her ultimatum: *If you love me, say so. If you don't, I'll leave.* He'd been cold and hard and unyielding, refusing to give an inch, refusing to lie even to save their marriage.

And so she had lost. She had issued an ultimatum, certain that he would tell her what she wanted to hear, and she had lost. As hard as it had been, as badly as it had hurt, she'd had no choice but to leave.

And now she was here, stepping back into the role of his wife as if she belonged. As if he might want her here. But she was used to not being wanted, needed or loved by Neil. She would stay, would wait and would pray, and when he was well, when he had made it through this crisis, then she would go back to her lonely apartment. Back to her lonely life.

Chapter Two

Time passed slowly. One hour, two hours, three. Elizabeth and Roy talked little. He paced back and forth, and she stood at the window, staring at the mountains that marked the location of the ranch. Carol Anderson had returned once, almost an hour ago, to tell them Neil was out of surgery and that the CAT scan, to determine how serious the head injury was, would be done next. She had promised to return with the doctor once Neil was settled in intensive care.

Very critical. That was all she had said when Roy had asked about Neil's condition. Elizabeth had been too frightened to ask the question herself. She had turned back to the window, repeating the answer in her mind, then had closed her eyes in silent prayer.

Now the door opened again. Carol was back, as promised, and behind her was a tired-looking man wearing a white lab coat buttoned over a hospital-green scrub suit. Carol introduced him as Dr. Adam Carter, then suggested that they all sit down.

Elizabeth's legs felt rubbery as she sank onto the sofa next to Carol. Her eyes were on the doctor, their expression a mix of hope and fear, expectation and dread, all colored by love. "How is Neil?"

The doctor rubbed the back of his neck with one hand. "He came through the surgery pretty well, considering. The ground was rocky where he fell, and he suffered blunt trauma to the head and abdomen.

He had an intracranial injury resulting in cerebral edema, along with a stellate fracture of the dome of the liver, multiple capsular tears and a ruptured... Well, Carol can put that in simpler terms for you. We're going to keep him sedated for a couple of days, until the swelling of the brain subsides. His condition is still critical, but at the present it's stable. Your husband is a very lucky man, Mrs. Sullivan."

"So he's going to be all right."

The doctor hedged. "Well, as I said, his condition is stable, and his vital signs are good, so we're hopeful."

Hopeful. That didn't begin to describe the way Elizabeth felt inside. It made her next question easier. "When can I see him?"

Dr. Carter looked at his watch. "You can go in for a couple of minutes in another hour or so."

Elizabeth shook her head. "I want to stay with him."

"No."

"I won't get in the way, Dr. Carter. I just want to be there."

"No." He pushed himself out of the low chair, then looked from her to Carol and back again. "Do you have any other questions?"

Elizabeth shook her head. She wouldn't argue with him about staying with Neil. There were other people who could arrange that for her. She stood up and extended her hand to the man. "Thank you very much."

When he had gone, Carol touched Elizabeth's arm, signalling her to sit down again. "When you see your husband, Mrs. Sullivan, you need to be prepared. He's been through a very traumatic event. He's lost a lot of blood, and he won't be conscious for several days.

He's on a ventilator, to help him breathe, and he's full of tubes, numerous IV lines, wound drains, EKG electrodes. It's all going to look very frightening, but it's all there to take care of him."

Elizabeth shuddered uncontrollably, and the fingers of her right hand moved to twist the ring on her left hand. "I want to stay with him, Mrs. Anderson."

"I'm sorry, but that's against hospital policy."

The door swung open once more. Elizabeth turned in her seat to see Karl Nelson, the hospital administrator and a friend of Neil's. Karl was one of those people who could arrange things for her. She greeted him with a faint smile.

Nelson extended his hand, then pulled her to her feet and hugged her close. "Elizabeth, I just heard about Neil's accident. Is there anything at all I can do for you?"

Her response, when it came, was directed to the nurse. "We were just discussing hospital policy. When you donate as much money to places like this as Neil does, you get to make your own policy, don't you, Karl?"

"What do you mean? What's going on here?" he asked, releasing her and taking a step back so he could see her face.

"Mrs. Sullivan wants to stay with her husband in the unit." Carol didn't wait for him to reply, but continued the conversation with Elizabeth. "Try to understand, Mrs. Sullivan, that your husband is still very sick. He's not out of the woods yet. The cubicle that he's in is small and already filled with equipment. There's barely enough room for the nursing team to work. There isn't room for family."

"*You* try to understand: I need to be with him." But it was more than that. For the first time in their lives, Neil wasn't strong, wasn't capable and self-sufficient. For the first time in their lives, he *needed* her, and she had to be there.

Carol was sympathetic, but her first duty was to the patient, not the patient's wife. She tried once more. "Consider Mr. Sullivan's condition—"

Elizabeth's blue eyes grew frigid and dark. "I'm not going to do anything to endanger Neil."

"No, of course not, Elizabeth, that's not what Carol meant," Nelson interjected, laying a soothing hand on her shoulder. "Listen, I'll talk to Dr. Carter and see what can be arranged. Now, why don't you come and have lunch with me, and by the time you get back, you can see Neil."

She knew she couldn't eat, but as long as Karl could arrange permission for her to stay with Neil, she would do whatever he said. She stood, picking up her coat and purse. "Roy, will you come with us?"

He got to his feet, too. "No, Elizabeth, I'd better get back to the ranch. There's work to be done. If you need anything, give us a call, all right?"

"I will. And I'll let you know what's happening." Impulsively she embraced the older man. "It will mean a lot to Neil that you were here." Then she turned from him to the nurse. She felt badly for going over the woman's head to the administrator, but she'd done what she'd had to. "Thank you, Mrs. Anderson."

Carol nodded. "I'll be around the unit. If there's anything I can help you with, let me know."

Karl guided Elizabeth to the cafeteria at the opposite end of the hospital. She accepted a cup of coffee but couldn't bring herself to eat anything, not yet. Maybe after she saw Neil, saw with her own eyes that he was all right . . .

After lunch, Karl left her in the waiting room again while he talked to Dr. Carter. The doctor was annoyed at having his orders countermanded, but he grudgingly showed Elizabeth to the tiny cubicle where Neil lay. "You can stay for only ten minutes this time," he said flatly, pausing outside the room. When she started to protest, he raised one hand. "Starting tomorrow, you can stay as long as you want, but not today. We've got too much to do."

When she nodded her understanding, he opened the door and stepped back so she could enter.

Elizabeth hesitated. Two more steps and she would see Neil for the first time in a year. He would be on his back, with machines breathing for him, monitoring every heartbeat, every change in his condition. He would be helpless, vulnerable and weak for the first time in his life. When he woke up, his fierce pride wouldn't like the fact that she had seen him this way.

She closed her eyes to gather her strength, then took the two steps.

Even with Carol's warning, she wasn't prepared for the sight that greeted her. The room was dimly lit, and the single bed was flanked by numerous machines. Bags of intravenous fluids and blood hung above the bed, giving life with their steady drips. There were tubes in his nose that were connected to various machines, IV needles in his neck and chest, as well as in one wrist and the back of the other hand. He was pale, his features drawn and still. Oh, God, he was *so* still.

Elizabeth walked slowly to the bed, leaned her arms on the side rails and looked at her husband. Although he was motionless, he was alive. She saw the steady beat of his heart, displayed on the monitor over the bed, and heard the slow, even flow of mechanical breathing to prove it.

She touched his hand, careful of the needle taped to the side of his wrist, and the tears that she'd been damming inside slipped out, hot, salty, full of sorrow and grief and joy. He was alive. Thank God, he was alive.

"Mrs. Sullivan?" Dr. Carter closed the door behind him and approached the bed. "You have to go now."

She had circled to the opposite side of the bed, her fingertips resting lightly on Neil's left hand. "Why is his wedding ring taped?" she asked, her voice soft and quiet and sad.

"They didn't have time to remove it in the emergency room. We'll take the tape off, and you can take it home with you, if you'd like."

Her eyes, when she lifted them to his face, were wide and startled. "No, don't do that." Like her, Neil had always worn his wedding band. If they took it from him, the fragile bond that she shared with him might be broken.

"You have to go now, Mrs. Sullivan."

She ignored his command. "He looks so..." She couldn't say it aloud. Dead. The steady heartbeat and even breathing that had comforted her only moments ago were disturbing now. His heart beat only because he breathed, and he breathed only because the ventilator beside the bed was forcing oxygen into his lungs. "Can he breathe on his own?"

"Yes."

"Then why...?" She indicated the machine with a nod.

"The ventilator assists his breathing—helps regulate it, sort of like a pacemaker helps regulate the heartbeat. We'll take him off it in a couple of days." He paused briefly, then added more softly, "He's critical, Mrs. Sullivan, but stable. That's the best that we could hope for."

"That's supposed to be reassuring, isn't it?" Elizabeth asked, her smile sad. "Because he isn't getting worse. But it also means that he isn't getting better."

"It takes time."

Slowly she drew her hand away from Neil's, gathered her belongings and walked to the door. There she paused to look at the doctor again. "I know you'll only be letting me stay here because Karl Nelson asked you to. I appreciate it very much, Doctor. I won't abuse the privilege."

He looked at his patient for a moment, then went outside with her. "Leave your number at the desk, go home and get some rest. There's no sense in hanging around here any longer today."

She considered his suggestion, but the idea of leaving the hospital—of leaving Neil—was frightening. She shook her head. "I think I'd like to stay here a little longer."

"Mrs. Sullivan—is it all right if I call you Elizabeth?" At her assent, he continued. "I told you, Elizabeth, he's stable and, as you pointed out, that means nothing is changing. Go home. If something happens, we'll call you, and you can be back in ten, fifteen minutes. If you're going to spend tomorrow with him, you need to rest today."

Once again she shook her head. It was too risky. Neil's life was at stake. She had to be there.

The doctor gave a shrug. He had already learned that Neil Sullivan was a fighter—the man should have died, but he was stubbornly hanging on. It seemed that his wife was as strong. "Don't tire yourself out, or you'll be no good at all to him when he needs you."

She thanked him once more, then walked down the hall to the big waiting room. An elderly man sat in a wheelchair in front of the television, laughing at the stale jokes of a game show host. A young mother, her husband and their daughter exclaimed over Polaroids of their newborn baby. A teenage boy, his leg encased in a cast, was flirting with a nurse's aide, who was signing the plaster with a bright red pen.

Elizabeth felt lost, empty. For a brief moment she wished that she could walk past those happy people, down the hall and out the door and just keep on going. She had lived so much of her life for Neil, and what had it brought her besides heartache? The weeks after she had moved out of his house last year had been the most miserable of her life. If she stayed here now, she would fall under his spell again, and it would be more painful than ever to break free again, because their relationship was *stable*, she thought with a grim smile. Nothing had changed. She loved him, and he didn't love her. Simple facts. Cold facts.

But she couldn't walk away, even if it *was* the only way of protecting herself this time. As long as Neil was unconscious and in danger, she would stay with him. She would love him and pray for him and will him to live. When he awoke and no longer needed her, then she would leave. And this time, she promised herself, she would never see him again.

Chapter Three

It was cold on Tuesday morning, the bleak sky promising snow and failing to deliver. Elizabeth stood at the single window in the cubicle that served as Neil's room and stared outside. Neil lay in the bed behind her, looking the same as when she'd seen him yesterday. Motionless. Lifeless.

Everything was fine, Dr. Carter had told her on his morning rounds. Last night had been peaceful, uneventful, and the results of the testing they had done were encouraging. Others besides the doctor went in and out of the room all morning—nurses, a respiratory therapist, lab technicians, the anesthesiologist who had been with Neil in surgery. They tested, examined, checked the equipment, drew blood, and through it all Neil never moved, never flinched, never responded in any way to this invasion of privacy and dignity.

"I'm through now," the nurse said, removing the surgical gloves she wore and tossing them into the wastebasket. When she had begun changing the wound dressing, Elizabeth had watched, curious to see what they had done to him. But when the nurse had removed the soiled Telfa and gauze dressing and Elizabeth had seen the incision, nearly twelve inches long, that cut from the middle of his chest down, she had turned away, sickened with guilt and shock and sorrow. He must have been in so much pain, and she hadn't been there with him.

Now she walked to the side of the bed, touching her fingers to his left hand, looking down at him with teary eyes. He was a handsome man, tall and broad-shouldered, but lean. His hair was black, a soft, hazy, dull-edged color, and his eyes steel gray. They were the most beautiful eyes she had ever seen, quick to laugh, quicker to turn cold and hard. His mouth was finely shaped, softened in the early months of their marriage by a smile, but often fixed in a stern, tight-lipped scowl at the end.

She rubbed her fingertip over his wedding band. The tape had been removed, but bits of adhesive remained, dulling the gold. When she had placed it on his finger two years ago it had been bright, shiny, new, full of promise. Now there were tiny scratches and imperfections, and the luster was gone. It was a fitting symbol of their marriage.

How had they come to this? she wondered sorrowfully. When she had married Neil, she had envisioned fifty or more anniversaries—cheerful, happy occasions that called for joyous celebrations, reaffirmations of their love. Not days like their first anniversary. Certainly not days like yesterday. But when she had married him, she had believed that he loved her. He hadn't mentioned love, but he had talked about marriage and children and forever, and she had been convinced that it meant the same.

How long had it taken her to realize that something was wrong? Six months? Seven? When had her perfect husband grown distant, inattentive, almost bored with her? She had ignored it, had made excuses, had pretended that it wasn't happening. But by the time their anniversary had arrived, she had long since forgotten how to ignore, how to pretend. By then she had been so hungry, so desperate to have his love, that she had gambled everything on it—her own love, her marriage, her future. And she had lost.

"Oh, Neil," she whispered, her voice thick with tears. "I didn't want to leave you, didn't want to lose you. I only wanted you to love me. I couldn't stay without your love. Why was that more than you could give?"

But there was no answer. Just the cadence of his breathing—slow, steady, unchanging.

As she had done the day before, Elizabeth spent all of Wednesday at Neil's bedside, rarely speaking but always touching him, willing him to feel her presence, to come back to life—and to her.

It was late that evening when Dr. Carter stopped in. "We're going to let him wake up tomorrow," he announced, leaning on the bed rails across from Elizabeth.

Tomorrow was Thanksgiving, she realized. How appropriate. If Neil was all right, she would be thankful for the rest of her life. "Are you sure you can do that?" she asked cautiously. "He looks the same as always. Nothing's changed."

"Things *have* changed. The swelling of the brain has gone down, he's gotten stronger, and his body is already starting to heal itself."

But those things were happening inside, out of sight. All she could see was that the outside hadn't changed. There was no movement, no response to the pain, not even an involuntary eye movement. The only outward change was the heavy stubble that now covered his jaw. "Are you sure he isn't in a coma?"

"Actually, he is. It's called a drug-induced coma. There's nothing to worry about, Elizabeth. Today's CAT scan looked good, so tomorrow morning he'll wake up naturally. He'll be in pain when he awakes, and he might not remember what happened right away, but that's to be expected. He's been through a pretty traumatic experience."

She closed her eyes and murmured a prayer. In one more day Neil would be awake and, thank God, he would be all right.

. . . And in one more day she would have to leave. She could handle an unconscious, helpless Neil; that way he had no power to hurt her. But awake, flowing with vitality and power—that Neil could destroy her. That Neil had never needed her, had only rarely wanted her. It wouldn't matter to him one way or the other if she was here, just as it hadn't mattered to him whether or not she lived with him.

Careful of the IV, she squeezed his fingers tightly. It would be hard—to not see him again, to not touch him or talk to him, to once again be out of his life— but other things had been hard, and she had survived. She would survive this, too.

"You *will* be here when he wakes up, won't you?"

She looked up at the doctor. "I'm not sure that Neil would want me here." Not sure that she could handle being here.

He considered that for a moment, weighing it against her obvious love for her husband and the heartrending pain that darkened her eyes. "If that's the case, then he can throw you out when he's strong enough. But I want you here tomorrow, all right? It might be easier for him if there's a familiar face.''

Easier for him . . . but harder than ever for her. She would have to look at his dear face, into his beautiful eyes, awake and alert, and see once again the cold proof that he didn't love her. But she nodded her agreement anyway, confirming it with her quiet words. ''I'll be here. But only until he's awake, until you're sure he's all right. Then I have to go.'' Then she would go back to her quiet, lonely life, and she would deal with the fresh breaks in her already broken heart.

The powerful sedative that had been routinely injected into the IV in Neil's hand was conspicuous in its absence Thursday morning. Elizabeth waited nervously beside the bed while the nurse finished changing the dressing. The sight of the wound, long and red, with its row of metal clips holding the skin together in place of sutures, didn't disturb her as it had only two days ago. It would leave a long, thin scar, but that was a small price to pay for the return of his life.

''How long will it take him to wake up?''

''Probably a couple of hours,'' the nurse replied. She gave Elizabeth a smile. ''We're having Thanksgiving dinner in the cafeteria today. You're welcome to join us.''

It was a tempting offer. Maybe she could arrange to be out of the room when Neil was finally awake. She could avoid having to see him, having to hear him say that he didn't want her with him. She could get the bad news from the doctor; then she could go home and mourn in private. ''No, thank you,'' she murmured anyway. ''I'll stay here.''

* * *

If pain had a color it was white—bright, blinding, take-your-breath-away white. It surrounded him, burned him, set his entire body aflame. He tried to move to ease it, but his body refused to obey. He tried to groan, but there was no sound. There was only the pain.

He was alive, Neil thought with a vague sense of relief. He had to be—he couldn't be dead and hurt this badly. He tried again to move and failed, tried again to speak. When his voice refused to work, he felt the panic growing inside him, expanding, filling his chest. What was wrong with him? Why was his mind so fuzzy, his body so uncooperative?

He tried to calm himself, rationally, logically. He was alive, but maybe he wasn't awake. Maybe this feeling of helplessness was all part of a dream. If he opened his eyes, he would know.

His lids moved, then fluttered open. His vision was blurry, the colors washed out. He blinked several times, struggling to bring the objects before him into focus. There was a white sheet covering him, a beige wall in front of him, a tiled ceiling above him and machines beside him. He was in a hospital, he realized. At least that explained the pain.

Slowly he folded the fingers of his left hand into a fist, enclosing his thumb in the center so that he could feel the cool metal of his wedding ring. The movement caused the tape on the back of his hand to pull tautly, tugging at the skin and hair.

A sound echoed around the room. A sigh, he thought. His body might not be working very well, but his ears were better than ever, amplifying that faint exhalation several times over. He became aware of another sound, rushing like the wind, in and out, matching the rhythm of his breathing, and identified it as the machine beside his bed. He must have been in pretty bad shape, he acknowledged, to merit all this equipment.

Shifting his eyes to the left, he looked for the person who had sighed and found her standing in front of the window: tall, slim, blond-haired. Elizabeth.

He must be dreaming after all, he thought sadly, because Elizabeth had left him. He had disappointed her, had cheated her once too often, and she had left him, and nothing he could do would ever bring her back. Once she had loved him, but he had turned that love to hate. Once she had wanted him, but he'd destroyed that, too. She would never come back to him now, except in his dreams.

The door on his right opened, but he didn't turn to look at the newcomer. His eyes, still a bit unfocused, were on the woman who looked so much like his wife.

"For once I timed my visit just right," Dr. Carter said when he saw that his patient was awake. He came to stand beside the bed. "Can you hear me, Neil?"

At the doctor's question, Elizabeth whirled away from the window and found Neil's gaze, unsteady, dazed, locked on her. Tears came to her own eyes, but she blinked them away and hesitantly approached the bed.

"Talk to him, Elizabeth," the doctor urged.

She looked down at him and felt the tears turning again. "Neil..." How could she talk to him when all she wanted to say was, "I love you"?

She touched his fist, and he uncurled his fingers long enough to accept hers. He lacked the strength to grasp her hand tightly, but he held on the best he could.

God, she was really here—and even more beautiful than he had remembered. Her hair, swinging past her shoulders, was blond and as soft as silk. Her eyes were lowered, but he had never forgotten their clear blue shade, their warmth, their gentleness, their love. If he could see into them now, would he see the love still there, or had it been replaced by hate—or, worse, nothing at all?

He tried to speak, to say her name. The noise that came from his throat was his voice, but it didn't form "Elizabeth." It was only a sound, hoarse, harsh, painful, and it frightened him.

"Don't try to talk," Dr. Carter instructed. "You have a couple of tubes in your throat. You can't talk until we take one of them out, and even then your throat's going to be sore for several days." He slid his hands into the pockets of his lab coat. "I'm Dr. Carter. You were brought here four days ago after a riding accident. Do you remember that?"

Slowly Neil nodded. It had been cold that morning, and he'd been thinking about Elizabeth when suddenly, somehow, the stallion had thrown him. There had been such pain, then... He couldn't remember what had happened next.

"You had a concussion and a ruptured liver. We repaired the liver in surgery, and we've been keeping you sedated because of the head injury. Elizabeth has been here with you the whole time," Carter filled in. "Are you feeling any pain now?"

Once again he nodded, and he felt Elizabeth's fingers tighten around his. The doctor gently touched his belly, asking, "Here?" and Neil winced.

"It's going to be tender for a while. What about your head? Does that hurt?"

He remembered the blood flowing down his face and the ache that had centered in his forehead. It hurt now, but not badly, so he shook his head.

"We can give you something for the pain—"

He signaled no again. He had lost four days—four days that Elizabeth had spent at his side. He wouldn't lose another minute with her.

Dr. Carter nodded approvingly. It was a good sign that the pain wasn't bad enough to require medication. "I'm going to send a lab tech in here to draw some blood. If we find that everything's all right, we'll disconnect the ventilator and remove the nasotracheal tube, and you'll be able to talk soon."

There were a million things he wanted to say, Neil thought, shifting his gaze to Elizabeth again. He wanted to tell her how glad he was to see her, how sorry he was for hurting her, how much he loved her. He wanted to ask her to forgive him, to ask her, plead with her, to go home with him, to make a life with him.

"Any questions?" Carter looked from Neil to Elizabeth. When they both gave negative responses, he spoke again in his most authoritative manner. "All right, then, Neil, I want you to get some rest. You're going to be weak for a while, and once the tube comes out I imagine you'll have a few things to say to your wife, so rest. Elizabeth, you're going down to the cafeteria to eat. You've been skipping too many meals the past few days, and if you don't start eating, you're going to end up in a bed here yourself. Understand?"

She started to protest, to tell him that she wasn't hungry, but on second thought, she closed her mouth on the words. Eating lunch would give her a little time away from Neil, time that she needed to prepare herself. When he could talk, he probably *would* have a few things to say to her—very likely unpleasant, hurtful things. She leaned over the bed, hoping that he was still too disoriented to read anything in her eyes, and asked softly, "Do you mind?"

Selfishly he wanted to say yes, to insist that she stay with him. Even if he couldn't talk, he could look at her, and, after more than a year without her, just looking was a gift to be treasured. But grimly he shook his head and released her hand, signaling her to go.

He looked like a lost little boy, left behind by all his friends, Elizabeth thought, and it made her smile faintly. "I'll be back."

She left the room, followed closely by the doctor, his hand on her shoulder. Neil willed the tension at that sight to leave his body and turned his mind to more pleasant thoughts.

Elizabeth was still in love with him. She might deny it later or put it down to emotion, but he knew that had been love in her eyes when she leaned over him. He hadn't seen it in a long time, but he would never forget it, and this time he wouldn't lose it.

He was awfully optimistic for a man lying helpless in a hospital bed, unable even to speak, he thought with a hint of bitterness. He was already a two-time loser with Elizabeth; why should this time be any different?

Because this time nothing was going to stand in his way—not his pride or his ego or Elizabeth herself. This time he was going to love her so thoroughly that she could never, not even in her darkest, weakest moment, doubt him. This time he was going to give her everything she'd ever wanted: his heart, his body, his soul, his self.

Besides—he managed a weak smile as his eyes closed—the third time is the charm.

She was dawdling, Elizabeth admitted, setting her mouth in a firm line as she hung up the phone. More than two hours had passed since she'd left Neil's room-time she'd spent in the cafeteria, sharing Thanksgiving dinner with two of his nurses, lingering over pumpkin pie and coffee and on the phone, placing calls to the ranch, to Peg and to her parents. She gave details of Neil's condition to Clara and Peg and somberly wished her parents a happy holiday.

She was afraid to face him again. If he couldn't talk yet, the silence would be awkward and uncomfortable. If he could talk ... well, she was afraid of what he would say. Whether he wanted her to stay or go, to care for him or to get out of his life, she was afraid. If he wanted her to stay, she would say yes, and she would be lost in the heartache once more. If he wanted her to go, she would leave, but the heartache would still be there. Could she possibly protect herself from him, one way or the other?

She went to his room, slowly pushing the door open. She was so used to seeing him there unconscious, motionless, that it was something of a surprise to see his head swivel around, his dark gray eyes open and alert, watching her enter. She saw immediately that the ventilator was disconnected, and the tube hooked up to it removed. Now he could talk. Now he could tell her to go or stay. She didn't know which she would rather hear from him.

"Elizabeth." His voice was a hoarse, harsh parody of its normal low, smooth-as-silk self.

Protect herself? she thought, closing the door and approaching the bed. What a joke. With one word, one rasping, rough word, he had her trembling inside and out. He could destroy her, and she couldn't stop him.

She stopped a safe distance away, too far for him to touch her, and clasped her hands together. "How do you feel?"

"Awful." He paused, swallowing carefully over the soreness in his throat, then continued. "It hurts."

That brought her a few steps closer. She knew that it hurt, knew that he wouldn't even have mentioned the pain if it hadn't been strong. "Do you want me to call the nurse?"

"No." He lifted his right hand, extending it to her. "Please," he murmured when she hesitated.

She took his hand, lacing her fingers through his, feeling the weakness in his grasp. His vulnerability touched the love deep inside her, filling her with it to overflowing. Lord, how could she love him so much when he had hurt her so badly?

"Thank you for coming back." She had been gone so long that he'd begun to suspect she had run away, leaving him and the hospital behind. That was what she always did when she was hurt or angry or fed up. The first time she had fled to Wyoming, then Colorado, then drifted to California before returning here to Helena nine years later. The second time she had run only twenty miles, to a tiny apartment and a job in Peg's shop. If she left him a third time, how far would she go?

With her free hand, she brushed his hair, thick and heavy, from his forehead. "Maybe you shouldn't talk,

Neil. Dr. Carter said your throat would be sore. Let it heal.''

"Then you talk." He was tired again. His eyes wanted to close, but he struggled to keep them open, to keep Elizabeth in focus. "Tell me that you'll stay.... Please...stay..."

She continued to stroke her fingers across his forehead in slow, soothing movements. When his eyes closed, so did hers, to hide the tears. "I'll stay, Neil," she whispered. It was a decision that might cost more than she could bear to pay, but whether it was only a few days or—please, God—a few weeks, as long as he needed her, she would stay.

Chapter Four

Being with Neil again was easy—frighteningly easy, Elizabeth realized when she returned each night to her apartment. He was weak and often slept, but when he was awake... Oh, when he was awake, she found such pleasure in his company, just like before. She found herself hoping that this time the pleasure would last, but such hopes were futile. It hadn't lasted the first time, or the second. Why should this time be different?

But she still hoped, still prayed. She had to, because she was in such danger. Every hour she spent with him, every time he looked at her or spoke to her or touched her, she fell a little farther into the trap of her love. She was so close to forgetting that he didn't love her or, worse, deciding that it didn't matter. All that mattered was being with him.

At the sound of his voice, still faintly hoarse but raised in irritation, she turned from the window. He was feeling better today, the one-week anniversary of his surgery. She could tell, because he had argued with every nurse and aide foolish enough to enter his room, about everything from the soft diet they were feeding him to the gown he was forced to wear instead of pajamas to the question of whether or not he could shave himself.

"Neil, quit being so difficult and let the woman do her job," Elizabeth said, going to stand beside the bed.

She gave the nurse a sympathetic smile. "He was much better behaved in intensive care."

Neil scowled at her. "I was unconscious then."

Laughing, she laid her hand on his arm. "Precisely." She extended her other hand to the nurse. "Let me shave him. I've done it a time or two before."

The nurse gladly handed over the supplies and left the room, mumbling to herself.

"I can shave myself," he grumbled. "I've been doing it since I was sixteen."

"You heard what she said. You're still weak." She smoothed handfuls of lather over his beard, cleaned her hands and picked up the razor.

"I'm not that weak, sweetheart," he muttered as she sat on the mattress facing him. He definitely wasn't too weak to appreciate the scent of her perfume as she leaned over him, or the touch of her hands on his face, or the warmth radiating from her body, and he wasn't too weak to respond physically to those things. He shifted uncomfortably under the covers, bringing a frown to Elizabeth's face.

"You have to be still," she chided, lifting the razor from his throat. "I'd hate to give Dr. Carter another cut to sew up."

"How do you expect me to be still when you're this close?"

"Hush."

For once he obeyed her, closing his mouth and his eyes. He inhaled deeply of her sensual fragrance, wondering how much of it was perfume and how much was Elizabeth. It was a scent that, even after a year, seemed to permeate his house, his bedroom, his bed, even though he knew it existed only in his mind. In his dreams.

Elizabeth made long, clean strokes with the sharp blade, shaving away the black beard, revealing the dark, smooth skin underneath. His face was too handsome, too dear, to hide under a beard, she had decided long ago, and he had remained clean-shaven ever since. "There," she said softly, using a damp towel to wipe away the remaining traces of shaving cream. "Without even a nick."

She started to draw back, but Neil stopped her with the gentle touch of his hand. "Elizabeth..." His eyes held hers while his fingers traced lightly over her jaw, down her throat to the pulse at its base. There were so many things he wanted to say, but none of them would come, nothing but the sweet sound of her name. "Elizabeth."

Taking his hand in hers, she lifted it away, laying it on the covers as she stood up. "It's time for your walk," she said, her voice soft and unsteady, her hands unsteady, too, as they picked up his robe. "Let's see how far you can go."

That was exactly what he intended, Neil thought as he let her help him with the robe and slippers. He wanted to see if he could go all the way. With her. Forever.

Tuesday afternoon Dr. Carter came in to remove the wound clips. Neil watched, his attention divided between the incision and Elizabeth's reaction to it. She had always managed to be elsewhere when the wound was uncovered, because it bothered her. Was she one of those people who couldn't bear physical imperfection? Or did it upset her because it was evidence of the pain he'd suffered?

Elizabeth stood beside the bed, viewing the scar for the first time since that day in intensive care. That day she had reacted with guilt, sorrow. Since then, she had avoided seeing it for other reasons. When the scar was exposed, so was a good portion of his body—his strong chest, hard stomach, flat abdomen. She was having enough problems without dealing with her physical response to his body.

Dr. Carter removed the clips, replacing them with narrow strips of porous tape. "We'll use the Steri-strips for a few days, just to make sure that the wound edges don't separate," he explained, then surveyed his handiwork with obvious pleasure. "I do good work, don't I?"

It was Elizabeth who replied. "Very good. It looks nice." Strong. Masculine. Erotic.

The thick mat of black curls that had covered his chest and abdomen had been shaved during surgery, but was now growing back. Neil rubbed his hand over his chest absently. "You don't need to tape a bandage on again, do you?"

"No. We'll just check to make sure it's not draining." Carter flipped his surgical gloves toward the wastebasket, grinning when they landed inside. "In another week or so we'll be letting you out of here. I bet you'll both be glad to see the last of this place."

Elizabeth smiled vaguely, but Neil wasn't sure how he felt about leaving. Of course it would be great to go home again, to be able to wear clothes and eat a regular diet and not have to follow any bossy nurse's instructions. But he hadn't yet figured out how to convince Elizabeth to go home with him. It was just possible that in leaving the hospital, he would also be leaving her, and that was something he couldn't bear to think about.

He waited until the doctor was gone and they were getting ready for another walk around the hospital corridors to broach the subject. "I'm probably going to need someone to stay with me for a while when I get out of here," he remarked casually. "Just for a few days or so, until I get back to work."

Elizabeth knelt to slide the rubber-soled slippers onto his feet. "You have Clara." The housekeeper was already busy, but she would be more than willing to take on the extra mothering duties. She already treated Neil like a son, anyway.

"Clara only spends a few hours a day at the house. The rest of the time she's got to take care of her own house and her own husband."

Standing, Elizabeth extended her arm to him, steadying him as she always did when he first stood up. In spite of his progress, a fall now would be disastrous. "Her own husband?" she echoed. "I suppose that means that your own wife should be taking care of you?"

His grin was boyish and charming and untouched by guilt. "It would be nice."

"You know, you could hire a nurse to live in for a few weeks." She stopped in the hallway and asked, "Which way?"

He was scowling as he turned to the right. "I've had enough of nurses here."

Elizabeth gave him a teasing, commiserating smile. "You haven't won a single argument with them, have you? It must be hard on your ego. But they all think you're the handsomest patient on the floor."

"And what do you think, Elizabeth?"

His voice had grown low, intimate, reminding her of long-ago nights and long, easy loving. It made her warm inside, made her ache with a need that she had tried for more than a year to forget. Staring straight ahead, painfully aware of her flushed cheeks, she answered with a lightness she didn't feel. "Fishing for compliments, Neil? I thought you were too sure of yourself for that."

"But I've never been too sure of you." He had always known that she loved him, but he had never known how to keep her, how to make her happy, how to please her. The day she had married him, vowing to stay with him forever—even then he had known that someday she would leave him. And she had, because he couldn't say, "I love you."

And he couldn't say it now, either. Then it had been a foolish promise that had kept the words inside, a vow made eleven years ago in anger, a vow that he would never say those words to her again. Now it was fear that, even if he found the courage to say them, he would see only sadness and disbelief in her eyes. After all that had passed between them, how *could* she believe him?

"Come home with me, Elizabeth."

She looked sharply at him. She had expected this, somewhere deep inside, had even planned how she would respond—with a polite, firm, unemotional, "No thanks." But she was surprised, too, because the refusal didn't come automatically. Because tantalizing images of the ranch, of being home with Neil, filled her mind. Because, more than anything in the world, she wanted to say yes.

He didn't love her, she reminded herself harshly. The last months of their marriage had been miserable ones for her, because she'd kept looking for signs that the love she'd taken for granted really existed and kept finding nothing. How could she condemn herself to that kind of life again?

But she wasn't looking for love this time. This time she knew that he didn't love her. He felt fondness, affection, lust, desire—there were a dozen different names for the way Neil felt about her, but none of them was love. As long as she didn't expect miracles, she couldn't be hurt by their failure to occur.

Encouraged by her silence, Neil continued. "You could give up your job for a while, move back home, see your friends there. We could try again, Elizabeth."

She gave a soft sigh and turned her head away from him as they walked. "We've already tried twice, Neil, and failed both times."

"Haven't you ever heard? The third time's the charm."

"Yeah. I've also heard another old saying. Three strikes and you're out."

Taking her arm, he steered her into the waiting room, empty at this time of day, and over to the windows. "Look out there. There's hardly a place in Helena where you can't see the Sleeping Giant. Tell me you don't think of the ranch every time you see it. Tell me you don't miss living out there."

She remained silent rather than lie.

Gently he forced her to look at him. "Tell me you don't miss *me*, Elizabeth. Tell me you don't wake up in the middle of the night wondering where I am, that you don't miss the rides we used to take, the picnics, the winter nights in front of the fireplace ... the loving."

"It's easy for you to talk about trying again, Neil, because it's different for you," she replied, her voice immeasurably sad. "You didn't risk anything. You didn't lose anything. *I* lost everything."

His hand fell away, and he took a step back, so cold inside that he felt nothing else. He had played his role so well, had protected himself so well, that she believed what she was saying. She didn't know that her leaving had almost killed him, that he, too, had lost everything because, without her, nothing else mattered. She didn't even suspect that he had loved her.

He walked away, and after a moment Elizabeth followed him. They remained silent until they reached the nursery window. Neil stopped there and watched the babies. He had always wanted children, at least half a dozen, and so had Elizabeth, but they hadn't been so lucky. Maybe a baby would have strengthened their rapidly failing marriage. Maybe a baby would have given him the courage to break that foolish vow and tell Elizabeth that he loved her.

Then again, he admitted with a sigh, maybe not. He had been stubborn. Those first months he had shown her in every way he knew how that he loved her, but she had refused to recognize it. It had been in his actions, his attitude, his eyes, his touch, but without the words, she had refused to believe. By the time she'd asked for them, it was too late. There was nothing left of the marriage to save. She had already drawn so far away that he couldn't reach her. They didn't talk, didn't touch, didn't make love. Even if he had swallowed his pride and sacrificed his honor, he still would have lost her. Too much damage had been done.

He looked tired, Elizabeth thought. His gray eyes were bleak, his face drained of color. She knew the weariness was emotional this time, not physical, but she responded just the same. "We'd better go back, Neil. You need to rest."

He nodded in agreement, accepting her arm around his waist. They made the trip in silence. At the door of his room, Neil paused, gazing down into Elizabeth's face. "If you've already lost everything," he asked softly, "then what more could you lose by going home with me?"

While she searched for an answer, he moved away, shuffling over to the bed and climbing in. He settled on his back, closed his eyes, turned his face away from her and left her to consider his question.

What *did* she have to lose? Her hopes? She didn't have any. Her dreams? She'd forgotten how to dream a long time ago. Her heart? It was already broken into a million tiny pieces; it couldn't break any more. So what could she lose? Maybe nothing.

Or maybe whatever little bit of pride, of life, he'd left her.

The only visitors that Neil had during the week were the ranch employees, the closest thing he had to a family. But on Sunday afternoon people began showing up. It seemed to Elizabeth that every friend he had in the city had chosen today to drop by and see how he was—and to see her. The news that she had spent the past two weeks at his bedside had circulated quickly, she thought with some bitterness, and more than a few of his "visitors" had come to see for themselves if it was true.

After several uncomfortable hours she excused herself and went to the cafeteria for a cup of coffee. She was alone at a table when Dr. Carter joined her.

"I went by to see your husband, but he had a roomful of friends."

She simply nodded as she stirred sugar into her coffee.

"You know he's being released tomorrow."

Again she nodded.

"Are you going home with him?"

"He's asked me."

"But you haven't decided." He paused to take a bite of his sandwich. "If you decide to go, meet me in his room tomorrow morning around eleven. We'll go over the restrictions he'll be under for the next few months."

Elizabeth's forehead wrinkled into a frown. Of course Neil had talked about needing someone to stay with him at home, but she had assumed that he was simply playing on her sympathies to get his own way. "What sort of restrictions?"

"On his activities. No driving, no heavy lifting, no working, no strenuous activity at all. That sort of thing."

She thought of Neil's comments a few days earlier, when he had asked her to go home with him. *Just for a few days or so. Until I get back to work.* "How long until he'll be able to ride again?"

"Probably three or four months from the time of the accident, provided that everything heals nicely."

She looked appalled. "You can't keep Neil off a horse for three or four months! He rides every day."

"Well, he's going to have to give it up for a while if he wants to stay alive." He studied her curiously. "Do you think he'll follow the restrictions?"

"I don't know." She was still dismayed by the notion that Neil couldn't ride again until spring. "Are they really necessary? He looks so much better and he's getting stronger every day."

"The body needs time to heal, Elizabeth—in this case, a lot of time. The liver is fragile, easy to injure and difficult to repair. Until it's completely healed, he can't do anything that will present the slightest risk of further injury."

She tasted her coffee, found it cold and pushed it away, folding her hands together. "He thinks he'll be able to go back to work when he gets out of here."

Dr. Carter shook his head solemnly. "He might be up to handling paperwork in a few weeks. As far as physical labor around the ranch...two and a half months, *maybe* two."

"What is he supposed to do until then?" she asked in disbelief.

"Rest. Slow down. Heal."

She shook her head emphatically, setting her hair swinging. "No...no. Neil doesn't rest. He doesn't slow down. He's worked hard all his life. He doesn't know *how* to slow down."

The doctor loaded his empty dishes onto his tray. "Then he'd better learn. Elizabeth, we're not talking about a matter of choice. The man was more dead than alive when he came in here, and it's a miracle that he's still alive. If he wants to stay that way..."

The unfinished warning made her shiver ominously. She looked up at him, her eyes shadowed and confused. "But you're releasing him. I thought that meant everything was fine."

"No, it just means that he doesn't need hospitalization any longer. He *does* need common sense and good judgment. If he doesn't have it, Elizabeth, you'd better provide it for him, or he still might make a widow out of you.''

As he walked away, she called his name. ''Is it okay if I talk to him about this today?''

He gave a shrug. ''If you think it will help. I'll go over it with him tomorrow anyway.''

She remained at the table long after he left, staring sightlessly at her hands. *Do you think he'll follow the restrictions?* Not on your life, she thought with a bitter sigh. Then she winced at her choice of words. Not unless he had changed drastically in the past year, and she'd seen no evidence of that. He was the same as ever—teasing, pleasing, charming, determined and stubborn as hell. If he decided to return home and pick up his regular duties right away, no one could stop him.

Except her. She was the only one here at the hospital whom he hadn't argued with, the only one he had willingly obeyed. If she made it a condition of her return, if she traded her presence at the ranch for his best behavior, maybe that would keep him in line.

Caution. She needed to handle this with caution. She would tell him what the doctor had said, would judge his response to it before she made any decision. Before she committed herself to something she might not come out of in one piece.

''What do you mean, I can't ride again for three or four months?''

Elizabeth winced at the thunder of Neil's voice. He wasn't taking this any better than she had expected. All his life he'd worked long hours and hard jobs. Sitting out the next few months couldn't seem very appealing to him. ''It's the doctor's orders.''

He faced her, his expression stormy and disbelieving. "You're kidding, aren't you?"

Slowly she shook her head.

"Is this Carter's idea of a joke?"

Another shake.

He exhaled deeply, tugging his fingers through his hair in frustration. "When can I go back to work?"

"Sometime in February."

Her quiet response brought another explosion. "That's ridiculous! I feel perfectly all right."

"Sure you do. That's why you sleep all night and half the day. That's why walking down the hall to the nursery and back wears you out. You don't have any choice in this, Neil."

Her calm fed his anger. He forced himself out of bed and walked across the room to her, stopping only inches away, glaring down into her cool blue eyes. "*All* the choices are mine," he said in a low, cold voice. "If you think I'm going to spend twenty-four hours a day alone in that house with nothing to do for the next three months, you're crazy—and so is Carter."

"I didn't know you had a death wish."

"Nothing is going to happen to me. He's just trying to scare you!"

For the first time in months, her hold on her temper broke, anger spilling out, fueled by two weeks of intense emotion. "Let me tell you about being scared! I was here while you were in surgery! They couldn't even wait for me to get here to sign the consent forms because you were *dying*, Neil! I stayed in that room with you, with the tubes and the lines and the machines keeping you alive, and I talked to you when you couldn't hear anything and held your hand when you couldn't feel anything, and I prayed—I begged God to keep you alive!'' She didn't realize she was crying until the tears fell on her hand. She touched her fingers to her face, and they came away wet. ''I can't go through that again, Neil,'' she whispered sadly. ''I *can't.*''

Reaching out, he pulled her into his arms, pressing her head into the niche of his shoulder. ''It's all right, Elizabeth,'' he murmured, stroking her hair. ''Sweetheart, it's all right.''

He held her for a long time, his eyes closed, his words soft and soothing. There had been times in the past two weeks when the pain had been unbearable, but now he knew that he'd had the easier role. For the first time he put himself in Elizabeth's place, considering how he would feel if *she* were near death, not knowing if she would survive, if she would ever be all right again. He couldn't cope as well as she had. He wasn't that strong.

When the tears stopped, Elizabeth lifted her head, wiping ineffectually at the damp spot on his robe. ''I'm sorry,'' she said, still sniffling.

Neil brushed her hair from her face, his hand lingering on its softness. ''No. Don't ever apologize for caring.''

It would be so easy to kiss her now, to bend his head the few inches that separated them and touch his lips to hers. He did it slowly, to savor the moment, to give her time to pull away. But she didn't pull away, and then his mouth was on hers. Her taste filled him, streaking through him, making him want and need, making him live. He teased her lips open, then her teeth, and was welcomed by her tongue into the moist warmth of her mouth. He sampled, stroking, thrusting, feeling the hunger spread through his body, through hers.

Then, suddenly, she was gone.

He watched as she gathered her defenses, a slight smile touching his lips. "Elizabeth?"

Swallowing hard, she risked a glance at him. "We . . . we can't do that."

He nodded once. "With all the other restrictions Carter has on me, I'm sure he must have one against feeling that good."

She smiled nervously, uneasily, then looked out the window at the darkening sky. "I'd better go home."

"It's still early."

"I have some things to do." The talk with Carter, the argument, the kiss—all were pulling her in different directions, but one thing had become clear. If she had any influence at all on Neil, if her presence would have any effect on his behavior, she would go home with him. Because one other thing was clear: she couldn't lose him again. She might never have all of him, but God help her, she would take what he chose to give. "I'll see you tomorrow," she said, managing a bittersweet smile. "We'll go home tomorrow."

Chapter Five

Only showers instead of baths until the incision was completely healed. Extra care on the stairs and lots of rest. No driving for two weeks. No work for two weeks. No heavy lifting for two months. No physical labor for two and a half months. No riding for three months.

Neil listened to Carter's instructions, his face impassive, determined not to show his dismay. He had followed orders for the week and a half he'd been conscious in the hospital, and by God he would follow them at home, even if the boredom and frustration killed him. He would do it for Elizabeth.

She was late this morning. She had called to say that she needed to take care of a few things before she picked him up. He still hadn't quite accepted that she was going home with him. He knew that she loved him, but he also knew that she didn't want to live with him. Hadn't her leaving proven that? He would have preferred to have her back because she wanted to be with him, but he would take her any way he could get her. Pity, concern, worry—those were all right if they brought her back to him.

"Ah, let's see ... there are no restrictions on your diet, no medications.... Do you have any questions?" Dr. Carter asked from his seat on the bed.

Neil leaned back in the only chair, stretched his legs out and leveled a blank gaze on the doctor. "You left out one thing."

"What's that?"

It was difficult to ask. Carter knew that he and Elizabeth had been separated for a long time, probably knew that she wasn't thrilled about going home with him. He'd probably left out that one restriction, figuring that it wasn't necessary to include it.

Neil's silence was easy to read, making the doctor smile. "As for resuming...intimate relations with your wife, it will be all right in another week or two, provided that she takes the...ah, superior position. Anything more...vigorous, you'll have to wait a couple of months."

A couple of months. Would she even be with him in a couple of months? Neil wondered bitterly. Or would she leave him again when she saw that he was being a good patient and was convalescing well?

"Anything else?" Dr. Carter waited but got no response. "I would like to see you in my office in two weeks, and again two weeks after that. If you have any problems before then, don't hesitate to call me." He stood up and extended his hand. Neil cautiously rose and accepted it. "I guess that's it. You're free to go as soon as Elizabeth gets here. Take care of yourself, Neil. I don't like patching up the same patient twice."

"Thanks for everything, Doctor." He remained standing until Carter left the room, then turned the chair so he could see out the window and sat down again. He was going home today. To the ranch. With Elizabeth. He had dreamed of this day, but now that it was here, he didn't know how to feel, how to act. Was she coming for a few weeks, or even a few months, only to keep an eye on him? Or was she accepting his offer of another chance, another try at being husband and wife? He didn't know if he had the courage to ask her.

The door swung open with a whoosh, and Elizabeth dropped a bag, her purse, coat, gloves and scarf on the bed. "Hi," she greeted him breathlessly. "Did I miss Dr. Carter?" She had rushed through her errands this morning, fearing that if she took her time, she would change her mind. She had given notice on her apartment, quit her job with Peg. They were big steps to take, but if she was going to risk trying again with Neil, she was going to risk everything.

"He just left." He stood up and turned from the window to look at her. Her cheeks were flushed from the cold, giving her face a rosy glow. She wore a simple royal-blue dress that was belted at her slender waist and made her look elegant and incredibly beautiful. It was a long moment before he remembered to speak again. "He laid out the rules."

"Good." She picked up the bag and began removing clothing for him. "Do you think you can follow them?"

He reached for the jeans she'd laid down, running the worn, faded denim through his hands. He recognized the shirt, too, and even the old running shoes. She'd gone to the ranch, either last night or this morning. Had she taken her own clothes out there?

Elizabeth touched his hand, prompting him. "Neil?"

"You know, except for our honeymoon, I haven't taken any time off work in...seven years," he remarked in a distant tone, then sighed. "Yes, I'll follow his rules." Dropping the jeans, he turned his hand over, capturing hers. "What about your rules, Elizabeth? Are you going to tell me that I can't touch you, can't kiss you or try to seduce you? Are you going to remind me that you're doing this only because you feel obligated, because you're concerned about my condition?"

She held her head high, her eyes clear and honest when they met his. She had given this decision a great deal of thought last night and had acknowledged that she had no other choice. She loved Neil and needed to be with him, was happy only with him. It meant living without love, being satisfied with his affection, his caring, his desire. But she could accept that. She didn't expect love anymore, didn't hope for it, didn't dream of it.

So did she have any rules to live by? Not for him. Only for herself. "No," she replied simply. Leaning forward, she brushed her lips across his, then laid the rest of his clothes on the bed: briefs, socks, a coat. "Do you need any help getting dressed?"

The smile he gave her was slow, teasing, sly. "You can wait in the hall."

When the door closed behind her, he drew the drapes at the window, then removed his robe and the plain cotton gown. He had never realized how much bending and maneuvering were required to get dressed, with each movement pulling at the tender, foot-long incision. By the time he finished with the clothing, he was sore and, to his dismay, too tired to bother with his shoes. Sinking into the chair, he called Elizabeth back in.

Without being asked, she knelt on the floor in front of him and slipped his feet into the shoes she'd brought. The boots he normally wore had been un-

suitable—too much tugging for a man in his condition—so she'd had to rummage through two closets to
find the scuffed, worn tennis shoes.

Neil watched as she efficiently laced them. Her hair
fell forward to hide her face, and reaching out, he
captured a swinging strand of it between his fingers.
It was soft and smelled of shampoo, the scent faint,
sweet, clean. He loved its color—blond in regular
light, but gleaming gold in sunlight and silver in
moonlight—loved to touch it, to feel it, to simply look
at it.

"Elizabeth?"

"Hmm." She didn't look up from the second shoe.

"Thank you."

Then she did look up and smiled. "For tying your
shoes?"

"For everything. For coming here, staying with
me . . . for going home with me."

She cleared her throat to ease the tightness, then
rose lightly to her feet. "I didn't have much choice, did
I? I don't think you could have hired a nurse to do it.
You now have a well-deserved reputation as the best-
looking and most ill-tempered patient in this hospital's history."

He stood up and drew her close, bending his head
to breathe in the scent of her perfume. "I'll be good
for you," he promised huskily.

"Be good *to* me. That's all I ask."

His eyes darkened to match the sunless sky outside.
It wasn't so long ago that she had asked for love, for
forever. She had lowered her expectations quite a bit,
it seemed. But before he could comment, a nurse came
in, pushing a wheelchair, ready to escort him out. He

released Elizabeth and scowled at the chair. "Is that for me?"

The nurse nodded.

"For a week and a half you've been telling me to walk, even though it hurt like hell, and now that I feel better, you want me to ride in that?" Dismay echoed in his voice, along with resignation. He knew he could argue until he turned blue, but he would never win. Still glaring, he reluctantly lowered himself into the wheelchair.

Within ten minutes he was settled into the passenger seat of Elizabeth's car and she was driving out of the parking lot. He tilted his head back, closed his eyes and gave a deep sigh of relief. "I thought I'd never get out of there. Let's stop someplace for lunch and celebrate with some food."

"You know darned well that Clara will have lunch waiting for us—probably all your favorite foods."

"Does she know you're staying?"

This time it was Elizabeth who sighed as she pulled onto the interstate. "She knows I'm bringing you." She hadn't known what to say to the housekeeper when she'd called yesterday, hadn't known what her status would be. Was she returning to the ranch as Neil's wife, his friend or simply his nursemaid? Was it temporary or permanent? Would he continue wanting her this time, or like before would it end all too soon?

Neil stared out the window at the Sleeping Giant. Occasionally it disappeared from sight as the highway dipped and curved, but it always reappeared, coming closer, holding the promise of home. When he could see, in the distance, the cluster of buildings that was his ranch, he smiled slowly, gratefully.

Elizabeth glanced at him. She knew what he was feeling, because she felt it, too. The ranch was the only real home Neil had ever had, the happiest home she'd ever had. Coming back like this, together, was enough to quiet her last few misgivings about her decision. "You've missed it."

He met her brief gaze. "Not as much as I've missed you. It's not the same without you, Elizabeth."

"Well, I'm back now," she replied with forced cheerfulness.

But Neil couldn't help wondering: for how long? How long would she stay this time? How long before he lost her again?

She'd been right about lunch. Clara had the meal on the table within minutes of their arrival. Elizabeth hadn't had a chance to bring in her suitcases, to ask Neil about sleeping arrangements, even to take a look around her old home. The housekeeper welcomed her with a kiss and a hug and fussed over her as much as Neil, urging her to eat, then to relax with Neil in front of the fire in the living room.

She stood in the doorway, reluctant to enter. Their last conversation in this house had taken place in this room, and the memories were still strong. He had stood at the window, she at the fireplace, and he'd watched her in cold, cruel silence while she had asked, pleaded, practically begged for his love. Even now she could hear the ghostly echo. *Do you love me?*

Neil turned from examining the fire, saw that the color had drained from her face and knew that she was remembering. For weeks after that night he'd been unable to come in here without seeing her, hearing her, in his mind. Her question had haunted his dreams and tormented his waking hours. *Do you love me?*

Lord, yes, he had loved her, more than life, but he hadn't told her so. When she'd left him ten years earlier, he had sworn that he would never again say those words to her. Then he had been poor, and all he'd had of value was Elizabeth and his word, his honor. He had lost her, but he wouldn't lose his honor. He had made a promise, and by God he had kept it. But it had cost him his marriage. It had meant losing her again.

It had been such a simple conversation, Elizabeth thought, moving slowly into the room. She had pleaded, and Neil had said nothing. *Nothing.* Without a word, he had ended their marriage, shattered her dreams, broken her heart.

He met her halfway, wrapped his arms around her, held her close. "Don't think about that night," he whispered against the softness of her hair. "Forget the past."

"I have too many good memories to forget." Slowly she settled her arms around his waist, linking her hands together behind him. "There's just a lot of pain...."

"I know. But we can make it go away."

She wasn't sure about that. Affection and desire could ease a lot of hurts, but not the hurt of finding out that the love she'd believed in, had gambled her future on, didn't exist.

She turned her thoughts away from that. She wasn't expecting miracles, wasn't living in dreams. If affection and desire were all she could have, they would have to be enough.

"Where do you want me to sleep, Neil?" There were three guest rooms upstairs, rooms that they had planned to fill with children, but unfortunately—or was it fortunately?—the marriage had ended before they'd started their family. She doubted that he had a preference as to which room she used, but there was no harm in asking.

The simple question sent a sudden need trembling through him. His breathing was uneven, his skin grew flushed and hot, and lower there was the impossible-to-hide swelling of long-unsatisfied hunger. He wanted her in his bed, at his side, where he could touch her, feel her, love her. "Do you have to ask?"

She felt his hunger, felt a corresponding need inside herself. It had been so long, and she had missed so much. She would like to share his room, his bed . . . but not yet. Not until they were used to each other again. Not until she was certain that he really cared, that all his sweet talk in the hospital about trying again hadn't been just talk. Not until she knew that they could make it work.

Lifting her head from his shoulder, she gave him a long, chiding look. "You just got out of the hospital, Neil. How can you possibly be thinking of that?"

His grin was easy and natural, his gray eyes sparkling. "It was my liver that was damaged, Elizabeth, not my—"

She cut off the rest of his reply with her fingers over his mouth. "I'll ask Clara to prepare the front guest room, all right?"

Neil gave a heavy, put-upon sigh. The front room was across the hall from his—*their* room. But it was better than the alternative; she could have chosen the room at the opposite end of the house. "All right," he agreed, letting her go as she pulled away. He watched her walk toward the door, admiring the graceful sway of her hips. "Elizabeth?"

She paused, glancing back at him.

"Welcome home."

The days passed quickly for Elizabeth. The first week was hardly different from the days at the hospital—Neil was still weak, still tired easily and spent long daylight hours asleep or resting on the sofa—but the second week he was stronger, more impatient to return to his normal activities. Only his promise to be good for her kept that impatience under control.

"Take a walk with me," he demanded crossly Friday afternoon.

She could tell by his frown that he expected her to refuse, so she closed the book she'd been reading, got to her feet and extended her hand to him. "Where do you want to go?"

"To the stables."

She'd known that, sooner or later, he would want to see the stallion, though she certainly hadn't intended to go along with him. But, without comment, she bundled up and went out into the cold, walking alongside him, holding back only when they came near the horse.

Thunder. One of the previous owners had given him that name, the story went, because his hooves when he ran sounded like rolling thunder. Because he was as powerful, as vicious, as savage as the fiercest storm, Elizabeth thought privately. She flinched when Neil left her and went to the animal, talking softly to him, stroking him.

Neil glanced over his shoulder at her and grinned. "Isn't he beautiful?" It didn't bother him that she didn't answer. He knew her feelings toward the horse. "By the time I get to ride him again, he'll have forgotten what it's like to have a saddle on his back."

Spinning around, Elizabeth left the building, stepping into the frigid cold, not feeling the bite of the wind on her face. She heard Neil call her name, but she didn't turn back, didn't stop for him.

When he caught up with her, he grabbed her arm and swung her around to face him. "Where the hell are you going?"

"That damned horse almost killed you, and you're planning to ride him again! Why don't you get rid of him?"

He gazed down at the concern, the anger and the love that filled her eyes. "The accident was my fault, not Thunder's. I was careless. I was thinking about you, wondering if you would ever come back, if the emptiness you left behind would ever go away, if the pain would ever stop. I was missing you and not paying attention to the horse. It was my fault, sweetheart."

"Why do you have to ride him again?" she whispered, her eyes glistening with unshed tears.

He rubbed his fingers over her cheek until they rested on her lips, soft and full and sweet. "Everyone deserves another chance, Elizabeth. Even Thunder." He replaced his fingers with his mouth, brushing his lips back and forth over hers. "Even me."

Burning with the emotions that swirled inside her, she slid her hands into his hair and pulled his head down, forcing him to deepen the kiss immediately. She craved the sweet, hot taste of him, needed it to satisfy the longing that had been building inside her these past weeks. These past months.

Neil's groan was low, broken. There had been kisses, embraces, caresses, in the past two weeks, but none like this, fueled by this desperate hunger that made him tremble, that made her quake. For the first time he allowed himself to hope that finally he could make love to her, finally he could ease the ache that left him hard and throbbing for her every night, every day.

He freed the buttons of her coat and slid his ungloved hand inside, over the heavy knit of her sweater, to cup her breasts. Her nipples were hard, aching, needing his kisses . . . but not here. Not outside where anyone could see.

Reluctantly he ended the kiss, dragged his hands from her breasts and refastened the buttons of her coat. "Come inside with me," he suggested in a thick, unsteady voice. "Let me make love to you, sweetheart. Let me—"

Elizabeth clasped both his hands in hers, her gloves warm against his cold skin. Her face was flushed, from need, from hunger, and her breathing was uneven. She wanted him—Neil could see it in her eyes—but he could also see that her answer was no.

"What is it you want from me, Elizabeth?" he asked grimly. "Promises of forever? Vows of love?" He could give those. She might not believe them—yet—but he could offer them.

"No," Elizabeth answered bluntly, gently. He couldn't give her the certainty that this was right—that could only come from within herself—and, at this moment, she simply wasn't sure.

His eyes intently searched her face, but he saw nothing to help him. "Will you answer one question for me?"

She nodded.

"Is the time going to come when you'll say yes?"

Again, slowly this time, she nodded.

Neil slid his arm around her shoulders as they walked to the house. What had she just said yes to? he wondered. Making love? Or accepting his love?

Chapter Six

When Elizabeth came downstairs from an afternoon nap Saturday, she found Neil in the living room, surrounded by boxes, studying a tall, fat tree in the corner whose branches reached to the high ceiling. "Where did that come from?"

He looped his arm around her waist and pulled her close. "It's called a tree. It grows outside, in the ground."

She gave him a withering look. "We don't exactly have a surplus of trees in this part of the state. You shouldn't be cutting them down."

"It wasn't cut down—it was dug up." He showed her the root ball, securely wrapped. "After Christmas I—" At her disapproving glance, he amended that. "The men will plant it at the side of the house. Will you help me decorate it?"

She looked at the boxes, the tree and then him, and smiled. "Sure. I haven't decorated a tree—"

"Since the Christmas after we got married. Neither have I." He'd found no joy in the Christmas season last year, not without her.

The boxes were filled with ornaments—some cheap, some costly, some plain, some breathtakingly beautiful—but each one special. Each one filled with memories. Elizabeth handled them carefully, remembering the hopes and dreams and joy and, yes, love that they represented. So much love...

She lifted a shiny glass ball from its box. It was one of the cheap ones; it had come in a set of six for under a dollar. They had bought them that first year, when money had been tight, when Neil had worked two jobs full-time to scrape together enough for them to get married. Their holiday that year had been simple, because of lack of money, but they'd had something more important; they'd had love.

The logs in the fireplace crackled and fell as she gently replaced the ball in its box. Neil laid another ornament in her hand, folding her fingers over it. "Remember this?"

It was leaded glass in Montana sky blue, poured into a metal frame that formed the ranch brand. On a whim she'd had it made for him two years ago, because he was so proud of his ranch. Just as he'd been so proud of his wife... "Yes," she murmured, turning it in her hands. She slid a hook through the loop and hung it on a branch sturdy enough to support its weight. "Do you remember our first tree?"

His smile, bright and warm and so damn charming, chased away the gloom that had settled over her. "That was the sorriest-looking excuse for a Christmas tree I've ever seen."

"It was a beautiful tree," she disagreed. "It was perfect."

Calling it to mind, Neil grinned. It had been barely four feet tall, lopsided, crooked and had lost most of its needles on the way to her apartment. But she was right. It had been perfect, because *they* had been perfect. They hadn't had any money or any of the material comforts that surrounded them now, but they'd had each other, and a love they had thought would last forever.

Maybe it still could.

"Your dream came true," she murmured as she hung a fragile glass angel on a high branch.

"I had a lot of dreams, Elizabeth. Which one are you referring to?"

"You used to say that someday you would have a big Christmas tree in a beautiful house, with the money to buy all the gifts you'd ever wanted." She indicated the room around them. "You've got all that."

He stopped her as she reached for a tiny wooden Santa. "When I had that dream, I thought you would be here to share it with me. You were in all my dreams, Elizabeth."

"You were in my dreams, too, but you weren't in my life." In spite of her best intentions, bitterness crept into her voice, subtly shading it. "You were so busy working to save money for us that I never saw you. I didn't exist for you anymore."

He traced one fingertip over her jaw. "I wanted to give you everything. A nice home, a good life..." The kind of life that she'd deserved, and for that he had needed money. She had never understood that he'd worked so hard for *her*, that he had, for a time, been forced to neglect her so that he could build a future for them. Instead she had seen his neglect as evidence that his words of love were a lie. By the time the future had been built, she was gone. "I'm sorry..."

She clasped his hand, pressed a kiss to his palm, then returned to hanging decorations on the tree. "I'm not criticizing you. It was a long time ago. It doesn't matter anymore."

But it *did* matter. Everything that had ever happened between them was still affecting them today.

She had left him a year ago because he wouldn't tell her that he loved her, and he hadn't told her because, when she'd left him eleven years ago, he'd sworn never to say those words again. It was the only promise to her that he'd ever kept.

He lifted an ornament from its box, letting it dangle by a thin gold cord. It was a sturdy porcelain heart—white, painted with a delicate holly-and-berries motif. He had bought it for Elizabeth two years ago, for their only Christmas together as husband and wife. "Do you remember—" As he turned toward the tree, Elizabeth bumped him, and the cord slipped from his fingers. Together they watched as the heart hit the wooden floor and broke into four jagged pieces.

Elizabeth stared at the heart for a long, still moment; then, blinking against the tears that filled her eyes, she knelt and picked up the pieces, standing again with Neil's help.

"Honey, I'm sorry," he said, pulling her close. "I didn't mean to break..." Laying his forehead against hers, he muttered a curse, then thickly whispered, "Oh, God, Elizabeth, I never meant to break your heart."

Hours later, Elizabeth lay in bed, her eyes open, staring into the darkness. Neil's apology had continued, the words rushing out in an uncontrolled flow—words of regret, of promise, of sadness. She had listened as long as she could, as long as she could bear the pain of what he was saying; then she had fled the room in tears. Now, safe in her own room, the words echoed in her head until she wanted to scream.

You were my wife, my life. I wanted to make you happy, wanted to live with you forever, wanted you to love me forever. . . . Sweetheart, I never meant to hurt you.

He was saying that he had loved her. Even though he had denied her the words, even though he had let her walk out of his life rather than say them, he had loved her.

She didn't believe him. She *couldn't* believe him. It had taken her too many painful months to give up her hopes of love, her dreams that someday he would love her the way that she had always loved him. If she began to believe again, began to hope and dream again, she would be destroyed once again. *As long as she didn't expect miracles . . .*

But it was Christmas. The season of miracles.

Rolling onto her side, she looked at the nightstand where a shaft of moonlight touched the pieces of her ornament with its cold, silvery glow. The porcelain heart was a fitting symbol of her own heart. Broken. Irreparable. No miracle in the world could make it as good as new again, and no miracle in the world could fix *her* heart, either.

Neil stuffed an extra pillow under his head, crossed his propped feet at the other end of the sofa, laced his fingers loosely together and sighed loudly. Dramatically. In the easy chair across from him, Elizabeth looked up, as he'd known she would, and offered him a warm, gentle smile. "What's wrong?"

"I'm bored."

She glanced at the television, tuned in to a football game with the sound turned off. "You can listen to that, if you want. It won't bother me."

He shook his head. He didn't like football, didn't like any sports. Rodeo was the only one he could identify with.

"What would you like to do?"

He would like to lift her in his arms, he thought with a sly smile, and carry her upstairs to his room—to their room. There he would strip off her clothes, lay her on the bed and make love to her sweetly, tenderly, thoroughly. Then the smile faded. He couldn't lift her, couldn't carry her, couldn't make love to her. In fact, since Friday, he'd been lucky to get more than a few chaste kisses from her. "Let's talk."

"All right. About what?"

About how long she was going to stay with him. About when she would be ready to accept his love-making. About whether she would ever accept his love. But he didn't have the courage on this dreary, cold Sunday afternoon to ask questions that would upset the snug, cozy warmth they shared. "Do you date?" He deliberately made his tone light, casual, so she wouldn't take offense.

Elizabeth left the chair, lifted his feet from the sofa and slid underneath, leaning against the arm to face him. He automatically shifted, making room for her legs on one side, so her feet could stay warm beneath his back, then settled his own feet comfortably across her stomach. It was a familiar position, one that allowed them to share their warmth, to be close without being intimate. "Do I date?" she asked when she was settled. "What kind of question is that to ask your..."

"Wife," he supplied, annoyed by her hesitation. What had she wanted to say? Estranged wife? "You're still my wife, Elizabeth, and it's a nosy question, but I think I'm entitled. Do you?"

"No." She paused only a moment before asking curiously, "Do you?"

"No. If I can't have you, I don't want anyone."

She tried to ignore the shiver of pleasure that coursed through her at his matter-of-fact statement, but it touched every part of her. She understood what he meant. Occasionally Peg had pointed out various single men to her, offering to arrange introductions or dinners, but Elizabeth had always refused. No explanation had been necessary, because Peg had understood; however nice and attractive these men were, they weren't Neil. "Is that why you still wear your wedding ring?"

He held up his hand and gazed at the gold band. "I wear it because I'm a married man. Because, even if you don't want to be my wife, Elizabeth, I will always be your husband."

Always. It was one of those little words that made her squirm, like love and forever. One of those words that made her want to believe, however foolishly, in miracles.

"Always, Elizabeth," he repeated. "Whether or not you believe me, whether or not you stay with me, whether or not you love me."

To keep her hands from trembling, she began rubbing his feet, encased in thick, white socks. She couldn't think of some light comeback, of any easy way to respond to what he'd said. "Sometimes 'always' doesn't last very long, Neil, does it?"

"It will last as long as I live."

"Will it?" she asked cynically.

"The problem with us, Elizabeth, is *your* 'always.' *I* never left you. *I* never walked away. *I* was the one who got left behind."

She shook her head in disagreement. "By the time I left, I had already lost you in every way that counted."

This time it was Neil who disagreed. "You never lost me, Elizabeth. You threw me away."

Their gazes locked for a long, tense moment; then slowly, coolly, she smiled. "They say that if five people witness an accident, they'll give five different versions of what happened. I guess we're not different from anybody else."

He wasn't amused. "What are you looking for, Elizabeth? Why did you agree to come back here? What do you want from me?"

Again she smiled. "I've learned one lesson in my thirty-one years: if you don't ask for anything, then you can't be disappointed when you don't get it."

"I disappointed you, didn't I, Elizabeth?" he asked quietly, sitting up so he could touch his fingers gently to her face. "I didn't give you what you wanted, what you needed."

"No, you didn't. But you taught me another lesson."

"What? How to live without love? How to quit trusting in it? How to settle for nothing when you could have everything?"

She sat up, too, catching his hand in hers. "You taught me that there's a time when you have to quit dreaming and be satisfied with what you can have."

"No," he disagreed solemnly. "No one should ever give up their dreams."

She rubbed her finger over his wedding band for a long time before meeting his gaze. "I don't have any dreams, Neil."

"Then share mine." He searched her face for any sign of unwillingness before kissing her sweetly, fiercely, his tongue probing her mouth, giving, taking, arousing. His caresses shared the same sweetness and fierce urgency as his hands slid beneath her sweater to cover her breasts, teasing her nipples into aching crests, making her heart thud, her blood rush.

She shivered when he leaned back and pulled the sweater over her head, letting it fall to the floor. His fingers trembled over the clasp of her bra; then it fell, too, leaving her breasts naked and hungry for his touch.

Neil's gray gaze moved like a caress over her satiny skin, her rose-peaked breasts. "You are so beautiful," he murmured, laying his hand flat across her stomach. "Do you know how long I've wanted you? How many nights I've dreamed about loving you?"

There it was again—one of those little words. If only he did love her. If she could have his love, she could... She closed her eyes on his dear, handsome face. If she believed in his love, she'd be believing in miracles, and she didn't. She couldn't. For the sake of her sanity, her heart, her life, she couldn't believe in miracles.

He felt her withdrawal like a chill through his soul. He clasped his hands together so he wouldn't reach for her, wouldn't try to change her mind, wouldn't consider taking her away.

When she opened her eyes, she avoided looking at him as she retrieved her sweater and tugged it over her head, pulling it down to cover her suddenly cold flesh.

"How long do I have to wait?" he asked, his voice hard and edgy and barely controlled.

Like him, Elizabeth laced her fingers tightly together. "Until it's right."

"Until it's right?" he echoed derisively. "And, of course, that's some arbitrary decision that *you* get to make, isn't it?" He didn't wait for her to answer before he continued accusingly. "I've been waiting for more than a year, Elizabeth. For more than a lifetime."

"For what? To have sex?"

"I want to make love with you."

"But *I'm* not ready to make love, Neil! All I have to give right now is sex." She stood up and paced the length of the room, stopping at last in front of the fireplace. "I'm sorry. I thought it would be easier. I thought I could forget about everything that's happened and move in here and be your wife again, but I can't." She leaned against the heavy stone mantel, resting her forehead on her arm, closing her eyes against the tears that burned. "I need..." Time. Reassurance. Love. God help her, she needed love.

This time it was Neil who found the easy way out. He came to stand beside her, wrapping his arms around her, hugging her close. "You'd never believe from the way I've been acting that I turned thirty-three on my last birthday, would you?"

She turned in his arms, hiding her tear-stained face against his chest. "Neil, I'm sor—"

"Don't apologize, Elizabeth. *I* was wrong. I can't take what you can't give." He raised her head so he could look at her. "Come on, sweetheart, don't cry. We just had our first real argument, and we're still speaking—that counts for something, doesn't it?"

She didn't answer. She couldn't. All she could think of was how she had fooled herself into believing that she could be happy living with Neil and knowing that he didn't love her.

It seemed she still had her own dreams, after all.

Following Neil's appointment with Dr. Carter Tuesday morning, they went shopping, then made the long drive back to the ranch. Elizabeth had gifts for Clara, Roy and Peg in her bags, along with two small presents for Neil: the newest book by his favorite author and an ornament, a beautiful horse in delicate, tinted glass. She had felt awkward shopping for him—she was his wife but not his lover, his companion but not his friend. So many gift suggestions had seemed too personal for the circumstances, so she had opted instead for the impersonal.

While she put her packages in her room, Neil went into the living room. It smelled sweetly of pine and was bright and warm, a pleasant contrast to the stark view outside the big window. This was the dreariest winter he'd ever seen—all dark skies, heavy clouds, bone-chilling cold. They should have had snow by now, but all the sky offered was empty promises.

Sort of like him.

With a deep sigh, he turned away from the window as Elizabeth came into the room.

"That sounds ominous," she commented lightly. "What are you thinking about?"

She was a vision to brighten even the bleakest day. In a royal-blue sweater and navy corduroy slacks, with her blond hair pushed back behind her ears, she was achingly beautiful, and she made him long to hold her, to love her, to please her. But he couldn't. Not until she could accept what he had to give.

She'd been pretending since Sunday afternoon—pretending that nothing was wrong, that the situation between them was comfortable and light and easy, that the scene that afternoon hadn't affected her at all. But he could see through her act. He had spent the past two nights awake in his bed, remembering the things that she'd told him.

If you don't ask for anything, then you can't be disappointed when you don't get it. There's a time when you have to quit dreaming and be satisfied with what you can have.

She had asked for his love once, and it had broken her heart when he hadn't offered it. Had he taken her dreams from her, too?

As much as he hated to admit it, he knew that the answer was yes. Now he wanted to give them back, along with so much more. He wanted to give her everything. To do that, he had to explain why, a year ago, he had denied her everything.

Elizabeth asked her question again, and he answered it quietly. "Do you remember the first time you left me?"

His question caught her off guard, in the middle of removing her shoes. She paused before letting the second one fall to the floor with a thud. Stalling for time before answering, she sat down in the chair, tucking her feet beneath her, spreading one of Clara's hand-crocheted throws over her legs. "The first time?" she echoed. "You make it sound as though I made a regular habit of it."

He sat down on the raised hearth, rubbing his hand over the rose-colored granite. "Didn't you?" he asked dryly, then shook his head impatiently. He didn't want to criticize, to lay blame, to anger her. "That night you said, 'You're the man who claims to love me, but all you've given are the words, and words mean nothing.'" It was an exact quote. The hurtful accusation had been burned into his soul, and he would never forget it.

She clasped her hands together in her lap, holding them so tightly that her fingertips turned white. She didn't want to remember. She had enough unhappy memories without going back that far for more.

"Do you remember what *I* said?"

"No," she lied. "I don't want to play 'remember when?' with you."

"It's important," he insisted. He left his seat and knelt in front of her, forcing her hands apart so he could hold them. "Elizabeth, we can't have a future together until we settle the past."

She tried to pull her hands away, but he held them tighter. "The past is settled. It happened the way it did, and nothing we say can change that."

Stubbornly he continued, forcing her to listen. "Words mean nothing, you said, and my answer was, 'You'll never hear them from me again, sweetheart.' Do you remember now? Do you remember the rest of it?"

Closing her eyes, she could hear his voice from that long-ago night—cold, cruel, threatening. Words that had been uttered in anger, that had been intended to hurt. Words that had broken her heart.

"'I swear before God...'" Even after eleven years, it was hard for Neil to say it aloud. "'...I'll never say *I love you* to you again.'" He looked up, his dark eyes shadowed with pain. "Do you understand, Elizabeth? Do you understand why I couldn't answer your question when you left me last year? Do you understand what I'm trying to say?''

She stared at him, the color drained from her face, her blue eyes just as pained. A promise—that was why he'd let her go. That was why he'd destroyed their marriage with his refusal to tell her that he loved her. A stupid, angry promise.

"I've made a lot of promises to you, Elizabeth. Love, happiness, children. A perfect life with no wants, no needs. But I've only kept one, and it was the wrong one. And I am so damn sorry."

"Why didn't you tell me?" Her voice was unsteady, laced with sorrow and dismay. "Why didn't you break that promise and answer my question?"

Releasing her hands, he stood up and walked over to the Christmas tree, touching a miniature bell, making it tinkle. "Companionship, consideration, tenderness. That's how I was supposed to prove my love to you. Not with words, but with actions." He glanced over his shoulder at her and saw that she remembered that part of their long-ago conversation, too. "So that's what I did when we got married. I spent time with you, I talked with you, I made you the center of my life. I treated you the best way I knew how, but it wasn't enough. The actions weren't enough. You demanded the words—the words that, eleven years ago, meant nothing to you."

She got to her feet, unable to sit still any longer. "I didn't demand anything until the day I left you, when our marriage was already dead!"

He tilted his head back to study the angel on top of the tree. With her beautiful face and lovely blue eyes and golden halo of hair, she reminded him of Elizabeth. That was why he'd bought it years ago. "Didn't you?'' he challenged mildly. ''What about when you started telling me that you loved me, then waited expectantly for me to say it, too, and looked so disappointed when I didn't? What about all those nights you pretended to be asleep when I went to bed, so I wouldn't touch you? What about when you *stopped* telling me that you loved me? You didn't want to talk to me, to spend time with me, to look at me or make love with me, unless I said I loved you. Those were demands, Elizabeth. Maybe not as plain, as blunt, as the day you left, but demands just the same.''

''That's not true,'' she protested weakly. But it was. How had she ignored the truth for so long? How had she viewed the same situation that he'd seen and considered herself blameless? She had rejected the very things that she had demanded of him the first time, had pleaded for the very words that she'd once thrown back in his face as meaningless. *She* was responsible, too. This last year of misery had been her fault as much as his.

''But, Neil . . . why didn't you tell me?'' she asked again.

''It was too late. Everything between us was already falling apart. You would have believed that I said 'I love you' only to keep you with me, not because I meant it. It never would have been enough to replace what we'd already lost.''

Her protest died unspoken. Maybe he was right. She had been so insecure, so unsure of him and herself. Eventually she would have wondered if he'd really loved her, or if he'd given her the words only to placate her, and the uncertainty would have torn her—and them—apart. ''Oh, Neil . . .''

"We can have another chance, Elizabeth." He walked over to her and raised his hand to her hair. In all the years, with all his money, he'd never found anything as soft, as silky, as beautiful, as her hair. "It isn't so hard. If something breaks, it can be put back together. Problems can be resolved, promises renewed, dreams rebuilt."

That meant trusting—in Neil, in love, in miracles. Could she afford to take that risk? Could she believe in promises and dreams and miracles, only to be destroyed once again? Could she survive another disappointment, another heartache?

She didn't think so. This time it had to be forever... or not at all. She couldn't risk her heart—her very soul—only to lose again.

Neil watched her consider his plea. The thoughtful look in her eyes was replaced by fear, pain, then sorrow. There was no hope there, just the memories of two heartaches, of two painful endings. Sadly, he knew what her response would be.

"I'm sorry, Neil."

Her whisper sliced through his heart like a blade. He tried to think of a response that would ease their pain, but there was nothing he could say, nothing he could do. He raised his fingers to her cheek, but, her eyes damp, she quickly stepped back and walked away.

He wanted to chase after her, to plead with her, to beg her, but he remained where he was. Even though it broke his heart... he let her go.

Chapter Seven

It had been a long, draining week, and Elizabeth went to the privacy of her room Saturday night, as she had the previous four nights, with a feeling of great relief. Neil hadn't started any more intense discussions since Tuesday—in fact, she'd seen very little of him. He had spent every day in his office, catching up on the paperwork that had been neglected since his accident. To fill her suddenly empty hours, she had offered her services to Clara, helping with the housework, the cooking and the seemingly endless holiday baking. She had decorated so many sugar-cookie trees, snowmen, Santas, stars and wreaths that she could do it with her eyes shut. It certainly hadn't been enough to keep her mind occupied.

And all she'd been able to think about was Neil. She was a coward, she had decided, pure and simple. He was offering her the things that she'd dreamed of most of her life—a future, a happy marriage. Maybe even love. All she had to do was accept them—reach out and take them.

But she couldn't. She was afraid—afraid to dream when her dreams had been so cruelly shattered twice before. Afraid to believe that this time could be right, that this time could be forever. Everything she wanted was right there before her, but she was too afraid to take it.

She sat down on the bed to remove her shoes. There on the nightstand, never out of sight, was the porcelain heart. She really ought to throw it away, she thought, rubbing the tip of one finger over the largest piece. It had once been so beautiful, but now nothing could be done to save it. The fragments were just a depressing reminder of how easily—and how permanently—things could break. Hearts, marriages, dreams, people.

She scooped up the pieces, intending to carry them to the wastebasket across the room, but impulsively she laid them on the bedspread in front of her, fitting them together, careful of the sharp edges.

For a long time she sat very still, staring at the heart, her eyes damp and stinging with tears. It was beautiful. Oh, tiny chips were gone, marring the perfection of the painted surface, and thin, jagged lines showed the path of the cracks, but it was still beautiful. It would never be as good as new again, but none of the flaws would diminish its value. It would always be precious to her, would always be Neil's gift to her. It would mean even more, because she had thought it was ruined, and now it was whole again.

If something breaks, it can be put together. Problems can be resolved, promises renewed, dreams rebuilt.

Was Neil right? Could their broken marriage be put back together? Could it be just as good as—maybe even better than—before? Could she, with his help, renew her promises and rebuild her dreams?

It was a risk. If she took it and was disappointed again, she feared the damage would last forever. She would never find the courage to love again. But could

she live the rest of her life like this—wanting, needing, craving love, but too fearful to accept it?

She could have it all—or she could end up with
nothing. The choice was hers.

Gently she returned the pieces to the nightstand,
then left the room, closing the door with a quiet click
behind her. Underneath Neil's door across the hall, a
narrow line of light revealed that he was still awake,
too.

She found the bottle of glue that she needed in the
kitchen and made her way through the darkness to her
room. Settling in on the bed, she opened the bottle,
picked up the heart and set to work.

Across the hall, Neil heard Elizabeth leave her
room, then return a few moments later. He wondered
why she was up at this hour of the night, but he didn't
leave his position sitting on the hearth to check on her.
The stones were warm, the fire hot against his bare
back, the room still. If he thought there was any
chance of sleeping, he would be in bed now—he could
use the rest—but sleep had been hard to come by these
last few nights.

It was Elizabeth's fault, he thought with a scowl.
She made his days as perfect, as pleasant and comfortable as could be, then made his nights hell, while
she slept like a baby across the hall. When he slept, he
dreamed of her—of the love and the sorrow—and
woke up feeling more tired than the night before. He
didn't know how much longer he could go on like this.

The worst part of it was, he'd done it to himself. She
loved him—he was as sure of that as he was of his own
love—but he had hurt her so badly that she couldn't
believe in him. She didn't have the luxury of cer-

tainty, like he did. She would have to accept him on faith, when he had betrayed her faith twice before.

He let his head hang limply, stretching the taut muscles in his neck, then grew very still. Lifting his head, he saw that he hadn't imagined the faint click. The door was open, and Elizabeth was standing there. He sat straighter, but didn't rise from the hearth. Silently, his heart pounding, he waited.

She took great care in closing the door before she approached him. Stopping a few feet in front of him, she knelt on the floor, her robe settling around her like a cloud. "Neil."

Her voice was breathy, a soft, insubstantial whisper of need, and it made his hunger unbearable. If she walked away from him again, this time he would surely die from the ache.

He raised his hand to her hair, and it trembled. How long had it been since he'd made love to her? He couldn't remember. *Too long*. But tonight she was asking him to. He didn't know why—whether she wanted that chance they had talked about, or if her longing had finally gotten the better of her judgment—and right now he didn't care. He would accept this precious gift that she was offering and worry about the reason later.

He moved to his knees in front of her, fumbling fingers undoing the buttons of her robe. It was heavy, soft, white, warm, and her skin underneath it was warm, too. He slid it off her shoulders and pushed it away, then slipped his hand beneath the thin straps of her nightgown. Her breasts were heavy, her nipples swollen, hard against his palms. Impatiently, he pulled off the gown and tossed it aside.

The firelight turned her skin golden—warm, soft gold. Neil gently laid her back on the braided rug, and for a long moment, he simply looked at her, his throat too tight to speak. He had known her, had loved her, for nearly half his life, and he had never tired of looking at her. She was so beautiful, so incredibly perfect, so deeply loved . . . and she didn't even know it.

She grew warm under his heated gaze, and the warmth fed her hunger. She reached for him, but he brushed her hands away. When his mouth closed over her nipple, she gasped, arching her back. He suckled it, dragged the rough wet surface of his tongue back and forth over it, sending shudders of desire that were almost painfully intense through her. At last, gritting her teeth over a low moan, she pushed him away and rose again to her knees, facing him.

For the first time since his release from the hospital, she saw his scar, extending six inches above his jeans. Her fingers gently grazed over it, following the thin line to his waist and the wide leather belt there. She opened the buckle then reached for his jeans. They were fastened with a row of buttons, and she took great pleasure in loosening each button, her questing fingers sliding between cool metal, warm fabric and the hard flesh beneath.

The weakness that troubled him in the last month was back, and he laid his hands on her bare shoulders for support. Opening the last button, she slid both hands inside the worn denim, underneath the soft cotton briefs, and with his help pushed them away, her hands leaving a hot trail down his hips and legs, then up again. She found the hard, heavy length of him and gently caressed him at the same time that she lifted her head to claim his mouth with hers.

"Now." Her whisper shimmered between them, then faded as Neil kissed her.

Finally he released her and pulled her, protesting, to her feet. "In bed," he murmured, then kissed her again, his tongue exploring the warmth of her mouth, as he guided her with his hands at her waist to the bed, gently lowering her, following her down. She tugged impatiently at him, but he refused to be moved. Reluctantly he leaned on one arm and gazed down at her, his free hand stroking over her, his eyes dark and hungry. "I can't..."

Her fingers closed around him once again and she wet his nipple, once flat, now hard, with the tip of her tongue. "I need you, Neil."

It was a simple, pure statement that made him swell even more. "Oh, sweetheart, I need you, too, but...the doctor said...not for a couple of months...."

Slowly she smiled with understanding. As she rose from the bed, she pushed him down, flat on his back, and shifted until she was astride him. "Did the doctor say that this is all right?"

His groan was the answer as she took him inside herself, slowly, deeper, tighter, until he filled her. She sat still, her eyes closed, savoring, feeling, loving. She had never forgotten this perfection, this glory. She never would.

In the light from the fire, Neil saw the tear that slipped down her cheek and lifted his hand to wipe it away. His fingers slid to her chin, their slight pressure encouraging her to meet his gaze. "You are my life,

Elizabeth," he solemnly promised. "Always. Forever."

Those words again, she thought with a teary smile. Only this time she believed them. This time she accepted them.

Careful to support her weight above him, she gave him a long, sweet kiss. Her breasts rubbed tantalizingly against his chest, and he raised his hands to capture them, to stroke them, to fan the flame burning low in her belly. When she could stand it no longer, she moved her hips against him, returning the torment, feeding his own need, until it exploded in bright, heated light, then faded to a warm, soft, golden glow.

Mindful of his injury, Elizabeth moved to Neil's side, and he pulled her close, his arm possessively around her, his shoulder her pillow. His heartbeat beneath her stroking hand was still rapid, erratic. Pressing a kiss to his damp skin, she asked huskily, "Are you sure Dr. Carter said this was all right?"

"Oh, it was better than all right, sweetheart," he teased, stroking her hair. Turning onto his side, he kissed her. "You are so beautiful.... God, I've missed you."

"I won't leave again." She offered the assurance quietly, without hesitation. There were few things in life that she was certain of, but that was one. She would never stop loving him, never stop needing him, and never again leave him of her own will.

"You'll give up your apartment and your job?"

"I've already done that."

"You'll be my wife? Live with me? Have my babies? Grow old with me?"

She nodded solemnly. "Yes."

He opened his mouth to ask the next question, faltered, then finally, in a husky, thick voice, asked it. "You'll love me?"

It took her as long to answer. "Always," she whispered. "Always, Neil."

He held her tightly, hiding his face in her hair, as the wonder of her promise swelled through him, wrapping around his heart, weaving into his soul. When he drew back, he raised his hand tenderly to her face. "Elizabeth . . ."

She knew what he was going to say, could read it in his eyes even in the dimly lit room, but she covered his mouth with her fingers. "No demands, Neil." She had made demands before, and it had almost destroyed them. She wouldn't let it happen again. "Just accept my love. Let me love you, and that will be enough."

He wanted to tell her that it wouldn't be enough, not for him—wanted to tell her that he loved her so much that he thought he would die with it—but she was touching him, kissing him, stroking and arousing him, and the words died unspoken, forgotten in the torment of need.

No demands, she'd said. Neil was scowling as he tugged on the jeans he'd discarded the night before, then added another log to the fire. Couldn't she see that he wanted—*needed*, after so many years—to acknowledge his love? Was she afraid that he would feel obligated, that because she'd said she loved him, duty would drive him to make the same claim? Was she still unable to believe in his love?

When the fire was burning brightly, he sat down on the hearth, his back to the flames, and studied Elizabeth across the room. She lay on her back, her hair a delicate tangle across his pillow, her expression as she slept one of complete satisfaction. God, she was so beautiful that looking at her made him ache. What was he going to do with her? he wondered forlornly. She was offering him everything...and asking for nothing in return. Not even his love.

Warmed by the fire, he went to the nearest window, pushing the curtain back. It was gray and cold and dismal outside. They should have had snow by now, he thought with a sigh. Snow for Christmas.

"Having regrets?"

As he turned to look over his shoulder, his smile came slowly, gently. "I have a lot of regrets," he replied. "I regret each time I lost you. Each time I hurt you. Each time I could have made you smile but didn't. Each day I spent without you."

She sat up, holding the sheet in front of her. "Do you regret last night?" she asked softly, fearful of his answer. She had assumed so much when she'd come here last night—that he would want her as much as she wanted him, that it would mean as much to him as it had to her. Had she been wrong?

He turned to face her then, folding his arms over his chest, leaning against the window frame, slowly, confidently shaking his head. "Not one second of it." Well...just one, when she had stopped him from telling her that he loved her.

Her shoulders rounded with relief, Elizabeth sank lower beneath the covers. "Then what was that sigh for?"

"I was just wishing it would snow. After all, tomorrow is Christmas." The last word echoed in his mind. Christmas—a time of joy, of celebration, of miracles. Also a time of gift-giving. He had bought

Elizabeth gifts—foolish, expensive gifts calculated to bribe a woman who couldn't be bribed, to buy love from a woman who gave it freely. But he had another gift for her, he realized. One more important than the emerald earrings, one more valuable than the diamond necklace, one that she wouldn't demand, wouldn't ask for. . . but surely she would accept it if it was given the way she gave—freely, honestly, sincerely.

Elizabeth watched him. She knew there was more on his mind than the lack of snow for Christmas, and she suspected what it was—her unwillingness to hear any words of love from him last night. She wished she could explain to him that she didn't need the words any longer. Oh, they would be nice, of course, but the real proof would come in his actions—in the way he kissed her so sweetly, in the way he looked at her so warmly, in the way he touched her so tenderly. In their lovemaking, their meals together, their quiet evenings in front of the fireplace—in all the hours they spent together, loving or talking or laughing or fighting or doing nothing at all, she would find the proof of his love.

He was such a handsome man. Standing there barefoot, bare-chested, the metal buttons of his jeans undone, he made her pulse flutter unevenly, made her throat tighten, made her think about loving, about heat and possession. He made her ache.

"Neil?"

He knew what she wanted before she spoke—knew because he wanted it, too. He couldn't remember a day in his life when he hadn't wanted her, couldn't imagine a day in his future when he wouldn't need her. He walked to the bed, stepped out of the jeans, ready and hungry for her, and joined her in the bed.

"Love me, Elizabeth," he muttered hoarsely as he shifted her into position above him. "Oh, God, sweetheart . . . please love me. . . ."

Elizabeth sat at Neil's desk, measuring wrapping paper to fit the small, flat box she'd found in the attic, smiling at the faint creaks above her. Neil was moving her things from the guest room to his room— *their* room. She had slept her last night in any bed other than his, he had insisted over dinner, and he was making the move himself while she wrapped this final small gift.

Although his office had never been off-limits to her, this was the first time she'd entered it in well over a year. Surprisingly, nothing had changed. Their wedding picture still sat on his desk, and another photo, of her alone, still hung on the wall. She wouldn't have blamed him if he had destroyed every memory of her in this house, but he hadn't. Because he had loved her.

Smiling serenely and humming Christmas carols to herself, she folded the edges of the paper, making tight, neat corners and taping them securely. It was a small package, wrapped in green and gold stripes, sporting a tiny, shiny gold bow. Neil would never notice it under the big tree until she was ready to give it to him.

She took the gift to the living room, adding it to the pile already beneath the tree, then stepped back to admire the scene. Neil stopped in the doorway to do the same. With the decorated tree, the brightly wrapped presents, the blazing fire and Elizabeth in a rich green dress, it was the perfect Christmas scene. All it needed was half a dozen small children and a loving husband and father.

Sensing his presence, she turned, a welcoming smile on her lips. "Are you finished upstairs?"

He nodded, coming to wrap his arms around her. "Have you looked outside? It's snowing."

Her gaze followed his to the window. At the sight of the fat, white flakes falling heavily, she smiled again. "Merry Christmas."

He bent to nuzzle her throat, then kissed her mouth. "Merry Christmas."

She turned back to the tree. "Sit down and let me give you your gifts now."

"But it's only Christmas Eve." He said it with a grin, knowing that it didn't matter to her. In her family, gifts had always been opened at home on Christmas Eve, so Christmas Day could be spent at her grandparents' houses. Since he'd had no family traditions, they had adopted hers, including this one.

Elizabeth gave him a look of mock annoyance, then smiled so sweetly that he willingly obeyed her, taking a seat on the sofa. She retrieved the three packages, leaving the smallest one on the end table, then handing him the book. It had been so suitable when she'd bought it only a week ago, but now, considering the changes between them, it seemed too impersonal; not even the inscription inside the front cover could change that.

The ornament came next. "It reminded me of Thunder," she said softly as he cradled the delicate glass in his big hands. "I guess, since I'm going to live here again, I'm going to have to get used to the beast . . . but I'll never like him."

He gently laid the glass horse on the coffee table, then leaned forward to kiss her. "He can't be all bad, can he? He got us back together again.... Thank you, Elizabeth."

He collected her gifts from under the tree and returned to sit beside her. Holding two of the three packages in his hands, he looked somberly from one to the other. He knew that, when she saw the expensive jewels, she would smile and tell him that they were lovely, but they wouldn't excite her. They wouldn't touch her heart.

And she did smile, told him that they were beautiful, admired their cold, icy sparkle. She would treasure them, not for their beauty or their monetary value, but simply because they were from Neil. But he had been right; they didn't excite her. They didn't touch her heart.

He offered her the third package.

It was a small box, and Elizabeth's fingers fumbled over the ribbon. Finally she uncovered the box and lifted the lid, giving a gasp of pure pleasure. "Oh, Neil . . ."

Inside was a Christmas ornament, a small white porcelain heart. It was identical to the one he'd given her two years ago, the broken one, but was painted in a mistletoe-and-berries motif instead of holly. She lifted the heart by its gold cord and let it dangle from her finger, her hand cupped underneath to protect it from harm.

He reached over to touch it. "I broke your other heart, Elizabeth," he said, though he knew the reminder was unnecessary. "I wanted to give you a new one—one that's never been broken and never will be."

She knew she would cherish this heart as much as the broken one. Together they symbolized her own heart, her marriage, hope and courage and understanding. Blinking back tears, she replaced it in its box and reached for her final gift for Neil, but with his hand on her arm, he stopped her.

"I have one more thing to give you. This one couldn't be wrapped and placed under the tree. You can't hold it in your hands or see it with your eyes, but it's something you can feel...something you can trust...something that will be with you for the rest of our lives." His hands were trembling, and he stilled them by grasping hers tightly. "I love you, Elizabeth. I loved you the day we met, and in all the years since, whether we were together or apart, I've always loved you. I always will."

Elizabeth stared at him for a long time, until her sight blurred. There were a dozen things she wanted to say to him, starting and ending with "I love you," but her throat wouldn't work. All she could get out was his name on a soft sigh. "Oh, Neil..."

He couldn't judge anything by her whisper, and her eyes were closed so the tears could flow. Was she happy because she believed him, or sad because she didn't? "I know I've given you good reason not to trust me, sweetheart, not to believe in me, but—"

"Don't, Neil," she interrupted. She pulled free and got the last package from the end table, thrusting it into his hands. "Before you say anything else, open that."

His eyes dark and confused, he ripped the paper off the box and opened it. When he saw the heart inside, he looked at Elizabeth, even more confused.

"I was so afraid to try again, Neil. Our marriage was broken, my heart was broken, *I* was broken, and I was convinced that none of it could be fixed. But you told me that if something breaks, it can be put back together. This heart is proof of that; it was broken, and now it's whole again. It gave me the courage to try, to hope, to dream." She smiled through her tears. "No one should ever give up their dreams. You've given mine back to me."

"Then you believe me." The wonder he'd felt when she had come to him last night was back. He had hoped, and he had prayed, but he hadn't known if she would ever accept his love. "You believe that I love you."

"Yes, Neil," she said, going into his arms. "I believe. And I love you."

He held her close and kissed her, with all the gentleness and tenderness and love inside him. When he released her, she remained in his embrace, her head on his shoulder, her left hand with its shiny gold ring flat against his chest, above his heart.

He had given her so much, she thought with a contented sigh—the gift of trust, the gift of faith, the gift of dreams. They were precious, and she vowed that she would never lose them again. But being loved by him, hearing him say those words that she hadn't heard in eleven years—that was the greatest gift of all.

* * * * *

Author's Note

A year after we got married, my husband, Bob, began dropping hints about going back into the Navy. Thoughts of travel and life in exotic places filling my mind, I instantly agreed, and he reenlisted. His first duty station, we were told, would be Pearl Harbor, Hawaii—exotic enough for this Oklahoma girl. As time to leave approached, though, plans were changed—typically Navy—and we were sent instead to South Carolina.

Being a Navy wife meant adapting. For one thing, I spent a lot of time alone in new homes in strange cities, with no one but our son, Brandon, for company, while Bob was off being a sailor. For another, the Navy has a language all its own: a grocery store is a commissary, a vacation is leave, and six o'clock at night is eighteen hundred hours. I had to learn to communicate all over again.

Another change the Navy brought was not always being able to go home for Christmas, an important family holiday for us. Those first few years we *were* able to go back, so there were no holiday celebrations in our own home, but the fourth year it happened: Christmas came, and we couldn't go home. With a small child, we had to provide our own holiday spirit, our own tree, decorations and, eventually, our own traditions.

The holiday begins after Thanksgiving, when we begin unpacking the decorations, the Christmas china, the cedar crèche. Our tree goes up the first Sunday in December, trimmed with our individual ornament collections, along with ornaments from each place we visit when we travel. The following week is spent decorating the outside of the house with wreaths, garlands and hundreds of brightly colored lights—at night, of course, so we can judge our work as we go. We attend the Christmas parade and watch every Christmas special, movie and cartoon, recording our favorites to view again. We also borrow freely from others' traditions—two of our favorites are St. Nicholas' Eve, when children leave their shoes on the windowsill and get gifts if they've been good or coal if they've been bad, and *farolitos*, the New Mexican custom of candles in sand-filled paper bags lining the driveway and the steps.

Over the years, these traditions have provided a certain stability to our lives. Whether we live in the Deep South or sunny California, whether our home is a house, an apartment or a condo, we carry with us these familiar objects and familiar rituals that make Christmas extra special.

So, to my husband and my son, to my mother, my sisters, Jacki and Sharon, and their husbands, to my nieces Lauren and Katelyn, to my mother-in-law, my brother-in-law, Tom, and his wife, and my nephew, Eric, and to my family and friends and especially to you, the readers, I wish you the merriest of Christmases.

Marilyn Pappano

THE VOICE OF
THE TURTLES

Lass Small

A recipe from Lass Small:

CHRISTMAS CANDY

Dried and seeded apricots
Dried and seeded dates
Pecan halves
Powdered sugar

Pull the dried fruits apart slightly. Put a pecan half into center of each fruit. Press and roll fruit in powdered sugar.

Results in sticky hands, watering mouth, closed-eyes savoring, gained pounds and guilty conscience.

Chapter One

On a hot Wednesday in August, Jethro Hanna left his farm to drive into Hadley. It was the county seat in a sparsely populated area of north-central Indiana, and a loner like Jethro was by nature reluctant to expose himself to the townspeople. In a community the size of Hadley, the residents didn't have enough to occupy their minds, and they were trying to marry him off.

The women said variations of: "You ought to try again. There're a lot of nice women out there. My cousin (niece/sister/daughter) is coming for dinner (lunch/coffee/square dancing/whatever) next week. You come, too."

Jethro was running out of excuses; and even he knew that a flat "No" was rude.

The men groused with rough humor: "For Pete's sake, get married! Get the women off our backs. You can't be the only lucky man around."

Jethro parked his pickup in the square, facing the curb. It was one of the things peculiar to Hadley. That kind of parking had begun with wagons when the horses were secured to hitching posts. Even with the coming of motored vehicles, parallel parking still hadn't caught on. Habits tend to linger in small towns.

But changes could happen. Jethro blessed the fact that their town would now have a medical office. That might give local tongues something to wag about besides him.

As he'd figured, there was almost triple the usual number of loungers sitting on the benches or standing around on the courthouse side of the square, facing the new doctor's office. It would occupy the first floor of the last private house on the square. The office furniture had arrived the day before, and now the nurse was out on the sidewalk to supervise the arrival of the medical equipment.

Jethro remembered the nurse would have an apartment on the second floor of the house. He noted that she was wearing slacks, that she was young and neatly built, and that her dark hair was curly but short. Although he "saw" her, he wasn't interested.

He thought it was a good thing that the doctor had decided to set up an office there. Even with the really intensive courses Hadley's two policemen and the volunteer firemen had had to pass, the town needed somebody around who knew exactly what he was doing in case of medical emergencies. Jethro wondered if having a doctor there only two days a week would be enough—probably.

Jethro was tall and dark-haired, with brown eyes. The farm work was physical and his body was well muscled and lithe, so he moved with ease. He got out of his truck and checked in with the square's benchsitters. He ambled over, standing quietly and giving several separately aimed nods to the upper members of the hierarchy who were present.

There were nods back and even a couple of acknowledging "Jethros" before the phalanx went back to watching the nurse.

At thirty-five, Jethro was still conscious of the fact that there were no women around on the courthouse side of the square. Nice women didn't loiter on the square. They could sit on the benches in front of the stores if they were older or had a protective coating of children; young women used the sidewalk on the store-side of the street, or if they had to sit down, they went to the ice-cream parlor. It was an ironclad, unwritten rule.

Jethro found himself wondering if any woman had ever been accosted by a stranger in Hadley. Jethro was certain that none had, or he'd still be hearing about it in the record-keeping gossip. And he was struck by the question of why a woman couldn't sit on the benches of the square without being labeled "fast." It was then that Jethro decided it wasn't the women who were the arbiters of social conduct—it was these old turtles.

Feeling intolerant, Jethro looked over the old men who managed the whole community with their gossip. Without a flicker of an eyelash, he discarded them all. They were useless, gossipy old men. After they died off, things might not be so rigid.

"Can't see a damned thing," the eldest turtle groused.

"You got the glasses the wrong way," another told him.

Slowly the old man turned the field glasses and looked again. "Well, that does make a difference." He chuckled. He was laying down their evaluation of the nurse. "Blue-eyed with that dark hair."

"Pretty," said a fellow turtle.

"Gonna cause a stir," said another.

That brought wheezing laughter; and sly looks were exchanged. But it was the bony elbow in Jethro's ribs that really ticked him off. Without another glance in the nurse's direction, he hardened his heart against her. The turtles were starting to pair them up. Damned if he would go along with it.

Just then, Peter Calhoun's pickup came careening around the corner toward the square and screeched to a halt in the middle of the street.

Jethro recognized such an obvious emergency and had started toward the pickup when Pete erupted from it and ran to the doctor's new office. Pete's face was distorted and his arms waved as he started yelling for the nurse, who ran from the office.

Jethro was already there and heard Pete shout, "—have the baby."

Jethro looked back at Pete's truck, and there was Christy with her chin tucked down to her chest and her face squinched. Jethro ran to her, and the nurse got in his way. She shoved against his shoulder, but he reached out past her and opened the truck door. The nurse exclaimed crossly as she tried to catch Christy's tumbling body.

Jethro grabbed Christy and banged his head on the edge of the truck door, cutting a gash, but he kept Christy from hitting the pavement. The nurse made another sound of impatience, and Jethro knew she was annoyed that the Calhouns had waited so long before going to the doctor.

Then his beeper went off.

That was one of the old men's innovations. All the volunteer firemen had beepers. And Jethro's had just beeped at a very trying time. Another emergency! He had to get this one organized first. He pushed everyone aside, lifted Christy and then looked around. What was he to do with her?

"This way," said a practical, female voice.

Jethro looked down in surprise. The nurse. Now where did she think he was supposed to take Pete's wife, who was making such urgent noises? The truck bed, of course!

But again the nurse stopped him as she said, "This way. Bring her in here. We have the table up. Come along now."

To Jethro she appeared calm, as if there was no undue hurry. She thought she could get the doctor there in time? Hah! Even *he* knew no doctor would make it for the birth unless a doctor was one of those standing around. So. It was up to *him*! He would have to deliver this baby by himself. He couldn't think, just then, how he was supposed to begin, or what he was to do next. He looked down at the contorted face of Pete's wife and he said, "Breathe."

Pete said, "Give her to me."

Jethro replied, "Don't worry."

The nurse put her hand on Jethro's shoulder and said clearly, enunciating precisely, "Bring her into the office and lay her on the table. Come *now*."

She was talking to him exactly as he had spoken to the bull when it had gotten loose some years back and he had had no idea which way the damned bull would go. She had used a tone that was calmingly authoritative. She was treating *him* like a loose bull!

Jethro gave the nurse a dismissive look, and as he turned toward the office, he effectively dislodged Pete with a swing of Christy's feet and carried her inside.

The place was a mess.

In that same tone she had just used on him, the nurse said, "Here. Put her here." And she brought her pointed finger down on the table.

She needn't have pointed. It was the only table around and it was reasonably clean. He laid Pete's wife on the mobile table.

The nurse took Christy's pulse and looked into her eyes as she laid her hand on that mound of a stomach. Then she turned and said to the crowding onlookers, "Please leave." Nobody moved. She said, "Out!"

In a low voice, Jethro told the crowd, "You heard her." He moved toward them and simply buffaloed them with his size. He closed the door and said to the nurse in a logical way, "I have to get to the phone. My beeper went off."

She exclaimed incredulously, "You're the emergency help?"

He blinked to assimilate that.

She elaborated as if to a child: "I punched the emergency alarm."

"You called me. I do fires and wrecks." Then, so that she wouldn't panic, he added, "I took childbirthing." He remembered the lesson to act as if you knew what you were doing and to keep everybody calm. "I'm here."

The nurse's lips parted on an indrawn breath, but she didn't comment. She said, "Do you have oxygen? I doubt we need it, but I would like it nearby."

"This is the emergency?"

With some relief at the opportunity to get rid of him, she smiled a little. "Check out the call. The phone is over there."

He hesitated as he looked at Pete's wife. Pete was holding her hands and crying. He was saying "Pant."

Jethro remembered that panting came late in the birthing. He went to the phone and called in; the nurse was right—she needed him.

He went over to the table, crowded in by the nurse and edged her aside, asking, "Do you have gloves?"

She indicated those on her hands.

He told her the obvious: "*I* need gloves."

She lowered her glance for an instant, then smiled faintly before she looked up at him guilelessly. "Go into the other room—and scrub."

It was a part of the instructions, and he did that. He was still scrubbing when he heard a baby cry. He went to the door with his dripping hands and was shocked. Through the exuberant exclamations of the parents and the tiny sounds of the baby, Jethro objected crossly, "You didn't wait for me!"

The nurse put the baby on his mother's stomach and smiled at Jethro.

He watched how easy it was to take care of a birth. He could have done it without any trouble at all. He gave the nurse a disgruntled look. She prepared the umbilical cord with the two plastic clamps and handed Pete the bandage scissors.

Jethro moved over and objected, "I can do that."

The bossy nurse replied, "It's symbolic."

The ambulance came wailing along, and it drew up at the curb in front of the clinic. It was a modified station wagon that the old turtles had chosen. It had more flashing lights than any other ambulance on the entire North American continent.

Jethro stood there, with his clean hands, watching everyone else being busy getting Pete and his wife and their new baby ready to go over to the little hospital in

Creighton. The doctor was to meet them there and finish the job.

It was all over. Jethro felt a little letdown. He hadn't had control.

The nurse put a big towel over Jethro's clean hands and asked, "Would you carry the baby to the ambulance?"

Sweat broke out on Jethro's forehead and his arms trembled as he accepted the tiny bundle into his big hands and held it against his hard chest. His stare was glued to the baby. The kid looked just like the old men on the square. A new little turtle. A delicate one that was helpless. And that bossy, interfering nurse said *Jethro* was to carry him—from there, clear outside to the ambulance. Jethro told himself, You can do it; pretend it's a new pig. But it wasn't. It was a new little boy.

He carried the baby carefully and put him in the vehicle in a backward-facing baby seat. Then, since it was John Beal who was driving the ambulance, Jethro got into his pickup and followed the station wagon all the way to Creighton. John had eleven kids, but he'd never delivered one. And Pete had only taken the father part of a labor. Jethro felt he should follow them to the hospital, then he'd be handy if Pete's wife should need any help in that ten-mile drive with two inexperienced men.

When Jethro returned to Hadley, he was a big enough man to go around and tell the nurse, "You did very well."

It was obvious that before then, no one had ever had cause to compliment her, because she didn't know how to handle it. She gasped in shock, then she couldn't control her self-conscious laughter. But she did try. It is the mark of intelligent people that they know when they haven't handled things just right. He thought that she needed to be complimented more, so that she could be smooth about hearing such.

And she was pretty. Jethro could recognize that, even though he wasn't in the market for another wife. Then he was surprised that he could think so easily of Betsy. The pain had lessened. It was just a kind of regretful twinge now. That was amazing, for he'd suffered when she'd left him.

The nurse said, "Sit down and let me fix your head. You must have cut it on the truck door when Christy fell out." She said this with some irony so he would remember that, if he hadn't interfered, it would have all gone smoother.

He did sit, but he put a hand up to his head and felt the forgotten gash. "It's okay." Then his forehead chose to hurt spitefully.

She said, "Hold still."

His eyes were level with her nice breasts, so he lowered his gaze but then he was looking at the tops of her legs where they joined. He closed his eyes as he asked ruefully, "What's this gonna cost me?"

She made herself be patient. "It's free."

He became conscious of his clean but work-worn shirt and jeans. "I don't need charity. I can pay." He started to get up.

"It's reciprocity to a colleague." She thought he'd laugh at that, but he gave an accepting nod, sat back down and allowed her to administer to him.

He instructed: "Clean it first."

Only then did she realize he must think she was an office clerk. She said, "You do know that I'm a registered nurse? And I have additional training as a surgical nurse.''

He nodded politely. "How many babies have you delivered?" He spoke as if to a fellow obstetrician.

She replied, "This was my first solo."

"You did very well."

"Thank you." She applied antibiotic to the cut and began to tape it. She wondered how many babies he'd delivered. In that sparse area and with his take-over attitude, the people must depend on him for everything, whether or not they were willing. His name was at the head of her emergency list. "How many have you delivered?"

"Quite a few."

She was impressed. He'd lost actual count of how many.

"It's different when they're alive this way."

That startled her.

He went on, "With the rubber ones, in practice, you don't realize it hurts that way, getting the kid out. Did you get the stuff in his eyes okay? And clear out his nose?"

It took a minute before she realized her hands had gentled, so her voice sharpened as she said "Yes."

"Good. Cleaning their eyes is important."

With dispatch, she completed the bandaging. Then she stepped back as she said "There," in a very final way.

He stood up and looked down at her. Remembering that she needed practice in accepting compliments, he stooped and pretended to look at the bandage in the reflection of the empty glass-fronted cabinet. He said, "You did a good job of it. Thank you."

"It's quite bruised, you know. You'll have a black eye."

Thinking of his isolation, he scoffed, "Lady won't mind."

"Is that her name?"

"Whose?"

"Is Lady your wife?"

He didn't turn away at the familiar questioning, or look down at the floor as once he would have. "Naw. Lady's my dog. My wife left a long time ago." For no reason, this time he went on in a slow, earnest voice: "She didn't like being on a farm. She thought it was...lonesome." He was still puzzled how that could have been.

"People are different."

She had said that as if she shrugged her shoulders over the variance in people, as if she had been confronted by that fact and had accepted it.

He wondered what "different" person had affected her life. What man?

Chapter Two

Leaving the doctor's office, Jethro surreptitiously removed the neat bandage from his forehead. He didn't want to attract any sympathetic attention. Sometimes women tended to get carried away about men who were hurt.

He went about his delayed errands and almost immediately heard a woman question, "Why, Jethro! What happened to your forehead?"

He replied as he tried to walk on past, "It's okay."

The next exclamation was "You've hurt yourself!"

He resisted saying "Really?" and just said, "It's okay."

Then someone asked, "How did you do that?"

By then, he wished he'd left the bandage on the scratch. Even as he was annoyed by the alarmed Florence Nightingales, he understood such concern was important to other people. He just thanked God he didn't live in town.

He loaded his purchases into his truck and drove out of Hadley toward freedom. And he thought how strange it was that people felt the need to gather together in towns, while he longed for the farm and felt uncomfortable away from it. He would be contented to live entirely alone.

But Betsy had complained about living "clear out there" with just him. The nurse was right. People were different. Some women just weren't made to live on a farm. Betsy had hated it when the dirt had blown across plowed fields. And she disliked the animals that had to have care. She'd complained about the long hours and her tired muscles, when all she had to do was learn to pace herself.

In spite of the unpredictable weather, farming gave Jethro great satisfaction. It was like a game of chance—some years you won. But taking the risk just wasn't for everybody.

Jethro loved the land, the "silence" of the sounds of nature. He couldn't change. Betsy had pleaded with him to move into town and commute to the farm. And he had tried, but he'd felt stifled. He just couldn't live in a town—not even one the size of little Hadley. There, he'd become a part of a different situation, one that the old turtles controlled.

It wasn't that he didn't appreciate the advantages gained by living among other people. He'd gone to Purdue University and gotten his degree. He'd been to Chicago. It had seemed frantic to him. He'd seen the things the city had to offer, and he was glad that he had; but he wasn't in any hurry to make a habit of going back.

With his thirty-fifth birthday, Jethro had faced the fact that he would probably never remarry. Although he regretted not having children, he'd accepted his unmarried state with some relief. But while he didn't need a woman for companionship or to clean or to cook for him, he longed for the time when his body would quit hungering.

He drove along the gravel road, resting his dark gaze on the expanse of land divided by tree lines into fields of soybeans and standing corn. There was the heaviness of full maturity in the growing things. They were fulfilled, their fruit ready; the growing season was finished. Now, in the night, he heard the cries of migrating flocks. Winter would come, and there'd be times when he would be snowbound. He'd be alone. He remembered other winters.

Gradually he became conscious of the fact that he was wondering what the nurse's name was. He shifted his position on the car seat, looked around briskly and drove on to his farmyard, stopping his truck beside Lady. She was small, black, mostly Scots collie, and she greeted him with calm affection.

Jethro remembered when he was first married and Betsy used to burst from the house when he came home. She'd yell "Jethro!" with such gladness. It took him a while before he understood that it wasn't him she wanted necessarily; just someone around to be with her. Making Betsy live out there was just the opposite of caging a bird. On the open farm, Betsy had felt trapped.

Jethro squatted down and asked the dog, "Aren't you going to ask me about my forehead?"

Lady sat in front of him and smiled, her tongue out as she panted in the lazy August heat.

"She's a looker, that one, that nurse that fixed my cut. I helped to deliver a baby today. Women make a lot more fuss over it than you ever did." He patted the dog, who was now spayed.

She pulled in her tongue as she turned her head and perked her ears at some sound Jethro hadn't heard. Having satisfied herself about the sound, the dog gave him her attention again.

"I wonder what she's called. That nurse. I wonder what her name is."

The dog just looked at him.

He stood and stretched, listening to the familiar sounds around him. Finally he focused on his yard. He looked more closely and frowned. He was getting careless.

There were no longer flower gardens. They'd died after Betsy left, and he hadn't replaced them. It was easier without them because they'd interrupted mowing. He spent the next hour mowing and trimming, then another hour sanding and painting the porch swing that hung from a branch of an enormous maple.

After he surveyed the yard with satisfaction, he went inside and looked around. He scrubbed the clean kitchen, put away the dishes from the dishwasher he'd bought for Betsy. Then he vacuumed and did three loads of wash. As he folded the last of the laundry, he paused to consider why he was making the house ready. For company? No way.

Dr. Cory Lombard was a young, energetic, competent medical man. He came on the following Tuesday for his first clinic day in Hadley. The office was in excellent shape, and he was pleased to have a full list of patients, but not too many. He could take a little extra time with each one, getting acquainted.

One of the first was Dan Seymore, who was the oldest citizen of Hadley and one of those who had recruited Dr. Lombard to set up this office. Dan told the doctor, "It was worth the effort to get you here, just to have your nurse around. She is a treat to the eyes."

Cory replied, "She's told me about you people."

The old man faked an earnest protest: "I didn't pinch her that day. I couldn't get through the crowd around Pete and his wife in all the excitement last week.''

Cory grinned. "See what a guilty conscience will do to you? She told me how kind everyone had been here in Hadley."

Dan chuckled. "That gal's a doer. She's got the farmers promising to bring in trees to plant in the courthouse lawn. We lost all our trees to Dutch elm disease about twenty years ago. We just never got around to planting any more."

"She's a good woman." Cory smiled at the elderly man. "Any complaints?"

"None. I'll last another eighty years. Just wanted to tell you welcome to our town."

Cory rose and held out his hand. "Thank you." After they smiled at each other, the doctor escorted the old man into the hall and indicated the exit door. Then Cory went to the half partition and asked Meg to send in the next patient.

Meg checked the sign-in list and looked over the room. "Jethro Hanna?" She watched him stand up and as he came closer she asked, "How's your head?"

He'd forgotten the healing cut and replied soberly, "Still on."

"I bet you took the bandage off as soon as you left here! It needed the support of the tape. It will probably scar."

"It's okay. I'm not entering any beauty contests."

As she led him into the doctor's office, she found herself thinking, but he could. With his dark good looks he could enter a "beauty" contest. And he'd win. She said, "Doctor Lombard, this is Jethro Hanna, who is first on the emergency list, and he was here last week when the Calhouns had their baby."

Jethro shook hands with the doctor and didn't realize that he and his nurse had shared a brief, communicating glance, so the doctor's smile seemed only friendly.

Before the nurse could leave the room, Jethro said very seriously, "Your nurse handled herself well." She had to learn to accept compliments, and he would help in that whenever he could.

"Meg is very competent," the doctor replied in a kind and noncommittal way, and his smile stayed.

Meg, Jethro thought. Her name is Meg. Meg wasn't flowing enough. It was too short, too abrupt; like her hair.

"Did you come to see about the gash on your forehead? It looks fine. No infection."

"No. I just came to sign up and assure you of my support. I'm never sick, but I think it's fine that you're coming here. I'll set up a physical so you'll have some business."

"We appreciate it."

Jethro accepted that.

After Jethro had departed ten minutes later, Cory stopped at Meg's desk and advised, "Hook that fish. He's an original."

"You know I've signed up for only two years, so find another woman for him. I've been cured."

"All men are different, Meg, you know that. Not every man would be like Jack. I believe Jethro—what a great name that is—I believe Jethro would be worth the time and effort."

"Baloney."

But there were other people who felt the same way Dr. Lombard did. With no communication, really, the town of Hadley paired off Jethro and Meg Bailey. It was all mental. No matter how they plotted, the two were like slippery eels. They avoided every single attempt to get them together.

Jethro understood the town and knew immediately what was afoot. He was practiced in avoidance. Meg, too, was clever about entrapment, so they never met. They acknowledged each other when they met by accident, but they didn't even comment on the weather! In Indiana, the weather was grist for any conversational mill.

It was the middle of September when little David Calhoun was baptized. Meg had been flattered when she was asked to be godmother. It didn't surprise her too much, since she'd delivered the baby, and most people around that sparsely populated area were already godparents to enough kids. Old Dan Seymore claimed half the county were his godchildren.

The Calhouns had no close family. They were special to the area because that was unique, so most of the town was there for the baptism and were already in the church when the godfather arrived. It was Jethro. It was the first time Meg had seen him in a suit, shirt and tie; and he looked terriff—very nice. The two godparents were stiff and only nodded.

Perfunctorily, Jethro told Meg, "You look like a bride in that pretty dress with the flowers on your shoulder." He meant to compliment her, to give her practice; but he saw that she tightened her lips.

He kept his distance until the preacher told them to come forward to the baptismal font. And Jethro saw that as Meg held the baby, the neckline of her dress had buckled out. Looking over her shoulder at the baby, Jethro could see a disturbing amount of Meg's bosom. He said, "Let me hold him."

Meg's arms tightened possessively and she replied, "Never mind."

But for his own sake, Jethro put a firm hand on Meg's back and put his other big hand under the baby's bottom, thereby adjusting the line of Meg's dress. That way, Jethro ought to have been able to listen to the preacher; but his hand reminded him that it was against Meg's back—and that it liked being there.

Although everyone watched avidly, neither godparent appeared aware of the other, and those witnesses left the celebration disappointed.

After the newness of having a doctor in town on a regular basis wore off, the only thing of any interest that happened was that Pete Calhoun got his pilot's license.

"It's a fool thing to do." Old Dan Seymore was positive. But then, he was still adjusting to cars.

Then Pete got a single-engine plane, and he gave his Ultra Light to Jethro. It was one of those little mosquito things consisting of a seat, footrest, wings and a motor. There were few rules about flying such a contraption, and you didn't need a pilot's license. Anybody could buy one, or order a kit and put it together. Or he could contrive his own. It was a dumb thing to fly one—a lot of the people said so—but a lot of eyes watched Jethro putt across the sky, and they yelled and waved to him.

On the courthouse square, the turtles watched, in the magical late-September weather; and they had grave reservations about a solid man, like Jethro, who showed such odd tendencies in his mid-thirties.

Then Jethro got a bigger mosquito plane and offered free rides. The shocker was that Dan Seymore was first in line. He didn't get there first; he just hobbled past everyone else and took first place. And they let him.

After the flight, when Jethro had landed the craft, the two men sat there for a while as Dan adjusted to being back on earth. He got off the seat with aged difficulty, and the spectators all waited to hear what he would say. He looked at them—those waiting and the larger group of onlookers—and he pronounced, "I'm going to start being good."

They all howled with laughter.

And Meg got in line.

Seeing her get in line made Jethro excessively aware of the fact that she would be sitting closely behind him—very close. He hadn't paid that much attention to the others who had to practically ride his hips. He'd shared the flight with them, the magic, and now he would share the magic and that extreme closeness with . . . Meg.

Now why should that rattle him?

Two more until Meg. One more. Then it was her turn. His palms sweated. He didn't just let her crawl into that limited space. He got off, held the plane, and he helped her. She was a little excited, he could see that. The fact excited him. Why? Why should he be nervous because she'd be so close to him as they climbed into the sky where she could look around from the back of this mosquito he was piloting?

He carefully settled in front of her and had only to lower his gaze to see her knees on either side of him. His skin could feel her only about an inch from his back.

He said, "The barf bags are on the ground right under the plane. Please aim carefully." She laughed breathlessly in his ear. He lifted off after only a hop and a skip, and they skimmed away. She put her hands around his belt and hung on. He was tempted to show off a little, but he did refrain.

She said almost giddy *oh*'s and *ah*'s and she was just charming. He laughed out loud, and she joined in. She said, "Oh, Jethro..." And she said it again, "Oh, Jethro—" the exact same way.

That was how the flying affected him, in that silly little lighter-than-air magical nonsense.

Then his beeper beeped.

Chapter Three

Jethro turned back to land in the same spot, and the instant the field came into sight, he saw that all the others had left. They'd stranded Meg with him. So he turned the tiny craft toward his place. That the townspeople would deliberately trap him with Meg made his blood pressure elevate and his breath come more quickly. His consciousness of her seated so close, just in back of him, became exquisite.

Turning his chin to his shoulder he told her: "I'm going to have to take you to my place. I don't know what the problem is, but I'll call in. If I have to leave, and I probably will, you can drive my car into town. Can you drive?"

"Yes."

With her brief, aloof reply, he knew she was equally aware that they'd been trapped by the matchmakers. But he found that he was piqued that she sounded as irritated by it as he.

As he approached his house, he was pleased that the yard was neat and the house clean. For once, something positive had happened. Positive? What did he mean by thinking it was positive that his house would look good to this woman? He hardened his heart and stiffened.

As silently as they'd landed, they rode the frail craft into its storage shed where he tethered it. She got off by herself before he could ignore her. She looked around. He said, "Hold it a minute." Then he ran to the house and phoned in. There was a fire at McHenry's. The barn.

He ran outside to her, waiting there, and flipped the keys to her. "The car's over there in the garage. McHenry's barn's on fire. I'll pick up the car later. Just park it in the square. Leave the keys on the floor under the passenger seat."

And he was gone.

She stood watching his truck disappear before she went over to the garage. She opened the doors in order to back out his sassy red car. It still smelled new and it was at least three years old. There were only two thousand miles on it. She sat there thoughtfully. Then she got out, closed the garage doors and turned to look at his house.

It was newly painted. The swing under the maple tree was freshly painted, too. The yard was mowed. She walked across the gravel drive and went up onto his porch. The door wasn't locked. She looked around, seeing what he saw from his porch. Then she went inside.

It was ordinary. Clean. It was a house, not a home. There was nothing to distinguish it from a basically bland, middle-class house, its furnishings chosen from a catalog with no imagination at all. It was just that the house wasn't at all important to whomever it was who lived there. Its purpose was to provide comfort and utility.

The dog was there when Meg went to the door to leave. Meg hesitated for a minute, not sure if the animal would allow her to leave. How embarrassing it would be if she was trapped inside by the dog until Jethro came home. Ye gods.

Meg opened the door a slit, and the dog was interested and watched. Meg widened the gap, ready to slam it shut. But the dog didn't move. Still ready to retreat instantly, Meg stepped onto the porch, but the dog—Lady, that was its name. "Hello, Lady. You caught me being nosy, didn't you?"

The dog smiled a little.

"I was just very curious. You have a very interesting man as your patron. I realize he doesn't own you and you're in charge, really. May I take a giant step to that car? I do have permission to use it, you know. It will be returned." Meg edged off the porch and headed for the car. Lady got up unthreateningly and leisurely followed Meg.

Meg got in and closed the door quickly. Lady sat and smiled widely as if very amused by such a strange woman.

Meg rolled down the window a little and said, "You're a rotten watchdog. And I know you understand every word I've said, but at least you can't blab."

That had the effect of making Lady get to her feet and lean her nose to the ground as she walked a couple of paces. Then she sat down again, with that wide, wide grin on her face and her tongue out, panting as if with silent laughter.

"Goodbye."

And the damned dog gave a soft bark.

The McHenry farm pond hadn't been cleaned lately, so water weeds clogged the hoses and strained the pumps. It was maddening. The volunteer firemen struggled to save the other buildings, and McHenry worked silently with them. All of that year's hay had been stored in the burning barn.

Jethro stripped and waded into the pond and cleaned the filter on the intake valve yet again. He remained in the water, trying to keep the weeds clear of the valve. The water was cold.

One of the McHenrys took over the job in the pond, and after that, it was always a McHenry in the water. They acknowledged their mistake.

Jethro had put on his heavy coat and helmet, pulled the boots and gloves back on and took one hose to direct the water with calculated skill on a building next to the barn. The shed had a tractor inside.

A McHenry son yelled to Jethro, "Cover me with water. That tractor has a full tank. If it explodes, the house'll go." The roof was burning, and the air was scorching.

Jethro yelled back, "No! I have protective clothing. Is the key there?" He was really the only man there who wasn't committed to a family. He was used to taking the lead, to risking the dangers. It wasn't anything but an automatic reflex. He didn't have a hero complex.

"The key's on the wall to the right of the door, shoulder high."

Jethro handed him the hose and said, "I can do it quicker. Keep the hose on the tank." In his heavy clothing and boots, he ran inside. He had to take his glove off to handle the key and the key was red-hot. He grimaced and ignored it, got on the tractor, started the motor with his heart in his mouth, and drove it out of the shed, expecting the world to blow any minute. But it didn't.

He didn't dare sit down on the seat, so standing up and one-handedly, he drove on away, clear of everything, knocking down a fence in the doing of it. He let go of the steering wheel, took off his other glove and looked at his hands. The key had burned into his fingers.

"Here." One of the other volunteers had a bucket of water.

"Put your hand in this," Mark, the chief, urged. "That was a damned fool thing to do, Jethro."

"The tank was full."

Mark was furious. "Anybody that would let a pond get clogged . . . No, I don't mean that."

They'd had a bad fire. All their hay had gone up in high, billowing flames. There'd been no wind. Hot, tired and dirty, they'd finally controlled it.

Mark asked Jethro, "Let me see your hand. You ought to go into town to the clinic and get that taken care of."

"A little grease will do it."

"No." Mark was adamant as several others came over. "The blisters are broken. It needs an antibiotic."

One of the others agreed with Mark. "Don't hang around. The worst is over. The rest of us can handle it now. Get going."

They helped him get out of his protective clothing. Somebody found his shirt. They were all careful with him, and the McHenrys were almost sick with their gratitude.

By then it was late afternoon. Jethro put on his shirt, his hand objecting strongly to being used. He got into his truck and started it; his adrenaline was used up and he was suddenly very tired. He was strongly tempted to just go on home, but his hand hurt like hell, and he drove in to the clinic. He was somewhat befuddled to find that he wanted Meg to see him this way. His clothes were still wet from his early turn in the pond. He was dirty and wounded. He was a warrior coming home?

A wounded warrior? Now where did a committed bachelor get such a fanciful idea? Thinking that way was dangerous. He didn't want Meg to admire him. His hand did need some care. She could wrap it better than he could. His going to the clinic was only practical.

He drove up and honked twice. Then he sat there for a minute, gathering the effort to get out of the truck. He was really tired.

He went up and lifted his left hand to knock on the door, when she opened it. Her eyes were big as they avidly roved over him. "What happened?"

"They lost the barn and this year's hay."

She backed away, drawing him inside.

"We got the tractor out."

"Your hand?" She'd made a quick survey of him, and other than the burn, he appeared to be intact. "Anything else?"

"No." He sighed deeply.

"Let me see."

"A little grease and some pain pills?"

"I need to clean it." She squinted. "This won't be fun."

"I can handle it."

She turned on the lights in one examination room. Then she held his hand and looked it over carefully. She took him over to the lavatory and set his hand in a sterile bowl before she turned the spigot so that the water flowed into the bowl around his hand. It felt good, cooling.

She hooked the toes of one foot on a stool and rolled it over. "Sit. I'll call the doctor and see if he needs to see you tonight. Just a minute." She left him there.

He heard the murmur of her voice as she discussed his burns. He put his head down on his arms, all the fight gone from his body.

She came back and found him asleep. She allowed that for a while, leaving the water running into the bowl.

Hovering over him, unaware that she hovered, she watched him sleep. His eyelashes were dark on his sun-browned, fire-reddened cheeks. His dark hair was mussed and a little singed. He was a broad-shouldered man. His body was built by hard work. The hair on his arms was black and his fingers were blunt on his big hands. She remembered him holding Christy's new little baby. Thinking of that made looking at him do things inside her chest. So she looked elsewhere. There wasn't anything around in that room that caught her attention, and she looked back at Jethro Hanna.

After a while, when she'd judged that his exhaustion had lightened, she gently moved his hand, cleaning the wounds. He stirred, his consciousness flickering to awareness.

"You must have worked hard on that fire."

He murmured, "It's always such a hell-bent job. So much counts on time. We're really good at it. We work hard. We don't have very many fires around here. We're careful, mostly. If their pond had been cleaned properly, it wouldn't have been so hairy." He hadn't intended the pun.

Neither interrupted the following silence. She worked on his hand, covered it, then wrapped it loosely to protect the covering. Then she put her hand under his chin and studied his face. He looked at her, and his heart almost stopped, because he thought she was going to kiss him. His lips parted— But she turned away to get a soft cloth, which she soaped. Then she cleaned his face and smoothed a soothing lotion over it.

She found a plastic bag and gave it to him, saying, "Shower when you get home, but use the plastic bag over your hand to keep the dressing dry. Don't wash your face yet. Take one of these pills. If you waken in the night, take the other if you need it. I don't think you'll waken, you're too tired. In the morning you need to go into Creighton to see Dr. Lombard and let him take a look at that hand." She watched him. "Will you be okay, driving back to your house tonight?"

"No problem."

"You've had supper?"

"Mrs. McHenry had food for us most of the time."

"You do remember that your car is here? Would you prefer to drive it instead of the truck? It handles like a dream."

"I'm too dirty. I'll come get it tomorrow." He patted his empty pockets. "I left my wallet at home. I never take anything with me on an emergency. I'll have to pay you tomorrow, too."

"This was for the car rental."

He started to object, but she was a little stiff waiting for just such an objection, so he said, "Thank you."

She replied, "You're welcome."

He drove back to his house. The dog greeted him and didn't tattle about Meg being inside his house, but he knew. Because he'd left the door handle just a bit off kilter, he knew someone had been inside. She was curious about him?

He went inside and looked at his house through a stranger's eyes. And he saw the same old things.

He checked his valuables, and they hadn't been touched. Nor were any of his other common clues to betray the pause of an 1nvader. So she'd just come inside and looked around. Why?

Chapter Four

Jethro went into the back bedroom, stripped, walked down the hall to the bathroom and turned on the shower. He found himself staring at the dry dressing Meg had put on his hand. She'd wanted him to keep it dry.

He sighed in disgust and went to retrieve the plastic bag to put it carefully on his hand and secured it with rubber bands. Then he took a one-handed shower. Two hands came in handier.

He dried himself awkwardly, took the pill, and went into his bedroom at the back of the house. Naked, he crawled into bed and covered himself with the sheet and a light blanket. He lay on his back, and for the first time in all his life, he felt that he was alone.

He studied that problem, dismissed it, turned over and went to sleep. He dreamed. He dreamed of fires and danger. He dreamed of flying—without even his fragile craft. He dreamed of falling. He dreamed of Meg reaching out to him. And he dreamed of making love.

He wakened in the darkness and his hand hurt like bloody hell. He got up and groped his way to the bathroom and took the other pill. He thought sourly that she'd been positive he'd sleep like a log the whole night, and here he was, taking the second pill. Then he saw that it was five-thirty and heard the birds were talking. It was almost dawn, but he'd already taken the pill.

There was the choice between getting rid of the pill, or going back to sleep. He went back to bed and slept instantly.

The phone rang a couple of times, almost rousing him, but he thought to hell with it and went back to sleep.

He wakened at noon and felt great. His hand didn't hurt unduly as he stretched and rolled over. He felt contented.

Ravenous, he got up and fixed his breakfast, automatically using that hand with no drastic objections from it. He ate with relish and scoffed at his remembered feelings of loneliness. Him? Hog wash.

He was shaving with his left hand when the phone rang again. He picked it up and said, "Yeah?"

Meg's voice questioned in his ear, "Are you okay?"

"Yeah."

"Dr. Lombard called, asking what happened to you. You were supposed to let him have a look at that hand."

"No need. It's fine. I let it help cook breakfast just a while ago. That second pill was a dilly. I just got up."

"You wakened in the night?"

"Yeah."

"That surprises me. That pill is potent."

"I dreamed fires and disasters all night long." He didn't mention that he'd made love to her, too. But he was conscious of the fact that he was prolonging the conversation. "If you don't need it, I'll get the car today."

"If you don't need it until evening, I'll have someone follow me out and return it then."

"Uh." What was his tongue doing? He listened in astonishment as he heard himself saying with slow carefulness: "Why don't you drive it out and I'll take you back? No need to bother anyone else with this problem."

She hesitated before deciding, "All right."

He heard her reluctance, but he said "Fine" and hung up the phone without saying goodbye. He walked differently, going back to finish his shave. And he smiled at himself in the bathroom mirror. Then he frowned and became businesslike as he forced his right hand to agree to take over the job and do a better shave.

He went out and looked around the yard. He'd been keeping it very neat lately. No problem. He went back inside and looked around and straightened, here and there. It was already clean. He was restless and got out the tiny aircraft to fly over his land and feel the satisfaction in seeing his property. He had a very nice farm. Enough land, no debts, enough profit and freedom. He was his own man. He felt a little sinful pride.

He returned to his house early because he was afraid he might miss her. He decided he'd invite her for a flight. It would be pretty. The leaves on the trees were just starting to turn nicely, and the air was cool. He would need to give her something warm to wear. He found several pairs of coveralls in the barn and washed them. He dug out a yellow sweater for her to wear under the coveralls. The yellow would be pretty with her dark hair. When the dryer was finished, he folded the best pair of coveralls and laid them and the sweater in a pile on his bed and looked at them.

Restlessly he walked around, then he dug out a roast and thawed it in the microwave before he put it into his conventional oven to bake with potatoes, carrots and onions. He decided at the last minute, that he could be surprised it was suppertime and could ask her to stay for it.

He put one of his grandmother's apple pies out to thaw on its own. His grandmaw lived down near Lafayette. She made him twelve pies at a time. He would share one with Meg.

When she arrived, he stood on his porch as she got out of his car, and his body's delight startled him. But the thought that she looked good to him shook him as he stood there in his yard. He bit his lower lip and decided he'd take her back to town right that minute. He went down the steps toward her to tell her that and asked, "What's your full name?" The question shocked them both. "Is Meg a nickname?"

"What? My name? It's Megan."

His mouth tasted it: "Megan." Then it went right on and asked, "Would you like to fly around for a while? I was out earlier and I'd be glad to take you up. It's still light enough to see the tree colors." His words made his face freeze and he was immobilized.

After a very long pause, she replied starkly, "All right."

To his indignation, his mouth couldn't wait to go right on: "You'll need something warmer. I have some coveralls." And he realized they were very obviously ready on his bed. "I'll see if I can find something." He belatedly began to take control back from his busy tongue.

"This is Lady?" Meg pretended to be surprised by the dog, but they shared a look of recognition, and the dog smiled knowingly.

"Yeah. Lady. Lady, this is...Megan."

His tone of voice saying her name made Meg's spine prickle oddly and her nipples peak. She shot a glance at him, but he was smiling at the dog in a dreamy sort of way. She was going to fly off the ground, into the sky, in that flimsy-winged nothing—with this man? The fact that he ever would fly around in something that silly proved something. And it cast large questions about her, if she went along. "We needn't—"

"You don't have to take off your clothes. My coveralls are big enough to fit over your..." His voice trailed away as he considered how his clothes would be so intimate with her body. He blinked. This was all a big mistake. He clapped his hands together once and said, "Come on in, and we'll get moving." Then he heard what he'd said and was appalled how she might think he meant— He stopped cold and stared. What would she think of him?

She would think he wasn't stable.

He hastened to explain: "This time, I'll show you how to steer, how to work your feet and the joystick...." And again he was silenced as he stared at her.

She replied busily, "I really—"

"We can just take a quick one." His soul groaned. Maybe Meg was incapable of accepting compliments, but he couldn't even talk right. He took a deep breath and turned his back on her, shoving his hands into his coverall pockets. "Meg— Really. We'll just go for a short hop. Then I'll take you home."

She knew that she wasn't going to be able to gracefully get out of flying with him. She would have to go for at least a short flight. He *was* capable. He could fly that foolish little thing. She could go along for that, then she'd be free to ask him to take her home. Or she could walk. Or "How about flying me into town?" Her mind applauded: brilliant!

He was already shaking his head. "You have to know they are trying to match us up. If we land in town, I'll have to walk you home, and *everybody* will know. It's best this way. I'll drive you back after the flight. Okay?"

"Everybody already knows I've had your car and—"

"They know why, too. They deserted you at the field when we were up flying, and with the emergency at McHenry's, I had to bring you back here, and you had to have a way back into town. It was the only solution then, but now, if I fly you into town, they'll think we're playing around." And his body loved the words.

"Okay. Just a short flight."

"Right." He went up on the porch, taking the steps two at a time, then he turned and looked back at her. She *really* looked good in his yard. "Come on. I've got a sweater for you that's sure to be big enough." He smiled.

She looked at the beautiful size of him, took a slow breath, and walked sedately to the steps, keeping her back straight as she mounted them precisely. This incident would pass. She would eventually be home again, in the apartment above the clinic, where she would have some hot cocoa; and in a couple of weeks she would take out this memory and view it safely. Now she'd just concentrate on getting through it.

He watched her to see if she would look around in a new-viewing way. She did. That confused him, because his house wasn't anything to look at a second time, and he wondered if maybe it hadn't been Megan who'd been inside. If not her, who? He said to her, "Wait here a minute."

She stood there by the door.

His feet thunked along the bare hallway to a back room, and he knew she heard him as he needlessly opened doors and opened and shut drawers. He took the stack off the bed and returned to the living room with clean, folded coveralls and the yellow sweater. He smiled as he handed them to her.

She stood uncertainly, holding the garments on her hands.

He went over to one side of the long hall, opened a closet door and brought back two knitted caps. "My mother makes these by the dozens, calculated by how many in each family. Being single again, and with no kids, I get more hats then any of the others." He frowned at her and explained further: "Mother gets a guilt trip if she makes only one for me, so I get several."

With him talking about a mother and family members, he seemed more real, so she turned and set the stack of clothing on the sofa. Then she pulled the sweater on over her head. Her curls were briefly flattened, then sprang back into their halo.

He watched that intently as he blurted, "I'd like your hair longer."

Primly she replied, "This length is convenient. I can scrub for an operation in nothing flat."

He looked down her and thought of what she scrubbed so routinely and without any real appreciation. He caught his thoughts and cleared his throat.

She was getting into the coveralls, and they were far too large. He went to her and squatted down, but she stumbled over the excess cloth to move away from him.

"Hold still," he cautioned. He lifted one of her feet to his knee and rolled the leg of the coveralls to a decent length.

As he did the other leg, she finally saw his hand as one she'd bandaged. She asked, "How's your hand?"

He then rose effortlessly, saying "No problem." He folded the sleeves, then stepped back to survey her. "You look like you're wearing your big brother's clothes, trying to look grown-up."

"I'm over thirty." Her tone was parsimonious.

"My, that is impressive. I'm thirty-five."

His look was so male that she hurried to ask, "Did you keep the bandage dry?"

"Yes, ma'am."

But she saw the indulgent amusement. Yet another time, she wished she could be ten inches past five feet, instead of just five inches.

He brought the knitted hat to her and would have teasingly pulled it onto her head, but she ducked and took it from him, putting it on herself.

"Do you wear glasses? It keeps the bugs and dirt out of your eyes. No? Well, I have these carpentry glasses. They'll do. Here."

They were ready. He went to the door and remembered to allow her to go through first. She saw that he wasn't used to caring about a woman. He was a natural loner.

He said, "Hold it," and went to the kitchen and fiddled with the stove. He returned to her and said, "I've got supper in the oven."

Lady walked beside them to the mosquito plane, and again, just seeing the fragile nothingness of it,

Meg's qualms returned. Oddly, he seemed to understand her hesitation because he said, "It sure looks stupid, doesn't it? But it's safe as long as there aren't any sudden winds. We fly under all the other planes and we watch out for kite strings. Let's go."

And she was lifted by a spirit of adventure.

Chapter Five

The evening was calm, the sun was setting, and it was a glorious time. Jethro took the plane up with Megan riding his hips and clinging to the back of his belt. The wind created by their movement was invigorating, like vintage wine. There was the smell of fall, of soil that had fulfilled the cycle of growth. The panorama was breathtaking, since the craft had no sides, it seemed they flew on a witch's broomstick. It was indeed magic.

And Jethro shared it silently with Megan.

They flew until the last of the sun's rays shone and then returned to land with their final glimmer. He'd pushed it. But he'd been reluctant to end such a flight. As amazing as the craft was, and as wildly free as it made his soul, the experience had been enhanced by sharing it with Megan.

It became dead dark right after they landed, and it was fortunate he had a flashlight in the pocket of the leg of his coveralls. He shone its beam ahead of them and picked up the shine of Lady's eyes as the dog waited for them. He called, "Lead us home, Lady."

The dog turned obediently and Jethro's craft followed through the first dark of the fall night. Soon the moon would rise—a harvest moon. It would be something to fly in such a sky. But he wasn't skilled enough yet.

Still curled behind Jethro, Megan was silent as she clung to his belt. He looked over his shoulder at her. "Are you frozen?"

"Not . . . quite. It was beautiful."

"Yes."

"Thank you."

"You're welcome."

"I want to learn to fly one."

"I'll teach you."

"I want to build my own."

"I'll help you."

"It's just wonderful."

"Yes." It had been the same for her as it was for him.

He put the plane away, and silent, they walked back to the house. He longed to be able to say ordinary things. He prayed for an agile, easy tongue; but the skill eluded him. He said, "I saw little David today. He called me Jeth."

"He's not old enough to say words yet."

A little offended, Jethro reiterated: "I distinctly heard him say 'Jeth.'"

"Undoubtedly." She was being sarcastic, but she relented and added, "Christy brought him into the office to say hello."

"If he couldn't say 'Jeth,' he couldn't say 'hello.'"

Megan sighed, but the darkness covered her smile. What a stubborn man. Arrogant. Male.

With calculation he said, "I'm starved. Have you eaten?"

She recognized an awkward confrontation. She could say yes and be stuck on the porch while he ate in the kitchen. Or she could admit she was ravenously hungry. It was late, and the aroma of the roast with its onions was sneaking from the open house. It lured her. She said, "No. I'm hungry, too."

"Good."

She waited, but he didn't invite her to eat with him. She said, "I'll just change—"

He looked surprised. "Don't you want to eat first? It's ready."

"I have on too many clothes. You probably aren't wearing any—" She stopped.

"You're hot?" He looked down her body, then bit his tongue for such silly words. "Want some help?"

"Why, yes. Thank you."

Taking off the coveralls suddenly seemed like a sexual teasing, and she turned her back. She slid them off and faltered, but he was there to catch her arm, squat down and help her get her foot out of the rolled-up trouser leg. He grinned up at her. "You're little."

"No."

"I didn't mean helpless. You're a firm, pushy woman. But you're littler than me."

She straightened and bent a cool stare down her nose as he grinned up at her. "Pushy?" she inquired in a rather hostile way.

"Yeah." He peeled the other coverall leg off hers. "You tend to take over. When I delivered David—"

She was positive: "*I* delivered David."

"You got in the way."

She couldn't think of anything that was equally snubbing and yet tactful enough for his overbearing male ego, so she was silent.

"I'll dish up. How about setting the table? There're dishes in that cabinet, and the knives and forks are in that drawer."

Before she began, she automatically washed her hands.

He then washed his left hand and the fingertips of his bandaged right hand. He was exquisitely conscious of her being there. His body was. He took quick side glances at her moving around there in his kitchen. Not long ago, she had been wearing his coveralls. His coveralls had been against her, rubbing on her body— He'd better not think about that.

They sat down in the silence and hungrily ate the good meal. It was delicious. She thought he would make someone a good husband since he could cook that well. But she wasn't in the market.

"My grandmother made the rolls."

"They're just right."

"Do you bake?"

"Not at all," she lied.

He was silent.

So he was looking for someone to cook for him? Not she.

"It's a good thing I had this cooking. You were hungry."

"I enjoyed it." Brilliant conversation. He was really a very nice man—if someone wanted one. But she wasn't interested. That meant that she wouldn't fly with him again. She'd have to give it up until after she left Hadley. No sense in inviting a closer relationship.

"I understand you're not here permanently." He encouraged her to talk.

"No."

"Good people here."

"Yes."

"Why would you leave?"

She was amazed that he would be so sincere in his question. Obviously he saw nothing in the world better than Hadley. Hadley? She smiled. "I'm a city girl. Cory is an old friend and he helped me out once, some years back. I'm repaying the favor getting this office started here in Hadley. Once it's well established, I'll go on."

"You won't find better people anywhere else in this whole world than those here, in this place."

"They've been very kind to me." She was as non-committal as she could be, and it was true. It was just that she hadn't mentioned how nosy they'd all been or how curious they were about her. They had been so blatant with their questions that she was sometimes stalled dead in her tracks trying to be tactful about not replying. Salt of the earth or not, they were darned near rude.

"Of course," he admitted generously, "the turtles think they run the place."

Cautiously she inquired, "Turtles?"

He nodded. "The old men on the square. They set the rules. Everybody thinks the old women run things in a place, and that could be so in other places, but here it's the old men. And Dan Seymore is the worst one in the whole bunch."

She laughed. Jethro called them turtles. Perfect! There was hope for this man. He had an imagination! Yes, and he loved flying that mosquito of a plane.

He was almost startled by her laughter. His ears soaked it up. How long had it been since a woman had laughed in that house? And he wondered if Betsy had ever laughed out loud. He tried to remember. He said, "I think I told you I was married once."

Megan didn't know what to say, so she just looked over at him to acknowledge that he'd spoken.

"She hated it here." He looked around, still not understanding.

Megan, too, glanced about the blah house.

"She didn't take the long view. Any setback was terrible, and any gain wasn't enough. She felt...caged here on the land." His puzzlement was obvious as he frowned over such an amazing thing.

Again Megan gave him the reply "People are different."

"Somebody dump you?"

She shouldn't have been astonished by his bluntness since she'd had over a month of those kinds of questions. She gave him a bland look and inquired, "Why do you ask?"

He explained, "You seem to understand."

She immediately stopped any feeling he might have of rapport. "Only that people are different. No one gets to my age without knowing that."

"Yeah," he said with amusement. "You've been on this earth a long time."

"Long enough." She rose, saying, "I see you have a dishwasher."

"I got it for Betsy. She was always so burdened with work."

"What did she do?"

"Cooking, housework, the chickens before I got rid of them."

"I thought I heard a hen."

"I got some back last year. I missed the rooster crowing mornings."

He was an interesting man. That flash of imagination in calling the old men turtles was something she'd never dreamed of finding in him. But she thrust the thought aside and efficiently piled the dishes into the dishwasher.

"Boy, you got that done quick."

She hesitated, wondering why he thought she was so fast, but it would be an opening for more talk about his ex-wife, and Megan didn't want to hear about her. Instead she asked, "Did…Betsy furnish this house?"

"My great-uncle. He got the stuff from a catalog. It's comfortable, a little dull. Betsy hated this place."

Megan had heard enough about Betsy. "I need to get back."

"Yeah. I'm glad you ate with me. It's been nice. I'll give you the catalog about the Ultra Lights. That's what the planes are called. You can pick one out, and I'll help you put it together."

"That's kind of you, but I realize that it's more complicated than that. I think I'll wait awhile. I enjoyed the flight. Thank you. And you're an exceptionally good cook…for a man." He was so damned male-chauvinistic that she couldn't resist that snub.

"Show me how women cook."

She should have expected that, but she bit her tongue against a sassy reply and just grinned. "Touché."

"That's a prick of a sword. I didn't mean it that way. I was inviting you to pay me back a meal."

He might not be practiced, but he was quick. She said, "You'd be appalled."

"Try me." He looked at her body, then he quickly tore his glance away and looked aside. "I have a VCR. How about a movie?"

"No, thanks. I must get back. I'm sorry to make you drive into town. I know with the harvesting you must be in the fields for long hours, and the evenings are short.''

He said with nice humor to dismiss the inconvenience: ''I can handle a drive into town. It's a pretty night.''

She stilled. He wouldn't suggest going somewhere to…park? Surely he was too old for that sort of stuff? She vowed that if she ever got back to town, she'd never leave again—or that she'd drive her own car. With all the matchmakers in Hadley, surely he wasn't beginning to get the idea himself, was he? Of course not.

''If there was a snowstorm, there's plenty of room here. You could stay over.'' He startled himself. But—

''Hardly. It's September. Not too many snowstorms in September.'' She gave him a diminishing look.

He grinned at her with great charm and murmured, ''Darn.''

And through her streaked the most startling electric bolt that she'd ever felt. How shocking.

He seemed to come out of a trance and said, ''Okay.'' As if that meant anything at all. Then he said, ''I'll drive.''

That confused Megan. Had he thought her so pushy that she'd insist on driving?

He went out the door ahead of her, but held the screen open for her. Lady was on the porch and gave Megan an amused look. She returned an ironic one.

They used the little red car and he drove silently along in the moonlight. It was strangely peaceful in the car. They didn't talk at all. He pulled up by the clinic door, got out and barely made it in time to watch her unlock the door. She ducked inside and hooked the screen door as she said "Thank you."

He replied, "You're welcome," and stood there.

She closed and locked the door, went up the stairs next to the door and glanced down from the landing. He was standing on the sidewalk, looking up. He saw her and lifted his bandaged hand to show he'd seen her. She could have died because he'd caught her looking. Why had she?

Getting ready for bed, she felt irritated. She had no idea why she was annoyed, but she was restless and impatient. She scrubbed her teeth but left enough enamel, then she brushed her hair ruthlessly, and showered, washing herself vigorously. It was almost as if . . . as if she was *angry*?

She dried herself with gentle abstraction while trying to puzzle out her conduct. There was no way that she would become involved with another man. Jethro was a classic male. Their lives would never fit. She would be exasperated with him all her life, and just watch, he would become one of those courthouse-square turtles who dictated the county conduct. Yes, he would. That's exactly what would happen to Jethro Hanna.

Chapter Six

Almost a week passed and Megan didn't hear from Jethro. It was frustrating not to use any of her studied and cool rejections of all sorts of innocuous invitations. She had practiced diminishing looks in her mirror, and punished her very clean teeth with her toothbrush. It was difficult to spurn an absent man.

With no warning at all, the first of fall's storms appeared in early October. The forecast had been for partly cloudy. The storm was mentioned, but the brunt of it was supposed to miss northern Indiana. It came in like any unpleasant surprise: mean, sloppy, erratic, with hail and driving, freezing rains. Everybody was disgusted. Some crops still unharvested were harmed. Susie Fillmore's best quilt was torn off the line and nobody ever found it.

People were still sour when the alarm went off. There was a plane down. Nobody could fault the pilot. No one had known the storm would veer off course that way. But someone saw the crash, and Jethro went.

Later, carrying a bundle, he came into the clinic to Megan. He was very upset. He jerked his head to indicate she was to follow him, and he went into one of the back examining rooms. He stood there starkly, waiting.

She frowned at him. "What *is* it?"

His mouth crumpled like a little boy's. He swallowed and shook his head once, then he squinted his eyes and said tersely, "It was Pete. They're dead. It was Pete and Christy. Christy said, 'Take care of Pete,' but he was already dead." Jethro gestured in a helpless way, then one hand indicated the examining table. "David's okay. He was cushioned. Check him out."

Megan looked at the table and saw the bundle move. With her heart in her mouth, she carefully opened the blanket, dreading what she might find. David looked back at her solemnly and yawned very big. Then he moved his mouth a little and looked around, frowning at the bright light. He was two months old.

"Can he stay here for now?" Jethro asked Megan.

"Of course."

"I'll get things organized and come get him then."

"He can stay here. Don't worry about him."

"Yeah. It'd help if you can handle him until I can get somebody to stay with him."

"Jethro, there's no problem. He can be right here. I can keep an eye on him. Don't go to any bother now. This can all be sorted out. There's no rush." She saw that Jethro was having a hard time. She heard her voice soften as she said "I'm sorry about Pete and Christy."

"Oh, God, Megan—"

"I know you were very fond of them."

"I told them I'd take care of David." His deep voice squeaked upward oddly. "I never thought I really would."

"Don't worry about that now." She soothed the one worry she could. "There's no hurry. David's fine, right here. I know how to take care of a baby, and we can get it all figured out after this initial shock is over. Is there anything I can do for you?"

She had meant to help with Pete and Christy. But he took her literally and came to her in a stumble to put his arms around her and awkwardly lean his head down by hers. He shuddered in his grief.

Megan was overwhelmed with unexpected answering emotion. Her arms went around Jethro. She held him, moving her hands on his back and murmuring soothing sounds. Her own tears trembled on her lashes and escaped to her cheeks. As sad as the deaths were, it was for Jethro's grief that she cried.

His voice was unsteady as he told her, "We used to play together in the pond at the farm. We've known each other all our lives."

"Yes," she murmured.

"Christy always loved Pete."

"Yes."

"I thought Betsy would be like Christy."

Megan understood, then, that Jethro had always envied Pete. And now that Pete and Christy were both dead, Jethro felt guilty for the envy. She knew then how sensitive Jethro was, and her hands were very gentle on his back.

"My nose is dripping."

"Here." She reached for a tissue box and gave him some, and they both looked down on David who was staring cross-eyed at his hands, tightly held together, unable to release one another.

Jethro blew into the tissue. "I never cry." His voice was gritty. After a pause, he admitted: "Once, when my great-uncle died." Then he added, "When Red was hit by a car. When—I guess I'm a crybaby."

"No."

"Did I embarrass you?"

She took her own tissue. "No."

"You hardly knew them. Are you crying for David? I'll take care of him. You have to know that."

"I'm his godmother."

"Yeah, but I'm his godfather, and he's a boy."

"We'll get it figured out."

"I can't believe this is true. They looked like the make-believe disaster victims. For practice, you know? It didn't seem real."

"I know."

"I couldn't think of anything to say to Christy. I just said, 'Don't worry.'" He gestured helplessly. "That I was there."

"It was the perfect thing to've said."

"Nobody ever told me I'd have to do that for people I know. It was awful. Nothing worked. I tried." His voice trembled. He turned and breathed deeply and walked around a little. He faced her again. "I'm glad you were here."

"Yes."

"There was no one else I could have talked to."

From the hall an old voice called strongly, "Jethro!"

Quietly, Jethro told Megan, "It's Dan Seymore."

She had turned toward the door. She glanced back and said, "I'll tell him."

Jethro nodded, his face taut, his eyes so sad. She saw him as he leaned over the baby and said softly: "I'm here. You got nothing to worry about. I'll take care of you."

The whole town mourned, especially since there were no relatives to mourn. It was bad enough to lose young people, but it made it worse that there were no family members to help with the grief. And there was David.

The evening after the funeral, Jethro came to Megan's door and rang the bell.

The sound wakened David. It was dark outside. Megan peeked from the landing and saw that Jethro had stepped back so that she could see who it was standing there.

Megan went down and opened the door. "What's the matter?"

"How's David? Is he all right?"

"Yes. Cory came down right away that first day and looked him over, and he saw him yesterday after the funeral. David is perfect. No injuries. No problems. He eats like a little pig, and he sleeps like…a log." She almost said "like the dead," but stopped in time.

"He's awake. Can I see him?"

"Sure."

Jethro went up the steps ahead of her, moving tiredly. He was dirty. He'd been harvesting corn all the day.

"Have you eaten?" she asked.

"No. I'll stop by one of the fast-food places."

That was a well-worn local joke. The town was probably the only place in the whole Northern Hemisphere that didn't have a McDonald's.

"I could fix you a sandwich," she offered, trying to think if she had enough bread.

"Good." He followed David's fretting sound and leaned over the crib set in Megan's room. "You okay?" he asked the baby.

From the doorway, Megan saw that David stopped crying and stared at Jethro.

Jethro asked with tenderness, "You crying for your mommy?"

David listened and waved his arms without control.

"I know you want to be picked up, but I'm really dirty. Just wait until I wash, then I'll hold you. I know you miss your folks. But I'm here now. You don't have to worry about a thing."

Jethro then went into the bath and closed the door.

From the kitchen Megan blinked at the wall when she heard her shower turned on. Then she became a little indignant as she realized Jethro was taking a shower! He was in there, in *her* shower, naked. She stared into space and just thought about that.

He came out in a clean white T-shirt and jeans, with his hair still wet. He put a bundle down on the floor by the door—his dirty clothes. Then he went in and lifted David up to his shoulder and took the now sleepy baby into the kitchen and sat at the table.

Megan said in censure, "You took a shower?"

Not paying any attention, Jethro was stirring up the baby with sounds and tickling his cheek with one comparatively enormous finger. He replied reasonably and offhand, "Yeah, I knew David would be in bed and would probably be clean so I—"

She gasped indignantly. "He would *probably* be—"

"—knew I'd have to shower or you'd probably raise hell with me getting him all sweaty and dirty."

She agreed huffily, "Probably."

"You're taking good care of him."

"He's a healthy kid." She put a plate of sandwiches in front of him with a glass of milk and watched in wonder as he consumed everything. She replenished the sandwiches and milk, then watched as those disappeared. She was amazed as the Tollhouse cookies vanished—and more milk. She'd not seen anything like it since her little brother had been eighteen.

Replete, Jethro sat back and sighed. He rested his solemn gaze on Megan for a silent while.

She didn't know whether he needed to talk, or if the companionship was enough. She didn't say anything, waiting to see if he needed to talk. David was asleep on the table next to Jethro. He picked the baby up and held him carefully. Then he carried the infant back and laid him in his crib.

Jethro looked around Megan's room—at the colors, at the nasturtiums on the marble-topped walnut commode. The quilt on the bed was in yellows and oranges, with browns scattered through it. The room was pretty.

He moved to the doorway and Megan stepped back to allow him to go through into her living room. There he stood and looked around. The colors were rich. There were pillows on the sofa. It was a welcoming room.

He looked at Megan. She seemed wary. He smiled at her as unthreateningly as he would at a confused dog that someone had dropped off in the countryside. Her expression didn't change. Someone had abused her. He said to her, "I'm bushed. I think I'll get on home. If you need anything, call me. I have an answering machine. If it's an emergency, use the beeper." He patted the instrument. "Good night, Megan."

"G'night," she replied and stood at the top of the stairs to watch as he went down and opened the front door. He tested the lock. Then, standing in the reflection of the outside night-light, he looked up at her for a while, very seriously, then he said, "Thanks. I needed to be with you tonight." And he left.

What a strange man. He had irritated her since she'd first laid eyes on him, that day when she was supervising the movers. She had seen him get out of his pickup in that slow, male way some men have of moving. Then Christy— Yes…Christy. Megan stood. Sadly.

She went in to tidy the kitchen, noted all that was left were cookie crumbs and bread crumbs. Jethro was like a plague of locusts.

She went into the bathroom to shower and was in it, under the warm stream, when she suddenly remembered that was exactly where he'd been not too long ago: standing right there—naked. Yes. And her breathing became erratic and her entire naked body blushed. She was embarrassed for *him* that he'd been so unmannered as to just walk into her apartment—a stranger's apartment—and take a shower. He was without any knowledge of what was proper. How disgusting, she thought, as her hands slowed in their soaping of her body.

She jerked to awareness. Hurriedly she finished her shower, scrubbed her sensitive flesh dry with a towel and pulled on her usual oversize T-shirt and old cotton panties. She ruffled her hair in the steamy mirror, and with it fogged, she could pretend that her hair was long and unruly. He'd had the gall to say Meg was too short a name for her, just like her hair was too short. Who'd asked him?

Slowly she turned off the lights and went into her bedroom to look down at David, sleeping like a baby should. Relaxed. Safe. With her.

Chapter Seven

Baby David was the answer to all Megan's frustrations. She didn't want another man, but she was a little appalled that she'd be so pleased that she now had the chance to have her own child—in David. She was so thrilled to be responsible for him that she felt a little guilty. And she applied to be his foster parent, with adoption as soon as it could be arranged.

She had expected some resistance from the authorities, but she learned that there are a lot of single adoptive parents. It was no longer unusual. She even found Dan Seymore had volunteered as one of her character witnesses—before she had even applied. Phyllis Lowman at the welfare-department desk in the courthouse said, "Oh, Dan Seymore already gave you a recommendation." Phyllis smiled. "So did a bunch of others. But Dan got here first."

So, as no recorded lady had done before her, Megan went boldly over to the courthouse square where Dan sat in the Indian-summer sun. And in the middle of all those turtles, she told old Dan, "I appreciate it—that you spoke up for me as David's foster mother."

Dan's cohorts hadn't risen, for long ago they had decided that no loose woman who invaded the courthouse square unchaperoned, should be given that courtesy. Dan stood, firmly took Megan's arm and led her back to her side of the street as he said, "I was glad to. Godmotherhood has some clout. You'll be a good mother." He smiled his crinkled old smile.

"I specialized in pediatrics in undergrad. I'm prepared."

Old Dan replied smugly, "I know."

Megan thought he probably even knew her scars, warts and moles. He had the time to satisfy all curiosities about other people.

From her side of the street, Megan watched the old man shuffle back to his bench, with the traffic stopping in order not to interfere with his crossing. The problem was: Dan *assumed* the traffic would stop. What if the driver of the car had been a stranger?

A stranger? Megan was startled to think that she considered herself one of the townspeople already. Here it was, October. She'd only been in Hadley since August, but she considered herself one of the natives. How droll.

That night Jethro came to see David again. And darned if he didn't bring clothes and take another shower just as if he was a boarder. Clean in jeans and T-shirt, he scooped up the sleeping David and carried him into the kitchen and sat at the table. He held the baby against his chest and looked up at Megan. "What've you got for me tonight?" And he smiled.

It was just a lucky thing she'd replenished her bread and cookie supply.

When he left, he asked her, "You're off tomorrow—Wednesday? How about bringing David out for a picnic lunch by my pond? Bring a suit if you're going to swim and you're modest. David can go in raw. It's been so hot that the water's still warm in the shallows. I'll be in from the field about twelve-thirty. I'll have sun tea, cheese, weiners and buns. You bring anything else you'd like. Okay?''

Foolishly, she nodded

The next morning Megan laid David on the kitchen table and prepared a feast to take out. No man should work as hard as Jethro and eat only hot dogs and buns. Of course not.

She packed her car in plenty of time and drove out through the gloriously colored, autumn countryside. She didn't really notice it. She was a little excited. Why should she be excited? She decided it was because this was David's first outing with her.

Jethro had said twelve-thirty, but she managed to get to his pond a little early. Since farm ponds were calculated for fire safety, Jethro's house wasn't far from his. It was a natural pool, and trees and bushes of various kinds grew close to its edge. All the leaves were in the full variety of fall colors, and the blendings and contrasts were lovely.

Lady came along and smiled at Megan; but this time the dog came close and lifted her head, pulling her ears down and almost closing her eyes, waiting to be petted. Megan was a stickler about clean hands and babies, so she thanked the dog for the honor but declined. The dog laughed.

Megan told Lady to guard the baby, who was concentrating on the leaves above his head. Megan unpacked the banquet for six, which she lugged from her car. She laid down a tablecloth, added some fat, needlepoint-covered feather pillows, and a hand-thrown blue pot she'd made one summer in a craft class. She'd filled it with a riot of mums.

It was exactly noon. She had a half hour to wait. Everything was ready.

She listened to the silence, looked at the trees, and was filled with a peace she'd never known. The day was a perfect example of Indian summer. Outrageously colorful. What a marvel. She turned back toward the pond, and emerging from it was a naked man!

It was Jethro. He stood and walked closer in the shallow water that was only midcalf. Pausing, he looked back over the pond in a way almost identical to the way Megan had been looking around in appreciation. The water dripped from his body—so male— as he stood quietly, half turned from her.

She couldn't tear her eyes from him but stood there, like a dolt, with her lips parted so that she could breathe. He was beautiful.

He turned slowly and looked right at her, and his eyes flared briefly in his surprise. She gasped. The impact of his stare was like a physical encounter. He smiled just a little and said, "You're early." Then, with an élan Megan had never realized he could possibly possess, he picked up a towel from the weeds close by the edge of the water, and wrapped it around his waist.

With her still acting like a moonstruck child, there at high noon, Jethro came over to the feast she'd spread. He squatted, tempting the towel to unwrap, as he reached to touch the watching David's cheek. Then he rose effortlessly and leaned to place a soft kiss on the mesmerized Megan's parted lips. "Never seen a naked man before?"

She said, "Uhh." But some of the pond water was still dripping from his hair and a light sprinkling of it helped her to focus. "I hadn't expected you this soon."

He laughed in his throat.

The sound was very low and shiveringly sexy. It was then that Megan knew positively that Betsy had been a fool to leave this magic man. With amazed insight, Megan understood that nobody in the town of Hadley had any inkling what the real Jethro Hanna was really like. He appeared normal. But if they only realized it, they had a good clue to the basic man in that Ultra Light mosquito he flew.

He reached around, peeking into containers, and smiled. He took a crusty, fried drumstick and crunched into it. Then he rose and gave her immobilized mouth another kiss. She watched him lick his lips as if she'd never realized people could do that, and heard him ask, "Are you going to swim?" And only her strict upbringing, which was so ingrained that it took conscious determination to counter it, prevented her from ripping off her clothes and luring him back into the water. That she would be tempted to do such a thing did shock her a little, but in a very thrilling way. If she *did* do that, what would he do? And she was sorely tempted to find out.

Her ingrained upbringing made her shake her head twice; but the movement was slow, as if she could *possibly* change her mind—or have it changed.

He grinned at her, and she knew how Lady had learned that knowing grin. He coaxed, "I'll watch the baby. The water's great." He began to peel off David's little shirt and diaper.

"You're taking him in?" Ponds were muddy.

"Sure. It's a baptism of another sort. Once he's been in the pond water, he'll be a native."

She laughed.

He smiled up at her, rising, and said, "Come along."

And she capitulated. She undid her wraparound skirt and pulled off her sleeveless top and actually flung them aside as, in her swimsuit, she ran past Jethro and splashed into the shallow water until she could push off and swim. She swam a ways, then turned back, wondering when he would . . . discard . . . the . . . towel.

Rats! He was already in the water and the baby was splashing and gave a squeal! The baby laughed. And Jethro's delighted rumble of a laugh made David wide-eyed. Jethro knew to lay David's head on his wrist and hold the opposite arm and to take a similar grip on his opposite thigh. That way, Jethro had a firm hold on the slippery child.

Excessively conscious that Jethro was naked, Megan swam nearby, but not close.

He looked over at her and said, "Now you're a native."

She scoffed. "I'm a city girl."

He nodded as he watched her. "A newly baptized native of the city of Hadley."

She laughed, listening to the sound bounce merrily on the water, and she knew he was teasing. The *city* of Hadley? Yes, indeed. He was such a tease. In more ways than that. He wasn't very far from her, and in the water he was stark, staring naked—just standing there. The idea of it excited her in a very strange way. She'd been attracted to men before, but never like this.

It was understandable. There really were no single men around in the sparsely populated county. She'd been there for three months and there had been no other man her age who was as attractive. And Jethro had seemed immune to women. That had lowered her guard.

She really didn't want another man. One had been enough forever. But Jethro was more complicated than he'd first seemed. The idea of knowing him better had become alluring. How had he done that?

She swam to the shallow edge of the pond and stood up on sand. She turned back to speak to Jethro and found he was very close, and about to stand up, so she quickly turned away. Why couldn't she be as casual as he? It was he who was naked. But she stayed turned aside, her eyes cast down as she walked out of the water and onto the shaggy grasses.

She picked up her clothes, and never glancing back, went to her car and got dry panties to trade for the wet bathing suit. She dressed and returned to the picnic cloth to find Jethro there in clean jeans and T-shirt, expertly putting a diaper on David. Instead of exclaiming "You've dressed!" she asked, "How did you learn to diaper a baby?"

"It's part of the training. Naturally I know how to get a man out of his clothes, but I can undress a woman or a baby, and I can put them into protective clothing. I have all kinds of handy abilities. Name anything you need—" he looked up at her in a shockingly sexy way "—and I can handle whatever you want me to do."

The reaction of her body was really scandalous. It embarrassed her and she blushed, bit her lower lip and sightlessly looked off to the side. This picnic was probably a really big mistake.

He already knew about the chicken and explored the other insulated bowls containing their treasures: corn on the cob, chilled tomato slices, hot rolls already buttered, and a chocolate cake with thick icing. He ate with gusto. He murmured appreciation. He knew all the tricks. That ex-wife of his had been dumb.

Then, replete, he lay down on the tablecloth in the midst of all the debris, with David on his chest, and he went sound asleep.

What is it about a contented man that pleases a woman to such an extent of satisfaction? Why does a woman have to feel so pleased that she has pleased a man that way? Megan filled her eyes with the sight of that man, with that small baby sleeping on his chest. And she experienced a great contentment.

Chapter Eight

Jethro wakened easily. His eyes opened and he looked up at the tree branches above him. The backlighting sun-washed the translucent leaves' colors. There was the soft drone of faraway tractors, the lazy hum of nearby bees, and the soft stir of leaves. It was a perfect day.

Jethro looked down at the baby, sleeping on his chest, and he lay a hand on the baby's back. Then he turned his head a little and looked at Megan.

She was sitting about five feet from him with her back to a silver maple. Her ankles were crossed and her hands lay peacefully in her lap. She watched him.

His look was different. It was intense, and he didn't look away. He kept her gaze captive with his. And the feeling between them was hotly communicating.

He said, "I want to make love to you."

She licked her lips nervously. Then she cleared her throat to dispel the need to agree, and she replied, "I'm leaving Hadley when my stint is finished." She was distracted by the point that she had not said a final "No."

In a slow, husky way, he told her, "If you left, and I hadn't made love with you, I'd regret it all my life."

Now where had he found words like that? Words that could lure a woman into being convinced she was only being a humanitarian if she agreed to make love with him, so that he wouldn't have any regrets. That was the mosquito flyer, the nude swimmer, talking.

But what about her regrets? Could she make love to Jethro Hanna and leave? If she knew how it was to be loved by this man of such surprises, could she give it up? Him? Could she dance in the flames and not get burned to a crisp? Who would have believed that Jethro could be such a stunning temptation?

He eased little David from his chest and laid the baby on his side with an upside-down bowl to support his back. Then, unthreateningly, Jethro slowly moved over to Megan and put his head on her lap, scaring her into delicious shivers.

She wanted to cup his head, pull up her knees and bury his face in her breasts. She put her hands firmly on the ground beside her hips and took a steadying breath.

Jethro watched her indrawn breath raise her chest and he closed his eyes against the strong erotic reaction in his body. He opened his eyes again. His breathing had quickened and was a little harsh. He said, "Love me."

"I don't dare."

"I have protection for you."

That surprised her. But then she remembered he'd come to her with his grief. It wasn't just to see David that had brought him to her. She said a very timid "I don't think so."

"This is a day for love—for being here and making love. These days don't come much. Look at it. Doesn't it make you want to be a part of it? All the seeds are falling. And the earth takes them—"

"I thought you said you had protection."

"I do. Let me love you. I wouldn't let any harm come to you. I'll take care of you."

He sat up, and with gentle care, he took her into his arms. He pulled her across his thighs with a strength that she felt move under her hands on his shoulders. She wanted the kiss; just the kiss. She allowed him one—and lost all of her brain cells to ecstasy.

She felt him tremble! Such a man could be that affected by her? His breath was steam in that warm, lazy day. His hot hands were earnest and his sounds were appreciating. He sounded very much as he had when she fed him: he was feasting on her. His mouth was scalding on her body... and she realized her clothes were askew.

She made a feeble attempt to regain control, but was easily coaxed to cooperate, to move so that the impeding material could be removed. She was going to allow him to make love to her. This once. Not only so that he would never have to be regretful, but in order to know how it could be with this different man; with this surprising man, who wasn't at all as she'd cataloged him.

He laid her back and looked into her eyes. He was excited, stimulated, aroused. He smiled and leaned to kiss along under her ear, and she felt sorry for the woman who had had him for her own and had turned him away.

He said, "Tell me what you want."

And her wobbly voice whispered, "You."

He laughed a deep rumble in his chest and urged, "Do you like this?" And with his scalding breath tickling her sensitive skin, his tongue touched inside her ear. He asked, "How about this?" and his tongue touched into other places, as he licked and suckled and teased. He touched and kneaded and smoothed with his scorching hands. And he made her frantic.

He did protect her, and he made love to her there on that perfect day in that perfect place. And it was marvelous.

They lay, still coupled, reluctant to be through. He parted from her carefully, to lie beside her and hold her hand. He said, "It was exactly as I knew it would be."

She couldn't reply. It had been uniquely wonderful. It had been perfect.

He moved her head up onto his shoulder. He had to touch her. He kissed her cheek, and he told her she was beautiful. Wasn't her hair a little longer? Would she allow it to grow now? Her eyes were so pretty, he said. Were her lashes real? Did she know she had little freckles on her nose and three on her right cheek and two on her left cheek?

And he kissed her. Again. Then again. And he made love to her leisurely with long, slow strokes and tender care, and he held her tightly as they climaxed.

With Lady watching the sleeping child, the lovers went into the pond to rinse themselves, and to kiss, standing there in the water. "You're a hot woman," he told her. "You've steamed out the pond."

"I only came for lunch."

"We had a feast fit for a king."

Hand in hand, they went back to their clothes. He dried her tenderly and helped her to dress. That only made her wonder, What had been the matter with Betsy?

Again they lay by the tree and dozed. He held her against him and their bodies were contented. He told her, "You're keeping me from the fields, you know. I need to work hard while the weather is still nice. It's hell being on a tractor when the windchill is minus twenty."

"That sounds uncomfortable."

"It is."

"What are you harvesting now?"

"Just finished the corn silage. Now I'm doing soybeans, and in those fields, I'm planting winter wheat. The wheat's harvested next July. The cornstalks that you see standing in winter will be disced into the soil...oh...in December, or whenever it can be done before the ground is too hard.

"The canning companies are urging us to diversify and plant more vegetables. I've done peas and carrots...potatoes. The vegetable crops take more time; they're less hardy.

"I have an orchard over beyond the house—apples. My grandmaw uses those when she makes the apple pies. If you behave, I'll let you share another one.

"My family gets a lot of what I produce. The chickens are just for me, with occasional ones for visitors. The hens give brown eggs, which taste the best. I use most of the eggs. Farming is hungry work. I eat a lot," he explained unnecessarily.

"I have some livestock, again, and in the fall my mother, dad and grandmaw spend a couple of days making up stew to freeze. It's just great. And my grandmaw makes rolls. She loves to cook. It satisfies something in her to feed people."

While he talked on about the farm, Megan thought that David could never again be orphaned. No matter what happened, he would be a part of Jethro's extended family. They were people who cared about others, and they would include David automatically. It was a comforting thought. No one in Megan's family would be so welcoming. They might be concerned, but it wouldn't occur to any of them simply to take in a stranger.

Jethro was saying "I have to go refuel the tractor and put it in another field. I'll be back in just a minute. Don't go away." He leaned and kissed her as if it was the most natural thing in the world. Then he grinned at her, rolled effortlessly to his feet, glanced back and said, "Don't move." And he left her there.

How strange it was that everything could change in just the course of one afternoon—in a part of one. She'd come there a beginning friend, and now she was his lover. How amazing.

Megan waited in the silence. No. There was the sound of other tractors working. If she listened closely she could tell just about how far they were from where she sat. There was the sound of a car on the main road. She heard a dog bark at a distance, and Lady perked her ears, but apparently it was just a regular bark and not one that needed a reply.

Megan thought how wonderful it was that she would have almost two full years to explore this interesting man. She had almost the full two years to enjoy him. Megan heard Jethro start his tractor. There was the change in pitch as it was moved. After a while she heard the motor cut off, and she listened for him to return.

She heard him whistling before she saw him. She watched him coming to her through the trees and bushes, a primal male. A man. Her sated body thrilled to him, and she laughed over such foolishness.

And he laughed in response. He came to her and hunkered down and leaned with one hand against the tree so that he could kiss her. Then he rose, tugged her to her feet and hugged her closely. He said, "You are so sweet. I want you again."

"No." There was that "No" that had eluded her not long ago, and she was glad it had been lost.

"Let me convince you."

She shook her head but her lips puffed in a tempting, tiny smile that was rather shocking.

So of course he kissed her. But he did let her go. He helped tidy up, he carried the picnic debris to the car, then fetched the sleeping David and slid him undisturbed into the child's seat and buckled the belt.

Jethro turned to Megan. "If you behave, I'll bring some of my grandmaw's stew and some of her rolls to dinner tonight. But I have to be sure you deserve to share in it."

She slowly opened the car door and got in the driver's seat before she looked up at him. "What do I have to do?"

He didn't want her to leave. He put his hands on the windowsill and stooped down so that he could see her. "I'll think of something." Then he leaned in and kissed her yet again.

He watched her drive out of sight.

She drove into town and pulled up by the clinic entrance. Getting out, she lifted a waking David from the car seat and carried him inside. She came back downstairs to fetch the picnic things and found old Dan standing by her car.

He asked, "Been on a picnic?"

"David and I went out to fly some kites."

He commented, "At Jethro's pond."

Megan was surprised. "How'd you know that?"

Dan was delighted. "I didn't. Just guessed."

She snubbed him. "You're impertinent." And she walked away with her burdens and closed the clinic door after her.

Old Dan laughed.

Chapter Nine

Jethro brought his grandmother's beef stew and rolls over after dark that night. Soberly Megan watched him walk up her stairs, grinning at her, the humor overflowing from his eyes with naughtiness. He told her, "I met a wood nymph today, and I'm some depleted."

She didn't reply, but he didn't seem to need a response. He leaned and kissed her mouth, then carried the frozen beef stew into her kitchen, found a pot and emptied the container into it. He set the pot to heat and put out the thawing rolls to rise. He kissed her again in passing, as he went into her bedroom to lean over David and smile at the sleeping baby. Then Jethro went on into her bathroom, showered and emerged in clean clothes—as if that was now the most natural thing in all this world.

And to Megan, it felt that way. She was so glad to see that he was real. Jethro's first kiss made her forget old Dan's fretful innuendos, and with the second she began to look forward to the third...and...

He wanted to know: "Are you going to make love to me while the stew's heating? There's exactly enough time. Come here, woman."

And Megan went.

It was just as it had been, but hotter, faster, wilder. Their bodies strained together. Their hands were hard, their fingers digging, their mouths open and hungry.

They rolled on her rug, somehow their clothes were discarded, and their coupling was like lightning striking and thunder crashing, as if the whole world had gone mad.

Shuddering to a standstill, they collapsed and were silent. It had been shattering. He finally lifted his head and asked, "Exactly who are you, Megan Bailey?"

"An innocent who's become entangled in a serious collision with some wood satyr."

"I'm no goat. No beard."

"You've shaved."

"My eyebrows aren't peaked."

"How do you know so much about satyrs?"

He laughed helplessly. "I can't laugh; I'm too weakened by this wood nymph."

"I was standing in my own house—"

"Standing temptingly."

"Minding my own business—"

"Looking ready."

"And this satyr came—"

"Oh, yes."

The timer went off in the kitchen. They separated carefully, with groans, and washed. Then they drooped around, baking the rolls, setting the table, dishing out the stew, eating, yawning, smiling, holding hands. He coaxed to spend the night, but she was firm that he would not. So he took a long time telling her good-night.

In the days that followed, the lovers met when they could. Megan was asked if she and David could be in the Christmas pageant as the Child and Mary.

Megan mentioned: "I'm brunette."

Jennifer Yeager replied, "We're tolerant. Mary was more than likely dark. The Europeans tended to adjust things their way. They were the ones who made Mary a blonde.''

October continued to be unrelentingly gorgeous, so that one could be convinced that a hard winter could be avoided.

The two lovers worked hard. His farm was tended; her patients were, too. The two admired and cared for David, and they made eager love. Their lives were perfect.

On Halloween, they dressed themselves and David like clowns and took him trick-or-treating in the town. They were so amused with each other that they didn't notice the avid looks of the Hadley citizens who found them at their doors, nor did they guess at the intense interest they engendered there.

Everyone had exclaimed at how amazing it was for it to be so warm so late in the year. Even the lovers discussed it. Megan told Jethro, ''This was a day to fly. Look at that moon! Wouldn't it be wonderful to fly tonight? Why don't we?''

''I've covered the plane, put it on a pulley and stored it in the top of the barn.''

''For the winter?''

''Until David's through college. I'm responsible for him, and while there aren't too many flyers killed flying the Ultra Lights, there're a lot of injuries, especially spinal ones. I can't risk being unable to take care of him.''

''I'm his godmother.''

''I appreciate the backup.''

Backup? She remarked slowly, ''You know that I've applied to adopt him.''

Jethro stopped on the sidewalk. ''Oh?''

''I'm his foster mother, and I want to adopt him.''

"Then you mean to stay here?"

"No."

"You'd take him away from here?"

"He could visit."

"What made you rush right out and file on him?"

"I'm also his godmother."

"You might have asked me if it was all right. I told Pete that I'd take care of David. That's my job."

"With my job, I can take care of him more easily than you. You'd have to hire someone to watch him."

"He's mine."

"Jethro—"

"Marry me. We'll share him. We'll live anywhere around here you want, but marry me. I love you, Megan."

"Jethro, you *know* that when this job is through, I'll leave and—"

He stared at her, frowning, and his breathing was quick. He was appalled by her. Did he mean nothing to her? He asked, "Don't you want to stay with me?" Another Betsy. Worse—she wasn't Betsy; she was Megan. She was all he'd ever wanted, and one that he'd never hoped to find. She could leave him? After what they had, could she really just—leave? "Do you mean to leave me?"

"You know that I've never intended to stay here."

"But after all we've had, you could just . . . leave?"

"Oh, Jethro. You have to know that . . . being with you has been . . . wonderful. But I'm a city girl. I've told you that from the beginning."

"And that's still more important to you than I am?"

"I've never said I'd stay, or live with you."

"But I thought you cared for me."

"I do. But—" Her words stopped.

Bitterly he supplied the rest: "But not enough." Dressed as a clown, he saw not the made-up clown that was Megan. He saw her and his failure with women. Two now. He said, "You can live wherever you want, you can see David whenever you want, but he lives here with me. If you try to take him away, I'll fight you." He looked down at her, still thinking she'd have to change her mind.

Megan was discomforted by their stern words, their schism. Who would have thought he could be so adamant about the baby? He *really* thought of David as his.

But then she knew how important the baby was to her. If Jethro was ready to fight for David, so was she. And yet, she had known David's parents so briefly compared to the lifetime that Jethro had known them. Could she interfere to that extent in David's life?

Yes.

In silence, they walked back to her apartment. Jethro carried David up the stairs and laid him in the crib. He turned to Megan and said, "With the field-work done, I can take David home tomorrow. I appreciate it that you've taken care of him all this time, but now I'll take over. I'll come with the pickup in the morning and get him and his things."

She was stunned.

He saw that she was, and his voice gentled. "I know you love him. But you have to know that I promised Pete. And Megan, I'll be a good dad to David. I promise you that. I'll take good care of him. You can come to see him. I'll give you a key, and you come out any time. If we're gone, you go inside and wait for us. We'll be back." But then he said, "I'll come and get him about ten tomorrow. I have a crib. You can leave this up, and David can spend the night with you now and then. That would be all right with me. Megan—'' But he didn't say anything more. He turned and left, going down the stairs and out the door, which closed with such a final click.

The next day was again beautiful, but Megan had a terrible headache. She hadn't slept all night. How could life go from ecstatic to blah in less than twenty-four hours? She could clearly remember how, after Jethro had made love to her that first time, she'd thought she had the world by the tail. But she was the tail and she was being whirled by the world. Rats! Everything had been ruined. And instead of gloating that she had almost the full two years there, she now had almost two interminably empty ones to endure.

Even worse, out the street window, she could see Jethro with David over there on the square, talking to the turtles. Jethro ought to know a mother was more important to a baby than a daddy. Well, she did know that both, together, were better, but she was better qualified to take care of David. Anyone would agree to that.

Not Jethro.

That man thought he was God's solution to any situation. Look how he'd barged in and tried to take over when David was born! What a precious man. But she could not give up David. No matter how precious Jethro was, or how skilled at handling a little baby, she was better.

The thing to do was to get the adoption settled. That would give her a leg up. And possession was nine-tenths of the law. That was true. So she couldn't give up David. She would keep him.

That was selfish. She sighed. She wished she could just—

Old Dan came in and said, "Jethro needs the formula for David."

"Why." It was a statement.

"It's his turn to take care of David. He's filed as foster parent and then for adoption. Did you know that?"

She felt the blood drain from her head and thought she might experience a faint for the first time in her life. But she didn't. Indignation came to her rescue. "I filed first."

"We have to look over all applicants. There were a slew of people at first who were interested, but then they found out David's parents were up to their ears in debt. That plane didn't help. The insurance will only pay current debts. The farm will be sold."

"I don't need any money. I make enough for us."

"Well, it isn't up to me." The old man was the picture of innocence. "It's up to the judge."

"Your son." She pointed that out.

"An independent cuss." Old Dan sighed.

"As I recall the gossip given me that first day I was here, Judge Seymore wanted to be a marine biologist."

"So he had some goldfish."

"Can he be bribed?"

"Hah! A dirty character trait."

"I just wondered if Jethro had tried."

Old Dan laughed all the way out of the clinic.

The leaves fell. The oaks and firs were the only nonnaked trees, and it seemed there were an unusual number of gloomy, draggy days. More than normal. And Megan was lonely for the first time in her solitary life.

The days passed and Thanksgiving came and went. Megan had had David once a week, and she'd spent almost one entire night holding him and talking to him. His subconscious might absorb her and there might be a bonding. Bonding was the catchphrase at that time.

The first of December, County Judge Seymore solemnly gave Jethro Hanna and Megan Bailey *joint custody*!

Megan tore her hair; Jethro smiled. He said, "Why don't you move out to the farm? It's an easy commute, and you can see more of our son."

"Yeah. Right down the hall from you."

"Oh, did you want a room of your own?"

She snarled at him.

"You're feisty. Our circumstances are just like a divorced couple's, except that I don't have to pay alimony. You have your time with David, and I have mine."

They had a joint luncheon celebration at Rose's Café. Good plain food. And David sat wobbly in the high chair balanced by a diaper bag and Megan's purse. He had mashed potatoes that he rolled on his tongue and thought about as he watched the people come up and congratulate the new parents.

But Jethro took David home, and Megan went back to her apartment empty-armed.

The first rehearsal for the Christmas pageant was in the middle of the second week of December. Everybody else had been practicing for a month, learning lines and how they'd move around. Megan and David had nothing to do but sit. The chairs were placed, and Megan waited. Jethro was supposed to bring David into town for the rehearsal.

Sitting there, watching as she waited, Megan was surprised how many of the people she already knew. The Abbott boy, who'd had an endless supply of colds and was going to an allergist. There was the twelve-year-old Denton boy who had grown a foot taller in just one year and had had so many falls that he was taking ballet. That had been an interesting hassle, but he was doing so much better in basketball since then, that a couple of the bullyboys had signed up for ballet.

And Megan smiled a little at not only knowing names, but the ramifications of the families.

Then Jethro came in as Joseph. She'd never thought to ask if there'd be a Joseph. Naturally, it would be Jethro. He was an Old Testament man if ever there was one, and a natural choice to portray one. He was a caretaker. His scar from when Christy fell from the truck was evidence of that.

He studied Megan all the way across the gym. It was as if he targeted her. Then, as he came near, he looked down at the baby in his arms and gave David to her.

Christy couldn't have loved her son any more than Megan did. She reached eagerly and took him. He was just right in her arms, against her bosom; his head perfect between her shoulder and cheek. She felt her eyes prickle. She was so glad to hold him. And she grieved for Christy not to be there with her son.

Jethro saw that Megan was shaken by holding David. He was appalled that she should suffer because he had taken David from her. Jethro didn't know what to do. He stood there, listening to the earnest little children's voices as they fumbled through their lines and stumbled through their paces, but he was conscious only of Megan. Aware only that she grieved.

Chapter Ten

One night, in the middle of December, just before supper, Jethro called Megan and said tersely, "David isn't feeling well."

Even through the sleet, Megan was out to Jethro's farm in ten hairy minutes.

Jethro met her as she drove up and eased the car to a slithering stop. He held her arm as she slipped on the steps and skidded across the porch. They entered the front door and closed it against the cold. Megan looked at Jethro fleetingly, then she looked at David.

The baby was down on the floor with Lady, laughing up at Megan. He was almost five months old, pink-cheeked and perfectly all right. He was on his stomach, braced up on his hands, rocking. He lifted one hand to reach toward her, and found he'd fallen over. He rolled over and laughed, with his hands and feet in the air.

Jethro was taking her coat off her shoulders, and Megan felt the need to mention, "He's not sick."

"He *told* me he felt awful and he *whined* and begged 'Miggie,' so I called you. My mother says kids are always well by the time the doctor arrives. He's a normal child."

Megan inquired, "'Miggie'?"

"It's the best he can do. If you kiss me, I'll let you feel his first tooth. This is on my time with him, but I'm graciously sharing."

"I'll wait."

"You'll have the time," he replied enigmatically.

She bit her lip. He was very pleased with himself as he smiled and looked smug. He asked, "Stay for supper? Grandmaw's stew and one of her apple pies."

It was only then that she became aware of anything besides David and Jethro. She saw that Jethro had put up a real Christmas tree and the lights were on. There was also the aroma of the apple pie teasing through the house. It was a home, not an apartment above a clinic.

She took an appreciating breath and said with satisfaction, "You fight dirty."

"Yes," Jethro agreed. And he smiled as the sleet relentlessly hit the north and west windows. He turned on Christmas carols, and set the volume rather high.

He gave her a quick look to see if she realized what he was doing, and saw that he needn't have bothered. She was down on the floor with David, her entire concentration was on him. Then Jethro felt bad to have fooled her. She'd been so alarmed about David that she hadn't even noticed the weather. Jethro felt a little envy of his new son.

But it had worked. She was there. Dan had told Jethro when to call her. And now she was trapped there, for at least a couple of days. Jethro smiled. That old turtle had known exactly what to do. Now, if it only worked.

Jethro set himself to behave very carefully. Not too friendly. Totally unthreatening. Pleasant. Patient. The last was the hardest. She was going to sleep in his bed tonight. He wished that he could have gotten her on his own and hadn't had to use the baby this way. But he was willing to try whatever it took to trap her. All's fair in love and war. Now he really understood that saying.

Jethro knew that Megan liked him, and that she *could* come to love him. David would help with that. She really loved that little baby. Maybe they could have another kid.... But he cautioned himself that he ought not push that right away. Just get her compromised, threatened with scandal that would risk her custody, and trap her. That was first.

When she begged him to marry her, he would be kind.

He went into the kitchen in order to quit staring at her, and she got up and followed him. "You're sure there's enough for me, too?"

"Absolutely."

"I'll set the table."

He gave her a pleased look. "I'll dish up."

"Is there a penalty if I feel his tooth on your time?"

"Of course not. Parents share."

"I already felt it."

"Why Megan Bailey! You sneak!"

"Yes. Are you going to invite me to spend the night?"

He couldn't breathe and turned carefully to peek at her.

She was very elaborately casual as she placed the flatware just so. "I had to drive like a fool to make it at all. I...probably...won't be able to...leave until...oh, maybe not until Friday. The weather station has been talking for three days about nothing but this storm. It is going to be a doozy."

He was getting a little dizzy from not breathing or something.

She turned and looked at him. "I've been very lonesome without you. I knew David was all right. He's so healthy that germs don't even try with him."

"You—"

"I'm a city girl. You'll have to take me into the city now and then."

He said it again: "Absolutely." And he was scared out of his shoes. Dan and his son were slated to come tomorrow and "surprise" the pair stranded by the weather with only a dog and a child as chaperons. Jethro knew he had to prevent Megan from ever knowing they'd all plotted against her, and he needed to call Dan as soon as possible.

Offhandedly she mentioned, "I thought you might kiss me when I told you that. Have you changed your m-m-m—?"

He was kissing her. He hadn't needed any coaxing at all. It was delicious to be held again against his strong body. She made contented sounds, and he groaned. When he lifted his mouth and they could breathe, she murmured, "Then you're not indifferent?"

"No."

She would have liked a few more words, but he was kissing her again, and that was almost satisfying.

Lady made a pitiful sound, and the pair surfaced and looked over. David had one of Lady's ears and was gnawing on it with that tooth. It took both adults to get Lady free from that clutching little hand.

Megan took David in to wash the dog hair out of his mouth and came back as Jethro was putting down the phone. She asked, "What's the matter? Is something wrong?"

He replied rather starkly, "The phone's dead."

Logically she told him, "With this storm, that's no surprise. You still have the ham radio. Who did you need to contact?"

"Uhh . . . Nobody."

"You're a little strange." She considered him. "But I've really decided on you. I'll accept that you're weird."

He laughed out loud and hugged her. Then he kissed her very seriously.

When he allowed the opportunity, she asked, "Are you still interested?" She had to hear some reassurance.

And he promised softly, "Absolutely."

"Do you know other words? You seem hung up on that one."

"I love you, Megan. I can't believe you really want me. That you're here and that you want to stay with me. I thought you would only come to see David."

"I've found, in researching my feelings for you, that I've loved you ever since I delivered David and you kept interfering."

"I delivered David."

"You were washing your hands."

"Well, I *would* have, if you hadn't been so pushy."

"You were marvelous."

"I can be perfect for you, Megan. Give me the chance."

"I'd be bored with a perfect man."

"You don't think I'm perfect?"

She laughed.

His grandmother's stew had to be warmed up. They ate holding hands, feeding David pieces of mashed carrot and bits of mashed potato, which he gummed and tongued thoughtfully. He made sounds and looked around. He shared bits of food with Lady, who didn't mind his sticky hands, but the dog licked the baby's fingers clean. Megan closed her eyes.

Jethro assured her: "All boys have to have a certain amount of dog saliva in order to thrive."

She said, "Ugh."

Thoughtfully he confided: "Megan, you're weird. But I've decided on you, and I can adjust to your being weird."

She leaned over and ruffled his hair, and they kissed.

David watched with some interest. He was put to bed a little before he was ready to go to sleep. He held one pajama-footed foot and talked to the night-light, until Lady came in and lay beside his crib.

While Megan was in the bathroom, Jethro frantically tried the phone again, and again was unsuccessful. He went in to try the ham radio and turned it on— as Megan came into the room.

She asked, "Trouble?"

"Uh, just checking it out."

"You worry too much. They'll call if they need you." He looked at her so seriously that she was concerned. "Is anything wrong?"

"I need you."

She looked blank as she rearranged her thinking, then she said "Do you, now?" as she lowered her eyelids and smiled. "I believe I have a solution."

Still very serious, he asked, "What would that be?"

"Instead of sleeping in the spare room, I could sleep in your bed. Then you'd be warm and co—"

"I'm burning now."

"Oh," she said. "Well, then, I suppose I should try to go on home, if you don't need me . . . to warm you in this ice storm."

"I'm afraid of ice."

She laughed as she tenderly touched the scar on his forehead.

He said, "Your freckles are fading."

"If you're burning, you might toast me and see if that brings the freckles back out." She gave him an innocuous look.

"We could try."

"How do you go about it?"

"Take off your clothes."

"Oh." She feigned elaborate interest. "Like a tanning bed?"

"Something like that." He helped her pull off her sweater.

As she undid her wool slacks and slid them off her hips, she looked around at the rather elaborate ham-radio equipment and asked brightly, "Where's the tanning machine?"

He showed her.

"A portable!"

Then he laughed. He laughed and hugged her, picked her up and carried her out into the hall and down to his room, to lay her on his unmade bed. He sprawled beside her, half covering her and said, "How could I have finally found you? I've searched for you all my life, and I'd given up."

"You never had a chance. I just needed a little convincing."

"What convinced you?" He thought it was the picnic by the pond.

"The Christmas pageant."

That really puzzled him. And since she was a tease, he pulled back to see her eyes: "The *pageant*?"

"All the people. I was surprised how much I knew about so many of them in just this short time. And I cared about them. I think this is a great place for kids. Are you willing to have a bunch? I would like to see what your kids are like. I think they'll be interesting to know. You're an original man. I love you, Jethro."

His eyes prickled, his heart melted, his conscience writhed. "Megan, I have to tell you something."

"You have five wives?"

"No. You see, honey, I didn't know how to handle you. You're so independent and pushy that you don't hold still for a man to get a handle on you. I wanted—"

"*Pushy*? You've used that word before."

He noted that she wasn't annoyed. That did astonish him, but he went recklessly on, so that she could understand him: "Well, you do tend to take over, like when David was—"

"I had no idea you were so adroit at all things. You have to remember that I was new in town. If I'd known you then, I would have stepped aside and let you take over."

"Megan, don't push. I have to admit I wasn't sure what to do next and—"

"You faked it well."

"I didn't even know what to do with Christy when she fell out of the truck. I was going to put her on the truck bed. Bed. I knew she ought to be flat. That seemed a good place."

"You appeared in control."

"Well, they tell us to act that way—it calms people. If everybody is calm, then people can be helpful.

You were helpful that day. You did a good job delivering David.''

Megan looked at her man and smiled. She limited her reply to "Thank you."

"You're welcome."

"Megan. Megan," he tried again. "Honey, I need to tell you that you aren't here by chance. You see—"

"Dan told me."

"Yes. I asked him what to do about you that day of the pageant, and he—"

"Said to wait for the storm, call me and tell me David was sick."

Jethro pulled back in shock. "How did you know?"

"He told me. He thought it was hilarious. He set you up. He thinks we ought to get married."

"Why, that conniving old turtle."

"Want to back out? I can still make it home. I have country tires."

"No. I can't risk you. You'd probably sue me if you bent a fender. I have some kids to send through college, and I can't afford to be sued."

"Kids? Plural? Whose?"

He slid his hands under her body and squeezed her close to him as he said a growly "Ours."

"You'll have to marry me."

"Yes."

"Dan suggested Christmas Eve. Everyone will be there."

Jethro laughed. "Those old turtles. They rule. Maybe they are what the Bible meant when it was written that the voice of the turtle was heard throughout the land. They control all our lives."

"I believe the Bible turtles were in the spring and it was turtle *doves* that they heard."

"Our 'turtles' are no doves. They just interfere." Jethro sighed enduringly. "Because of them, here we are in bed together, stranded in an ice storm, compromised, soon to be married and worrying about educating our kids."

"We're back to having kids?"

"Yeah."

"And how do we go about that?"

It took a long, involved, fascinating time for him to demonstrate all of that process. She was a doubter, but he was positive and made her repeat parts of it.

At a crucial time, she wiggled out from under him, got up and went to the dresser mirror. To the sound of the pinging of ice against the windows, Megan studied herself. She noted her longer hair was in disarray, her lips were reddened and a little pouty, and her chest was selectively red.

He inquired softly, "Are you all right?"

She told him, "There's no difference."

Puzzled he asked, "What *are* you talking about?"

She shifted her mirrored gaze to the frustrated, naked man on the bed in back of her and replied, "I see no difference in my freckles."

There was a startled silence. Then he said silkily, "To do it right, it takes a while. It could take all winter. Come here."

* * * * *

Author's Note

It was the summer before I was eight. I remember the Texas heat and how the sun seemed to put its hand on my head as I crossed our yard and went inside our house. Mother was ironing my daddy's shirts and taking notes on a baseball game. My daddy loved baseball, and it was years before I realized my mother loathed it.

With Mother ironing in the heat and keeping track of the game, it probably wasn't the best time to tell her—in horror—that Buddy Connor didn't believe in Santa Claus.

Her reaction was not the profound shock I had anticipated. She looked at me patiently and replied, "Neither do you." I was stunned and started to question this amazing statement, but she said, "Run along."

I went out to my tree and climbed up to my place to think about such a strange thing. No Santa.

Fall came, then the Texas "winter," and in December the French doors to the living room were covered and closed. The living room was forbidden territory, not to be opened until Christmas Eve. I watched and listened, and I knew the strange summer happening would be proven one way or the other.

In the early dark of Christmas Eve, I listened critically to the traditional front-door slamming departure of Santa from the forbidden room and the sleigh bells (sounding very much like the spoon jar) ringing on the front porch.

We'd always run to the windows, but we'd never caught a glimpse of Santa. We'd hear the hoofbeats (rocks?) on the roof, and we'd run outside, but he'd be gone. Mother said he had a lot of stops to make.

That year, as always, Daddy came inside and was surprised he'd missed hearing Santa yet again. We went through the house toward the living room, and Mother opened the French doors to the magically decorated room with the lighted tree and all the presents. Neighborhood families came, and as we stood around talking, *Santa came in the back door*!

That magic being ho-ho-hoed and reached into his big bag and doled out gifts to all the kids. He knew all our names. While the kids were opening their presents, I figured now Buddy Connor would have to believe in Santa because he was standing right over there.

Then my daddy grinned very familiarly at Santa and asked softly, "What kept you so long?"

And Santa replied, "I got tangled up in that goddamned chicken wire."

Lass Small

A CHRISTMAS
FOR CAROLE

Bay Matthews

A recipe from Bay Matthews:

CHRISTMAS-CAKE COOKIES

2 eggs
2 lbs dates
1 lb pecans
½ lb candied cherries (4 oz red, 4 oz green)
½ lb candied pineapple (yellow)
2½ cups all-purpose flour
1½ cups sugar
1 cup butter
1 tsp baking soda
1 tsp salt
1 tsp cinnamon

Preheat oven to 400° F.

Chop all fruit and nuts. Combine and set aside. Sift together flour, salt, baking soda and cinnamon. Set aside. Cream butter. Add sugar. Beat until smooth. Add eggs and beat again. Add flour mixture. Stir until smooth. Add fruit and nuts. Blend until coated.

Drop mixture from teaspoon onto ungreased cookie sheet. Bake for 10 minutes. Makes 150 to 170 cookies.

Chapter One

Carole Chapman drew on her full-length Tibetan lamb coat, left her store and hurried through the Pierre Bossier Mall, dodging the hundreds of holiday shoppers who were frenziedly substantiating the hype that the day after Thanksgiving was indeed the biggest consumer event of the season.

The season of miracles. Ha! The only miracle was that anyone survived it with her sanity intact. Carole's feet hurt, her May-I-help-you smile felt frozen into place, and if she heard "Santa Claus Is Coming to Town" one more time, she would scream. She tried to ignore the fact that Christmas songs would be filling the air for another month and that she still had to decorate her shop, the Ultimate Man, for the holidays.

She'd put off the dreaded task long enough, though. Hers was the only store in the entire mall that wasn't yet festooned, beribboned or draped with tinsel.

An obese man plowed into her in an attempt to skirt a teenage couple in the throes of a "meaningful discussion." "Sorry," he murmured with an obscenely cheerful smile as he backed away and started off through the throng.

Carole didn't acknowledge his apology. She was too busy reading the words on his sweatshirt: The Fat Man Is Coming. "I hate to break it to you, sir," she mumbled inaudibly at his retreating back, "but he's already here." She headed her dragging footsteps toward the mall exit, trying to block out the shoppers' cheery chaos. Darn. She really did have to work on her attitude.

Outside, she took a deep breath and tipped her head back. The night was cold and clear, and silvery stars shone brightly, like twinkling decorations against the black velvet of the winter sky.

Decorations, she thought ruefully. She needed decorations.

With luck, the Paper Shack would still have some Christmas paraphernalia left, and the shop was no more than two blocks away. Suddenly she couldn't bear the thought of getting into her car and breathing its canned heat. Not when the night was so glorious. She would walk. Never mind that no one in Bossier City walked anywhere anymore or that it was eight-thirty at night and she could be mugged.

Carole glanced at the street. It was well lighted and busy with traffic. Then she looked at the high heels she was wearing and reminded herself that her feet were killing her. Still, she thought, she wanted to walk.

Hugging her coat more tightly around her, she started off across the parking lot toward the big Baptist church. Surely she'd be safe in that vicinity. Besides, if a mugger even thought of accosting her, she'd start singing "Santa Claus Is Coming to Town." That would get rid of him.

Christmas. Nothing but a commercial scam designed to eke as much money as possible from unsuspecting shoppers. While she couldn't deny that the season helped her business, she personally felt it was all a farce. People frittered away money they couldn't afford, charging their credit cards to the hilt, then spent the rest of the year paying for one day's enjoyment.

Why not just show your loved ones some care and consideration each day of the year, instead of trying to make up for the lapses in your relationships with a single lavish display of artificial affection?

Carole struggled to squelch the bitterness that stemmed from sixteen Christmases—sixteen years— spent in a church-affiliated children's home. Every year during the holidays the children had received generic gifts, tagged either "Boy" or "Girl," with the appropriate age alongside. Yet while gifts were plentiful, few of those "Christian" people who donated them took the time to come to the home to meet the nameless, faceless kids they had shopped for.

Ah, well, what did it matter?

She crossed the side street between the mall and the church and forced her thoughts to her store windows. Maybe she'd buy an assortment of glossy red and green shopping bags and tissue paper and have some sweaters, ties and belts spilling over the tops. Or maybe she'd—

A weak mewling sound brought her thoughts and her steps up short. She tilted her head and listened. There it was again! A faint squalling, like a baby crying. She looked across the street. Nothing there but the glass company's empty parking lot. There was no one behind her, no one ahead of her and nothing to her left but the floodlit nativity scene in front of the church's playground. Nothing unusual there, just the manger and the standard figurines of Joseph, Mary, three wise men and a donkey.

Lured by the sound, though, Carole started across the dry grass. The season really was getting to her, she thought as she stumbled over the uneven ground in her heels. She had flipped. Toppled over the edge. Yet she kept walking, drawn to the nativity scene by a force stronger than she. As she approached the manger, the sound grew louder.

What if the police saw her? she wondered suddenly. Would she be arrested for trespassing? Disturbing a crèche? What could she say? *"I'm sorry, officer, but I thought I heard a baby crying, and it sounded as if it was coming from this manger."* She shook her head crossly and covered the last few feet to the wooden trough filled with fresh yellow straw.

To her utter amazement, there, wrapped in a worn blanket and crying its little lungs out, lay a real live baby. Carole stared at the child and expelled the breath she hadn't been aware she was holding. So she hadn't gone off the deep end. This was no figment of her imagination. This was real. For a moment she was too stunned to move.

The infant didn't look newborn, but it wasn't very old, either. It was wearing a knitted cap, and a pacifier lay in the folds of the blanket near its head. Someone had abandoned the baby! Red-hot anger, fueled by the memory of her own similar circumstances as a two-year-old, filled her. What kind of person could leave a baby outside in the winter?

Without further thought, Carole retrieved the pacifier and, careful to support the baby's head—she'd heard that somewhere—scooped the infant into her arms. She didn't know much about babies, but she knew that pacifiers were supposed to keep them from crying. She gently thrust the plastic nipple into the tiny bow-shaped mouth. The crying stopped.

She sighed in relief and looked toward the busy street, once more realizing that she was standing in the floodlights illuminating the nativity scene. Good grief! What would people think? Opening her coat, she tucked the baby inside. Then, holding it close against her shoulder, she started toward her car. Obviously, buying decorations for the Ultimate Man would have to wait.

With a bouncing gait, she trekked eagerly to her car, aware of the baby's muffled sucking. She approached the red CRX with a prayer of thanksgiving. It wouldn't take long to warm up the interior. She unlocked the door and eased inside, turning on the ignition and setting the heater on high.

As warmth spilled from the vents, she took the baby from her shoulder and laid it on the seat. It promptly spit out the pacifier and began to cry again, its little mouth wide open and filling the car with ear-splitting shrieks. Carole tried to insert the pacifier again, but the wailing child was having no more of it.

Carole gnawed her bottom lip and wondered what she should do. Change its diapers? Feed it? She didn't have diapers or formula, but K-and-B drugs was just across the street, and...

Get real, Carole. You can't just keep the child. What are you going to do?

The seriousness of the situation finally struck her. She didn't know how to take care of a baby. She was a thirty-year-old businesswoman who knew more about fashion merchandising and changing window displays than she did about buying formula and changing diapers.

This baby had been abandoned—a situation the police should look into. But the thought of taking the baby to the police station was unbearable. What did a bunch of blue-uniformed men know about taking care of a baby? Probably even less than she did. She tried again to get the baby to take the pacifier.

"Please, God," she said frantically, her wide-eyed gaze shifting up to the windshield and the street, "help me."

Even as she uttered the prayer, her gaze landed on a billboard at the corner of Texas and Airline. For as long as she could remember, the billboard had advertised Bossier Medical Center. She blinked in surprise at the appropriateness of it.

Of course. The hospital. It was only a block away, and the baby should get medical attention. God alone knew how long it had been exposed to the cold night air or when it had been fed last. She put the car into gear and started out of the parking lot. Why hadn't she thought of it sooner?

An hour later, Carole wasn't sure the hospital had been such a good idea after all. The baby had been whisked away into some inner sanctum, and a pediatrician had been called. Carole had supposed she would drop off the infant and be free to go, but instead the hospital had called the police station and insisted that she stay until the officers arrived to ask her some questions.

Which they'd been doing for the past half hour.

"Are we finished, Officer Gibson?" she asked the heavyset, balding man who had been taking notes while his younger partner flirted with the woman at the emergency room desk. "I'd like to find out how the baby is doing and go home. It's been quite a day."

The man looked up with a tired smile. "Just one more question."

She nodded, her attention idling on the younger officer, who was heading through a nearby doorway. "Fine," she said. "But I really can't think of anything else to tell you."

"Is it yours?"

"I beg your pardon?" Carole asked, reaching for her coat and alligator purse.

"Is the baby yours?"

Her astonished gaze met his. "Mine? I'm not even married."

He shrugged. "All the more reason to dump a kid."

Carole let that soak in. Having been "dumped" herself, it wasn't an option she would ever consider— married or not. She tried to control her rising temper. "It is not my baby," she told him, enunciating carefully. "Why would you even think it was?"

"We had a similar situation a few years back. Someone left a baby right here on the hospital steps. A couple of bystanders said they saw a woman leaving."

"I fail to see the connection," Carole told him frostily.

"Sometimes even though a mother is abandoning a child, she wants to make certain it's being taken care of. That's probably why the other dame left hers here. It could be why you're sticking around to see what's happening to the kid."

Carole shook her head, her blunt-cut glossy brown hair brushing her cheeks. "You're wrong, Officer. I'm 'sticking around' because no one will let me go home."

"Hey, Al!" the young officer called as he came back through the doorway. "Come look at this."

Al Gibson rose and crossed the room. Seeing that the other policeman held the baby's blanket and a plastic bag, Carole went, too.

"What is it?" she asked, regarding the bag.

"A few baby things that were wrapped up next to her. Worn out but clean. And there was a bottle of water, too."

"Her?" Carole asked. "It's a girl?"

The young officer smiled. "Yeah. A girl named Katy. The mother left a note inside the blanket. Said she had four other kids, that her old man skipped out on her. Her milk dried up, and she couldn't afford to feed another one. She said God told her where to leave the baby. That he'd see to it she was found."

"What a nutso," Al said with a shake of his head.

But Carole hardly noticed. She was too busy remembering the unusual set of circumstances that had led her to the baby. Since when had she walked anywhere when she could drive? And why had she chosen to walk tonight when she was so tired and out of sorts? A faint, sick feeling swept through her when she realized how long it otherwise might have been before someone came along and found the child. Did children really have guardian angels?

"How is she?" she asked suddenly.

"Fine. Doc says she's a couple of months old. Healthy. Apparently she hadn't been out there too long. She was wrapped up good, but she was one hungry little girl."

Relief made Carole feel weak. She managed a slight smile.

"You can go now, if you like, Ms. Chapman," Al Gibson said kindly. "If we need you, we'll give you a call."

She nodded, suddenly very tired. "What's going to happen to...to Katy?"

"I've already called Chris to come and pick her up," Officer Gibson said.

"Chris?"

Al nodded. "Chris Nicholas. The police psychologist."

Chris Nicholas. A psychologist. A woman like that should be a safe bet to provide a good, stable environment for a baby, Carole thought.

"Chris is an approved foster parent who can pick up a child on short notice when we need to get one out of a bad situation. He'll keep her until we can find her mother or a permanent foster home."

"He?" Carole echoed in disbelief. But even as shock began to take hold, a reassuring thought occurred to her. "There *is* a Mrs. Nicholas, isn't there?"

Officer Gibson shook his head. "No. But don't worry; Chris is well qualified. He's a widower with three kids of his own."

Before Carole had a chance to digest this new information, Al gestured toward the door. "Here he comes now."

Carole turned toward the emergency room entrance. A station wagon covered with a film of red dust and sporting a dented right fender pulled to a screeching stop. Carole's eyes widened and her heart sank as a veritable giant of a man unfolded his length from the disreputable car's interior.

Chris Nicholas must have stood six foot four and was so broad through the shoulders that he looked as if he were wearing football gear. He sported a mane of too-long hair so blond it was almost white, which contrasted sharply with the dark mustache draped nonchalantly over his upper lip.

But that wasn't the worst of it, Carole realized as her horrified, style-conscious gaze roamed from the top of his head to his toes. If clothes made the man, as the fashion industry was fond of promulgating, this specimen of masculinity was in deep trouble. You couldn't get any farther from the "ultimate man" if you tried. He was wearing faded, raggedy jeans too tight for decency, much less for the obvious strain on the aged fly. She deliberately shifted her gaze from the disturbing masculine bulge to his torso. The view got worse. A plaid flannel shirt, half unbuttoned and its sleeves rolled to the elbow, boasting an unlikely combination of orange, black and teal, had been pulled on over a thermal undershirt and thrust haphazardly into the waistband of the scruffy jeans. Worn sneakers without socks covered large feet.

Carole gave a delicate shudder that had nothing to do with the draft of cold air accompanying the giant through the door. This was a psychologist? A qualified foster parent for Katy? This . . . this hobo who looked like a Salvation Army reject?

Chapter Two

How on earth could she let this man take Katy home with him?

"Hey, Chris!" the younger policeman said, holding out his hand. "Glad you could come."

The newcomer shook hands with both officers. "No problem. How's the kid?"

"Doc says she's great. She's gathering up some formula and stuff for you."

"Good."

Al Gibson gestured toward Carole. "This is Carole Chapman. She found Katy."

The police psychologist turned, his hand extended and the corners of his mustache lifting in a slow, incredibly sweet smile. "Hello, Carole Chapman. I'm Chris Nicholas."

Ingrained politeness made her offer her own hand, but manners had nothing to do with her reaction. Somehow, the warmth of his smile and the heat and strength of his fingers as they swallowed hers made Carole momentarily forget that he was dressed as a Paul Bunyan look-alike. Her hello was barely audible.

"You found Katy at the Baptist church?" he asked.

"Yes," she said, drawing her hand away a bit testily. She was tired of answering questions, she rationalized. She just wanted to make certain the baby was going to be well taken care of so that she could go home to a hot bath and a warm bed. Besides, she didn't like the breathless feeling she'd experienced when Chris Nicholas touched her.

"Look, are you sure you can take care of a baby?" she queried as a defense against her muddled emotions. "I mean, we aren't talking about a puppy here. She's going to cry during the night and need her diapers changed and—"

The towering psychologist smiled again, but there was a considering light in his sapphire-blue eyes. "I'm well aware of what babies do, Mrs. Chapman," he said. "And you can trust me to take good care of her. Believe me, I've had a lot of experience."

"Fine, then," she said, shrugging into her coat. "And it's *Ms.* Chapman."

"Ah," he said with a nod and another smile.

That particular smile grated on Carole's nerves. It seemed to say without words that, with her attitude, it was no wonder she was a Ms. instead of a Mrs. In response, she produced an insolent gaze and let it roam from his feet to his gleaming silvery hair—which was a mistake, she realized when her heart jumped into fifth gear. How could she have forgotten how broad his shoulders were and how well he filled out his jeans? Her libido, which she took great pains to keep under control, made a bid for freedom—an attempt she squelched with a facade of sarcasm.

"It's good to know Katy will be in such good hands," she snapped, grabbing her purse and slinging the narrow strap over her shoulder. "Goodbye, Mr. Nicholas. Meeting you has been...an experience."

The goodwill in his eyes faded, and his heavy blond eyebrows met in a frown. "Whoa!" he said. "What got your panties in a wad?"

Carole gasped. *Panties in a wad,* indeed! What an uncouth man! Her angry eyes made another scathing survey of him. Defying logic, defying the orders of her head, her heart sprinted forward. She struggled—and failed—to find a logical reason to offer for her antagonism. "You... Your choice of clothing is reprehensible," she sputtered at last.

"Well, that certainly clears things up, doesn't it?" he shot back with uncharacteristic temper. "Pardon me. If I'd known my wardrobe was going to be under scrutiny, I'd have worn my tux."

Vivid blue eyes locked with brown while Al Gibson and his partner looked on in astonishment.

Chris saw Carole's gaze waver, could almost see her mentally backing down. Was that a glimmer of pain in her eyes? Why? The male part of him, the part of him that thought she had the sexiest upper lip and the most gorgeous chocolate-brown hair he'd ever seen, stepped aside for the psychologist part of him.

"Look," he said, suddenly all therapist, "I'm sorry if we got off on the wrong foot. I apologize. You're right. I'm not exactly dressed to impress, but I didn't know I'd need to."

His sudden contrition took Carole by surprise. Maybe she'd judged him too harshly. Despite the wanton feelings he inspired in her and the fact that he dressed terribly, any man who took in children had to be a good person, didn't he?

She sighed and shook her head. "No, it was my fault. It's been a long day, and I'm tired. Chalk it up to bad manners and exhaustion."

"Here she is!" The words preceded a white-frocked nurse who cradled a small bundle against her ample bosom. She held her small burden out to Chris, who grinned and said, "'Lo, Margaret."

"Hello," she replied, transferring Katy to his waiting arms. "You got yourself a real beauty this time."

Chris's eyes crinkled in another smile. "Let's see." He pulled the blanket away from the baby's face. "She is pretty, isn't she?" He glanced up at Carole. "Wanna take a last look?"

Without answering, Carole closed the few feet separating her and Chris and, sidling closer, peeked at Katy. The infant was sleeping, her fair lashes fanning out over her sleep-pink cheeks. Carole felt the prickling of tears behind her eyelids. How could anyone just leave the life and fate of a baby to the care—or abuse—of strangers? Blinking back the threatening moisture and avoiding eye contact with Chris, she stepped away and said, "I'm sure you'll take excellent care of her."

Chris heard the emotion in her voice and wondered again why the situation was hitting her so hard. He wished she would look at him. "I'll do my best," he promised.

Carole nodded and started for the exit. Chris watched her hasty retreat and wished he knew what was bothering her.

Saturday, November 26

If possible, Saturday's shoppers seemed as eager to get on with their holiday purchasing as Friday's had been. Carole assigned her two helpers to handling the customers and the cash register while she set about transforming the store to conform with the season.

Strangely, the task wasn't as bad as she'd expected. Maybe because her mind wasn't really on decorating. Instead, her thoughts were filled with Katy and the woman who had left her behind. Unlike Carole's own mother, it appeared that Katy's mom was trying to give her daughter a chance at a better life. Still, Carole wasn't so sure.... What would happen to Katy now? Would she be placed in an orphanage or a series of foster homes, the way Carole had?

As she contemplated foster homes, Carole's thoughts drifted to Chris Nicholas. How long would Katy be allowed to stay with him? And, more to the point, how was she doing in his care? Reason told Carole that the psychologist must be more than competent to be called on the way he had been, but she would still like to see for herself how Katy was faring.

She fluffed a sheet of red tissue paper and shook her head. Checking on Katy would mean facing Chris Nicholas again. She didn't think that would be wise. Yet the idea wouldn't leave her alone. Worse, her heart unaccountably fluttered at the prospect. She decided to put the notion out of her head entirely.

But when she crawled into her solitary bed that night, her final thought was of Chris Nicholas's warm, friendly smile....

Sunday, November 27

Carole was thankful she didn't have to work on Sunday, even though the mall was open from one to five. By midafternoon, she had finished all her weekly chores, and she found herself staring out the window and thinking of Katy...again. On sudden impulse, she dialed the police station and asked for Officer Al Gibson.

"Yeah?" came his scratchy, familiar voice a few minutes later.

"Officer Gibson, this is Carole Chapman—I'm the one who found Katy the other night," she said without preamble.

"Oh, right!" he said. "How's it going, Ms. Chapman?"

"Fine." She paused. "I was wondering...do you know how Katy is doing?"

"No, can't say that I do. I haven't run into Chris since he picked her up the other night."

"Oh."

"Why don't you run on out and check on her yourself," he suggested. "Chris won't mind."

The thought left her breathless, even though a secret part of her heart whispered that Al Gibson's suggestion was only corroborating her own longing. She had no idea what was happening to her, but for some reason her heart's desires had been overriding her brain's dictates lately. "Oh, I don't know..."

"Let me give you the directions," the policeman said, "just in case."

Thirty minutes later, Carole was pulling into the driveway of Chris Nicholas's farm. The house, set in the midst of a small pecan grove, was a Cajun-style cedar with a porch across the front. Beyond the trees and a barn stretched acres of pastureland, brown now with dead grass. Several head of beef cattle munched on large rolls of hay, and half-a-dozen—no, seven, she counted—swans swam majestically across the smooth surface of a large pond, a flock of noisy ducks scooting along beside them. The barn looked freshly painted, and the fence stood straight and taut. Carole imagined that the scene before her would be gorgeous in the springtime, with green grass undulating in a soft breeze. It was the perfect environment for growing children. And, unlike its owner, the farm was well tended.

Wrapped in surprising contentment, she got out of the car and breathed in a deep draft of the fresh air. Though the temperature had gone down to freezing the night before, in typical Louisiana fashion the winter sunshine had sent the mercury soaring into the low sixties as the day progressed. It was a perfect afternoon for a country outing.

The melancholy sound of two turtledoves calling to each other evoked a sudden surge of uncertainty in Carole. Had she done the right thing by coming here?

Lost in thought, she watched a trio of colorful, exotic-looking hens parade across the lawn, followed by a cocky rooster obviously trying to keep them in line. Smiling at his nervous antics, Carole was once more propelled into action. She rounded the hood of the car and started for the front door.

A sudden honking and hissing assailed her ears, and at the same time an earsplitting yell escaped the interior of the house. Carole's wide-eyed gaze darted between the house and the six geese approaching her at a dead run, their wings outspread and mayhem obviously their intent. Making a quick decision, she raced back to the car. As she attempted an Olympics-style leap to the hood, the front door of the house burst open and a teenage boy flung himself off the porch, yelling, "Get the heck out of here!"

Chapter Three

Carole stared at the irate boy, unable to believe he was running her off the place so venomously. She automatically began to apologize for coming without calling first. "I'm sor—"

"Get out of here, you miserable pack of pillow stuffing!" the boy shouted, interrupting her faltering speech.

He wasn't talking to her at all! He was yelling at the gaggle of geese.

At the sound of his voice—or perhaps it was the waving of his arms—the geese stopped honking and ambled away from Carole.

Drawing a shaky breath, she eased her boot-shod feet to the ground and prayed her trembling legs would hold her. She had heard that geese made good watchdogs but had never seen them in action before.

"Sorry about that," the young man said with a wry smile, raking a hand through his short dark hair. "But those geese are a lot better at announcing strangers than Shep is." He gestured toward a Catahoula hog dog sleeping in a once-glorious bed of yellow and rust mums. In recognition of his name, the dog lifted his head, yawned and slapped his tail against the ground a couple of times.

Carole couldn't help smiling. "Shep looks like a ball of fire all right."

The boy smiled in return. "I'm Brian Nicholas. Can I help you with something?"

Before Carole could do more than register the fact that he must be Chris's son, a gravelly voice from inside the house screeched, "There's one!"

Seeing the look on her face, Brian grinned. "It's okay. That's only Sebastian."

"Sebastian?"

"Our parrot."

"Oh," Carole said, as in the dark as ever about what was going on inside. Then, realizing that Brian was staring at her questioningly, she said, "I'm Carole Chapman. I found Katy at the church the other night, and I just wanted to see how things were going."

Brian nodded. "Oh, yeah. I heard. Katy's fine. It's kinda wild in there right now, but come on in and see for yourself," he offered, starting toward the wide porch steps.

Wild hardly did justice to the scene that greeted Carole as she stepped into Chris Nicholas's house. It was bedlam. What calm remained after her encounter with the geese fled as she scanned the cluttered room and struggled to comprehend the activity.

Three boys of various sizes and descriptions, a little blond girl and a second dog, which looked like a mop, scrambled over the floor and under tables in pursuit of something, while a pretty teenager sat on the couch holding a bottle of nail polish out of harm's way. A huge Amazon parrot sat in the upper branches of a lemon tree.

"There's another one!"

Carole glanced toward the parrot, which was repeating its announcement, and caught sight of Chris standing across the room, holding Katy, who was screaming at the top of her lungs. Evidently there was so much going on that he didn't even see Carole. Something green leaped toward the girl on the sofa, who squealed and screamed, "Tad Nicholas, I'm going to kill you!"

The tow-haired boy lunged forward.

Carole realized with a start that he'd grabbed a frog.

"Yeah? You and what army?" Tad taunted, grinning and shaking his captive in the girl's face. The mutinous act elicited another panicked yell from the teenager and a thundering "Tad!" from Chris and Sebastian.

"How many is that, Jake?" Chris asked a teenage boy holding a big glass jar.

"Ten," Jake replied as Tad added his frog to the collection. "One to go."

"Chris," Brian said, taking advantage of the relative quiet, "Ms. Chapman is here." But Chris didn't hear. A chorus of cuckoos began chiming out the hour. Attempting to pinpoint the source of the sound, Carole counted no fewer than four cuckoo clocks in the room.

"Chris!" Brian yelled, struggling to make himself heard over the cuckoos and the barking dog, which had just spied Carole and obviously mistaken her coat for some sort of animal. Yapping furiously, it attacked the hem, planted its feet apart and pulled, shaking its head and snarling viciously.

Diverted from wondering why Brian called his father Chris, and almost in a state of shock, Carole bent over and tried to free her coat—her expensive lambswool coat—when yet another frog appeared out of nowhere, leaping toward her face with a deep, throaty, *rrribbitt*. Carole jumped and shrieked.

The dog released its hold and scrambled across the room to lunge onto a chair piled with what appeared to be clean laundry. Carole didn't know if it was due to the unfamiliar sound of her voice in the melee or the fact that, after announcing the time, the four calling birds retired to their respective clocks, that the room seemed suddenly quiet.

Her eyes found Chris's. He was looking at her in surprise, as were the children, and she felt like an alien in a strange land. Even Katy had quieted.

"Me got it," another youngster said, breaking the relative silence. He held the last frog aloft in both hands, a wide smile crinkling his almond-shaped eyes.

"Way to go, Mikey," Chris said, shifting his attention from Carole to the boy. Then he turned to Tad, who, Carole deduced, must actually *be* his son, if the name and the hair were anything to go by.

"Take those frogs back to their aquarium, and don't let them out again, do you hear me?"

"I didn't do it!" Tad objected. "Tina dropped the picnic basket."

Chris closed his eyes, making Carole wonder if he were counting to ten. "And what were they doing in the picnic basket?" he asked patiently.

"She was taking them for a walk."

"A walk?"

"Yeah. They were tired of being cooped up."

"Go to your room, Tad," Chris said wearily.

"And clean it while you're in there," Brian added.

"You wish," Tad said in true brotherly disdain. He jerked his head toward Carole. "Who's she?"

"Stop staring, Tad," the girl on the couch said.

"This is Ms. Chapman," Brian announced to the room at large. "She found Katy." Before anyone, including Chris, could reply, Brian asked, "Would you like to sit down?" He glanced at the nearest chair, where the dog was ensconced, and blushed before shooing the dog off the clothes and scooping them up in his arms.

"Thank you." Carole sank gratefully into the chair. She glanced up at Chris, who shifted Katy to his other shoulder and patted her back soothingly.

"I'm sorry about the confusion," he said with a rueful smile. "Please don't think it's always like this around here."

"I understand," she hastened to assure him. After all, it wasn't every day that frogs were unleashed on a household.

"Sometimes it's worse," he told her, his expression deadpan. Then she saw that his bright blue eyes were alight with mirth. "I just wanted to give you fair warning."

"Oh," was all she could think of to say.

"So, Carole Chapman, what can I do for you?"

She met his questioning gaze and felt her face flush with heat. "It was such a pretty day that I...I thought a drive would be nice, and I—"

"You wondered how Katy was doing," he stated baldly.

"Well, yes."

"She's doing fine." He squatted beside the chair and turned Katy so that Carole could see for herself. Katy's eyes were open, and she'd stopped crying. Her soft hair was brushed to the side. She looked well-fed and sleepy. And she smelled nice and clean, just as a baby should.

Smiling, Carole turned and looked at Chris, surprised at how close to her he was. His shoulders were so broad, she thought as her gaze traveled up over his square chin and the sultry curve of his upper lip beneath the sweep of his mustache.

She'd never kissed anyone with a mustache before, she thought randomly as her gaze drifted to his eyes, which were smiling warmly into hers. The latent sensuality hiding behind that innocent blue robbed her of her next breath.

"Well?" he questioned softly.

She licked her dry lips and struggled for air. "She looks . . . fine."

"She is fine. Actually, Katy has adapted very well. Insanity must run in her family, too." When Carole's eyes widened, so did Chris's smile. "Let me introduce you to the troops," he said, standing and giving her some breathing room. "You've obviously met Brian. He's a senior this year."

Glad for the reprieve from his overwhelming nearness, Carole nodded. "Brian saved me from the geese."

"Brian is my oldest. He's been a Nicholas for about six months now."

Carole was surprised. It was hard to believe that Chris had bothered to adopt a boy Brian's age, since he would soon be out on his own.

"The one over there who's afraid she's going to mess up her manicure is my daughter, Lisa, who is in the ninth grade."

Pretty, blond-haired Lisa wrinkled her nose at her father, but there was a familiar glint of mischief in her blue eyes, too. "Hello, Ms. Chapman."

Chris pointed to the boy holding the glass jar. "Jake Arnold, keeper of the frogs, has only been with us since school started. He's thirteen."

Jake ducked his head shyly. "Hi."

Chris reached out and ruffled the hair of the smiling boy with the Oriental look. "This is Mike. He's ten, and I'm trying to adopt him."

Mike offered Carole a bright-eyed smile. "Yeah!"

At second glance, Carole could see that Mike wasn't Oriental at all, but that he had the look of a child with Down's syndrome. Just for a moment her heart ached in pity, but with Mike's smile rivaling the afternoon sunshine streaming through the windows, the feeling passed.

Pointing at the thin boy with thick glasses and the blond culprit who owned the frogs, Chris said, "This is the Terrible Twosome. Tad is my own offspring— he's seven—and the eight-year-old boy genius is David Carter, who has all the makings of a computer whiz. What one of them doesn't think to get into, the other one generally does."

"Me, Daddy," the cute little girl who was holding on to Chris's leg for dear life said.

"I didn't forget about you, pretty girl," Chris said, placing a big hand atop her blond head. "This is Tina Nicholas. She's two and a half and just the tiniest bit *j-e-a-l-o-u-s* over the *b-a-b-y*." He smiled. "And, of course, you know Katy."

"Me, Daddy." The reminder came from Sebastian, who could obviously mimic anything he heard.

"Ah, yes," Chris said. "That's Sebastian. We're kind to animals around here, even ornery ones."

Carole remembered the menagerie outside. She was overwhelmed. And full of questions. For instance, where had all these kids come from, why was Chris adopting a Down's syndrome child, and what had happened to his wife? But instead of asking those questions she said, "You have three biological children—Lisa, Tad and Tina?"

"Right," he told her with a nod. Then, changing the subject abruptly, he asked, "Would you like some coffee?"

As his warm smile had the night she'd met him, his easy offer of hospitality took Carole by surprise. "Well, I..." She hesitated, wondering if she shouldn't simply leave while she was ahead. After all, she'd seen for herself that, despite the chaos of the household, Katy was fine. "A cup of coffee sounds wonderful," she heard herself say. "Thank you."

"Good. I think Lisa has some cookies baked." Chris turned to the roomful of children. "Get on your chores. P.D.Q."

To Carole's surprise, the room emptied as if he'd just told them a toxic gas had been turned loose, though she did hear some grumbling as they filed out.

"Not you, young lady," Chris said to Lisa, who was the last to leave.

Turning, she looked at him innocently. "What?"

"What?" Chris echoed. He looked at Carole. "She looks smart, doesn't she? But her memory is terrible."

"Daddy!" Lisa cried.

"Sorry, sweetie, but, wet nails or not, it's your turn to do the kitchen."

Lisa gave him a wounded look.

"Pronto."

"But you promised you'd take me to the mall to look for a dress for the Christmas dance."

"That was before we had eleven frogs escape and before company came," Chris said, pointing toward the kitchen. "Go."

Lisa went. As the door swung wide, Carole glimpsed a large kitchen with dirty dishes covering every inch of counter space. She sighed in sympathy for Lisa. Past experience had taught Carole how hard it was for a girl to stand on the threshold of womanhood with no one to guide her, no one to confide in about problems or the changes taking place in her life and her body...no one to help pick out party dresses.

But on the other hand, Lisa at least had a father who loved her and who was willing to try to stand in for the mother who was missing in Lisa's—in all the children's—life. It had to be hard on him, trying to bring up his own family without a wife and mother. And then to take on the added responsibility of five other children...

"Hold Katy, will you?" Chris asked, the simple request breaking into the somberness of Carole's thoughts.

She looked up, her excuse already forming. She didn't want to hold Katy, didn't want to feel any more tugging on her heartstrings. "I don't—" she began. Then her eyes met Chris's. There was a question in the clear blue depths, something that asked without words what was wrong. Carole realized suddenly that he was a very intuitive man.

He smiled at her. She wasn't certain she'd ever met a man who smiled so often—or had a smile so sweet. "If you don't hold Katy, Lisa will have to make the coffee. And if Lisa makes the coffee, you'll never come back."

Carole wasn't even aware that she held out her arms. Without a word, Chris placed Katy there and disappeared through the swinging door that led to the kitchen. Only when he'd gone did she wonder why it would matter to him whether she ever came back or not.

Chapter Four

While Chris was in the kitchen making coffee, Carole prowled the room, rubbing Katy's back and searching for clues to what made Chris Nicholas tick. Sebastian climbed up and down the branches of the lemon tree. A huge rock fireplace with a gun cabinet built on one side dominated the room. Matching bookcases on the other side balanced the wall. A mounted deer head and a huge largemouth bass hung on the far wall. Obviously Chris was an outdoorsman. A hunter. And a fisherman. But a well-read one, she thought, eyeing the magazines scattered about and the titles on the book spines. Everything from the classics to Ludlum was represented, including psychological journals and *Ranger Rick*.

Katy began to fuss, cutting Carole's tour short. She cradled the baby in her arms and bounced her up and down a couple of times. What would happen if Katy started crying in earnest? She glanced toward the kitchen. How long did it take to make coffee, anyway?

She looked at the baby in her arms, who gave a low, halfhearted wail and pursed her lips in a sucking motion. Was she hungry? "Oh, Katy," Carole begged, "please don't start crying."

"What's the matter? She hungry?"

Carole looked up and saw Tad, David and Mike standing in the doorway, three small witnesses to her quandary.

"Time Ka-dee eat?" Mike asked.

"Ka-dee eat?" Sebastian echoed.

"I don't know," Carole confessed, bouncing Katy in her arms.

"It's probably colic," David said, pushing his Coke-bottle-lens glasses farther up on his small nose. The trio sidled nearer.

"Horses have colic," Tad said disdainfully.

"Colic. Gas. It's all the same, nerd-o," David said.

"Nerd-o," the bird croaked.

David looked at the clock. "I think she eats in a little while. Want us to go ask Chris?"

"That might be a good idea," Carole said.

David and Tad left the room, but Mike stayed behind. She watched as he went to a stack of paraphernalia in the corner and came back with a dispenser of baby wipes, a diaper and a pacifier, which he held up with a triumphant smile. "Passie," he said, poking it into Katy's little bow-shaped mouth. Katy accepted the pacifier eagerly. Her eyes closed, and the fretting stopped.

"No cry-hing," Mike said, pleased with his solution. "Me tell Chris."

As he left the room in search of Chris, Carole's heart swelled with a strange blend of pity and pleasure. What a sweet child he was! Yet she wondered again why Chris would want to saddle himself with a child who had such obvious problems. It couldn't be easy bringing up so many children, and one with any kind of disability would surely require more work and worry.

Without forewarning, another thought worked its way insidiously into Carole's mind. There were so many healthy, normal kids, kids like she had been, looking for homes. Pain, as old as her memory, brought the sting of tears to her eyes.

She had thought that, as she grew older and came to a better comprehension of people and life in general, she would understand why no one had wanted to make her a part of their family when she was a child. But she was thirty, and she still didn't understand. She could still recall how she had convinced herself on three different occasions that the family she was living with was going to adopt her.

The first time she had been five and the couple had been young and attractive, parents any child would have been proud of. People had even commented on how much Carole resembled the woman, who was sterile and wanted a little girl. But after eight months, Marcia Brady had sent her back to the orphanage, saying that her husband wasn't sure he could handle the permanent responsibility of a child, since his business kept him on the road a lot and he wanted Marcia to travel with him.

The second time she had been told that the people loved her, but they really wanted to adopt a little boy. Carole couldn't remember what excuse she'd been given the third time. By then, she was twelve and convinced that something was wrong with her; otherwise, things would have turned out differently. She had loved them all and had wanted so much to be part of a family that loved her back. But somehow, no one ever returned her love, and after those three heartbreaking experiences, she had vowed she would never put herself in the position of being rejected again.

And she hadn't.

She had dated; she had even lost her virginity when she was twenty-five—late, by today's standards. But even though the man had tempted her aching heart with the promise of forever, she was afraid to trust her burgeoning feelings, afraid that he, like the others she had let herself care for, would walk away. In the end, it was she who had broken off with him.

Since that time, there had been no one significant. She had stopped accepting dinner invitations if they weren't business related, stopped trying to please anyone but herself. Her determination to keep her heart inviolate had given her more time to devote to her business, which had resulted in a growing clientele and a line of merchandise that drew businessmen from faraway Dallas, Little Rock and Houston. And if her decision made her a lonely woman, it had also made her a successful one. Success was something tangible, something she could hang on to.

Most of the time she didn't regret her choice, but she was smart enough to realize that she was cheating Mother Nature—which was why, she decided, Chris Nicholas had caused such unaccountable reactions in her. After all, she was a woman, and even if he dressed in clothes that looked as if they belonged among someone's castoffs, he was most definitely a man. As a matter of fact, she was beginning to suspect that his way of dressing fit his life-style just fine. And his rough-hewn good looks and impressive physique, combined with his gentle personality, added up to quite a man. Had she been wrong in assessing him as anything *but* a candidate for the ultimate man?

"Coffee's ready."

The sound of Chris's voice sent her guilty gaze to his face and silenced the clamoring of her wayward thoughts. "Good," she said, attempting to hide her feelings behind a too-bright smile.

Chris set two mugs on the coffee table and pulled a baby bottle from his shirt pocket. "Tad and David thought you might need this, but it looks as if you have everything under control."

"Thanks to Mike. He found Katy's pacifier."

"Works every time," he said with a grin. "Let me put her into bed so we can enjoy our coffee."

Carole nodded eagerly. Holding Katy made her nervous and brought back those feelings of inadequacy she usually managed to push aside. She held the baby out, and Chris leaned over, sliding his hands over hers to support Katy's back and neck as the exchange was made. The warmth of his callused palms made her uncomfortable, as did his smile, and once again she found herself struggling to control the wild beating of her heart.

She didn't say a word as he left the room with Katy cradled close.

When he returned, she was still pondering why this particular man should stir her emotions when she had managed to avoid that pitfall for the last five years.

"She's out like a light."

"That's good," Carole said, taking a sip of her coffee.

Chris sat down on the couch, facing her. "What's the matter?"

Startled, Carole avoided his eyes. "What makes you think anything's wrong?"

"It's my job to read people," he said. "And you've been angry, suspicious and generally prickly ever since

I met you at the hospital. I assure you that I'm dependable, sane and that I love these kids a lot. I'll take good care of Katy."

"I know that," Carole told him, and she realized that she meant it.

"Then what?"

"It's just the season, I guess."

"You talk in riddles, lady. Anyone ever tell you that?" he said with a shake of his head.

"The Christmas season," she said, rising and going to the window. "It always brings back so many memories."

"Not good ones, obviously."

"No. Not good ones." She turned to look at him. "I was raised in an orphanage and a series of foster homes, too, Mr. Nicholas."

"Chris."

"Chris," she repeated obediently. His name sounded right on her lips, just as the need to open up to him suddenly felt right. Seeing the children in his home, knowing that he was so giving, made her old hurts and doubts shoot straight to the surface. "Like Katy, I was abandoned," she confessed. "Only I was two when my mother left me on an orphanage doorstep."

"And you resent that."

Carole's laugh was short and bitter. "Wouldn't you resent knowing that someone loved you so little she could give you up without looking back?"

Chris shrugged his massive shoulders. "Maybe she was like Katy's mother. Maybe she did love you but didn't feel she could give you life's essentials, much less its advantages. At least in a children's home she knew you would have a roof over your head and get three square meals a day, even if no one was going to cuddle you at bedtime.''

Carole considered his suggestion. In truth, she had never looked at it that way.

"Why would you think she didn't love you?"

"Because no one has ever loved me," she blurted.

"That's a pretty strong statement," he said smoothly. "What do you base your assumption on?"

"I base it on the fact that even though I lived with and learned to love several families, no one cared enough to want to adopt me," she told him angrily, unaware, in her anger, just how much of her heart she was revealing.

"Adoption is a big decision, Carole," he told her calmly. "Some people who are fantastic foster parents don't want to make that final commitment for one reason or another. Sometimes they feel they can do more as that intermediate step between a bad situation and adoptive parents. And after a while, you realize that you can't adopt them all, so you have to choose."

"I can buy that," she said, "but how do you decide? Why would you adopt someone like Brian, who's almost grown? And why Mike, instead of Jake or David?"

Chris nodded, understanding what she was asking. "Like you, Brian needed to know someone loved him. He needed to know he had a family. He'd been through several foster families, wasn't doing well in his studies, and stayed in trouble with the law—nothing too terrible until he broke into the school with some other kids. The police picked him up, sent him to me, and over a period of time, I realized that he felt like he'd fallen through the cracks somewhere. He was too old to be adopted; the state was just waiting until he was of age so they could cut him loose. He was crying out for attention and love.''

And Chris had given him that, Carole knew. Brian's situation was so close to her own that she had to swallow back the lump in her throat.

''And you're wondering why I'm trying to adopt Mike instead of a so-called normal child. The answer is easy. First of all, kids with any kind of handicap seldom have a chance for adoption. Secondly, once you're around him for a little while, you'll see that Mike is a very lovable child. I hope that by the time he's Brian's age, he'll be able to function in the world at least enough for him to have some sort of independent life.''

Carole felt the sting of tears beneath her eyelids. ''What about the others?''

Chris's mouth curved in a gentle smile. ''There have been a lot of others through the years, but you must mean the kids I have now. Jake—'' He paused, and for a moment Carole saw a hint of anger in the depths of his blue eyes. ''Jake's only here temporarily. His father beat him on more than one occasion. His mother is in the process of getting a divorce and finding a decent job and a place for them to live. When we feel she's well enough established, he can go back to her.

''David's parents were killed in a car accident,'' he continued. ''He isn't eligible for adoption because he has an older sister—a career woman who doesn't want to be bothered with bringing up a child but who won't relinquish her rights to him.''

''That's terrible!'' Carole said.

''It is, but David's a survivor. And he's smart.''

"And how do *your* three kids feel about all this? Do they resent having their home invaded by strangers?"

"Not so far. Lisa is a typical teenager. She likes boys more than girls at this stage. Other girls are competition. Tad loves having someone to get into trouble with, and Tina just goes with the flow. I guess they accept it because Cathie and I always did it."

"Cathie? Your wife?"

Chris nodded. "She died having Tina." His blue gaze found Carole's. "It wasn't supposed to happen. No one dies in childbirth anymore." He sighed. "But she did."

"I'm sorry."

A hint of bittersweet sorrow lingered in his eyes. "Yeah. So am I. Besides the void her dying created in my life, it left me in a bit of a predicament as far as adoption goes. Not having a wife slows things down."

"Maybe you should marry again," Carole suggested practically.

His mustache crawled up at one corner in a derisive smile. "Hell, it's hard enough to find a date—" he waved his left arm in a wide arc "—much less anyone willing to take all this on." Sunlight glinted off the gold watch circling his brawny wrist, obviously reminding him of the time. "Damn."

"What is it?"

"I've got to get busy finding a baby-sitter."

"A baby-sitter?"

He nodded, already heading for the phone. "Tomorrow's Monday, and Mrs. Landry, who keeps Tina and whatever other preschoolers I have, called this morning and said she had the flu. I've got to round up someone else pretty quick."

He was going to leave Katy with a stranger? The thought brought an ache to Carole's heart.

"What are you doing tomorrow?" he asked out of the blue.

She looked at him questioningly. "Working. Why?"

"Can you get the day off?"

"What do you mean, can I— Oh, no," she said, seeing the contemplative gleam in his eyes. "I can't baby-sit. I own my own business."

"Then you could take the day off, couldn't you?"

"No."

"Sure you can. Only one day."

"No."

"Caa-role," he wheedled. "Come on. Tina is no trouble. And you've been worried about Katy. This'll give you an opportunity to see what her mother is missing. A chance for you to see that she's well taken care of—at least for a day."

"I don't know how to take care of a baby!" Carole cried, setting her mug on the coffee table with a thud. "I'm a businesswoman, remember?"

"You're a natural," he soothed with a tender smile. "Why, you had Katy asleep by the time I got here with her bottle. All you have to do is feed her, change her, give her a bath—"

"A bath!" she exclaimed.

He shook his head. "Never mind. I'll give her a bath tonight."

"I can't."

"You can." His blue eyes cajoled. "Please."

The softly uttered plea was her undoing. She exhaled softly. If her uncharacteristic response to him so far was any indication, she had a feeling that Chris

Nicholas could charm her into robbing a bank if that's what he wanted.

"You're a manipulator," she accused, pointing a well-manicured finger at him.

"I know," he confessed without an iota of remorse. "But when you're in my shoes, it helps."

Chapter Five

Carole called herself ten kinds of fool all the way home. Psychologist Chris Nicholas had learned his trade well, she thought as she pulled into her parking place at the apartment complex where she'd lived the past two years. He had learned which emotional buttons to push to get people to talk and which ones to push to get them to agree to whatever he wanted. She let herself into the apartment with a sigh. That wasn't a fair accusation. Not really. She could have said no to his preposterous idea that she stay with Tina and Katy the next day. She should have. But she hadn't, and now she was worrying herself sick about how she was going to handle things.

She fixed a salad she didn't eat, called her assistant manager and asked if he would take care of the store the next day, then turned on the television, only to find yet another Christmas special taking up prime time. Groaning, she pushed the remote control to change channels. A country singer and a high school chorus were doing a snappy rendition of "The Twelve Days of Christmas." What was the deal? she wondered grumpily. Where did all these specials come from? Were they cloning them on some Hollywood soundstage? In the end, because she planned to do some bookkeeping anyway, she decided on Dickens's *A Christmas Carol*.

Somewhere between the ghosts of Christmas past and present, Carole yawned and thought longingly of bed. Her eyes burned, the columns of numbers were blurring, and she was suddenly dead tired. All that housework she'd done before driving out to the Nicholas place must be catching up with her, she thought. She propped her head on her hand as a picture of Chris ambled through her tired mind. Now, why would she think of him on the heels of longing for her bed? she wondered, smothering another yawn.

Plopping the papers onto the coffee table, she scooted down until her head rested on the throw pillow. She'd finish the paperwork in just a minute, as soon as she had rested her aching eyes....

"Carole."

Chris was calling her. She forced her eyes open. She was at home... there was her bookkeeping from the store. She was lying on her sofa, but it wasn't her sofa, and it wasn't her house. She was at the orphanage. What was going on? she wondered. Chris's voice spoke her name again.

"Chris?" she replied. "Where are you?"

"Here."

She glanced to the foot of the sofa, and sure enough, there he stood, clad, as usual, in his disreputable Levi's and a garish flannel shirt. But there was a sort of glow around him that made her nervous.

"What are you doing here?" she squealed. "What am I doing here?"

"We're both here because I wanted to show you something about Christmas... about people."

"Sorry, I'm not interested. I know all I want to know."

"Maybe so. But you *need* to know a few more things." He held out his hand. "Come with me."

Carole regarded him warily. "Where are we going? Why do you look like that?"

"Just come."

For some reason she put her hand in his, and the next thing she knew she was standing in the center of Fairhope's recreation room. A huge tree stood in the corner with a veritable mountain of presents stacked around it. Mr. Nelson, the director of the orphanage, and Mrs. Hardy, the head housemother, were sorting the gifts into stacks.

"It's Christmas, and they're getting things ready for the kids," Carole observed. "So what?"

"Listen," Chris said as they drew nearer.

Carole tugged on his arm. "Stop!" she whispered. "They'll see us. Mrs. Hardy sees *everything*."

"They can't see us, Carole. No one can. Besides, Evelyn Hardy died two years ago."

"What!" she screeched.

"Will you just listen?" Chris said in exasperation, placing a finger over her lips.

"Look at this," Tom Nelson was saying, holding up the fancy porcelain doll Carole had received on her eighth Christmas. "This is for Carole."

"Isn't is beautiful?" Evelyn Hardy said. "I know she's going to love it."

Carole cast Chris a maligned look. "The doll was from Mrs. Charmichael. She always sent big presents at Christmas, but did she ever come to see one of us during the year? Did she ever think to ask us what we wanted? No. She just went to the store every December, bought a bunch of expensive toys and figured that she was okay with God for another year."

Chris arched his fair eyebrows. "You know that for a fact, huh? Maybe you'd better keep listening."

"I can't believe she does so much for us," Mrs. Hardy said, a sad look on her pleasant features. "Not when her medical bills are so high."

Mr. Nelson nodded. "I know. She sends that check faithfully every month, even though she can't come and see how much good her money is doing."

"It's too bad her dialysis forces her to stay so close to home," Mrs. Hardy said with a sorrowful shake of her head.

"Dialysis?" Carole echoed, looking at Chris.

"That's right," Chris said. "Mabel Charmichael was on a dialysis machine for years, but she still called the home and asked Evelyn Hardy what each child wanted. How else do you think she knew you wanted that porcelain doll? Even though she couldn't come to visit, she tried to make your Christmases happy. And Andy Franklin who sent the hobbyhorse lived in Tallahassee, Florida. And—"

"I get the picture," Carole interrupted with a sigh. "I judged them all wrongly."

"Not all," Chris said. "Some of them do just send a gift at Christmas and forget about the kids the rest of the year. Like you."

"What?"

"Don't you send a big check to the orphanage every year?" the ghostly Chris asked.

"W-well, yes, of course. It's the least I can do. . . ."

"And when was the last time you visited?"

It had always seemed too painful to go back to Fairhope, but now, at Chris's question, a new awareness washed through her. "I . . . I—" she stammered.

"The last time you were at Fairhope was when you walked out the door for good. Isn't that right?"

"Yes, but—"

"No buts. Come on, Carole. Let's go see the Bradys...."

When Carole woke up, the television screen was blank and the sound of static filled the room. Her neck had a crick in it. Clamping her teeth onto her bottom lip and stifling a groan, she pushed herself to a sitting position, her sleepy gaze finding the clock on the VCR. It was 2:00 a.m. Only four hours until she had to get up and go to Chris's.

Chris. Thoughts of him brought back her dream in full force. She remembered waking in the orphanage and seeing Chris—as the ghost of Christmas past? Following the episode with Tom Nelson and Evelyn Hardy, he took her...where? Oh, yes. To the Bradys', the young couple she had once hoped would adopt her. Marcia Brady was packing Carole's clothes and crying. Her husband tried to console her, telling her that he loved her but that he needed her to himself, at least for a while.

Carole realized that maybe, just maybe, Marcia Brady had loved her after all.

Finally, Chris took her to the orphanage door, where a sixteen-year-old girl stood telling Evelyn Hardy that she had found the little girl in her arms wandering along the sidewalk. The teenager thrust the toddler into Evelyn's arms. Didn't she belong there? When Evelyn denied it and went to find Tom Nelson, the girl ran away, into the nearby woods. They saw her huddled beneath a big oak tree, her tears falling freely.

It had been her mother, Carole realized now.

"Ridiculous!" she cried, leaping to her feet. It was only a dream. Some silly notions her mind had conjured up as a result of her talk with Chris, her weariness and falling asleep while *A Christmas Carol* was on television. It meant nothing, except that her past, Christmases and all, still bothered her.

She went to her room, set her alarm and, after stripping down to her French-cut panties, crawled into her king-size bed. Punching the pillow with unnecessary force, she flopped to her side. Chris Nicholas might make her heart beat like crazy. And he might be able to talk her into baby-sitting when she didn't want to. She would go to his house and watch Tina and Katy, but there was no way a single talk with him was going to change the way she perceived her past.

"Don't you send a big check to the orphanage every year?" Chris's voice, straight from the dream, filled her mind. *"And when was the last time you visited?"*

"Leave me alone," she said aloud. Her verbal command banished his voice from her mind, but she fell asleep with the uneasy feeling of hypocrisy in her heart.

Monday, November 28

Carole arrived at the farm at exactly seven-thirty. To her surprise, Chris had already gone to work. As Brian led her to the kitchen, she told herself smugly that Chris had taken the coward's way out. Hearing the sounds coming from behind the closed door, she had a sneaking suspicion why. Brian pushed the swinging door wide for Carole, who was followed by a waddling Sebastian squawking a loud, "Come on in." The big, cheerful room was filled with noise, and confusion reigned once more.

Jake was sitting at one end of the table doing some last-minute studying. Lisa, her makeup perfection, was desultorily sliding bits of pancake through the syrup pooled on her plate. Each offered her a halfhearted hello. Mike greeted Carole with a smile and the offer of "Wanna pancake?" David and Tad couldn't offer her a greeting because they were racing to see who could down his glass of juice first. Carole assumed that Katy was sleeping—though she didn't know how—in the bassinet against the far wall.

"Start eating those pancakes," Brian barked, sitting down next to Tina's high chair. "Come on, baby," he urged. "Eat."

Tina shook her head. "I want her to feed me," she said, pointing to Carole.

"That's Ms. Chapman," Brian said.

"Can I give you a kiss?" Tina asked. "Daddy didn't give me a kiss."

Carole felt a tug on her heartstrings.

"Tina!" Lisa cried. "Daddy was in a hurry—he told us it was an emergency. And he blew us all a kiss. Now leave Ms. Chapman alone."

"She's fine," Carole said, approaching the high chair. "And why don't you all call me Carole. It'll be easier."

"That's great," Brian said. "Look, do you mind feeding her, Carole? I still have to shower. I'm running late because I had to fix breakfast."

"Of course I don't mind."

"Thanks," he called, already heading for the door. "You're a lifesaver."

Carole took Brian's place and offered the child a bite of pancake. Tina smiled at her, a grin so like Chris's it stole Carole's breath . . . and just the slightest bit of her heart.

"I wanna kiss first," Tina told her.

"Of course," Carole said, leaning over to kiss the plump cheek. To her surprise, Tina's chubby hands reached up, one grabbing the sleeve of her silk shirt, the other pressing against her chin.

"Holy cow, Tina, look what you've done!" Jake said in disgust.

Carole drew back and looked at the sticky imprint of Tina's hand, complete with bits of gooey pancake, on her expensive shirt. "It's all right. Really."

"I'll keen it up," Tina said, grabbing for her napkin. As she reached, she bumped her juice glass and sent it toppling to its side. Before Carole could do more than gasp, orange juice cascaded off the edge of the tray, right into her lap.

"Tina!" four shocked voices chanted in perfect synchronization.

Automatically, Jake reached for a handful of napkins and thrust them at Carole. She looked up from the stain on her hundred-and-fifty-dollar pair of imported wool slacks and met Jake's wide-eyed gaze. His eyes held fear, a fear of retribution that far exceeded the crime. "I'm sorry," he said. "She didn't mean to do it. It was an accident."

"I'm sorry," Tina echoed.

As Carole looked at Jake, a remnant of her conversation with Chris flitted through her mind. *"Jake's father beat him on more than one occasion."* Her heart contracted with pain. Jake was afraid she would react the same way his father had.

"Are you mad at me?" Tina asked, her pretty little mouth trembling, her eyes wide and tear-glazed.

Carole promptly offered Jake a reassuring smile and took the napkins he held out.

"No," she said to Tina as she began to wipe up the spill, "I'm not mad at you."

The relief on Jake's face would have been comical if it hadn't been so tragic. The collective sigh that issued from the children was audible. Carole added her own sigh to theirs. Sweet heaven! What had she gotten herself into?

Chapter Six

Chris pulled into the driveway with a feeling of trepidation. Carole's car was still there. Why? It was almost six and already dark. He'd supposed she would head back to Bossier City as soon as the older kids got home from school. But she hadn't, and for some strange reason he was glad. He tried to ignore what his gut was telling him—that she definitely had the sexiest mouth he'd ever seen . . . and the longest legs—and concentrate on wondering how she'd managed with the girls. It was a lost effort.

His heart told him that he'd done the right thing by gently coercing her into staying with Tina and Katy for the day; his intellect told him that his plan might have backfired. He had sensed hostility in Carole that first night at the hospital, but it hadn't taken him long to realize that the hostility stemmed from some inner pain buried deep beneath the chic, efficient facade she presented to the world.

He'd thought about her a lot over the following weekend. She was a beautiful woman, and he was a healthy man who could appreciate beautiful women, even if there wasn't much opportunity for enjoying them. Despite her hostility, he'd wanted to see her again, which was surprising in itself, since no woman had made such an impression on him since Cathie died.

He had wanted to see if he could encourage her to open up and tell him why she was hurting, but he had been so busy getting Katy settled and doing the never-ending thousand and one things that had to be done on his days off that the weekend had slipped by without his ever getting a minute to look her up. Which, he had decided by Sunday afternoon, was probably for the best.

Carole Chapman wasn't his type, and if her scathing comment about his clothes was any indication, he certainly wasn't hers. Carole was a Neiman Marcus kind of woman, and he was a J.C. Penney kind of guy. She was filet mignon; he was frozen fish sticks. She was a savvy businesswoman, maybe even a swinging single. He was a cop looking for a woman as crazy as he was, someone who had a heart with enough love in it not only for him but for a hundred kids as well, give or take a few.

When things had calmed down after Sunday's frog fiasco and he'd realized that Carole was in his living room, his initial reaction was that she had come to check up on him. Which, he supposed, she had. But since he'd felt her concern for Katy was genuine, it was okay.

He still couldn't believe the way she'd opened up and told him about her past, but he supposed that the timing had been right and that finding a houseful of kids in her old predicament must have brought the painful memories out of hiding. Besides, everyone knew that sometimes it was easier to talk to a stranger than to someone you knew well.

He had a feeling there weren't too many people who knew how she felt about her past, about herself. Clearly she had pursued financial success so single-mindedly not only for security but also to boost her ego—to make her "okay"—because deep inside her past had made her feel that she was unlovable, unnecessary.

She needed to know that she was loved and needed. That's why he had suggested she take care of the girls for a day. There was no one more dependent than small children, no one who gave so much love unconditionally.

Chris opened the front door and said a brief, fervent prayer that his little scheme had worked.

"Dad's home!" Tad yelled the instant the door closed behind him.

Like metal filings drawn to a magnet, kids flocked to the living room. Chris was vaguely aware of Katy crying in the kitchen.

"Daddy, we've got to go look for a dress!" Lisa wailed.

Chris put his arm around her shoulders and gave her a hug. "Maybe tomorrow, huh? I'm beat, honey."

"Got an A," Mike said, waving a school paper.

"That's great," Chris said, mussing the boy's hair.

"We went to the wildlife museum today, Dad, and you shoulda seen the snakes and geela monster and stuff!" Tad cried excitedly.

"Gila," David corrected. "The *G* sounds like an *H*."

"Shut up, you four-eyed geek!" Tad said, elbowing David's ribs.

"Boys, please!" Chris said, holding up his hands in surrender. "Gimme a break!" He bent over and swung Tina, who had been tugging on his slacks, into his arms. "How's my baby girl?" he asked, rubbing her tip-tilted nose with his.

"Good," she giggled, tugging at his mustache.

"Gimme a break!" Sebastian squawked, hanging upside down on his perch.

"Katy's got the colic again." The calm statement came from Brian, who had just emerged from the kitchen.

"Wonderful," Chris replied, lowering Tina to the floor.

"Carole has her in the kitchen," Brian added.

"Move it," Chris said to the kids, who parted like the Red Sea at his command.

Once, just once, it would be nice to come home to quiet—the old clichéd slippers-and-pipe routine, maybe. A snifter of brandy and a little David Sanborn on the stereo. Cuddling in front of the fireplace with a beautiful woman... like Carole. He swore under his breath. It was a long time since Cathie died, his body had recently begun to remind him.

Dream on, Nicholas. Your romantic scenario doesn't quite jibe with the life you've chosen.

He squared his shoulders to face the chaos in the kitchen, but the sight that greeted him stopped him at the door.

With Katy cradled gently in her arms, Carole paced the black-and-white-tiled floor. She had discarded her shoes, and one bright red toenail poked through the toe of her panty hose. Her silk blouse—which had cost a hundred bucks if it had cost a penny—was hanging out in the back, and there was a big stain of some sort on the sleeve. Her high-style slacks were stained, too, with something orange. Her hair, usually combed to sleek perfection, was pulled back in a ridiculously short ponytail that stuck out at the nape of her neck. And her customarily impeccable makeup was reduced to smears of mascara around her tired-looking eyes.

As she turned in her pacing, she spotted Chris in the doorway. They stared at each other across the room.

"Are you all right?" he asked, starting toward her.

She nodded, but her bottom lip trembled the same way Tina's did when she was trying not to cry. Chris fought the urge to gather both her and Katy into his arms.

"Something's wrong with Katy," she said in a quavering voice.

"I know. Probably colic."

"She's been crying for an hour, and I didn't know what to do for her. She wouldn't take a bottle. I can't stand for her to hurt, and I just didn't know what to do." Her voice caught on a sob. "I tried to tell you I couldn't do this."

He saw her face crumple and her model-straight shoulders slump. Tears filled her dark brown eyes and began to slide down her cheeks. Chris didn't think; he acted. Half a dozen steps took him to her, and, without a word, he did the very thing he'd told himself he shouldn't do. He took her in his arms and drew her close, Katy sandwiched between them. His big hand cupped her ponytail, and he drew her head down until her cheek rested against his chest. Then he pulled the rubber band from her hair and began to knead the tight muscles at the base of her skull. His mouth moved against her sweet-smelling hair, murmuring words of comfort.

"Shh. Take it easy, honey. It's all right."

"I'm sorry," she sobbed.

"It isn't your fault. She's been having a touch of colic every night about this time."

Carole lifted her tear-ravaged face. "She has? I thought I'd done something wrong. She made a mess in her diaper, and I had to give her a bath after all, and I was afraid I'd done something to hurt her."

"You did fine. Babies are tougher than you think."

He released her and moved to the sink, where a roll of paper towels hung. He ripped one off and tilted Carole's chin up. Gently, as if she were as young and delicate as Tina, he wiped away her tears. Then he smiled, and the burden in Carole's heart became lighter.

"Come sit down," he told her, ushering her to a chair near the end of the table. "I have some drops I can give her. I should have told you about them, but I was called away so early this morning that I forgot. Stay put. I won't be long."

He was back, carrying a small bottle, in less than a minute. He took Katy and deftly squirted the prescribed amount of medicine into her mouth. "There you go, pretty girl," he said soothingly, easing her up to his shoulder.

"What now?" Carole asked, wiping her palms on her slacks.

"We wait for the stuff to work," Chris told her as he sat down in a ladder-backed rocker near the wood-burning stove.

"Oh."

He rocked Katy, patted her back and crooned soothing words to her, the same way he had comforted Carole moments before. Carole blotted her eyes. When she glanced at Chris, he was giving her that measuring look again.

Heat suffused her cheeks, and she raised her hands to her hair. "I must look a mess."

He shook his head. "Tired, maybe. I'm sorry you had such a bad day."

She tucked a strand of hair behind her ear and shrugged. "It wasn't so bad. Well, it wasn't *great*, but I coped fairly well with Tina's help."

"She's pretty good at fetching things," Chris agreed.

"She's an angel. I had no idea how smart two-year-olds could be."

"She is smart. Thanks. And how did you do with Katy—until this evening, I mean?"

"Okay, I guess," she said hesitantly. She looked at him. "I've been wondering..."

"What?"

She moved to stand beside the rocking chair. Reaching out, she placed her hand on Katy's downy blond hair, stroking softly. "Do you think she misses her mother? Do you think she knows we're different?"

"Probably on some level," he said. "Why do you ask?"

Carole shifted her gaze from Katy to Chris. "I don't want her to remember and hurt. I don't want her to grow up and feel the way I—" she paused "—that her mother...that no one loves her."

"She won't," Chris said, "because someone does love her."

"Who?" Carole asked.

"You. Me. The kids."

She turned away, crossing her arms over her breasts. "I don't love her. I hardly know her."

"You don't have to *know* babies to love them. You just do."

"Maybe so, for some people. But I don't."

"Then why have you been so worried about her?" he asked. "Why were you so upset that something was wrong with her?"

Carole cast him a look over her shoulder. "I don't like to see anyone suffer. But you may as well know that I can't make a habit of missing work and taking care of her. I have my own life to live."

"You're afraid to love her, aren't you, Carole? You're afraid that if you do, her mother will come back and take her away, or she'll be sent somewhere and you'll never see her again. Isn't that right?"

Carole met his steady gaze. He was too smart, she thought. He saw right through her. But he was right. Very right. "Yes," she told him, almost defiantly. "That's exactly what I'm afraid will happen."

"Come here," he said.

"What?"

"Come here. I want to show you something."

Reluctantly, Carole moved closer. Chris laid the now sleeping Katy on his knees. "Look at her. Look at her and tell me that you refuse to love her."

Carole looked. Katy's fair face was flushed from crying, and her eyelashes lay like tiny fans against her cheek. Her silky hair was damp, and one small fist was flung upward. Her fingernails were so small it was hard to believe. She was perfectly beautiful and tiny and helpless.

Chris reached for one of Carole's hands, which were clenched tightly at her sides. "You have to let yourself feel, Carole. You have to open yourself up to the possibility of pain as well as of pleasure."

"Why?" she cried, jerking her hand free of his disturbing touch. "Why do I have to take a chance of getting hurt?"

"Because every time you close up a part of yourself to the pain, you lose an equal capacity to feel love and pleasure. And you're far too beautiful and sensitive a woman not to live and love to the fullest."

Beautiful? He thought she was beautiful? It had been so long since she had heard a compliment from a man that for an instant, she was in shock. And sensitive? She'd never thought of herself as sensitive. She did, however, have a sneaking suspicion—had for some time—that something was missing from her life, that she wasn't living it to the fullest. She had thought that it was a man, a healthy sex life. Maybe she had been only partly right. Maybe it was a man...and not just sex, but love...and children. The thought of leaving and going to her lonely apartment was suddenly distasteful.

Get a grip on yourself, Carole. The man brainwashes for a living. Just because he's flattered you and because keeping a menagerie of kids is his thing doesn't mean that you should go all mushy inside.

"I think you need to take an interest in something besides your shop," Chris said. "Do things you've never done before...see what the world has to offer. And try giving love to someone, and just see if they don't give it back."

"Like who?" she asked.

"Like my kids, for starters. Do you work next Saturday?"

A feeling of déjà vu swept over Carole. Was he going to ask her to baby-sit again? "No."

"Then why don't you come out and help us hunt for a Christmas tree."

A Christmas tree! She couldn't hide her surprise. She had never had a real Christmas tree. But with all these kids, of course Chris would have a tree, and probably a mountain of presents, too. She thought again of her cheerless apartment.

Memory of her dream and what Chris had shown her about her past Christmases and the people in her life flashed through her mind, as it had intermittently throughout the day. Guilt and confusion over doing the very thing she had accused other people of doing suffused her. Without ever intending harm, she had become the Mabel Charmichael of the eighties, except she didn't have any excuse for not visiting the children at the home. None, perhaps, except fear. Maybe she should go back and try to make amends for her inadvertent neglect. They had been good to her at Fairhope. If she could just get past her fears, maybe she could give something back to the people there. After all, it wasn't their fault no one had adopted her—or that she had been left there in the first place. A tiny glimmering of hope flickered in the shadows of her heart.

"Well," Chris said, "what do you say? Are you going to come along, try to get out of your rut?"

Rut. He was right. That's exactly what she was in. She went to work, and she went home . . . to a solitary bed. And the next day she did it all over again. Maybe she would go on his family outing. She wasn't saying Chris was right about trying to love someone—that was going a bit too far—but she supposed it wouldn't hurt to tag along with the crazy clan.

Chapter Seven

Carole went down the wide steps of Fairhope toward the parking area, filled with a quiet glow of contentment she'd never expected to experience. Surprising herself, she had taken the day off and driven the seventy miles to the children's home where she'd grown up.

She told herself that the gesture had nothing to do with Chris's suggestion that she do something different with her life or try giving love to someone. It had to do with her very own dream and the ghost-Chris's statement about her contributions to the orphanage. She had never been able to tolerate hypocrisy, and she had never connected that failing with herself. The dream had made her realize that, in a practical sense, she was no better than the people she had always blamed for not caring enough.

She did care, which was why she sent money. She hadn't gone back to visit because she had built herself a new life and she hadn't wanted anything to remind her of the pain and disappointment of the old one.

But that was before she'd found Katy. Before she'd met Chris and all his kids. Despite the fact that determination and hard work had taken her far in life, her past had caught up to her with a vengeance. Lately, whether it was the memory of Katy's sleep-flushed face or the recollection of Mike's smile, something told her that she owed it to herself to try to come to terms with that past so that she could go on to a better future.

So she had returned to Fairhope.

Her first stop was the administration building, where Tom Nelson still had an office. Though he had officially retired, he came in two days a week in an advisory capacity. He had greeted Carole at the door.

Since it was Wednesday, the older children were in school, but Mr. Nelson—who'd told her to call him Tom, now that she had grown up—had taken Carole to see the preschoolers and infants. The sheer number of them saddened her, but at least she now realized that these children were fortunate in many important ways. As Chris had pointed out, they had a roof over their heads and three meals a day. The children living on the streets or with desperate, destitute parents were the ones to feel truly sorry for.

They went from building to building, Tom Nelson showing her the renovations, the additions and dredging up memories. As they talked and laughed, Carole realized with something of a start that she'd had a good life there. At the time, she had often been so lonely and afraid that she hadn't fully appreciated the better moments, the many advantages.

Now she recalled the years that she and some of the older girls had helped in the kitchen, preparing for the annual Christmas party. They had made hundreds of cut-out cookies and decorated them with colored icing and sugar sprinkles…and had a lot of laughs while they were doing it.

There were the May Day baskets she had made in elementary school and left on the doorsteps of the housemothers when they weren't looking.

There was the memory of her first dance, when she and Evelyn Hardy had stayed up until after midnight revamping a hand-me-down gown. It had been fun, and she'd looked darn pretty.

As she approached her car, Carole shook her head, thinking back over the rest of her eventful day. She had stayed until the older children got back from school, and then she'd let Tom talk her into joining them for dinner. After the prayer, he got up and introduced her to the group, telling them that she was a former Fairhope girl and what a success she had made of herself. Simultaneously humbled and proud, and wanting to show solidarity with the current residents of Fairhope, she volunteered to be a runner. It had been fun, sitting at the long table, with the bowls of stew and pitchers of lemonade passing among eager hands. As the bowls and pitchers were emptied, it had been her job to "run" to the kitchen to get them refilled.

After one of her runs, she had propped her elbows on the table to talk to the boy across from her, and the cafeteria had suddenly rung with a hundred voices singing a refrain she thought she'd forgotten:

"Get your elbows off the table, Carole Chapman! Get your elbows off the table, Carole Chapman! We have told you once or twice that it isn't very nice. Get your elbows off the table, Carole Chapman!"

Carole had blushed and laughed, feeling wholly at one with the children of Fairhope.

Before leaving, she had wanted to ask Tom about the Bradys, but at the last minute she'd changed her mind. What did it matter now? Her visit had been a memorable experience, and she promised herself she would repeat it soon. By the time she headed the red CRX out of Fairhope's gates and started toward Bossier City, it was dark, and she'd known without a doubt that what she had done was very right.

Saturday, December 3

The day dawned cold and crisp and sunny. As Carole tramped around the tree farm, she was thankful she had dressed in warm slacks and her red wool jacket. It was lovely December weather, and looking for the perfect Christmas tree was fun. She only regretted that Katy and Lisa, who was coming down with a sore throat, hadn't been able to come along.

Lisa had been fine on Thursday evening. Carole had been in the middle of a big sale when she'd looked up to see the whole Nicholas clan troop into the Ultimate Man. They had come to the mall to shop for Lisa's dress and to select something for Jake, who was going on his first "date" to a church Christmas party. Though they hadn't met with success for Lisa, Carole had found something just right for Jake's "coming out." Then, in high spirits, they had all trekked to the food court, where Chris treated them to dinner.

Carole couldn't remember when she had laughed so much or heard so much good-natured teasing or felt such closeness, such love. However, she'd had mixed feelings upon learning that Chris's parents were arriving from Dallas three days before Christmas and that his mother would fix a traditional holiday dinner, complete with turkey and dressing and all the trimmings. Obviously, the entire family was looking forward to Christmas; the only overtones of sadness were hers.

All she had to look forward to was dinner for one and a day alone in her apartment. But that was the way she'd spent all her Christmases since she left the orphanage—avoiding the crass commercialism of the season, she'd assured herself—and it had never bothered her before. What was the matter with her now?

"Hey! Come look at this one!" Brian yelled from several yards away, shattering Carole's pensive mood. He and Jake had been forging ahead among the rows of evergreens, carrying the saw and a measuring rod.

Chris waved at the boys and turned to Carole. "I'm glad you're back," he said.

Shielding her eyes from the bright sunlight, she looked at him. Her heart skipped a beat at the warmth she saw in his eyes, and her breath caught in her throat. Chris Nicholas was an extremely handsome man, and she'd spent entirely too much time thinking about him this past week.

Even though she couldn't recall having felt precisely this way before, she likened her seesawing emotions to what a teenager with a crush must suffer. She adamantly refused to consider that her feelings might represent more than that. She had dreaded spending the day with him, yet, contrarily, she couldn't wait for Saturday to come. And now that it had, she was totally confused.

"What do you mean, back?" she asked.

"You were here in body, but your thoughts must have been on another planet. I'll give you a penny for them," he offered.

She shook her head. Chris was too good at figuring her out as it was. If he knew she was the slightest bit interested in him, he'd probably die of mortification. Though she might be dumb enough to be attracted to him—on a purely physical level, of course—surely he was only being kind to her because he was a kind, generous person. A rescuer.

"It was nothing," she said. "I was just thinking about...things."

Chris reached out and brushed a stray lock of hair away from her mouth. His touch was gentle and lingering and kindled feelings Carole knew she'd be better off not feeling. She resisted the urge to hold his hand against her face and beg him to explain what was happening inside her.

"Hmm," he said, "sounds serious. And we aren't here to be serious. We're here to show you that hunting for a Christmas tree is fun and that parenting eight kids can be an almost normal state. No more serious thoughts, okay?"

"Okay," she agreed with a hesitant smile.

For a moment it seemed as if Chris couldn't look away. His blue eyes caressed her face, lingering on her lips. Carole knew it was a silly thought, but she imagined that she could almost feel the touch of his mouth against hers. Her tongue skimmed over her tingling lips. The involuntary action seemed to break the spell binding them. His eyes aglow with tenderness, Chris shifted Tina, who was sitting on his shoulders. "Come on, sweetheart, let's go find a tree."

Puzzled, Carole watched as he turned and started toward Brian and Jake. She knew he'd been speaking to Tina, but he'd been looking straight into *her* eyes.

"It's the prettiest tree we've ever had!" Lisa said two hours later.

"It is, isn't it?" Chris agreed.

Tina in her lap, Carole sat back and looked at their handiwork. Brian and Jake had found the perfect tree, and they had taken turns sawing it off at the base. Then Chris had helped tie it on top of the station wagon, and they had brought it home to decorate.

Lisa had helped Carole fix sandwiches while the guys fitted the tree in the stand and strung the lights. After they finished eating, all hands set to adding the tinsel and ornaments—everything from handmade construction-paper chains to an exquisite crystal sphere. Sebastian paraded back and forth, generally making a nuisance of himself and crowing, "A par-tri-idge in a pear treeeee."

"Let me do one!" Tina cried, wanting to take part in the fun.

"You're too little!" Tad said.

"Uh-*uh*!" Tina said emphatically. "I am not, am I, Daddy?"

"Of course you aren't," Chris said, producing a small wooden bear from the ornament box. "You can put this one on." He picked Tina up, handed her the bear and showed her where to put the wire hanger. "This is the one Mommy bought for you just before you were born."

"I don't have a Mommy," Tina reminded him with a shake of her head. "You said that she went to live in heaven."

Every eye in the room focused on Chris.

"That's right," he said, his voice huskier than usual. "She went to live in heaven, but she left you for me to love instead."

Tina's chubby hands carefully hung the bear. Then she looked at her father, her blue eyes wide and innocent. "Jake has a mommy."

"I know."

Tina placed her hands on Chris's cheeks. "I want a mommy, too," she said. "Please, Daddy."

Carole felt her throat tighten.

"Please, Daddy," Sebastian squawked, his timely interruption drawing attention away from Tina's wistful plea.

"Look," Tad said, pointing to the Christmas tree. "Sebastian is our top-of-the-tree decoration!" All eyes turned to the parrot, who, sure enough, was perched at the very tip of the tree. He bobbed his head and blinked, almost as if he were taking a bow, eliciting a round of hearty laughter. Even Tina giggled, her request momentarily forgotten.

"Just who in the heck do you think you are?" Brian asked, his hands planted on his hips.

"A par-tri-idge in a pear treeeee!" the bird croaked.

As coincidental as it was, his pronouncement sent everyone back into gales of laughter.

When the furor subsided, Tina demanded that Chris give her back to Carole. As she took his daughter from Chris's arms, Carole's eyes met his. She tried to look away but couldn't.

"She's really getting attached to you," he told Carole. In a whisper he added, "And all the boys have a crush on you." *Even me.*

"All of them?" she asked. *Even you?*

"All of them."

"But I thought Brian had a girlfriend."

"He does, and so does Jake, but that doesn't mean they can't care for you, too. I guess they like the advice you give them on their clothes and stuff.'' He grinned.

"Oh,'' Carole said with a slight smile. "I'm afraid I'm not too familiar with the way males think.''

"Stick around; you'll figure it out in no time,'' he said enigmatically.

Stick around. Heaven knew she wanted to, but she wasn't certain where all this was leading. She hadn't even been able to tell Chris about her trip to Fairhope yet. She had a feeling he would understand exactly how she'd felt. He would understand the peace the trip had brought her, and he would be glad for the changes taking place inside her.

But she herself wasn't so sure about those changes. Chris Nicholas had come into her life and turned it topsy-turvy. He had made her think about and face things she hadn't thought she could deal with. But what would happen when he was finished "rescuing'' her? What would happen when there were no more ghosts in her past? Would he still be eager for her company, her friendship?

The thought filled her with a sudden, inexplicable sadness. She wasn't certain she wanted Chris for a friend. She was afraid that her feelings, despite her firmest intentions, were swiftly mutating from wariness to something more—something she was afraid to even consider.

Chapter Eight

Tuesday, December 6

The Ultimate Man. Carole speaking. May I help you?"

"Hi."

The softly spoken greeting sent shivers of pleasure scampering throughout her. "Hello," she replied a trifle breathlessly. "How are you?"

"Other than facing a stack of paperwork a mile high, I'm fine," Chris said. "What about you? Any aftereffects from the day spent at the Nicholas zoo?"

Carole laughed with happiness and denied any ill effects.

"Are you working tonight?" he asked.

"That depends."

"On what?"

"Whether or not you want me to baby-sit," she told him.

He laughed. "No, I don't want you to baby-sit. I want you to come to dinner."

"Dinner?" she echoed, unable to hide her surprise.

"Yeah."

"Then, no, I'm not working, and I'd like very much to come."

"Good," he said. "Is six-thirty, okay?"

"Fine."

"I'll see you then."

Carole hung up the receiver, but the silly smile she was wearing refused to disappear.

"It was wonderful lasagne," Carole said as she and Chris carried their coffee cups into the living room. They'd left clean-up duty to the kids.

"Thank you. Maybe you'll return the honor sometime."

Carole felt overwhelmed. "I'm not certain I'd know how to feed this many people."

Chris smiled at her over the rim of his cup. "Then we'll have to make it just the two of us."

More confused than ever, she set her cup on the coffee table and sank into the wing chair across from the sofa. "That would be...nice."

Sensing her discomfort, Chris said, "In the meantime, would you like to go with us to see the Christmas play at the kids' school? Tad, Mike and David all have parts."

"When is it?" she asked. "If I'm not working, I'd love to go."

"Friday night at seven-thirty."

"I don't have to work, so I—"

"Daddy," Lisa interrupted from the door. "Can I talk to Carole a minute?"

"Sure," Chris said. "Come on in."

Lisa sat beside her father and leaned toward Carole earnestly. "I need to ask you about Kyle's tuxedo. Should he wait until I get my dress—" this was accompanied by a pointed look at her father "—before he chooses a style and color?"

Carole nodded. "It would be best, unless he goes with traditional black. He can't go wrong with that, no matter what you wear."

Lisa stood, a relieved look on her face. "Thanks. I knew you'd know. I'll tell Kyle."

"Just a minute, young lady," Chris said. "In all fairness, I think you should tell Carole that I've taken you several places to look for a dress, but we haven't found anything yet."

"That's true," Lisa said, leaning over and kissing his cheek. "You're an okay guy, Mr. Nicholas."

"Thanks," he said dryly. "Now, get back in there and finish the dishes while I entertain my guest."

Lisa shot him a knowing look, then glanced at Carole. "By all means," she said, heading toward the kitchen.

Friday, December 9

The school gymnasium was packed. Chairs had been set up facing the stage at one end, and families of the performers noisily filled every row. According to the mimeographed program, the play was called *A Visit to the North Pole*. Some of the children were featured in a speech choir, reciting quatrains about various toys, which then "came to life" courtesy of other costumed kids.

David, in the speech choir, caught sight of Chris and Carole and waved. They laughed, then cheered as Tad, along with several other youngsters, marched onstage in full military regalia while the piano played the "March of the Toy Soldier."

Mike was a superb robot, complete with flashing lights.

When the play was over and refreshments were being served in the library, the boys rushed up to Carole and Chris, wide smiles on their faces. They couldn't wait to introduce Carole to their teachers, who looked at Chris and Carole the same way Lisa had. Though Carole was embarrassed, a quick glance at Chris told her he was amused by the teachers' assumptions.

The memory of Chris's amused expression stayed with Carole as they took the boys to McDonald's for milk shakes. Did everyone assume she and Chris were an item? she wondered. Were her growing feelings for him that obvious? She shuddered and vowed to clamp down on her emotions.

Saturday, December 10

Carole rose before daybreak and stirred up a huge batch of sugar cookie dough, since the cookies were to be gifts for all the kids' friends. Armed with cookie cutters, food coloring, two bags of powdered sugar and a variety of sprinkles, she headed for the Nicholas farm.

A shirtless Chris met her at the door. He held a cup of coffee in one hand, while the other absently rubbed the dark mat of hair sprawling over his broad chest and down his flat stomach. She tried to appear nonchalant, but it took every ounce of willpower in her possession to keep her gaze from following the path of his hand.

"Hi," he said, stepping aside so she could enter. "I saw you coming up the drive and thought you could use this." He held out the cup of coffee.

"Thanks," she said, reaching for it and relinquishing her bag of baking supplies to him.

"Are you sure about doing this?" he asked, his eyes twinkling as if he knew something she didn't.

"Sure," she said blithely. "Why wouldn't I be?"

Three hours later, Carole knew the answer to that question—as well as why Chris had volunteered to watch Katy. She had barely survived a seemingly endless battle over who got what cookie cutter, who was using which icing, and who had the red or green sprinkles. Not to mention trying to keep a parrot off the table. Thank goodness Chris periodically stuck his head in the door to subdue the more vehement arguments.

She watched numbly as Tad licked some red icing off the spreader he was using to frost a cookie. Oh, well, what were a few germs? Mike was calmly eating chocolate sprinkles, all thoughts of decorating gone from his mind. Who cared? They were finishing up the last batch. All that was left was the cleaning up.

Carole's gaze drifted around the kitchen, and she put her hands to her cheeks and groaned in dismay. The room was a disaster! Blobs of icing dotted the table and floor, faces and clothes. A fine powdering of flour floated in the air, leaving a film over everything within a five-foot radius of the table. She was exhausted, and she still faced a mammoth cleanup operation.

"Don't eat those!" Brian said to Tina, who was plucking dragées from the front of a white-frosted snowman.

"I like them," Tina said, popping one of the tiny silver balls into her mouth.

"Tina! You're not supposed to eat those!" Brian shouted. "They have metal on them, for crying out loud! Dad!" he yelled, heading for the door.

"Spit it out, please," Carole said with an encouraging smile. "It could make you sick."

"Okay." Tina obediently spit the confection onto the table.

Carole automatically reached for a paper towel.

"Tina!" Chris bellowed from the doorway, a thunderous look on his face.

"She spit it out," Carole told him, averting a possible tearful confrontation between Chris and his daughter. She'd learned that Tina was incredibly sensitive to reprimands.

"Oh." He looked around the room. "Good grief! It looks as if the Pillsbury Doughboy and a few of his friends had a party in here."

"I'm sorry," Carole said, pushing her hair away from her face.

"It's not your fault." Planting his hands on his hips, he faced the true offenders. "Go change clothes, gang. I'll help Carole."

"We're not finished!" Tad cried.

"Oh, yes, you are. Now, git!"

The room emptied of kids, and Carole sank into a vacated chair.

"I tried to tell you this was going to be madness," Chris said, moistening a paper towel.

Carole looked up at him. "As I recall, you asked me if I was sure I wanted to do it."

"Same thing," he said, squatting beside her.

"What's wrong?" she asked, fighting the temptation to lean away from his nearness.

"You look like one of the kids, you have so much flour on your face."

She smiled wryly. "I imagine I do."

Grasping her chin in gentle fingers, Chris began to wipe the flour away. She lowered her eyes in an attempt to hide the pleasure his touch evoked.

"You have the most beautiful complexion," he commented softly, dabbing at a white smudge near her mouth. "And the most incredible mouth I've ever seen."

The words sent her gaze winging to his. He was so close that she could see the darker flecks of blue in his eyes. Too close! her thundering heart attested. Carole swallowed nervously as his face moved even closer. He was going to kiss her! she thought on a wave of excitement and fear.

"Hey, Dad!" Tad called, pushing through the swinging door.

"What?" Chris snapped, instantly putting several inches between him and Carole.

Tad stopped abruptly. "Are you kissin' her?"

"No," Chris said, standing, "I am not kissing her. I was washing the flour off her face."

Tad grinned. "Yeah. It was pretty bad."

"What do you want, Tad?" Chris asked with extreme patience.

"I wanna know if I can have a boa constrictor for Christmas. Lisa said you wouldn't let me."

"Lisa is right."

The sound of Tina crying in the living room filtered through the door. "What now?" Chris grumbled to no one in particular. He tossed the paper towel onto the cluttered table on his way to the door.

Carole sighed and stood up, uncertain of all but one thing. It looked as if she would be cleaning up by herself after all.

Thursday, December 15

On Thursday night, Katy stayed with a baby-sitter while the Nicholas crowd went Christmas caroling with a church group. Carole joined them, but her mind wasn't on singing. It was on the kiss she thought Chris had almost given her on Saturday and the fun she'd had as he and Lisa helped her clean up the cookie mess.

It hadn't escaped her attention that she was spending a lot of time with Chris and his family—and loving every minute of it. Monday night they had again gone looking for Lisa's dress, but Brian had a rescheduled basketball game, and their time together was cut short. Carole thought she saw regret in Chris's eyes when he'd told her goodbye. But whatever he was feeling, she knew that she was falling hard for him. It was stupid. Ridiculous. But she didn't seem to be able to help herself.

"Having fun?" Chris asked her.

"As a matter of fact, yes. It reminds me of when I was a kid and the orphanage used to—" She paused, realizing that she'd found another happy moment in her past.

"What?" he asked.

"I went to visit the children's home, Chris," she told him in a rush.

He nodded but didn't seem remotely surprised. "And how did it feel?"

"Good. It felt good." She still couldn't believe it had turned out so well. "I realized a lot of things while I was there, among them the fact that it wasn't such a bad place. I remembered a lot of good times, and I think the people there really cared."

Chris looked thoughtful for a moment. "I'm glad you went. I think it was a good move. A responsible, mature move. And I think it's going to open up a whole new world for you."

Carole hoped so. She offered him a tremulous smile.

"And, under the circumstances, I think it's okay for me to ask you a question."

"Sure. Anything," she said, wondering what it could be.

"I've been invited to a party Saturday night. It's going to be a black-tie affair with a lot of political bigwigs in attendance."

"And you want me to go with you?"

He nodded and shrugged. Carole thought he looked a little unsure of himself—a first, for the Chris Nicholas she knew. "I'm asking you for a date. I figure you've seen the kids, seen things at their worst. If you haven't been scared off so far, chances are you won't be." He took a deep breath. "So, what do you say?"

She nodded, a quiet joy filling her. "I say yes."

Chapter Nine

Carole's gown was a strapless black velvet with a center slit in the back that revealed a generous portion of her legs. A moiré sash swathed her slim hips and was gathered into a huge bow on her left hip. Her hair was pulled sleekly to the nape of her neck, where black silk flowers nestled becomingly. The style showed off her diamond drop earrings, the only jewelry she wore. Her nails were painted hot red, and her perfume was the drop-dead scent of Opium.

She was ready a full thirty minutes early.

And she was a nervous wreck.

The ball, hosted by a prominent state politician, would be a showcase for the Shreveport-Bossier area's social élite. It was even rumored that the governor would attend. Chris, a friend of the senator's, had been invited because of the invaluable work he had done on the police force. Although psychologists had long been part of many law-enforcement teams, their unique contributions were only recently being recognized and applauded by the public.

Carole checked her makeup for the tenth time and wondered what she could possibly say to people of the social strata she would be encountering tonight. If it wasn't too late, she would call Chris and cancel. As she glanced at the clock to see if that was a possibility, the doorbell rang. Casting a final look in the mirror, she went to greet Chris.

He stood before her in a black tuxedo that fit him to perfection. Why, she wondered a bit dazedly, had she ever thought the man had no clothes sense? She couldn't have done better if she'd chosen his attire herself. She registered a brief impression of a pleated white shirt and the whiff of Aramis before she heard him say, "You're beautiful."

Her gaze climbed from his chest past the black bow tie to the cleft in his chin, past his mouth and the neatly trimmed mustache to his vitally, tenderly blue eyes.

"You don't look so bad yourself," she said breathlessly.

His lazy smile sent the corners of his mustache crawling upward. "Not 'reprehensible'?"

Carole felt a blush creep over her face at his reference to her rudeness the night they had first met. "Are you ever going to let me live that down?"

"Probably not," he told her, tongue in cheek. "I have to have some defense, puny as it may be. Are you ready?"

Carole nodded, wondering what he meant about defenses. Obviously, though, he didn't intend to discuss it now. "Just let me get my wrap," she said. "I won't be but a minute."

Carole leaned back against the station wagon's upholstery and drew in a contented, weary sigh. The Bossier Civic Center had been crowded, and much to her surprise, she hadn't felt a bit uncomfortable. Actually, she'd known a great many of the people in attendance as regular customers at the Ultimate Man. In spite of her fears that she wouldn't fit in, several guests praised her business savvy and thanked her for carrying a line of quality clothing that made shopping trips to Dallas unnecessary.

Chris had been an attentive date, frequently bringing her wine and hors d'oeuvres. He had been teasing, complimentary and totally charming.

She hadn't lacked dancing partners, either, but she had always been glad to get back to Chris. Even though his dancing wasn't as smooth and practiced as some of the other men's, the feel of his arms around her had sent her onto the dance floor with him time after time. The feel of his arms and the soft thudding of his heart beneath her ear.

They rode to the apartment in silence, almost as if both were afraid words would break the spell between them. Carole knew the hour was approaching midnight and wondered if, at the chiming of the hour, she, like Cinderella, would be left with nothing but her memories. Then, out of nowhere, Chris's earlier comment came back to her. *"I have to have some defense..."*

At her apartment door, Carole was filled with questions. Should she ask him in? she wondered. Or was he ready to go home? She could make them some coffee or...

"Defense against what?" she heard herself say as she swung the door open.

"You," he said easily, letting her know the subject was on his mind, too.

Carole looked at him in disbelief, afraid to hope he meant what he seemed to mean. Before she could gather her wits and formulate her next question, he grasped her bare shoulders and propelled her into the apartment and toward the mirror over the couch.

"Look at you," he said to their reflections. "How could any man not go a little crazy over a woman like you?"

But Carole wasn't looking at herself. She was looking in the silvery glass at *him*, so tall and broad and virile-looking as he stood behind her. Their gazes meshed. "And are you?" she asked in a quavering voice.

"Yeah," he said with another of those disarming smiles, his hands skimming from her shoulders to her elbows and back. "I am. How do you feel about that?"

"I—I don't know," she said honestly.

He turned her toward him, took her face in his big hands and slowly lowered his mouth to hers. His lips were firm yet incredibly soft and mobile. Sparks flickered throughout her body, and she gave a shuddering sigh that was lost as Chris's mouth opened over hers, deepening the kiss. Her arms slid around his waist, and she leaned into his broad chest.

The delicious friction of his mouth against hers kindled and ignited the dormant flames of her desire, while the sensual brush of his mustache fanned the flames hotter, higher. Her breasts felt swollen and heavy, aching for his touch, while inside she was melting. As she'd known, she was hungry for a man's touch—no, Chris's touch. She had denied her body and her heart too long, and now that they were sampling passion, there would be no going back.

She felt rather than heard the downward slide of her zipper, felt the warmth of Chris's hands as they caressed her back. Then somehow she was on the couch, and he was beside her, the top of her gown pushed to her waist, her breasts bared to the smoldering heat of his gaze.

"Beautiful," he murmured, cupping one throbbing ivory globe in his hand. "So beautiful." Squeezing gently, he thumbed the rosy crest to pebble hardness and, lowering his head, took it into the fiery heat of his mouth.

Carole arched her back in pleasure and threaded her fingers through his gleaming blond hair, holding him to her. She wanted him. God help her, she *loved* him.

The realization had the effect of cold water thrown in her face. Desire died. Spiraling passion plummeted. And her newly born love lay in the cold ashes of her lifelong fear, fear that she would give her all to him, and when he tired of her, he would walk away as everyone else had. Embarrassment swept through her, leaving her cold and ashamed in its wake. Carole pushed at his shoulders and struggled to sit up, dragging the bodice of her dress up to shield her nakedness from him.

"Carole?" he said, releasing her and moving aside immediately. "What is it?"

When she refused to look at him, he grasped her chin in his hand, forcing her gaze upward. Her eyes were dark with anguish and swimming with tears.

"I'm sorry," she whispered. "I can't do this."

He was silent for long seconds. The only sound she could hear was the beating of her own heart.

"I understand," he said at last. "I've bungled things, rushed you. I mean, we really haven't known each other very long, but I—" He paused, and his lips twisted in a wry smile. "I have no excuse except that you go to my head, lady. I'm sorry."

Carole closed her eyes and clamped her lips together to keep from crying. She felt his mouth touch hers with feather softness, felt his thumb slide over the wetness of her lips, felt the warm vapor of his breath against her face as he said, "I'll give you time. I'll give you all the time you need."

Tell me you love me! her heart cried. *And maybe, just maybe, I won't need any time.*

She opened her eyes and looked into his, her heart breaking. She'd taken his advice. She'd offered her love and her heart to someone—him. But if she was lucky, he would never know it. If she gave in and let him make love to her, there was no way she could hide her feelings. And if she stayed around him long enough, there was no way she could resist him.

Which left only one thing to do.

"Time won't help, Chris," she said softly, tilting her chin up in a show of pride.

Chris reacted like a man, not a psychologist. Leaping to his feet, he grabbed her shoulders and gave her a hard shake. "Dammit! I'm not going to let you do this, Carole. You care for me whether you want to or not. I can feel it when I kiss you, and I can see it in your eyes."

"Maybe so," she acknowledged. "But it will go away." *When I'm dead and buried.* "It always does."

Dazed, Chris let his hands fall to his sides. She had simply slammed the door on him; there was no use pushing. Not now. He couldn't. Not when his own dreams were crumbling at his feet.

"I feel sorry for you, Carole. You could have a full, rich life, with people who love you, if you'd only let go of your fears. Despite what you think, you're a very lovable person. If you weren't, I'd never have fallen in love with you." Without another word, he crossed the room and let himself out of the apartment.

The words didn't sink in until she heard the sound of his car engine starting. He had said he loved her, and she had let him get away. Carole lifted a trembling hand to stifle the harsh sob fighting its way up her throat, and she glimpsed her reflection in the mirror. What she saw was a woman, her eyes brimming with tears, her hair and makeup lovingly mussed. Lovingly...

No. It was better this way, she told herself even as the hot tears started tracking her cheeks. Chris thought he loved her, but it was probably simply a case of raging hormones. Why should he love her? What did she possibly have to offer? No, it was better that she hurt a little now than for her to give herself to him and hurt a *lot* later.

Chapter Ten

Wednesday, December 21

The four days since Chris had walked out her door were the longest Carole had ever lived through. She was short with customers, short with her help and miserable in general. She missed the kids—Brian's steadfastness, Lisa's chatter, Tad's and David's wrangling, Mike's sweetness, Tina's hugs and Jake's seriousness. She even missed Katy's crying.

But most of all, she missed Chris.

Initially, she had wondered if he would call. After all, hadn't he said he loved her? But he hadn't called. And there was no way that she could call him—not after what she'd said.

Christmas was fast approaching. She had thought this year would be different; Chris had invited her to spend the day with his family, and, nervous yet excited, she'd bought everyone a gift. She'd finally sent the packages to the farm via UPS, but she hadn't heard a word from the Nicholas clan. It looked as if it would be the same old Christmas for her after all, at home, alone. Away from all the commercial nonsense, right? she thought bracingly.

She picked up a glossy fashion magazine, hoping to stop feeling sorry for herself, but she couldn't seem to help it. Today was the day Chris's parents were due to arrive from Dallas. Carole envisioned them laughing, joking, hugging. Disgusted with herself, she tossed the magazine onto the table and stretched out on the sofa. Maybe she could catch up on some rest, sleep the afternoon away.

She drew the afghan up and closed her eyes. She hoped Chris wouldn't return as the ghost of Christmas future and show her just how empty the years ahead would be, all because she was afraid to trust her heart. She didn't need anyone to show her her dismal future. She already suspected there would be precious little laughter or fun. Chances were, there wouldn't be any love either.

The phone was ringing. Carole struggled through a fog of sleep and reached for the receiver. "Hello."

"Is this Carole Chapman?" a vaguely familiar voice asked.

"Yes, it is," she said, pushing herself to one elbow. "Who's calling?"

"This is Officer Al Gibson."

She frowned. Al Gibson! What could the policeman who'd questioned her about finding Katy possibly want? "Yes?" she queried warily. "What can I do for you?"

"Chris Nicholas called me a little while ago and asked if I'd give you a call. He needs you to come out to the farm right away."

"Why?" she asked, panic rising. "What's the matter?"

"I don't know," the officer said. "He just wanted me to see if you'd drive out. Something about one of the kids."

Carole's heart clenched. What could it be? Was Lisa sick again? Was someone hurt? "Of course I'll go. I'm on my way. Thanks for calling."

It was a thirty-minute drive, but breaking every speed limit put Carole in Chris's driveway in less than twenty. She slammed the car door and raced up the steps to the front porch. It was just dusk, and the geese must have already turned in for the night. She raised her hand to knock, but before her knuckles made contact with the polished wood, the door opened and Chris stood before her, tall and handsome and rugged-looking in a bright red flannel shirt.

"What is it?" she asked in a rush. "What's wrong? Al Gibson said you needed me—something about one of the kids."

Chris nodded, and Carole's heart took a nosedive.

He took her elbow and ushered her inside, closing the door behind them. Part of her noted conversation and Christmas music in the background and the wonderful scent of cinnamon in the air. "Who is it?" she asked, swallowing hard. "Katy?"

"Yes," Chris told her with a nod. "It's Katy."

"What's wrong?"

"And Tina," he added.

"Tina?" she cried.

"And Tad and David and Mike."

For a moment, Carole was too stunned to speak. Then she realized that Chris was perfectly calm. Too calm. It didn't make sense. If something was wrong with all the kids, wouldn't he be upset? "Chris," she said softly, "what's going on? Al said—"

"I know what Al said. I told him to say it."

"What?"

"Hi, Ca-role," Mike said, entering the room with his arms outstretched and a wide smile on his face.

"Hey, Mikey," Carole said, giving him an abstracted hug. She looked at Chris. "He looks fine to me. What's wrong?"

Before Chris could answer, Tad burst into the room. "Hey, Dad, if I promise..." His voice trailed away when he saw Carole. Turning, he cupped his hands around his mouth and bellowed, "Hey, everybody, Carole's here!"

The sound of chatting ceased, and Carole heard the rest of the kids scrambling to get to the living room. One by one they entered, followed by a friendly-looking older couple.

"Dad. Mom," Chris said. "This is Carole Chapman."

"Hello, Carole Chapman," an older version of Chris said, unknowingly repeating the very thing Chris had said to her at their first meeting.

"Hello, dear," Chris's mother said. "It's a pleasure to meet you at last."

At last? "Hi," Carole said, in a bit of a quandary. She turned to Chris. "Chris—"

"I know. Something is supposed to be wrong. And it is. With all of us."

Her gaze scanned the sea of faces. Everyone looked fine to her.

"I need you, Carole," he said softly. "We all do."

"I'm having trouble with Kim," Brian said. "I swear, I don't understand women."

Carole shot Chris a look. "I—I don't understand men, either."

"I need you to help me pick out a present for my mom if you have time," Jake said. "I don't know what to get her."

"I'd be glad to help you, Jake," Carole said, blinking fast to hold back the tears. She was beginning to understand what was going on, and her heart swelled with so much love she wasn't sure she could bear it. Chris was trying to show her that they wanted her to be a part of their lives, that they did need her.

"Will you *please* take me shopping?" Lisa wailed. "Daddy finally brought home this awful dress, and I just can't wear it! Kyle would croak!"

Carole rolled her eyes. "After seeing a portion of your dad's wardrobe, I can imagine!" she managed to joke. "Of course we'll go shopping."

"My sister sent me a new computer program," David said, pushing his glasses up on his nose, "and I can't figure it out. Do you think you could help me?"

Carole smiled at him. "I can try."

"Well, I need someone to help me talk Dad into getting me a boa constrictor," Tad said.

"No!" Carole, along with everyone else, shouted.

"I need a hug," Mike said, putting his arms around Carole's waist.

"I need one, too," Tina said, making her way through her brothers to Carole, who reached down and picked her up. "And I need a mommy. Reeeel bad," she tacked on.

Swallowing hard, Carole chanced another look at Chris before she squeezed Tina and set her on the floor. His blue eyes were glowing with love—there was no mistaking it this time. "What about Katy?" she asked him.

He grinned, and Carole's heart turned over. "I imagine she needs changing."

"And Chris needs a woman who can put up with all this," Doris Nicholas said. "So far, you seem to be a good candidate."

Carole looked at Chris's mother in surprise. Like everyone else in the room, the woman was smiling.

"How about it, Carole?" Chris asked, taking her by the shoulders and drawing her close.

"How about what?" Carole wanted to make absolutely certain she wasn't misunderstanding.

"We want you to be a part of this family," he told her. "And I'm not talking about adoption."

Tears welled in her eyes, and she bit her lip to keep from crying.

"We love you, Carole. Will you marry us?"

She looked around the room once more. Brian—girl problems. Lisa—boy problems. Tad—pure mischief. And Mike with the sweet smile. It would be a challenge. It would be hard. It would be fun.

"Yes!" she cried, laughing and opening her arms to them all. "I'll marry you."

The kids rushed to her, laughing, shouting, each demanding her attention. Finally, an earsplitting whistle rent the air, and quiet reigned. "What about *me*?" Chris asked.

Carole went willingly into his arms, and his mouth descended on hers in a promise as sweet as the future she now knew would be hers.

"Wow..."

"Look at that!"

"Hmmph!"

"Daddy!"

"Way to go, Chris!"

"Children…children! Maybe we'd all better go into the kitchen and leave them alone for a few minutes. Come on, Tad!"

"Yuck!"

"Now!"

"Yes'm."

The door closed behind the group, leaving Chris and Carole alone in the living room. His kiss deepened, and his hands slid down to her hips, pulling her hard against the proof of his desire.

"Tomorrow?" he asked, his eyes blazing.

"Tomorrow," she promised before his hungry mouth found hers again.

"Way to go, Chris!" the parrot croaked from his perch on the lemon tree.

"Thanks, Sebastian," Chris said.

And Carole laughed. She had found her love. Her home. Her heart. The place she'd been seeking all her life. And she'd been guided there by a small, crying baby in a crêche.

* * * * *

Author's Note

When our children were growing up, Christmas at our house didn't mean spending lots of money. It *did*, however, mean having lots of presents. We learned early on that it didn't matter *what* the kids—Todd, Bret and Jennie—got, as long as there were tons of packages to open. Of course, "Santa" always brought what they wanted (or a reasonable facsimile, in case it was a new car), and my husband, Ken, and I always got them a "big" present. But the rest of the gifts were little things: art supplies, books, games, a coveted pocketknife or that special pair of earrings or bottle of perfume.

More important to us than the gifts, though, were the traditions we established. One year, Ken and I had just put up the Christmas tree, when Todd decided it was time to be born—two weeks early! Ever since, the tree is *always* put up on December 13, Todd's birthday.

Ours is a happily cluttered tree, laden with a hodgepodge of ornaments. Some are from the first Christmas Ken and I spent together, some are from my parents' collection, and some are antique treasures found at the Salvation Army thrift store. Added to those are stockings and decorations our children made at school over the years, some that *I* made as a child, and even a hanging Christmas card I received from a friend way back in the fourth grade, now covered with clear contact paper to preserve it. Top all that off with tinsel and icicles—put on one strand at a time—and you have our Christmas tree!

Several years ago I read of a mother who, after her daughter's birth, bought her an ornament each Christmas, so that when the girl grew up and had her own family, she would have a start for their own tree. I adopted that tradition, too, even though it involved some doubling up to catch up on the missed years.

Each holiday season my family and I bake cookies of all kinds (including my Christmas Cake Cookies) to give to friends. Making Christmas-cutout cookies, as Carole and the kids do in my story, has become a solid tradition with us...though by the time the last batch comes out of the oven, everyone is tired and good ole Mom winds up finishing the decorating. This year my two oldest grandchildren, Ambur and Zachery, both three years old, were introduced to cookie making. What an experience! Thankfully, Roman, age two, and Drew, ten months, were content simply to sample.

Ah, grandchildren. It's curious that they came along just when Ken and I were beginning to feel that Christmas morning had lost some of its zip. This year once more anticipation ran high, and the waiting was worth it when we heard Drew's happy chatter as he tried to mount his rocking horse, saw Ambur's dimples make an appearance as she ogled the fish in her aquarium, watched the surprise on Zachery's face as he sang into his microphone and, lo! heard his voice come through the speakers in the living room, and spotted Roman's mischievous grin as he peeked out from beneath the visor of his pilot's helmet.

Want another Christmas recipe? Here it is:

Families + Home + Love + Children = My Wish for You.

A very Merry Christmas.

Day Matthews

SILENT
NIGHT

Brittany Young

A recipe from Brittany Young:

Every year we have the same meal on Christmas Eve—a delicious stew made from one of my mother's recipes.

FIVE-HOUR STEW

6 carrots
5 celery stalks, chopped
3 potatoes, chopped bite-size
1 large onion, finely chopped
2 lbs stewing beef, cut in 1-inch chunks
2½ cups stewed tomatoes
4 tbsp tapioca
salt to taste
cracked black pepper to taste

Place all ingredients in a large baking kettle or oven-proof Dutch oven. Mix and cover. If you'd like to add more meat or vegetables, go ahead. They won't hurt the stew.

Place in a 250°F. oven for five hours. Don't open the oven or take off the pot lid to see how the stew's coming. In other words, no peeking until time is up.

Serve with fresh hot bread or cornbread, and baked apples stuffed with brown sugar, cinnamon and butter. This is one meal that's even more delicious as a leftover.

Chapter One

Marisa Alexander looked up with smiling gray eyes from her designing table when her secretary peeked around the door of her office. "Good morning, Denise."

Denise walked the rest of the way in and glanced at her watch. "Am I late or are you early?"

"I got here around four." Marisa tossed her pencil onto the desk and stretched, raising her arms high above her head. "I've figured out how to rebuild that one section of Mrs. Farrell's house to keep it in line with the way it was two hundred years ago."

"I hear a but in there somewhere."

"A big one. I don't think she's going to want to spend the kind of money it'll take to do it properly."

"What's her alternative?"

"To do it incorrectly, but for less money."

"Surely, if she went to the trouble of hiring you in the first place..."

"You'd think so, I know. That's not the way I read her, though." Marisa removed the wide red band from her ponytail and let her dark hair fall in thick tresses to her shoulders.

"Can I get you some tea?"

"Thanks, Denise. That would be nice." She snapped off the adjustable lamp and rose from her stool. "I think I'll lie down for a few minutes."

"Do you want me to call Mrs. Farrell to tell her the drawings are ready?"

"Not until this afternoon. I know she'll want to come over right away to pick them up."

"Fine." Denise walked to the window and closed the miniblinds to shut out the Chicago winter sun, then went to her own office while Marisa lay on her couch and covered herself with the quilt folded neatly at its foot.

When Denise walked in a few minutes later with a cup of hot tea, she found Marisa sound asleep. Backing out quietly, she gently closed the door behind her and put the tea on her own desk.

When the phone rang half an hour later, she grabbed it on the first ring. "Marisa Alexander's office. May I help you?"

The voice at the other end was obviously quite a distance from Chicago. "This is Dane Konrad," he said in a voice deliciously tinged with a light accent. "I'd like to speak with Miss Alexander, please."

Denise eyed the closed door. "She's actually quite busy at the moment . . ."

"Tell her that she comes highly recommended to me by Countess Sophia DiBrasi."

Denise's eyes widened. The Italian Mrs. DiBrasi had paid them a small fortune for the plans drawn up for restoration of her villa in Rome. "Where are you calling from, Mr. Konrad?"

"Salzburg, Austria."

Her eyes widened even more. "Hold on just a moment, please. I'll interrupt her."

Punching the button that put him on a silent hold, Denise ran into Marisa's office. "Marisa, wake up! You've got a phone call you have to take."

Marisa sleepily blinked her eyes against the light as Denise opened the blinds. "Who is it?"

"Dane Konrad from *Austria*."

"What does he want?" she asked as she pushed back the quilt, got up and walked over to her desk.

"I don't know, but whatever it is, it's probably big. He said he was referred to you by our favorite countess."

"Sophia?"

"The one and only."

"I'm impressed." Marisa lifted the phone from its hook. "This is Marisa Alexander," she said, her voice still a little husky from sleep.

"Miss Alexander, I am Dane Konrad. As I explained to your secretary, I got your name from Sophia Di Brasi. When I commented on the quality of the restoration of her villa, she told me you had done the drawings detailing the work and also designed many of the furnishings."

"That's right."

"I've just purchased a home in the mountains just outside Salzburg. It's been left vacant for more than a decade and requires extensive work, both inside and out. I'd also like a wing added, but would like it in keeping with the rest of the structure so that it matches the original part of the building."

Marisa picked up a pen and pulled a notepad toward her. "From what period does your home date?"

"Early 1800s. It was once used by the Hapsburgs as a hunting lodge."

Already she liked the sound of it. Homes like that were filled with fascinating history. "I'm very interested in seeing the lodge, Mr. Konrad." Marisa's calendar was open in front of her. She flipped through the pages. "I could come in March."

"I'd like you to come next week."

She blinked in surprise and looked up. "Next week? I'm afraid that's impossible. I have other clients I need to—"

"Miss Alexander, I can guarantee you that this project will be worth your while. Money isn't a consideration, as far as I'm concerned. The quality of the work is the most important thing."

She looked up at Denise who was standing in the doorway nodding her head and mouthing, "Go, go go."

They really could use the money. She flipped through her calendar, mentally trying to figure out which clients she could put off for just a little longer. Crooking her finger at Denise, who crossed the office to stand behind her, she pointed out a name and looked at her questioningly. The secretary studied it thoughtfully, then nodded. "All right, Mr. Konrad."

"Good. Come prepared to do your work here. I want to be able to have some input as you design."

"But that could take weeks. The way I normally work is to spend anywhere from a few days to a week getting to know a home, sketching the interior and exterior, then I bring my drawings to Chicago and draft what needs to be done. The drafting process alone can take more than a month. To be frank, I simply can't be away from my office that long."

"This won't take you a month. It's a small home. Only twelve rooms."

"But . . ."

"Miss Alexander, do you want the job or not?"

"Yes, I do, but—"

"Fine. If you'll contact me with your flight information, I'll have someone pick you up at the airport." He gave her a telephone number and she quickly scribbled it on the notepad. "Goodbye, Miss Alexander."

"Mr. Konrad—"

The line went dead at the other end. Marisa took the phone from her ear and stared at it for a moment before hanging up and looking at Denise. "Charming."

"Well?" Denise asked as she perched on the edge of the desk. "What's going on?"

"It would appear that I'm taking a trip to Austria in a week."

Denise clapped her hands and beamed. "That's wonderful! What kind of home?"

"An early 1800s hunting lodge."

"Sounds interesting. You haven't done anything like that yet." She looked at her boss and friend. "Why don't you seem more pleased?"

"He wants me to remain in Austria until the work is finished. Not just the sketches, mind you, but the actual drafting."

Denise grew thoughtful. "I'll go over your calendar and do what I can about delaying project due dates. I hope we can come through this without shooting ourselves in the foot. How long do you think it'll take?"

"He said the lodge has twelve rooms. I could be there anywhere from two to four weeks."

"Darn."

"What's wrong? Do you have a conflict?"

"Not really. I just wish he'd picked a different time of year to do this."

"Why?"

"It's almost Christmas. My children are starting their vacation in a few days."

"Oh, that's right. I forgot about that. I could hire some temporary help," she suggested after a moment.

"No. My mother's going to be staying with us, and Jeff has a few days off, too. Among the three of us, we can work out some kind of schedule with the children so that I'll be able to spend whatever time is necessary in the office."

"Are you sure?"

"Absolutely." Her eyes met Marisa's. "I guess this means that you won't be having Christmas dinner with us."

Marisa looked at her secretary affectionately. "I appreciate your trying to take care of me at Christmastime, but it's not necessary."

"Isn't it? Did you put up a tree this year?"

"No."

"Any decorations at all?"

"No."

Denise put her hand on her friend's shoulder. "Marisa, it's been three years since Peter died. You can't continue going into mourning every Christmas."

Pain darkened Marisa's lovely gray eyes. "I'm not in mourning," she said quietly. "But frankly, it's not a happy time for me, and there doesn't seem to be much I can do about that except try to survive the holiday season as best I can." She handed Denise a slip of paper. "This," she said, changing the subject, "is Dane Konrad's phone number. As soon as you've made my travel arrangements, call him with my arrival time."

Denise took the paper but kept her eyes on Marisa. "You look tired."

A quick smile flashed. "Thank you so much."

"I mean it. You haven't had a vacation for as long as I can remember."

"That's what happens when you have your own business."

"You haven't even taken a weekend off in months."

Marisa leaned back in her chair. "Why do I get the feeling that you're leading up to something?"

"Possibly because I am. Why wait a week to go to Austria? Why not leave tomorrow and take some time for yourself to go skiing? You have to pay the airfare anyway."

"That's a nice thought, Denise, but I couldn't. You'd be stuck alone in the office that much longer."

"I wouldn't have suggested it if I minded."

Marisa tapped the eraser end of her pencil on her desk. It was tempting. She really was tired. It was getting harder and harder to cover the shadows under her eyes.

"Come on," Denise coaxed. "Chances like this don't come up every week."

Marisa smiled suddenly. "All right. I'll do it."

"Good girl! I'll make the reservations. You go home, pack and get some rest."

"I think I will. Thanks."

"I've got to call my friend Mary."

"Why?"

"She was in Austria last year and she told me about this wonderful ski chalet where she stayed. I think she said that it was near Salzburg."

"It sounds perfect. And that way I'd only have to make one flight." Marisa rose and hugged Denise. "Thanks. I'm actually looking forward to it."

Denise hugged her back. "You're welcome. And make sure you have a good time. I don't want to put in that extra week alone here for nothing."

"I promise to do my best." Lifting her coat from the brass rack, Marisa slipped her arms into it then checked to make sure that her keys were in the pocket. By the time she got to the door, Denise was already on the phone.

It was a short drive home for Marisa, down the gray slushy streets. Snow, blackened by automobile exhaust, sand and salt, was piled depressingly along the curbs. Shoppers, bundled in their coats and hats, hurried along carrying their brightly colored bags. Department store windows along State Street were, as usual, decorated with scenes from fairy tales.

Stopped at a red light, Marisa looked around and tried to suppress the sadness that welled up in her at this time every year. She tried to see the beauty rather than the bleakness. Tried to take pleasure in the happiness of others rather than dwell on her own emptiness. Sometimes it worked and sometimes it didn't. Today it didn't. With any luck, maybe she'd miss Christmas altogether this year. This new job made that a distinct possibility.

The light changed, and she drove on until she got to her apartment on the lakeshore. Pressing the button on her remote control, she opened the wide garage door and headed into the underground parking lot, then took the elevator to her eighteenth-floor apartment. Her phone was ringing when she got there, so she hurriedly unlocked the door and ran inside. "Hello?"

"Marisa? It's me, Denise."

Marisa cradled the phone between her neck and her shoulder while she slipped out of her coat and tossed it over the back of the sectional couch. "What's up?"

"Your plane reservations are made. You leave tomorrow at one o'clock."

"That was fast."

"Pure luck. I called just seconds after someone else had canceled a reservation."

"Then tomorrow it is."

"And I've got you booked at a place called the Wechsberg Inn. Mary says it's exquisite. One of the most romantic places she's ever been. Tucked away on a mountain with roaring fireplaces, incredible scenery. The whole bit."

"It sounds perfect. Thanks, Denise. I appreciate all the trouble you went to."

"No problem. I'll have your ticket and the other information messengered over to you today."

"All right."

"Now, get some sleep."

"I think I'll pack first."

"And then get some sleep."

"Yes, Denise," she said with a smile.

Marisa slipped out of her sweater as she walked into her bedroom, then took off her jeans and pulled on her fluffy white terry-cloth robe. Standing on her tiptoes, she reached high into her closet to grasp the handle of a suitcase. As she pulled it from the shelf, something next to it fell onto the carpeting with a soft thud. Marisa set the suitcase on the floor, her eyes never leaving the package with the shiny red paper and big green bow that lay next to her bare foot. After a moment's hesitation, she picked it up. The top had a light coating of dust from sitting undisturbed for three years. She carried it to the bed cradled in her hands as though it contained something of impossible fragility and sat down, still staring at it. Her throat grew so tight it ached. With a tissue, she tenderly wiped away the dust and freshened the bow as best she could. Lifting her gaze just a little, Marisa found herself looking into a photograph's laughing blue eyes. Peter's eyes. Eyes she'd never look into again. One moment she'd been putting the finishing touches on their first Christmas tree as a surprise while she waited for him to get home from a business trip, and the next moment she'd taken the call that told her he'd died in a car accident.

Marisa rose and put the package back on the shelf. Picking up the framed photograph, she wrapped it in her arms and sank onto the bed, curling her body around it as she lay on her side, her dark hair spilling around her. "Oh, Peter," she whispered, her voice husky. "I do all right until Christmas. Help me get through this one."

Chapter Two

After getting her luggage, skis and all, through customs, Marisa had the skycap take it outside near the taxi stand. "Could you tell me how far it is to the Wechsberg Inn?"

"Only about ten miles from the center of Salzburg," he answered in careful English, "on Gaisberg Mountain. Is that where you're going?"

"If I can get a taxi."

"Oh, you have no need for a taxi. The Wechsberg and several of the other hotels send a driver every hour or so to pick up and deliver guests." He gazed down the row of taxis to some vans parked nearby. One of the vans started to pull away from the curb, and the skycap flagged it down. As soon as the van had stopped in front of them, the skycap opened the sliding side door and spoke in German to the driver. "Come, Miss," he said turning to Marisa and giving her a hand into the van. Two couples were already there. She handed him a generous tip then watched while he loaded her luggage.

As the van pulled into the flow of traffic, Marisa smiled quietly at the others, then sat back and relaxed, watching in wonder as the view changed from busy airport to a spectacular riot of snow-capped mountains strung out in bold relief against a bright blue sky. Looking at them like this, Marisa thought of Voltaire's description of the Alps: "Those haughty mountains which weigh down upon hell, and split the heavens." Her gaze drank in the sight.

The van left the main highway and headed down a narrower road that began a slow upward climb to a charming inn set on the outskirts of a mountain village. A small, simply designed church with a single white bell tower sat in a place of honor on a hill, overlooking everything with a benevolent gaze. A carved wood sign, in keeping with the nontourist atmosphere, identified the inn as the Wechsberg. While the driver collected her things from the back of the van, Marisa stepped out onto the snow-covered ground and took a deep breath of the bracingly cold mountain air. Denise had been absolutely right. This was just what she needed.

Following the driver into the inn, a smile lit her face as she looked around. It was exactly the way it should be. A huge fireplace dominated one stone wall, with a fire burning brightly within it. Couches and chairs that just asked a person to sink deeply into them surrounded the hearth and the cathedral ceiling with its dark wooden beams added to the atmosphere. People in ski gear walked past her on their way to the slopes, talking quietly and laughing.

Marisa followed the driver to the registration desk. It blended in so well with its surroundings that it would have been easy to overlook. After tipping the driver, she rang the small bell that sat on the highly polished wood of the curving desk. A white-haired man came out of a back room and flashed her a friendly smile as he greeted her in German.

"Do you speak English?" she asked.

"I do."

"Oh, good. I don't speak any German at all. My name is Marisa Alexander. I have a reservation."

"Indeed, you do," he said as he began going through a card file. "I took it myself. How was your flight?"

"Crowded."

"They always are this time of year." He pulled out a card and held it aloft triumphantly. "Here you are, Miss Alexander. You'll be staying with us for one week?"

"Yes. I have quite a bit of luggage. I'd appreciate being able to leave most of it here with you rather than taking it up to my room. I'll only be needing one suitcase."

"That's fine. I'll see to it. Now," he said as he put the card in front of her and handed her a pen, "you must fill this out, and I shall need your passport."

Marisa removed her passport from her purse and handed it to him, then answered all the questions on the card. As soon as she'd finished, the man walked around the desk. "Which suitcase will you be keeping with you?"

She touched the one nearest her. "This one."

He carried the remainder behind the desk, took a key from the wall and walked around the desk to pick up her suitcase. "If you'll follow me, I'll take you to your room. I think you'll like it. Most visitors enjoy the view."

They walked up a wide, curving stairway to the second floor. Her room was at the end of a long hall behind a heavy wood door. The atmosphere in the room was a lot like the lobby, with the dark wood floor, high ceiling and a working fireplace.

As soon as the man had shown her where everything was, he left. Marisa immediately crossed the room and opened the door leading to the balcony. Cold air flooded the room, but she didn't mind as she stepped outside. A light snow was beginning to fall, and a flake landed on the tip of her nose.

Resting her hands on the railing, Marisa raised her face to the sky and sighed.

Six days later, Marisa, her cheeks glowing from skiing in the crisp air and her eyes sparkling, walked into the inn. "Hello," she said with a smile to the clerk behind the desk. "Are there any messages for me?"

"Oh, yes, Miss Alexander. Herr Dane Konrad is here." He seemed impressed.

"He's here now?"

The clerk looked beyond her. "Yes. At least he was just a moment ago."

Marisa turned and looked as well.

"There he is," he said, pointing. "The man near the fireplace reading the newspaper."

"Thank you," she said as she spotted a very handsome man with dark blond hair.

The Austrian looked up and watched her as she approached, setting his paper aside and rising when he realized she was headed for him. He was so tall that Marisa had to tilt her head back to look at him as she extended her hand. "Hello. I'm Marisa Alexander. I understand you've been waiting for me."

Her hand was swallowed in his much larger one. He gazed at her with startling intensity for a long moment before speaking. "Yes," he finally said. "I have. I'm Dane Konrad."

Self-consciously aware of his touch, Marisa slipped her hand from his. "I'm sorry if I kept you waiting, Mr. Konrad, but I wasn't expecting you."

"Call me Dane, please, and it is I who should apologize. I asked my secretary to leave a message, but you obviously never received it." He waved her into a chair across from his. When they were both seated, he leaned back and studied her again.

Marisa gazed at him with direct gray eyes.

"You're very much younger than I expected." He didn't sound pleased.

"Is that bad?" she asked bluntly.

A slow smile unexpectedly curved his mouth and warmed his brown eyes. "No. Just, as I said, unexpected."

"How did you know I was here?"

"Your secretary called my home last night to tell me there was no need to pick you up at the airport—that you were in fact already in Austria. Since you're due at my home tomorrow, I thought I'd speed the process up and offer you a ride."

"That's very kind of you."

"Don't credit me with too much kindness, Miss Alexander. It's more impatience than anything else. I want to get started on the lodge."

"Call me Marisa, please. And if you don't mind waiting just a little longer, I can be packed and ready to go in less than fifteen minutes."

"I'll wait. Do you have any skiing equipment that needs to be collected?"

"Yes, I do. I checked it with the hotel staff down at the ski lift."

Dane rose, his dark eyes on her. "I'll pick it up for you and meet you here with my car."

Marisa stayed where she was for a long moment, watching his broad-shouldered back as he walked from the lobby then, deep in thought, went to her room to repack. After quickly brushing her wind-blown hair and checking her makeup—a vanity that surprised her as soon as she realized what she was doing—she picked up her suitcase and went downstairs.

Dane headed straight for her as soon as she got to the lobby and took the suitcase from her. "I already have your other luggage in the car."

She looked at him in surprise. "Thank you, but I still have to check out."

"That's already been taken care of." He reached into his pocket and pulled out her passport.

"But..."

"Just deduct the amount when you bill me for your work on the hunting lodge."

Marisa dropped the passport into her purse. "All right." Not sure she really liked his take-charge approach, she followed him outside to a black Volvo station wagon. After opening the passenger door for her, he loaded her suitcase into the back, then climbed in next to her and started the car.

"How far away from here do you live?"

"I have two homes. The lodge is on Monchsberg Mountain, but I don't consider it habitable at this point. You'll be staying in my home near Salzburg and traveling the short distance to the lodge for your work."

"I see." Marisa watched him from the corner of her eye, not really daring to stare outright. Except for that one earlier smile, he'd completely distanced himself from her. Was that cool, almost haughty arrogance his natural demeanor, or was he annoyed with her about something? She could usually gauge people very quickly after meeting them, but Dane Konrad was different.

He drove quickly over the roads, seemingly impervious to the snow, but Marisa was strangely at ease. A car belonging to Dane Konrad probably wouldn't dare skid. He wouldn't allow it. She smiled at the thought.

"You find something amusing?" he asked.

Marisa looked at him with startled eyes. "Excuse me?"

"You were smiling."

"Oh," she said, smiling again, "I'm sorry. I do that from time to time." Her tone was completely charming.

The Austrian glanced at her quickly, then turned his eyes to the road. They followed the shore of the Salzach River as it wound past Salzburg. Monchsberg Mountain loomed nearby. An enormous fortress or palace stared down at them, unblinking and impregnable. "What's that?" Marisa asked.

Dane followed the direction of her gaze. "The Hohensalzburg Fortress."

She waited for more, but he stopped talking. "I assume it has a history," she coaxed.

He was amused despite himself. She could see it in the depths of his brown eyes as he looked at her. "Of course. The fortress is over a thousand years old. The archbishops who ruled Salzburg lived there until the eighteen hundreds."

"Does anyone live there now?"

"It's mostly for tourists."

On they drove, until turning between two massive stone pillars onto a tree-lined road that led them to an utterly elegant castle. Marisa, unaware that she did it, moved forward on her seat to get a better look as they approached. It was built of stone, gently faded and softened by the centuries. Arched windows as tall as most single-story homes lined the front, broken only by a horseshoe stairway that curved up to the arched double doors. The castle was easily big enough to hold a hundred rooms.

The Austrian parked in front of the castle, walked to Marisa's side to open the door for her, then politely put his hand under her elbow as they walked up the steps. Before they got to the top, a formally dressed butler opened the door.

"Have Miss Alexander's luggage taken to her room," Dane said in English.

"Right away, sir," the butler answered, also in English, apparently in deference to Marisa's presence, as he helped them out of their coats.

On either side of where Marisa stood were curving staircases, duplicates of the one outside. She stepped forward into the cavernous octagonal foyer where a single chandelier loomed overhead, so large it probably would have filled her entire living room at home. The floor and walls were a creamy, pale marble. A heavy, gilt-framed mirror rose above an elaborately carved rectangular table along one of the eight walls.

Dane watched her expressive face. "What do you think?"

"It's beautiful."

"Am I wrong or do I sense an unspoken opinion in there somewhere?"

Marisa smiled. "You're putting me on the spot."

"I expect you've been there before," he said dryly. "What do you really think?"

"Well, it's beautiful, but rather cold. It's too formal to be user friendly."

"User friendly. That's an interesting way of putting it."

"How long has it been in your family?"

"Several hundred years. The only time it was unoccupied was for a brief period during World War Two. Most of the valuable paintings were stolen, but everything else was left intact."

"Did you ever get the paintings back?"

"A few. Most have disappeared."

Suddenly there was the surprising sound of running feet and children's delighted laughter. They came racing through a doorway and into the foyer, both of them stopping in sudden silence when they saw Marisa and Dane. The Austrian gave them a long look. "I don't want to have to tell you again about running in the house."

There was a boy who appeared to be about eight and a little girl who was perhaps five. The boy's shoulders straightened. "Yes, sir," he answered for both of them, then the girl, giggling, ran to Dane and threw herself into his welcoming arms. After setting her gently on the ground, he put his hand on the boy's shoulder and turned to Marisa. "Miss Alexander, this young man is Penn and this young lady is his sister, Justine."

Penn stepped forward and politely shook her hand, and the little girl followed.

"It's almost your dinner time," Dane said. "Go to your rooms and change your clothes."

In a remarkable burst of speed, they tore up the stairs.

"Walk!" he called out after them.

Smiling, Marisa followed them with her eyes. "They're delightful. I hadn't pictured you with children."

"Why not?"

The question was unexpected. All Marisa could do was answer honestly. "You seem rather too forbidding for fatherhood."

"Forbidding?" His eyes looked into hers. "Do you really think so?"

"I did until I saw you with Penn and Justine. It would appear that you're human after all."

A corner of his mouth involuntarily lifted. "Thank you so much for your revised appraisal."

Her lovely eyes sparkled. "Am I fired?"

"Not yet. And as it happens, the children aren't mine." An invisible wall suddenly slid into place between them as Dane looked at his watch. "Dinner is served promptly at eight. We'll be having guests this evening. I'll have the maid show you to your room so you can freshen up."

Before she could respond, he left the foyer and Marisa, unsure of what was expected of her, stayed where she was. Within moments, a uniformed woman, her dark hair just starting to go gray, approached her. "I'm Mina, Miss Alexander. Please, follow me."

They went upstairs and walked along what seemed to be a never-ending hallway. The room they finally entered was spacious, with thick white carpeting. There was a canopied bed, on a slightly raised platform at one end of the room, with a down comforter that was made to snuggle beneath. A fire crackled pleasantly in the fireplace. A heavy, antique armoire was centered against a wall, and her luggage had been placed next to it. Mina set one of the suitcases on a table and unfastened the clasps. "Do you know what you'd like to wear to dinner?" she asked.

Marisa crossed the room and pulled open the drapes, revealing one of the huge windows she'd seen from the outside. It went from ceiling to floor. "I don't really know how dressed up I should get."

"Then please, allow me to choose for you."

"I'd appreciate that, thank you," Marisa said gratefully.

"Would you also like me to run a bath for you?"

Marisa turned to her with a smile. "Oh, no, thank you, Mina. I'd rather do it myself."

The corners of Mina's eyes crinkled. "I forgot for a moment that you Americans prefer doing things for yourselves. The bathroom is through that door," she said, pointing.

Marisa sat on the window seat and watched the maid, her eyes thoughtful. "Do you mind if I ask you some questions?"

"Of course not."

"How long have you worked here?"

"Nearly twenty years." She shook out a dress and held it up. "This needs to be pressed. I'll see that it's taken care of."

"Thank you," Marisa said absently. "What's Mrs. Konrad like?"

"Mrs. Konrad? There is no Mrs. Konrad."

"Is Mr. Konrad divorced?"

"He's never married."

That surprised Marisa—pleasantly so. "I wonder why?" she said softly, almost to herself.

"I don't know." Mina sounded genuinely mystified. "I'm sure it's because he hasn't asked anyone, though, and not because he's been turned down."

Marisa nodded. "Do you know who else will be at dinner this evening?"

"I'm afraid not—except for Mr. Konrad's sister, Claudia von Shroft. She's visiting for a few days." She crossed to the armoire to hang some clothes.

"Are the children hers?"

"Oh, heavens, no. Penn and Justine are the children of Mr. Konrad's older brother. He died six months ago, and Mr. Konrad took the children in to live with him."

"What about their mother?"

"That one." Mina very nearly hissed. "She ran off years ago, right after Justine was born. No one has heard from her since. She undoubtedly has a new life now, with no room in it for the two children."

She hung more clothes, then closed the suitcase, set it on the carpeting, picked up another one and opened it. "You know, Miss, it's getting late. You really should start preparing yourself for dinner."

Marisa, still thinking about what she'd been told, crossed to the bathroom and looked inside. It was as large as her living room, complete with thick carpeting and black marble walls. The fixtures were gold; the shower separate from the bath. She leaned over the tub and turned on the water, running her hand under it and adjusting the hot and cold until it was just right.

"Here," Mina said, coming in behind her with her robe. "You'll be needing this."

"Thank you."

"If you want anything else, just call. I'll be outside until I finish with your unpacking."

It didn't take Marisa long to undress and sink into the deliciously warm water. Despite the blazing fireplace, her room was still cold.

Marisa's thoughts ran scattershot through her mind, making it difficult to focus on any one thing. She wondered about the house she was going to be working on. She wondered about the children she'd met earlier. But most of all, she found herself wondering about Dane Konrad.

How much time passed she didn't know, but she was startled out of her reverie when Mina knocked lightly on the closed door. "The unpacking is finished. I've laid a dress for this evening on your bed. Is there anything else?"

"No, thank you. What time is it?"

"Nearly quarter to eight."

"Quarter to eight!" Marisa immediately let the water out of the bath and stepped onto a thick towel while wrapping herself in another. Dashing into the bedroom, she stood in front of the fire and rubbed her skin until it glowed, then put on her stockings, slip and the V-necked black velvet dress that Mina had laid on the bed. The cream-colored satin belt had fallen onto the floor, and it took Marisa a moment to find it. Without a moment to lose, she slid into her black high heels as she wrapped the belt around her slender waist. After adding some color to her cheeks and putting on some soft rose lipstick, she brushed her hair until it hung in a silky wave to her shoulders. Stepping away from the mirror, Marisa gave herself a critical once-over. Something was missing.

Jewelry. Mina had placed her jewelry case on top of the carved dresser. She pulled it toward her and rummaged through it until she found what she was looking for. Pearl earrings. They were small, but perfect with the dress. As soon as she'd fastened them to her ears, she ran from her room and down the hall—the long hall—down the stairs then stood in the foyer, slightly out of breath, not sure where to go.

Justine walked into the foyer at that moment. Marisa smiled at her. "Hi."

The little girl beamed back, showing a perfect dimple in each cheek.

"I need your help, Justine. It seems I'm late for dinner with your uncle and I don't know where to go. Can you show me?"

She nodded her golden head and took Marisa's hand in hers, tugging on it lightly as she led her through the house to a room from which music, conversation and laughter spilled out into the hallway. It sounded like a lot of people. Justine opened the door and walked straight through to her uncle.

Dane seemed somehow separate from the rest of his guests as he stood with a drink in one hand, the other in the pocket of his trousers, staring silently into the fireplace. Justine touched his arm, and he brought his hand lightly to rest on her blond curls. As though sensing Marisa's presence, he turned his head at that moment, and their eyes met and held. Her heart went straight into her stomach. Strange how a look from him could do that to her.

Dane spoke quietly to Justine, and she skipped happily out of the room. Then he crossed to Marisa, his eyes never leaving hers. "I'm afraid you're too late for a drink," he said, without any hint of criticism. "We were just getting ready to sit down to dinner."

Her eyes locked irresistibly with his. "It's my own fault. I lost track of the time."

For a long time neither spoke, and their gazes never wavered.

A stunningly attractive woman with smartly styled short red hair came up to Dane at that moment and slipped her arm through his. She spoke in German.

He looked at Marisa a moment longer, then turned to the woman. "English, please, Claudia, and of course I'm going to introduce her. Marisa Alexander, this is my sister, Claudia von Shroft."

Marisa, her heart pounding, lowered her eyes to fully break the connection before raising them again and looking at the woman. Claudia was unabashedly sophisticated, but there lurked in her eyes an unmistakable twinkle. Marisa liked her instantly.

Claudia's reaction to Marisa was much the same. She turned to her brother as she dropped his arm and took Marisa's. "If you'll excuse us, Dane, I must introduce Marisa to the rest of your guests." And she did, making a complete tour of the room and the other twelve guests. Marisa barely heard the names. Her awareness centered on the man whose eyes she could feel following her.

As soon as Claudia had finished the last introduction, they all went into the dining room. Dane started to seat Marisa halfway down the length of the table, but Claudia tapped his arm with her finger. "Oh, no, you don't. I want her near me. It's so nice to have someone new to talk with."

With reluctance, or so it seemed to Marisa, he placed her to his left at the head of the table, just across from his sister, who sat to his right.

Claudia kept up a steady stream of amusing small talk, some of which caused Marisa to laugh out loud. But always she was aware of Dane. She could feel his dark eyes on her, intense. Almost brooding. His demeanor was in complete contrast to his sister's in that he spoke only when a question was addressed directly to him, and even then he answered with an economy of words.

Marisa was intrigued. Most of the men she came across professionally or socially felt an amazing need to divulge their entire life histories. But not this man.

The dinner was wonderful with a delicate, brothy soup, fish fillets poached in a wine and butter sauce, asparagus and saffron rice. Claudia noticed Marisa's left hand for the first time as dessert was being served. "Does your husband mind that your work often takes you away from home?"

"My husband?"

Claudia held up her left hand and indicated her ring finger by wiggling it.

"Oh," Marisa said quietly as she looked at her own hand and saw the simple gold wedding band that she'd never removed. Strange, but she hadn't thought about Peter all day. That had never happened before. "I'm a widow."

Claudia was genuinely shocked. "Oh, dear, I'm sorry. You're so young. I never dreamed..."

"Please, don't apologize."

"Did this happen recently?"

"Three years ago Christmas Eve."

"How long had you been married?"

"Claudia, for heaven's sake," Dane interrupted angrily, "that's enough."

Claudia was contrite. "You're right, of course." She smiled at Marisa. "It's just that I find I like you—which is rare for me when it comes to other women—and I let my curiosity get out of hand. Please forgive me."

Marisa returned her smile. "I like you, too, and there's nothing to forgive. In answer to your last question, we were only married one month, but we'd known each other since childhood." She had no idea of the depth of sadness in her voice as she spoke. Looking down at the crystal dish of homemade vanilla ice cream topped with fresh peaches, Marisa sighed. Her appetite was suddenly gone. "This looks lovely but I can't eat another bite."

"Would you prefer just coffee?" Dane asked. His voice was surprisingly kind.

Her eyes met his. "Nothing, thank you. Actually, I'm a little tired. If it's all the same to you, I think I'd like to go to my room."

Dane rose. "I'll walk with you."

"You don't have to do that."

Without saying anything, he moved behind her chair.

Claudia looked at her brother with a raised brow, but he wasn't paying attention to her. His eyes were on the top of Marisa's head.

Sliding her chair back with Dane's help, Marisa glanced at him over her shoulder as she rose. "Thank you."

He inclined his head.

Turning to the other guests, she bade them goodnight and walked from the dining room with Dane. His arm brushed against hers as they walked. Marisa felt the accidental contact as sharply as though she'd had an electrical shock and moved her arm away from him. When they got to her room, she put her hand on her door.

"What time would you like to go to the lodge in the morning?" It was the first thing Dane had said to her since they'd left the dining room.

Marisa turned and looked up at him. Their eyes met and held. "Eight o'clock."

"I'll take you to show you the way tomorrow, and to explain my thoughts about the lodge. After that you can have the use of one of my cars so you can go on your own."

"Thank you."

His eyes roamed over the smooth skin of her face, taking in the faint flush in her cheeks and her gray eyes—such a remarkable contrast with her dark hair.

At that moment, she felt one of her earrings drop onto her shoulder. From there it fell to the floor. Dane saw it also, and they both bent and reached for it at the same time, their hands colliding. Their eyes met as they slowly straightened. Dane held out his hand. The pearl lay nestled in his palm. With a hesitance she understood all too well, Marisa took it from him, her fingertips lightly brushing against his palm. "Thank you."

Dane looked at her for a long moment. "The thought of your husband still causes you great pain, doesn't it?"

"Yes." She raised her eyes to his. "but this is the first time I've also felt guilty."

"Guilty? Why?"

"Do you want the truth?"

"I've come to expect nothing less from you, Marisa," he said quietly.

Her gaze remained direct. "For the first time in a long time, I find myself looking at a man rather than through him. You're nothing at all like Peter, and yet you intrigue me."

"And you feel that's doing a disservice to his memory?"

"It's more like a betrayal."

Dane reached out and cupped her chin in his hand. "You're a young woman with your entire life in front of you. No amount of wishing is going to bring your husband back. Denying yourself the pleasure of another man's company, or of falling in love again, will accomplish nothing but to bring you unhappiness, Marisa. Just be careful about where you place your affection—and with whom you become intrigued." His hand fell to his side as his eyes roamed over her face and shoulders. He started to say something more, but stopped himself. "Good night, Marisa."

She looked at him a moment longer, then lowered her gaze. "Good night." As soon as she was in her room with the door closed between them, she leaned against the wood and shut her eyes tightly. Had she really said that? Or more importantly, how could she have said that? What was wrong with her that when asked a question she felt a need to always tell the truth? And his reaction had been to warn her away.

She opened her eyes. Well, it was too late now to retract her words. Dane was still standing outside her door. She could feel his presence. Then she heard him leave. Crossing the dimly lit room to the fireplace, Marisa stood in front of it, her hands stretched near the flames, absorbing the heat. She was filled with disquiet. What had happened to her was obvious. After years of being emotionally—and physically—numb, she now was feeling something. This man caused the transformation.

Deep in thought, she took off her clothes and slipped into a pale pink cotton nightgown whose large bottom ruffle swept the floor as she walked. The style was modest and old-fashioned. She lay the matching cotton robe at the foot of the bed then snuggled under the warmth of the down comforter until all that showed were her nose and eyes.

She was comfortable, she was warm, she was tired—and she couldn't sleep. Marisa tried lying on her back, her stomach, her right side, her left...she lay there for hours until finally giving up altogether. Her mind was racing, and she couldn't stop it.

A book. That was it. She needed a book, and there wasn't one in the room. Slipping into her robe, she padded barefoot across her room and peered into the semidark hallway. No one was there, and the house sounded quiet. Lifting her long robe and nightgown with one hand, she went downstairs and began looking into rooms. Surely in a house this size there was a library.

She found it. A fire burned low in the fireplace but gave off enough light to see some titles. Most of the books were in German, but she found some in French, Italian, Spanish and even Greek. The English books were on the wall opposite the fireplace. She pulled out one by an author whose work she enjoyed and took it over to the fire to look at it more closely.

"I thought you went to bed, Marisa," said a deep voice from the doorway.

Marisa gasped and looked up to find Dane watching her. "I did, but I couldn't sleep. I thought a book might help."

He walked toward her, took the book from her hands and looked at the title. "Do you enjoy Jane Austen?"

Her eyes were on his face. After what she'd said, it was impossible not to be self-conscious. "She's one of my favorites."

He handed the book back to her. "Feel free to borrow it, or any other book that you'd like."

"Thank you."

His gaze held hers for a long moment, then moved over her slender form, coming to rest on her unslippered feet peeping beneath the hem of the voluminous robe. "You'd better get back to your bed before you catch a cold."

Marisa looked down at her feet also. "Yes, I suppose I should." She started to leave the library, but looked back when she got to the door. Dane was staring into the fire. Light and shadow from the flames flickered gently over his serious face.

"Good night, Marisa," he said quietly without looking at her.

She was silent for just a moment. "Good night."

As soon as she was in her room, Marisa sank onto the window seat. Laying the book beside her, she hugged her knees to her chest and folded her nightgown around her toes to keep them warm. Light from the library below spilled onto the snow outside her window. Dane was still down there.

"Why do you look at me the way you do, so grave and unsmiling?" she whispered. "What are you thinking?"

Dane stared into the fire long after Marisa had gone. How was it possible for a man to meet a woman and to know before she'd uttered a single word that she was the one he'd been waiting for?

And how was he going to get through the coming weeks knowing that he could never have her?

Chapter Three

Marisa had to rush to make it downstairs by eight o'clock the next morning. Once she'd finally fallen asleep, it had been into a deep, uninterrupted slumber.

After brushing her dark hair into a ponytail, she put on a heavy yellow sweater and jeans, socks and hiking boots. Mina had left her drawing supplies in the suitcase, and Marisa took them out and put them into a backpack. All that was left were her yellow ski jacket and fuzzy white earmuffs. Grabbing her backpack, she tossed it over one shoulder and hurried to her door. For just a moment, her hand hovered over the handle. She was simply going to have to move beyond what she'd said the night before. It wouldn't do any good to be embarrassed. In fact, that would only make things worse. Taking a deep breath, she opened the door and quickly went down the stairs, reaching the bottom just as Dane came into the foyer.

"I thought you'd be sleeping late," he said as he stopped in front of her.

Her heart made a strange movement beneath her breast. "I almost did."

Dane turned away from her. "Do you have everything you're going to be needing for the day?" he asked as he picked up a set of keys from a table.

"Yes."

"Then let's go."

"Do you think the children might want to go with us?"

"I'm sure they'd love it, but they have school to-day."

She followed him outside to the car he'd picked her up in the day before. Just like last night, both of them reached for the door handle at the same time, and their fingers collided. He clasped his warmly over hers and lowered her hand to her side before opening the door for her. Marisa turned her head and found that her face was only inches from his. She could feel his breath wash warmly over her cool skin. "I'm afraid my manners are a little old-fashioned," he explained in his low voice, his eyes on hers.

Marisa's heart moved into her throat. "Please, don't apologize. It's a nice change," she somehow managed to say as she tore her eyes from his and slid into the car.

Dane closed the door after her and climbed behind the steering wheel. In silence he started the car and headed down the long drive away from his home. They encountered very little traffic as they drove toward the mountain and began the upward climb. It had snowed a little during the night and the dry powder swirled madly as the car streaked through it. She tried to pay attention to landmarks and to where he turned so she could find her way when she returned by herself the next time, but Marisa's gaze, as though it had a will of its own, kept turning to the man beside her. Her artist's eye found him irresistible. He had a wonderfully clean profile. His jaw was slightly squared with just a hint of a dimple in his chin. His dark blond hair was neatly trimmed. He was a wonderful-looking man, but his attractiveness went far beyond his looks. He had tremendous dignity—something rare in men these days.

Marisa turned her head and stared out the window. They were on the mountain, passing by villages spread over the valleys. Tiny churches sat prominently on hills overlooking the clusters of houses.

They continued upward until the part of the mountain they were on flattened out. The only road was the one they made as their tires crunched over the packed snow. It was much deeper here than it had been below.

"There it is," Dane said quietly as the lodge came into view.

It was pretty much what Marisa had expected. Not terribly large. The roof was white with snow. A strong wind had blown wet snow onto one side of the lodge, making it white, and it contrasted with the darkly stained wood of the rest of the building. Dane parked in front, walked around the car and opened the door for Marisa. She grasped the backpack that held her working materials and stepped outside, her booted feet sinking into the snow. "What exactly is it that you want done on the outside?" she asked, her expert eye already noting the lovely lines of the lodge. She was loath to tamper with something like that.

"I need an extension put on."

"Large or small?"

"One room, but good-sized. It's for the children. What I don't want to do, though, is ruin the balance or the overall look of the building."

Marisa nodded as she began to walk around. There was a small pond on one side, frozen over and perfect for ice skating. But it was the view that stopped Marisa in her tracks. The lodge, set in an upland pasture, looked down on a valley, and beyond that, Salzburg itself. She recognized the Salzach River and Hohensalzburg Fortress, even at this distance. But when she looked in the other direction, just across the valley, a massive, jagged line of mountains stretched as far as the eye could see, overwhelming her with its size to the point where she inhaled sharply.

Dane had been watching her for a reaction and was obviously pleased by it. "Intimidating, isn't it?"

"I've never seen anything like it."

"The thing about actually being in the middle of these mountains, the way we are now is that you're forced to deal with them, with their size, their sheer magnificence. There's nothing else in nature that makes you do that."

Marisa turned her gaze to Dane. "That's why you bought the lodge, isn't it?"

"I guess I wanted a place to escape to. A place where I can be completely alone with my thoughts. Of course, the children will be here at times, and I want them to be comfortable, but mostly the lodge is for me." His eyes met hers. "What are you thinking?"

Her gaze remained direct. "That you're a remarkably complicated man."

A corner of his mouth lifted, and for just a moment the barrier he seemed determined to keep between them slipped. "Not as complicated as most people think. I am, after all is said and done, just a man, like other men."

No, you're not, Marisa thought. *You're not like anyone else at all.* Afraid her eyes would give her away, she turned her head to look at the lodge. "The windows are rather small. They don't take advantage of the view. We could change that very easily."

"Then do it."

She felt his eyes on her profile and had to force herself not to look at him.

"I'll show you the inside."

Marisa fell into step beside him as they walked around to the side where the car was parked. He unlocked the heavy wood door and pushed it open, then guided Marisa in with his hand warmly pressed on the small of her back. "I'm afraid there's no electricity yet, but it's light enough in here to see without it during the day. If you're ever up here in the evenings, there are lanterns throughout."

Marisa was already engrossed in her surroundings. Everything was dark wood: the walls, floor, ceiling. Even the slightly spiraled staircase off to the right. Rugs, threadbare in places, covered some of the floor space. This was most definitely a hunting lodge.

Huge stone fireplaces dominated entire walls in most of the rooms. Furniture was sparse, and what was there had seen better days. But despite everything, there was a feeling of spaciousness—probably because of the high, beamed ceilings—and at the same time, a comforting coziness. Marisa liked it immediately. She crossed the living room to where two small windows had been plugged into the wall almost as an afterthought. "I think if we put in arched floor-to-ceiling windows right here, it'll almost pull the mountains into the room with you."

"What about just one large window?"

Marisa shook her head. "That's not in keeping with the general flavor of the lodge. It wouldn't look right. Inside, of course, you'll need new rugs. I wouldn't put in carpeting. This place needs to have wood floors. Most of the furniture that's here can be refinished, and what can't be found in antique shops I can design and have built." She stood in the center of the room and gazed around. "I really like it here. It's going to make a wonderful home."

"You like the lodge better than my other home, don't you?" he asked.

"I didn't say that."

"You didn't have to."

"I just like it—differently."

"You're hedging."

"All right," she conceded. "I'll admit that I prefer cozy to grand."

Dane looked around the room. "So do I," he said quietly.

Marisa looked at him in surprise.

Dane's eyes met hers. "I'm going for a walk. You, of course, may do whatever it is you need to do and let me know when you're ready to leave."

Her eyes followed him through the door. No matter what he said, Dane Konrad was indeed a complicated man. Setting her backpack on a table, she removed a notebook, pencils and sketch pad and went outside to sketch the lodge from every possible angle so that she could study the drawings later to get a feel for where an extension might best be placed. The glove on her right hand restricted her finger movement and interfered with her drawing, so she took it off while she drew, raising her hand to her mouth every so often to blow on her cold fingers. Her warm breath misted the air.

Marisa worked for hours, entirely oblivious to the world around her—until she saw Dane standing about fifty feet away from her, his hands in his trouser pockets, the collar of his dark jacket turned up. He was very still, his profile toward her, staring at the mountains. Almost unconsciously she turned the page in her sketchbook and with swift, clean lines captured his broad shoulders and long, lean body on paper. The face took longer. His expression was one she had trouble defining. Was he sad or simply pensive? Wistful, perhaps—a strange word for a man of such innate strength.

Dane moved his head ever so slightly, and his eyes met hers. For a long moment, neither of them moved. He turned and walked away. Her gaze followed him out of sight. He seemed to want to push her away, and yet there was something in his eyes when he looked at her that told Marisa otherwise.

Banishing the Austrian from her thoughts as best she could, Marisa went back to work, making her way around the house, losing track of time, as she always did.

It was getting dark when she saw Dane walking toward her. She glanced at her watch and apologized. "I'm sorry. I didn't realize how late it was."

"Ordinarily it wouldn't matter, but as it happens, tonight I promised the children I'd take them into Salzburg to buy a Christmas tree."

"To *buy* a tree?" she asked in surprise.

He understood what she meant. There were probably thousands of trees on both his properties. "I know, but Justine can't bear the thought of cutting down a tree. Somehow, to her five-year-old mind, there's a difference between one you cut down yourself and buying one that's already been cut down by a stranger." Suddenly, as though he felt he'd been a little too friendly with his explanation, Dane withdrew again.

"Why do you do that?"

There was no need to ask what. Dane knew. And he chose not to answer.

"You left some things in the lodge you'd better get, Marisa. I'll warm up the car." And with that, he walked away and left her standing there.

When she got into the car a few minutes later, Dane was as silent as he'd been on the drive up the mountain. Marisa was quiet, too. Thoughtful. Lights twinkled in patches on the mountain across from them and in the valley. It was as beautiful and peaceful out there as Marisa was in turmoil inside. She sighed aloud without realizing it.

"Is something wrong?" Dane asked.

She turned her head and gazed at his profile. "I was just envying the mountain its serenity. Nothing penetrates it. It sits there through the centuries, unaltered no matter how hard man might try to alter it. Indestructible, yet sometimes destructive. Challenging, yet often fatal to those who accept that challenge."

Dane met her gaze, then looked at the road. "For someone who's never been in the mountains before, you understand them very well."

"I don't think one can understand the mountains any more than one can completely understand another person. Take you, for example. There are times, such as when you're with the children, that I sense such warmth in you. But then the moment passes and you place yourself out of all reach. You become as impenetrable as the mountains."

"That's quite an analysis considering you've known me for less than two days."

"But accurate, don't you think?"

"I'm sure it is, from your perspective."

Marisa bowed her head and looked at her hands.

When they arrived at his home, light from the windows spilled onto the snow. Justine must have been watching for them, because she came running outside without her coat, leaving the door gaping open behind her as she raced down the steps and into her uncle's arms.

"Jussy," he scolded affectionately as he lifted her onto his shoulders, "you're going to catch a cold."

"No, I won't. Are we still going to town?"

"Yes." He walked around the car and opened Marisa's door.

"Are you coming with us?" Justine asked.

"I don't think so," Marisa said with a smile as she climbed out.

"Please."

"Thank you, Justine, but I have some work to do."

"You can do it later."

Marisa looked helplessly at Dane, well aware that he'd prefer she not join them.

"Please come," he said after a moment. "It will make Justine happy."

Still she hesitated.

Justine whispered something in his ear.

He looked up at the little girl and pinched her cheek, then turned to Marisa. "I'd like you to come. Salzburg at night during the Christmas season is a sight you shouldn't miss."

She understood, and he knew she understood, that he was only doing what Justine wanted. "All right," she agreed quietly. "Do I have time to change my clothes?"

"Of course."

The three of them went into the house, and Marisa continued up the stairs as Dane set Justine on the floor. "Find Penn and tell him to get ready."

Yelling her brother's name, she shot past Marisa on the staircase. Marisa smiled after her, unaware of the man watching from below.

Claudia had been standing in a doorway unobserved. She stepped into the foyer as soon as Marisa had disappeared upstairs. "She's lovely, isn't she?"

Dane turned and looked at his sister. "I didn't know you were there," he said in German.

"Obviously."

"We're going into Salzburg, Claudia. Would you like to join us?"

"Not this time, thank you, and please stop changing the subject, Dane."

"I have no intention of discussing Marisa Alexander with you." There was a warning in his tone that Claudia chose to ignore.

"Why not?"

"Because there's nothing to discuss."

"Who are you trying to convince of that? Me or yourself? I've seen the way you look at her."

"Claudia," he said, his dark eyes growing darker, "that's enough."

She touched his arm. "Dane," she said softly, all teasing gone from her voice, "if, after all these years, you've found the woman you want, don't turn away from her."

"You're wrong."

"No," she said as she shook her head, "I'm not."

He looked at the now deserted stairs. There was no mistaking the pain in his eyes. "Even if it were true, I have no choice," he said tightly. "You, of all people, know that."

"I don't know that. I don't know that at all. Don't let your misguided sense of gallantry get in the way of..."

"Misguided sense of gallantry? There is nothing misguided about my wanting to protect the woman I—care for."

"The woman you love," she corrected softly. "And unless my intuition is sadly off kilter, if Marisa isn't in love with you already, she soon will be."

"I won't allow that to happen."

"Love doesn't need your permission. If it's there, it's there. Marisa strikes me as a sensible woman. Surely, if you simply explain things to her..."

"Explain what, Claudia?" he asked as he walked away from her, dragging his fingers through his hair. "That if she falls in love with me there's a very good chance she'll be twice widowed?"

"There's an equally good chance that that won't happen."

"Oh, please, don't preach that optimistic half-full-glass nonsense at me."

"But it's true. Over the past one hundred years, only half of the Konrad men have died young. That means the other half haven't. They've married and had families and lived to see their children into adulthood. They've managed to grow old with the women they loved."

"Those words must have been cold comfort to our mother, widowed with three children before she was thirty, and to Penn and Justine, who are never going to see their father again."

"Dane, our father and brother were both under thirty-five when they died. All the Konrad men who've been victims of these sudden and unpredictable heart attacks have died before they turned thirty-five. You only have one year to go, then you'll be in the clear."

"One year can sometimes seem like an eternity," he said quietly.

"You should be with Marisa."

"No. If and when that year passes, then perhaps I'll go to her, but not until then."

"If Marisa is in love with you, she has a right to share that year with you. And if, God forbid, something should happen, at least the two of you will have had some time together. There will be pain, of course, but nothing to compare with the joy. And she'll have memories."

"Memories? Joy? Did you see the look on Marisa's face when you quizzed her about her husband at dinner? I never, ever want to be the cause for putting that look on her face again."

"Dane..."

"It's not a risk I'm willing to let her take. She's been through too much already."

"That's her decision to make, not yours."

Dane turned to his sister and leveled his gaze at her. "It's very much my decision, and that's the end of this conversation. Don't bring it up again. And don't discuss this with Marisa. Ever."

Claudia watched as he walked away from her, her heart in her eyes. She loved her brother dearly, but he could be impossibly stubborn. At times that stubbornness gave the appearance of arrogance. He'd surrounded himself with armor when he was a child and their father had died, and he'd readjusted it so that it was more securely in place when their brother had died.

But he hadn't counted on Marisa coming into his life. And if there was any way that Claudia could get the two of them together, she was going to do it.

Marisa finished changing into a calf-length dark blue skirt and matching sweater. Sitting on the edge of the bed, she pulled on some boots, then found herself staring off into space. She was almost—almost— tempted to run back to Chicago. Or more accurately, away from Dane Konrad. And why? She'd thought long and hard last night and had made peace with herself over Peter. The problem was that she'd closed herself off from normal feeling for so long that she wasn't used to the vulnerability Dane made her feel.

Made her feel. That, of course, was the real problem. He made her feel. And she knew that with the return of feeling came the possibility of pain. In fact, the probability of pain because he so obviously wanted nothing to do with her.

Marisa had always prided herself on her emotional stability. She never behaved rashly. She never believed in fate. Her reality was that each person was in charge of his or her own destiny. But if there was no such thing as fate, how could she explain the fact that she, practical and pragmatic Marisa Alexander, had fallen in love with a man she'd never even met until the day before? And she was in love with him. The knowledge settled on her softly, like a blanket.

Marisa's eyes focused on the wall in front of her. With a sigh, she rose from the bed, picked up her jacket and purse and headed downstairs.

She saw Claudia standing in the foyer and managed a friendly smile. "Hello. Are you going with us into Salzburg?" she asked, hoping Claudia would say yes.

"No. I'm going to stay home and do something decadent such as wash my hair and eat chocolates." She looped her arm through Marisa's. "Let's go sit in the library until the others are ready. Can I get you something to drink?"

"No, thank you. I'm not thirsty, but I'm hungry."

"Then you'll love Salzburg. You'll find vendors on the street with hot baked potatoes, soup, cider—almost anything."

"That sounds wonderful."

Claudia sat on the couch, and Marisa sat in a chair across from her. "It is. I always miss Salzburg when I'm away from it."

"Why do you leave?"

"Boredom. A contradiction, I know. Life is very quiet and very cultural here. But this time of year I enjoy coming home. Everyone should come to Salzburg for Christmas."

"I've heard that it's lovely."

"Incomparable, and I should know. I've been all over the world at various times, and with various of my husbands. But I particularly like coming home for the annual Christmas ball our family throws."

"When is that?"

"Christmas Day. You're coming, aren't you?"

"Well, I . . ."

"Oh, of course you are. It's a perfectly lovely evening. Everyone comes."

"I'm sure it is, but I think if your brother had wanted me there, he would have invited me."

Claudia smiled. "It's my ball as well, and I'm inviting you. Besides, I wouldn't be too sure that Dane doesn't want you there."

"What do you mean?"

"I mean that what you see with Dane isn't always what's really there." She leaned forward. "And I'll tell you something else, Marisa. I . . ."

"Are you ready, Marisa?" Dane asked from the doorway.

Claudia's head snapped up to look at him. "You shouldn't sneak up on people like that."

Marisa slipped her arms into the sleeves of her coat as she rose. "I'm ready."

"Let's go. It's getting late, and the children are already in the car."

Claudia touched Marisa's hand. "We'll make some time to talk later. Have fun."

Dane stood in the doorway after Marisa had passed and looked at his sister. "Claudia, mind your own business. If you don't, our relationship will be severed."

She looked at him in shock. "Dane, you don't mean it!"

"I don't say things I don't mean."

They were halfway to the door when Marisa stopped and turned to Dane. He seemed almost hostile toward her. "You know, if you don't want me to go, all you have to do is say so."

"Justine would never forgive me."

"I'll tell her I changed my mind."

"She'll still think it was my doing. She told me tonight that I wasn't very nice to you."

Marisa studied his face. "We have business together. That doesn't oblige you to enjoy my company."

"True. But the fact is that this is the children's first
Christmas without their father. It's been extremely
difficult for them, and if your going with us to pick
out the tree makes Jussy happy, I don't have the heart
to disappoint her. Do you?"

He was so distant and impersonal that he could have
been talking to a tree rather than a woman. She
searched his eyes, but there was nothing there she
could grasp. She felt something in the vicinity of her
heart and she realized it was the pain she'd dreaded.
In silence, Marisa slowly turned and went to the car.
The engine was running, and the inside was pleasantly warm as she slid into the passenger seat. Dane
got into the driver's side and looked into his rearview
mirror. "Jussy, Penn, put on your seat belts."

Two clicks sounded in the back, and Dane put the
car into gear. He glanced at Marisa. "You, too."

She snapped hers into place.

"Is Christmas in America different from Christmas here?" Penn asked.

Marisa turned slightly so she could see the children
and put a determined smile on her face. Just because
she was miserable was no reason to ruin this night for
Jussy and Penn. "I don't really know. I don't know
anything about your customs and celebrations."

"Do you have *Knecht Ruprecht*?" Justine asked.

She glanced at Dane. *"Knecht Ruprecht?"*

"Our version of Santa Claus," he answered.

"Oh, I see. Well, I guess we do, Justine, only we call
him by a different name."

They drove along the Salzach River and into Old Salzburg. The lights in the trees lining the main street sparkled like thousands of low-hung stars. Dane parked the car and they all got out, but no one was in a particular hurry to get the tree. Justine walked between Dane and Marisa, holding their hands, while Penn walked on his uncle's other side. He was too old to want to hold hands, but Dane clasped the boy's shoulder.

The buildings, all beautifully decorated, were close together, but rose several stories. There were narrow alleys between them, filled with shops, some so small that only two or three customers at a time could go inside.

But it was the spicy aromas that got to Marisa as they floated tantalizingly through the crisp air. Her empty stomach growled. They came to a vendor selling huge cookies. Jussy tugged on Dane's hand. "Please?"

"Did you have dinner?"

She nodded vigorously. "And I ate almost all of it. So did Penn."

Dane's eyes met Marisa's over the little girl's head. "Would you like one?"

"I'd love it."

He bought four cookies and passed them out, and they continued down the street. Jussy and Penn kept stopping and pressing their noses against the store windows, calling for their uncle to look at this and that, afraid they were going to miss something. In one window, a woman made silk flowers. In another, people crowded around to watch as a man worked with glass, shaping the red-hot globs into the most amazingly graceful animals with quick, deft movements.

Marisa joined the children, loath to leave. Justine pointed to a dove held aloft on a sliver of glass, its wings spread in flight. Penn watched in wonder as the man made a dolphin leaping from the sea, with splashes of water surrounding it.

As they started walking again, Marisa suddenly stopped. "Would you excuse me for a moment?" she asked Dane. Without waiting for an answer, she turned and disappeared into a group of people, returning a few minutes later with two boxes tied together with string. "Where to now?"

Dane looked at the boxes and then at her. "Straight ahead."

They walked along the Getreidegasse, sometimes following the alleys and the shops to narrow, arcaded courtyards. One of them was strung with a garland of red apples.

Marisa gazed up at the buildings while the children watched a woman making candy. "I'm surprised at how tall everything is."

Dane looked up as well. "As Salzburg grew, there was nowhere to go but up. We're sandwiched between two mountains and the river, not to mention the fortress."

They passed the Hotel Goldener Hirsch, a modernized sixteenth-century town house, and again the smell of food nearly made her weak at the knees. Marisa touched Dane's arm. "I'm sorry to be a bother, but the only thing I've had to eat today is that cookie, and I'm starving."

"My apologies, Marisa. I wasn't thinking. Of course you must eat. We can go in the hotel."

"No, thank you. That's too much trouble. Your sister said something about soup vendors."

"Are you sure that's what you want?"

"Positive."

"Come on, then." He touched the children's shoulders. "We're going to get Marisa something to eat."

They turned right, then right again, going through a passage to the Universitatsplatz market. There, straight ahead, was a soup stall. Dane bought her a cup of vegetable soup and carried the boxes so that Marisa could eat while they walked. The children kept darting here and there, but Dane kept a watchful eye on them. They passed a bookstore and this time it was Marisa whose nose was pressed against the window. There was an old, old copy of *Pride and Prejudice* by Jane Austen. In English, no less.

Dane came up behind her. She could feel his breath above her ear. "Do you like bookstores?"

She was suddenly very self-conscious and straightened away from the window. "I could spend days wandering through them."

"This one is the oldest in Austria. I think it has been here since something like 1594."

"Come on," Justine said as she tugged at his arm. "We're almost there."

"There" turned out to be the Christmas tree market. While Marisa stood off to one side finishing her soup, Dane and the children picked out not one but two trees and paid for them, then had them set aside to pick up later.

"Why two trees?" she asked Dane as he took the empty soup cup from her hand and dropped it into a wastebasket.

"One is decorated with crumbs for the birds and placed outside."

Marisa smiled. "What a lovely custom."

"We have a lot of lovely customs in Austria. Are you still hungry?"

"I hate to admit it, but, yes, I am."

"Then our last stop will be the Christkindlmarkt." They went through a high arcade and suddenly the aromas were terrific. "Warm donuts," she said, stopping in her tracks. "I smell warm donuts."

"And roasting chestnuts and hot rum punch." Dane went to a booth called Engelmann's and bought something of everything, much to the delight of the children. He handed Marisa a donut and some punch.

She took a sip and offered Dane some. He hesitated just a moment before accepting the cup and taking a drink, then handing it back to her. Their eyes met and held.

Marisa's heart started the steady beat that she was gradually becoming used to in his presence. "Thank you," she said suddenly.

"For what?"

"For making this such a pleasant evening."

"It has been, hasn't it?" he said quietly.

Again Jussy tugged on Dane's hand. "I want to go home."

"Justine, don't be such a baby," Penn said in disgust. "There's lots more to see."

"I'm not a baby," she informed him, "I'm just tired."

Penn didn't say anything, but rolled his eyes expressively.

They started walking, retracing some of their steps, taking some shortcuts, until they reached the car. They picked up the trees and tied them to the roof of the car, then headed for home. The children were tired and didn't talk much. Marisa was tired, too, and rested her head against the back of her seat, more aware than ever of the man beside her. To keep herself from looking at him, she closed her eyes. Without realizing it was happening, Marisa drifted off to sleep.

When they arrived home, Dane was the only one awake. He looked at the children and smiled. Then he looked at Marisa in the light that shone from the outside lamp. Her lashes were long and dark and fanned out over her cheeks. Her lips were slightly parted. Dane's eyes softened as he looked at her. He sat there for a long time in the cool silence, his eyes filled with a tenderness that would have surprised those who knew him. Leaning over, he touched his fingers to her cheek. "Marisa," he said softly.

"Um."

"We're here."

She slowly opened her eyes and found them locked with Dane's. For a long moment neither of them moved. His eyes roamed over her face. He started to say something but stopped himself and straightened away from her. "The children are both asleep."

She turned her head and looked in the back seat. "I'll carry Jussy."

"That's not necessary."

"I know, but I want to."

Without saying anything else, they got out of the car. Marisa unbuckled Jussy's seat belt and lifted her in her arms while Dane did the same with Penn.

Mina met them at the door, clucking in German and following behind as they climbed the stairs. The maid took Marisa into Jussy's room while Dane went on to

Penn's. Marisa lay the little girl on the bed and smiled softly. She was a beautiful child. With a gentle hand, Marisa pushed the blond hair from her forehead and bent to kiss her. "Good night," she whispered.

While Mina pulled out a nightgown and began helping the still sleeping Jussy out of her clothes, Marisa left the room and ran straight into Dane. He caught her shoulders in his hands to steady her, then immediately let go. With an inclination of his head, he went past her and down the stairs.

Instead of going downstairs, Marisa went to her room. Very methodically, she got ready for bed, then climbed onto it with her sketch pad and settled in to do some work. That, after all, was what she was here for.

There was a knock on her door. Marisa climbed off the bed and padded across the room to the door. She opened it to find Dane standing there.

"You left these in the car," he said, handing her the boxes.

"Thank you."

"I also wanted to tell you that I've changed my mind about having you stay until the plans for the lodge are completed. I'd prefer that you follow your usual routine, which is to accomplish what you need to here then finish the rest in Chicago."

Marisa felt as though he'd slapped her and had to swallow hard before responding. "I see."

"I'm going to be out of town on business for the next several days, so if you have any questions, just write them down and I'll get to them when I return. Or if it's something really important, relay the message to Claudia, and she'll see that I'm contacted."

"All right."

His eyes met and held hers. "You'll probably be gone by the time I get back, so have a safe flight. I wish you all the best."

It was a moment before Marisa could trust herself to speak. "That's all? You wish me all the best?"

Their eyes locked for a long moment. Dane clenched his jaw. His gaze moved over her face as though to memorize each feature. "That's all," he said quietly, then he turned and walked away.

Marisa couldn't let him leave like that. "Dane?"

He turned around.

"That's not all."

"What?"

"I said that's not all." She sounded more sure of herself than she felt.

Dane walked toward Marisa until he stood directly in front of her. "What are you talking about?"

Marisa went to her dresser to set down the boxes. Her hand bumped against a bottle of perfume and sent it crashing onto the wooden arm of a chair. "Damn," she said softly as shards of glass fell to the carpeting and scent filled the air. Kneeling, she began picking up the glass.

"Leave that, Marisa," Dane said as he crossed the room. "I'll send someone up to take care of it."

"No, thank you," she said tersely. "I can take care of it my—" She suddenly inhaled sharply.

"What's wrong?"

"I cut myself."

"Let me see." He knelt in front of her and cradled her hand in his. There was a small cut on her index finger that was bleeding profusely. He took a tissue from the dresser and wrapped it around the finger, then put his hand under her elbow and raised Marisa to her feet. "Go sit on the bed. I'll be right back."

Marisa sank onto the bedspread and waited. She could hear the water running in her bathroom. Then Dane came and sat next to her, taking her hand in his. After removing the tissue, he dabbed at the finger with a cool, damp washcloth and examined the cut more closely. "It doesn't look serious. A bandage should be sufficient."

Marisa's eyes rested on his face as he looked down.

Dane wrapped the cloth around her finger and sat with her hand in his as he applied some slight pressure. He raised his eyes and found them locked with hers. For a long moment he said nothing. "Does it hurt?"

She shook her head.

"What exactly was it that you wanted to talk to me about?"

Marisa had lost her momentum. The words she'd had in her mind just a few minutes earlier had vanished. Only the raw feelings were left. "Why are you sending me away?"

He clenched his jaw. "I'd hardly call it sending you away. I'm simply altering our business arrangement."

"Business?"

"That's why you're here. Business."

"Originally. But that's not the reason you're sending me away—and you *are* sending me away."

Dane looked back at her hand and unwound the cloth. "The bleeding seems to have stopped."

Marisa couldn't have cared less about her finger. "Dane, I..."

"No," he said quickly, his eyes burning into hers. "Don't."

Her lips were softly parted over her unspoken words. It was as though he knew what she was about to say.

Dane rose from the bed. "I'll send someone up with a bandage. Please be gone before I get back from my trip."

Marisa watched him leave in silence. He'd made his feelings painfully clear.

"All right, Marisa, now what are you going to do?" she asked herself.

Chapter Four

Several days later, Marisa went downstairs early, before anyone else was awake. It was Christmas Eve, and if all went well, she'd be finished that afternoon and could catch a plane to Chicago that night. She'd get the work done first, then worry about everything else. Grabbing the car keys from the hall table, she headed toward the door.

"Marisa?"

She turned with a startled gasp to find Claudia standing at the top of the staircase. "What are you doing up?"

"Trying to catch you," she said as she walked down the steps, her long robe trailing behind her. "You've been out every morning before anyone is awake and you don't get home until after we've all gone to bed."

"I've been very busy."

"Apparently." She stopped in front of Marisa. "Want to tell me what's going on?"

Marisa hesitated for just a moment. "Your brother wants me out of here before he returns." She looked at her watch. "And if I leave right now, I just might make it."

"You mean you're going to give up on him just like that?"

"Claudia, he doesn't want me. I'm not going to keep throwing myself at a man who doesn't want me."

"Is that what Dane told you?"

"I think the fact that he told me to leave is a pretty clear indication."

"There are times when things aren't always as they seem. There are things you don't know."

Marisa looked steadily into the other woman's eyes. "Then tell me."

Claudia opened her mouth to speak, but as she did, she remembered her brother's words. Aside from Penn and Justine, he was her only living relative. She couldn't lose him. "I'm sorry, but I can't."

It was the answer Marisa had expected. She reached out and gently touched Claudia's shoulder. "I've really grown fond of you, Claudia. I hope that we'll always keep in touch. But as far as Dane goes, stop trying to match the two of us. It won't work." She looked at her watch again. "I really have to be going. I'll be back late this afternoon for my things."

Claudia looked so crestfallen that Marisa leaned over and kissed her on the cheek. "Cheer up. And go back to bed. Things will seem a little better when you've had some more sleep."

"I seriously doubt that."

Marisa opened the door and stepped into the cold morning air. The sun hadn't quite come up yet. Snow had just begun to fall, lightly, gently, leading a peaceful hush.

The driving was easy, despite the snow, though it wouldn't have mattered if it had been treacherous. She was determined to finish before Dane got back to Salzburg.

Settling down to work inside the lodge, she kept her jacket on to ward off the chill and lit several of the lanterns. She'd already done all but three of the rooms. Now she finished those, taking one at a time, filling them with furniture on paper and deciding on everything from the design the area rugs should have to the color of the paint and wallpaper.

When she was nearly finished, Marisa looked at her watch. It was late afternoon, and she still had another hour of work. Bearing down, she drew as swiftly as she could, then went over each of the dozens of pages of drawings again to make sure she hadn't missed anything.

That was when she came across the one she'd done of Dane. Marisa looked at it for a long time, tracing the tip of her finger gently over the line of his stern profile. "Oh, Dane," she said quietly, "I could soften that look, if only you'd let me."

With a shake of her head, she turned to a fresh page. One more drawing. She knew exactly where the new wing should go and how it should look. Zipping up her jacket, she headed into the snow.

Dane, shaking the snow from his coat, stepped into the foyer and set his suitcase down. "Is anyone home?" he called out.

Jussy and Penn came running down the steps, and Claudia, looking a little the worse for wear, followed them.

"What happened to you?" he asked with a smile as he hugged the children.

"We've been playing a game," Claudia panted. "I'm 'it,' whatever that means."

"Not any more. Penn is," Jussy cried as she chased her brother out of the foyer.

As soon as they'd gone, Dane looked at his sister. "Is she gone?"

''By 'she,' I assume you mean Marisa. No. She went to the lodge this morning. I know she intended leaving sometime tonight, but she hasn't come back yet.''

''She's at the lodge now?''

''I assume so.''

''In this snow? She could be in a ditch somewhere. I'd better go make sure she's all right.'' He headed toward the door. ''If I'm not back in time, make sure the tree gets decorated. You know where the presents are.''

Claudia's mouth curved into a smile as soon as his back was turned. She raised her eyes heavenward and winked.

Marisa had been outside for an hour. The wind had picked up considerably, and the snow was beginning to slice through her. Between being in the cold lodge all day and standing out here, she wondered if she'd ever be warm again, but cold or not, she was determined to finish tonight.

She was standing on the mountain side of the lodge and was sketching exactly where she thought the addition should go, but she was also trying to show how harmoniously it would fit in with its surroundings, so after checking behind her to make sure she wasn't too close to the edge, she stepped back. Her perspective still wasn't quite right, though; she stepped back a little more, still a good five feet from the edge.

There was a strange noise—a loud, cracking sound. Marisa stopped drawing and looked up from her pad. It was hard to tell where it had come from.

After a moment, she went back to work. Almost immediately the noise came again, louder this time, and the ground beneath her vibrated. Her heart moved into her throat. Marisa knew she should move, but it was as though her legs were frozen. They wouldn't do what she willed them to do.

There was another loud crack, then a noise like thunder. The ground beneath her feet was disintegrating. Someone suddenly tackled her, hitting her hard and literally knocking her into the air and away from the edge. Strong arms wrapped protectively around her, and Dane turned his body so that he hit the ground first, cushioning her impact. Watching in horror from the ground, Marisa saw that the place where she'd been standing had disappeared down the mountainside.

She sat up and looked down the cliff. There was a sheer drop of more than two hundred feet. Dane looked, too, then stood and pulled her into his arms. He held her tightly, pressing her face into his shoulder. "My God," he said hoarsely, breathing hard.

Marisa pressed her hands against his chest and looked at him. "What happened? I wasn't anywhere near the edge."

"You were standing on false ground."

"False ground?"

"Snow that's been added to the edge of the cliff, then turned into ice until it has the appearance of solid ground. The winter has been strangely warm this year. At least it was until about a week ago. I guess the ice became less stable and broke under your weight." He cupped her face in his hands and gazed intensely into her eyes. "Are you sure you're all right?"

She nodded and covered his hands with hers, savoring their warmth on her cold face. "Where did you come from?"

"My sister said you'd been up here since early this morning. I was worried."

"Thank heavens."

Dane, his expression gentle, smoothed his thumbs over her cheeks then pulled her into his arms again. Marisa's entire body began to tremble, just a little at first, but then got so bad she could barely talk.

Without saying anything, Dane picked her up in his arms and carried her into the lodge. Placing her on the couch, he took off his coat and draped it snugly around her, then began building a fire with old wood that was already there.

Marisa's teeth chattered uncontrollably as she watched. "This is ridiculous," she finally managed to say. "I don't know why I'm so cold all of a sudden."

"It's shock—plus the fact that you've been up here in the cold all day." Within minutes a fire blazed brightly. Marisa moved from the couch to sit in front of the fire. "There aren't any blankets in the lodge," Dane said, "but I think there's one in my car. I'll be right back."

"You'll need your coat."

"I'll be fine. You keep it on."

"Oh, Dane!" she called as he got to the door. "My sketchbook. I dropped it."

"I'll find it for you."

"If it went down the mountain, I don't know what I'll do. All that work..."

Dane walked to her and put his finger under her chin to raise her face to his. "I'll find it. Just relax and concentrate on getting warm."

Marisa pulled his coat more tightly around her and stared into the flames, willing herself to stop trembling. Nothing helped. She clenched her teeth so hard to keep them from chattering that her jaw ached.

After ten minutes, Dane came in and stamped the snow from his boots. "There's a blizzard out there now."

Marisa turned and looked up at him. "Should we leave before it gets worse?"

"No." He handed her the sketchbook.

Marisa cradled it in her arms. "Thank you."

His gaze was warm. "You're welcome. The roads were already bad when I came up, and I don't want to risk going down until the storm is over. Right now it's impossible to see more than a few feet in front of you." He draped a blanket around her and rubbed his hands up and down her arms. "Are you feeling any better?"

"I'm still cold."

"Maybe this will help. I found a winter emergency kit." He tossed a couch cushion onto the floor and sat next to it as he opened the metal box. Inside were a small bottle of brandy, some crackers and chocolate and first-aid materials.

Dane opened the brandy and handed the bottle to Marisa. "Not very elegant, but better than nothing."

Marisa took a small sip.

"Come on. You can do better than that. It'll help warm you."

She took a longer drink and added a shiver of distaste to her trembling.

Smiling, Dane took the bottle from her and drank from it, his lips touching where hers had been.

The room around them was dark except for the single lantern she'd left burning and the flickering of the fire.

Marisa placed her sketch pad on the floor and pulled the blanket around her. "Your family's going to be worried."

"A little. I warned Claudia, though, that she should take care of Christmas for Jussy and Penn if we, for some reason, didn't make it back."

"Oh, no. I forgot about its being Christmas Eve. I'm so sorry, Dane. I really intended to be on my way to Chicago by now."

"Don't apologize, Marisa," he said softly. "Are you feeling better?"

Marisa nodded, then turned her gaze to the flames as she leaned her chin on her knee.

Dane watched her quietly. "What are you thinking?"

She turned her head slightly. Their eyes met and held. "I was thinking about you."

He was taken aback by the honesty of her answer, though by this time he shouldn't have been. "I'm almost afraid to ask, but specifically what about me?"

She wasn't trembling as much as she had been. "You're different from any man I've ever met. You can seem so forbidding and yet behind that is such warmth." She looked into the fire. "I thought when I lost Peter that I'd never be able to feel anything for any other man. For three years I've walked around barely aware of anyone else, avoiding Christmas because it was a reminder. I was hollow inside and I liked it that way. It was safe."

She grew silent for a moment, her eyes still on the flames. "Then I met you, and suddenly I wasn't safe any longer. From the beginning you've put a wall between us. I don't know why. But that didn't stop me from falling in love with you." Her eyes met his.

"There, I've said it out loud and I can't call it back. Despise me if you will, but there's nothing I can do about it." She sighed. "Well, you asked me what I was thinking, and that's what I was thinking."

Dane watched her in silence for a long time, a frown creasing his forehead. "This wasn't supposed to happen."

"It's certainly not your fault. You did everything you could to keep me at a distance. I don't even think it's my fault. From the moment I met you, I think I knew that this was inevitable."

He reached out with a gentle hand and turned her face to his. His eyes moved over her, feature by feature, coming to rest on her softly parted lips. With exquisite slowness, he leaned toward her, lowering his mouth to hers. At the first contact, a small gasp escaped Marisa. Dane raised his head and gazed into her eyes, then kissed her again, gently at first, searching. As the kiss grew deeper, so did Marisa's reaction. She rose to her knees, the blanket and his coat falling from her shoulders, and wrapped her arms around his neck. He pulled off the band holding her ponytail, freeing her hair to fall to her shoulders, and tangled his fingers in the silken tresses.

Marisa moved against him, and he inhaled sharply.

She pulled back and looked into his eyes, concern etched on her face. "What's wrong?"

"My shoulder. I must have hit it on a rock when I knocked you to the ground."

"Let me see." She unbuttoned his shirt and slid it from his shoulder. There was a large bruise on the left side. "That must hurt. Why didn't you say something?"

"I didn't notice it until now."

Marisa bent her head and gently touched her lips to the bruise and the skin around it.

"Marisa," Dane whispered.

Her hands moved over his muscled chest, and her mouth sensually followed, tasting his skin.

Dane closed his eyes. His breathing grew ragged until, with a groan, he cupped her head in his hands and raised her face to his, capturing her lips and kissing her deeply. Marisa could feel his heart beating against her breast. Or was it hers? The cold was forgotten as her body warmed, inside and out. Dane lowered her to the cushion on the floor as he gazed into her eyes. For a long time he just looked at her, then tenderly pushed her hair away from her face. "God, you're beautiful."

Marisa placed her hand alongside his face. He covered it with his hand and rubbed his mouth against it.

"Now it's my turn to ask what you're thinking," Marisa said softly as the firelight flickered over her face.

He trailed his finger over her smooth cheek. "It would be so easy for me to fall in love with you. I knew it the moment I saw you walking toward me. It was as though somehow, without my knowing it, I'd been waiting for you." Dane moved away from her and sat up, staring into the fire as he dragged his fingers through his hair.

Marisa sat up also, slightly behind him, and rested her cheek on his bare shoulder. "What's wrong?"

"This. What we're doing."

"How can it be wrong?"

He stood and walked away from her, pulling on his shirt and buttoning it in silence. After a moment he turned and looked at Marisa, his gaze full of warmth.

"It's wrong because nothing can come of it. You aren't the kind of woman a man makes love to without marrying. I can't marry you, but if we were to make love, I'm not sure I'd ever be able to let you go."

Marisa lowered her eyes to hide the pain that suddenly filled them. "I see."

"Do you?"

"Look, if you don't want me, all you have to do is say so. You don't have to paint some face-saving scenario for me."

"Oh, Marisa, don't, please," Dane said as he knelt in front of her, cupping her face in his hands and raising her face to his. "If I seemed cold to you at first, it was in order to avoid exactly what's happening between us now."

"Why? What's wrong with what we're feeling? What's wrong with acting on what we're feeling?"

"Because we have to face each other in the morning. And we're going to have to say goodbye."

"And then we'll go on about our lives and pretend that nothing has happened?"

Dane didn't say anything.

"Will you be able to do that?"

"I'll have to. We both will," he said.

"But why? Help me to understand, Dane."

"Things are the way they are and nothing is going to happen to change them." He pressed her against the cushion, reached for the blanket and lay beside her, covering them both with the blanket and pulling her against him so her body curved into his. "It looks like we're going to be here until morning. Try to sleep."

Marisa lay quietly, feeling his body against hers, savoring his warmth, his closeness. "I don't give up easily," she said after a moment.

Dane held her closer. "I know. Just believe me when I tell you that it's better this way," he whispered above her ear.

Marisa kept her thoughts to herself. She'd lost Peter, and there was nothing she could have done to prevent that, but there had to be something she could do about losing Dane.

They lay for a long time, unmoving. Then Dane stirred. "Are you awake?" he asked softly.

"Yes."

"Do you hear that?"

"Hear what?"

He rose and pulled her up by the hand. After wrapping her securely in the blanket, he walked with her to one of the windows on the mountain side of the lodge and pushed it open. It was still snowing, but more softly. The wind had died down. Church bells pealed, their music echoing off the mountains.

"It must be midnight," Dane said.

"It's beautiful."

"There's more."

The bells stopped after a few minutes, and she heard the voices. Beautiful voices, hundreds of them, drifting up from the valley. The words were German, but there was no mistaking the song "Silent Night."

Somehow, for those few moments, Marisa was filled with peace. It was impossible to hear that music and not believe that things would work out.

She leaned against Dane and his arms closed around her.

When they got to the main house the next morning, they were both tired from not having slept. The house was bustling with activity as it was readied for the ball that evening. Dane and Marisa were hardly noticed as they went to the library. The children were there, playing with their toys. Claudia sat in her robe, sipping a cup of coffee.

The tree stood in place of honor, decorated with shiny balls, foil-wrapped candy and gilded nuts. But what surprised Marisa the most were the lighted candles, rather than electric lights, placed on the tips of the branches. A bucket of water stood at the ready beside the tree.

Claudia saw them first and lifted an expressive brow. "Well, I'm glad to see you finally made it."

The children looked up and ran over to them, Penn to his uncle and Jussy to Marisa. "You missed Christmas."

Dane ruffled Penn's hair. "We didn't miss it. We're just a little late." He looked over at his sister. "Thank you, Claudia."

She lifted her cup and inclined her head. "Now," she said as she rose, "if you folks don't mind, I'm going back to bed."

Dane went to the tree with the children to look at their presents. Marisa reached out and caught Claudia's arm. "I need to talk with you."

Claudia tilted her head to one side and looked at her with a curious kind of dread. "That sounds serious."

"It is. Very."

"All right. You know where to find me when you want me," she said, leaving the library.

Justine walked over to Marisa carrying a small unwrapped box, "Merry Christmas," she said, smiling shyly.

Marisa knelt in front of her and opened the box. Jussy had baked and decorated cookies. They were obviously done by a child, and that made them all the more precious. She must have worked so hard on them. "Oh, Jussy, they're beautiful," she said as she folded the little girl in her arms. "Thank you."

"Do you really like them?"

"I think they're the most wonderful Christmas present I've ever received."

"See, Penn," she said turning to her brother. "I told you she'd like them." She took a box just like Marisa's to her uncle. Dane opened it and ate one, delighting the child. He pulled her onto his lap and had her explain to him in detail how she'd made each special cookie.

Penn walked over to Marisa and handed her a hand-carved deer that was about six inches high. She took it and examined it closely. "You didn't make this yourself, did you?"

His cheeks grew pink as he nodded.

"Penn, it's beautiful. You're very talented. How long have you been carving?"

"Since I was six. My father taught me."

Marisa shook her head in amazement. The detail was quite something. He'd captured the deer's alertness, the ears turned forward, the nose held high. "Thank you. I'll treasure this always." She held out her arms and Penn suffered her to hug him. "And if you'll excuse me for a moment, I have something for you in my room. I'll be right back."

Marisa ran upstairs and got the two boxes and one rolled paper tied with a ribbon. When she walked into the library, Dane looked up. Their eyes met and held. She moved forward and gave each of the children a box. Penn found the glass dolphin he'd admired in his, and Jussy got the dove. Then she handed Dane the paper. "I was planning on leaving this under the tree for you."

He took it from her and untied the ribbon. The paper unfurled, and Dane found himself looking at a wonderful sketch of Jussy and Penn. He stared at it for a long time then looked up at Marisa. "You're quite an artist."

"It's easy when you have those two as subjects."

Mina looked into the library. "Children, it's time to get dressed."

As they left, Dane went to his desk and returned with something in a plain brown wrapper that he handed to Marisa. She sat down on the couch to open it. The paper parted to reveal the *Pride and Prejudice* volume she'd seen in the bookstore. It was a first edition. She looked up at Dane. "You shouldn't have. This must have cost you a fortune."

"It gave me pleasure to buy it for you, Marisa."

"I don't know what to say." She looked into his eyes. "Dane, I..."

He touched his finger to her mouth. "Don't, Marisa. I want you to go upstairs and pack. I'll call the airlines and see about getting you a flight out." Then he turned away from her and left the room.

Marisa just sat there for a time. This was it. She wanted to know what was going on. She *had* to know. Picking up her book and other presents, she dropped them off in her room then went down the hall and knocked on Claudia's door.

"Come in, Marisa."

She found Claudia still in her robe, sitting in a chair near the window. "I thought you were going back to bed."

"I was until you told me you wanted to talk. After that I couldn't sleep."

Marisa sat in a chair across from her. "Then you already know what I want to ask."

"I have a pretty fair idea. You're in love with my brother, and my brother is in love with you. You want to know why he's sending you away."

"You know, don't you? That's what you were talking about yesterday morning."

Claudia didn't say anything for a long time. "My problem here, Marisa, is that if I do tell you, Dane might well never forgive me. And if I don't tell you, I might well never forgive myself."

Marisa waited.

"You've been through a lot since your husband died."

"What does that have to do with Dane?"

"Everything. Dane doesn't want you to have to go through anything like that again. Especially not because of him."

"Because of him? What are you talking about?"

"Marisa, I know you're aware that our brother died six months ago."

"Yes."

"Do you know how he died?"

"No one's mentioned it."

"His heart just stopped. There was no reason for it. He'd been checked just weeks before and nothing was found. The same thing happened to our father. The same thing has happened to too many cousins and uncles to list. It's even got a name. The Konrad Curse. There's no way of telling who has it and who doesn't. If he can make it to his **thirty-fifth** birthday then Dane will probably live to a ripe old age. No one with this disease has lived beyond that. But in the meantime, there's no way of knowing what the next year holds for him.''

Marisa felt as though she'd taken a direct blow to the heart. ''My God.''

''He would rather give you up than face the possibility that he'll cause you pain.''

Marisa didn't say anything. She was beyond speech. This was her worst nightmare coming true.

''You must talk to him about this.''

Still she said nothing.

''Marisa? Marisa?''

She slowly focused on the other woman. ''What?''

''I said that you must talk to Dane about this.''

''If I do, I'll have to tell him that you told me.''

Claudia sighed, then lifted her shoulders in resignation. ''So be it.''

Marisa bowed her head.

Claudia reached out and touched her hand. ''How do you feel?''

''I don't know.'' She looked at Claudia and the shock she was feeling was evident in her eyes. ''I just don't know.''

''Your choice is very clear. You can either stay here and fight to make him see that you have a future together, however long it may be, or you can leave and get on with your life.''

Marisa rose in silence and walked slowly to her room. She started to sit on the bed but rose almost immediately to pace back and forth.

She stopped suddenly in the middle of the room and stood like a statue, then, wrapping her arms around herself, she slowly sank to her knees as hot tears spilled down her cheeks. Her slender body was racked with painful sobs over which she had no control.

Gradually the sobs lessened, though the ache inside her remained. She slowly rose and walked over to a chair facing the window, sinking onto the cushions, her arms wrapped around her knees. The numbness that had taken over her mind receded to the point where she was able to think more rationally.

Here she was, through no fault of either hers or Dane's, in love with a man who might well die. For a moment—for just a moment—she wondered if she could put herself through the same situation again. But as quickly as the thought came, it left. It really wasn't a matter of choice any longer. She was in love with Dane, and in her heart she knew he was in love with her. She couldn't and wouldn't walk away from him.

Life itself was one giant risk. There were no guarantees. Peter wasn't supposed to die, but he had. Marisa asked herself whether or not, if she'd known before she'd married him what was going to happen, she would have still chosen to marry him, and the answer was an unequivocal yes. She wouldn't have traded in a minute of their time together.

There was a knock on her door. "Marisa, are you in there? It's Claudia."

Marisa didn't move from her chair. "Come in."

Claudia opened the door and narrowed her eyes in an effort to see. "It's a little dark in here, isn't it?" Crossing the room, her ball gown swishing as she moved, she turned on a small lamp, then walked to where Marisa was sitting. "Are you all right?"

Marisa nodded. "I've been thinking."

"And crying," Claudia said quietly as she looked at Marisa's stained cheeks.

"And crying," Marisa agreed.

"Have you made any kind of decision with regard to Dane?"

Marisa nodded. "I want to be with him. I don't care about anything else. All that matters is that we're together for however long that turns out to be."

Claudia beamed. "I take it you haven't spoken with him yet."

"No. I haven't been out of my room."

"I thought not. I just saw him, and he was perfectly civil to me. He told me that the earliest he was able to get you booked onto a plane is tomorrow morning. That means you can come to the ball."

"I don't really have anything to wear."

"You do now, if you don't mind borrowing one of my dresses."

"I'd appreciate it, thank you."

"Are you going to talk to him tonight?"

"I have to."

"He might not be receptive."

"I know." She looked at the other woman. "I may lose him, Claudia, but if I do, it isn't going to be because I didn't try."

Claudia smiled. "Quite right. I'll get the dress. You'd better wash your face in some cold water. The guests are going to start arriving any minute." Music was already drifting up the stairs.

As soon as Claudia had gone, Marisa went into the bathroom and splashed cold water onto her face, then took a brisk shower.

By the time she finished drying her hair and putting on makeup, no one would have guessed from looking at her how hard she'd cried earlier.

Claudia had placed a gown on the bed. It was a beauty. Rich blue silk that left her shoulders bare, hugged her waist then flared out to the floor. To wear under it were three stiff petticoats, in true ball-gown spirit.

Marisa left her hair down but wore it behind her ears, and clipped on delicate diamond earrings. With that, she was ready to go. Straightening her shoulders, she took a strengthening breath and went downstairs.

Everything was lovely. The house had been completely decorated. Elegantly dressed guests milled around the foyer. She smiled a greeting at them as she followed the sound of the music toward the ballroom.

Standing on the threshold, she looked into the vast room. It was comfortably filled with waltzing couples, but she barely noticed them. Her eyes went straight over their heads to Dane, standing there so straight and tall in his tuxedo, talking to another man.

He turned his head at that moment and their eyes locked. He hesitated only a moment before crossing to her. "I didn't think you were coming."

She smiled into his eyes. "I wanted to make a fashionably late entrance."

His eyes moved over her face. "You look utterly lovely," he said softly as he held out his hand. "Dance with me."

Marisa moved into his arms, and it was the most natural thing in the world. It was where she belonged. No one else in the vast room existed as they waltzed.

His hand was warm on her back, holding her body a whisper away from his. She looked up into his eyes and tried to read what he was thinking.

"Did Claudia tell you that your plane reservations to Chicago are for tomorrow morning?"

"Yes. I'm not going."

He stopped dancing. "What are you talking about?"

"I'm not going. I think that's pretty self-explanatory."

"Why not?"

"I'm not going to leave you."

Dane took her by the hand and pulled her through the people, out of the ballroom and into his library, closing the door firmly behind them. Then he turned and looked at her. "Marisa, we've already talked about this. You're going back to Chicago."

"I had a conversation with Claudia earlier."

Dane waited.

"She told me about your brother and father."

His expression didn't change, but his anger was obvious. "I see."

"Please, don't be angry with her. I didn't leave her much of a choice."

He rose from his chair and walked to a window where he stood with his back to her. "I don't want to discuss this with you."

"You have to."

He turned to look at her. "Marisa, the way things are is the way I want them."

"Do you love me?"

Dane didn't say anything.

"I asked if you love me."

His eyes locked with hers. "What I feel for you doesn't matter, because it doesn't change anything."

"It matters to me," she said softly.

Dane stood in front of Marisa and cupped her face in his hands as he cherished her with his eyes. "Yes, I love you. I loved you the moment I saw you, and I love you even more now. I tried not to, but how does a man defend himself against a woman like you?"

"You don't have to defend yourself. Why didn't you tell me what the problem was?"

"I didn't want to put you in the position of having to choose between the life you have now and whatever kind of life you might end up leading with me."

"But that's the point. This isn't just you we're talking about. I'm involved in this, too. It should be my decision, as well."

"The decision has been made."

"Dane..."

The eyes that looked at her were black with emotion. "God, Marisa, just go," he said hoarsely. "If you won't, I will."

"I love you," she said softly, "and whatever risks that love entails are worth it to me. Do you honestly believe that by sending me away now you're causing me any less pain than if I were able to spend at least part of my life with you?"

"With me, you won't have children, Marisa. I won't bring any into this world as long as there's a risk of my passing this problem on to them."

"We have Justine and Penn."

Dane shook his head as he looked into her eyes. "No."

Without saying anything else, he walked past her and through the door.

Chapter Five

Marisa's hand fluttered to her stomach as she sank onto the couch. She was shaking in reaction.

Claudia opened the door and looked inside. "There you are," she said, coming all the way in. "I saw Dane drag you in here, then he stormed out the front door. What happened?"

"What happened is that I've just been rejected about as thoroughly as a woman can be."

"You're not giving up, are you?"

"Never. I'm just taking a break between rounds."

Claudia smiled at her. "I can see that my brother has met his match."

"You can see it, and I can see it, so why can't he?"

"He's a very stubborn man—and he thinks he's right."

Marisa rose. "You said he left. Do you know where he went?"

"No."

"Probably the lodge," she said more to herself than to Claudia. "May I use one of the cars?"

"Certainly. You know where the keys are."

"Thanks." Marisa ran upstairs and changed out of the dress, grabbed her coat and went downstairs to get the keys. The set for the Volvo were still there, so Dane had taken a different car. She took the Volvo keys, smiled politely at the people in the foyer and rushed out into the cold.

It was dark, but the road wasn't slippery. She sped along. When she arrived at the lodge, she saw his car and parked alongside it. Relief flooded through her, and it wasn't until that moment that she realized she wasn't absolutely sure this was where he'd be.

Marisa took a deep breath. The rest of her life was going to be determined by what happened in the next few minutes.

Getting out of the car, she crunched her way across the snow to the lodge. She started to knock, but changed her mind and just walked in. "Dane?" she called.

There was no answer.

Closing the door behind her, she walked into the dark living room. "Dane?" she called again.

Still there was no answer. Where could he be?

With a sigh, she walked over to the window and looked out at the mountain. The moon was almost full and its light washed over the snow. Dane was there, standing absolutely still, staring into the distance.

Marisa started to open the window to let him know she was there, but stopped. She just watched him, her hand against the cold glass, her heart filling with such joy that she ached with it. Oh, how she loved him. She had to make him understand.

Dane lowered his head and turned to the lodge. She turned from the window and waited. She heard the door open and close, then Dane was in the room with her.

"Hello," she said softly.

He looked up and saw her standing in the light of the moon. "Marisa?"

"Yes."

"What are you doing here?"

"Looking for you."

Dane walked to the fireplace and stacked some logs in it, then set them alight and stood in silence as he stared into the flames.

Marisa moved next to him and touched his arm. "Dane, I told you before and I'll tell you again that I'm not leaving you. Your trying to avoid me isn't going to change that. Your standing here and not speaking to me isn't going to change that."

"You don't know what you're doing."

"I know exactly what I'm doing. I'm fighting for the man I love like I've never fought for anything before. I want you to understand, the way I've come to in the past twenty-four hours, that what happens in our lives—and who we love—is more often a matter of fate than of choice. I'm not looking for any guarantee of happiness. It doesn't exist. Peter wasn't supposed to die, but he did. It can happen to anyone at any time. Am I supposed to not love you because you might die?"

Dane was silent.

"Tell me something, Dane. If the situation were reversed—if I was the one who might die—would you walk away from me just on the chance of that happening? Or would you want to stay with me, accepting each day that we have together as a gift?"

He didn't answer for a long time. Then he turned and looked down at her. "You are the most stubborn woman I've ever met."

"And you love me."

"I love you," he conceded tenderly. "And if the situation were reversed, no power on earth could make me leave you."

"I rest my case."

He looked into her eyes and shook his head as the corners of his mouth lifted. "I knew you were going to be trouble the minute I saw you."

"I'm glad I didn't disappoint you."

Dane lowered his head and gently kissed her, then pulled her into his strong arms and held her tightly against him. "Of all the things that have happened to me in my life, I think losing you would be the hardest to bear."

"So you surrender?"

"Completely."

Marisa leaned back, still secure in the circle of his arms, and cupped his face in her hands, her eyes filled with such love that it took Dane's breath away. "I didn't know that I could feel this way. It's wonderful—and a little frightening—but as long as I know you love me I can face the future, whatever it brings."

Dane kissed her again, deeply. A delicious warmth grew in Marisa as he pulled her body close to his. "I want to marry you," he said, his forehead against hers. "Tonight. While it's still Christmas."

"Can we do that?"

"We can do anything we want."

Marisa put her cheek against his shoulder and closed her eyes. Her throat was tight with emotion. She was here, with the man she loved, and there was nothing else she wanted.

Dane kissed the top of her head. "What's going on in that delightful mind of yours?" he asked.

"I was just thinking about how I used to dread Christmas. But no longer." She looked up at him. "From now on it's going to be my favorite time of year. A time of joy instead of pain because it gave me you.''

"Happy Christmas, darling," he said tenderly.

Epilogue

Marisa lay in the big bed feeling warm and wonderfully drowsy. She heard the church bells in the distant valleys. When they stopped, she held her breath, waiting for the voices. They came faintly through the lodge walls.

Lifting her head from Dane's bare shoulder, she whispered, "Do you hear it?"

"Yes," he whispered, his lips against her hair.

"Do you remember the first time we heard it together?"

"Exactly three years ago tonight."

"I wonder if the children are listening."

"They're sound asleep by now."

"I suppose." She kissed his shoulder. "I'm glad we went to bed early."

Dane smiled into the darkness as he held her closely. "Mm," he said sleepily. "So am I."

They listened for a long time until the singing stopped.

"Happy anniversary, Mrs. Konrad," Dane said.

Marisa lifted her head from the pillow beside Dane and looked into his eyes. For a long time neither of them spoke.

Dane pushed her silky hair away from her face and trailed his fingers down her cheek. "Any regrets?"

"None. How could I have? Do you?"

His eyes rested on hers. "When we got married, I thought that I couldn't possibly love you more than I did at that moment. As the months have passed, I've watched you with Justine and Penn, becoming the mother they never had, and I've seen how you've turned this lodge and the other house into homes filled with warmth and caring. I've seen you do your job and wondered at the depth of your creativity and skill. Each and every time we make love, I want you more, not less. You fill my senses. You give me life. You've made me realize that the love I feel for you knows no boundaries. It's beyond anything I ever imagined." He kissed her long and lingeringly, then lifted his head and gazed at her. "What's this?" he asked tenderly as he touched a tear that escaped from the corner of Marisa's eye.

"My heart's so full, it aches."

He kissed the tear away, then lay back and pulled Marisa into his arms. Her cheek rested on his shoulder. His chin touched her hair. "I'll never leave you," he said quietly, telling her that he knew what she was thinking.

The most amazing thing suddenly happened. Marisa was filled with such a sense of quiet—of peace—that it radiated from her. Before, even when Dane's age had passed thirty-five, that magic number of safety, she'd still felt some fear...that she was still going to lose him. But at that moment, somehow, somewhere deep inside herself, she knew that he spoke the truth. He'd never leave her.

"What is it?" Dane asked, aware that something was going on, sensitive as he always was with her.

Marisa shook her head. "I can't really explain it," she said softly, "but I think I've just been given the most wonderful Christmas present of all."

* * * * *

Author's Note

When I was a child, I used to wonder how I'd know for sure that I was grown-up. One sure sign would be that Christmas would turn into an ordeal to be endured rather than a pleasure to be savored. Well, I'm in my thirties, and I still love Christmas. Even more now than I did as a child.

We start early in December when my daughter, Ariel, son, Ryan, and I begin decorating the house, wrapping banisters with fresh, beribboned evergreen garlands and hanging wreaths over the fireplaces. The house gradually begins to fill with the fresh scent of pine and the twinkle of tiny lights.

On Christmas Eve, we light the fireplace in the library and huddle together under a blanket while we watch *It's A Wonderful Life* and eat popcorn. Just before bedtime, we take turns reciting "'Twas the Night Before Christmas" from memory—or at least we try. I'm not sure the author would recognize our end result. Then the children go to bed, and my husband assembles whatever toys need assembling—mumbling language appropriate for the occasion—while I wrap presents and arrange them under the tree.

Our children are still young enough that watching them open their gifts on Christmas morning is a joy. A little later on, the pine scent in the house becomes mixed with the spicy smell of homemade pumpkin and mincemeat pies baking in the kitchen. A turkey browns in the oven. Our home fills with family, most of whom, remarkably, live in the same city. I look around me and think of earlier Christmases and the faces of loved ones who are no longer with us, remembering them with a sweet ache.

Oh, yes, I still love Christmas. And if that means I'm not quite grown-up yet, that's fine with me.

READERS' COMMENTS ON
SILHOUETTE ROMANCES:

"The best time of my day is when I put my children to bed at naptime and sit down to read a Silhouette Romance. Keep up the good work."

P.M.*, Allegan, MI

"I am very fond of the quality of your Silhouette Romances. They are so real. I have tried to read some of the other romances, but I always come back to Silhouette."

C.S., Mechanicsburg, PA

"I feel that Silhouette Books offer a wider choice and/or variety than any of the other romance books available."

R.R., Aberdeen, WA

"I have enjoyed reading Silhouette Romances for many years now. They are light and refreshing. You can always put yourself in the main characters' place, feeling alive and beautiful."

J.M.K., San Antonio, TX

"My boyfriend always teases me about Silhouette Books. He asks me, how's my love life and naturally I say terrific, but I tell him that there is always room for a little more romance from Silhouette."

F.N., Ontario, Canada

*names available on request